Ternaria

Legacy of a Careless Age

a novel by

Robert C.A. Goff

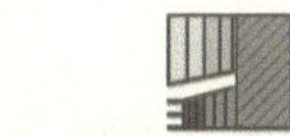

Dreamsplice
Christiansburg, Virginia

This book is a work of fiction.

TERNARIA: Legacy of a Careless Age

Dreamsplice
3462 Dairy Road
Christiansburg, VA 24073

www.dreamsplice.com/books

ISBN-13: 978-0-9761559-5-9
ISBN-10: 0-9761559-5-8
Library of Congress Control Number: 2017917419
First Edition: January 2018

For Hayden and Amberle.

Robert C.A. Goff

The Counterspell Chronicle

Counterspell: Guardian of the Ruins
Counterspell: the Second Law
Counterspell: Age of Fools (upcoming)

From the world of Counterspell

Ternaria: Legacy of a Careless Age

TABLE OF CONTENTS

MAPS

TERNARIA
Thistlepix Land
Partha
Domes
Oakhaven
Nettle River
Faerie Ring
Telia
Nart
Kizikum
Lake Willow
Westbng
The Great West Road
Mount Easley
Nettle Falls
N
Salceda
Lilac
Moonglow
Ost
Kikumbee
Elby
Wither
Quince
Saracet Land
Mount Gurush
Wiley
Seraz
Wab
Nettle River
Chive Crossing
Shibam
Tewesh

The endless wars between Faerie and Thistlepix took their toll, without either race recognizing its own contribution to the recurrence of those wars.

Kurash: *History of Ternaria*

CHAPTER 1—EGG OF AN OAK

"So, how far can you take it?" Dobar asked. He hastily tucked the bottom of his tattered, forest green blouse into the new, light green lizard jowl trousers he had received only yesterday. Stepping from the base of the thistle tower, he cinched his belt. His new trousers were still a bit large for his hips. A new, green leather sheath dangled from his belt, holding his obsidian shard.

"No limit," Romek replied. "While you were getting that lizard fitted, Ringar gave me the nod." The older Pix—older by a full year—leaned close to Dobar's face and plucked a fragment of lavender colored petal from the younger's head. "Wisteria blossom. You should really comb your hair every morning, Dobar." He flicked it away, then ran his slender fingers through Dobar's hair. "There." He smiled. "Much better." Romek tucked a stray edge of Dobar's blouse, then punched the cuffs of Dobar's trousers down into the tops of his boots. "Now you're fit to be a rider."

"You can go anywhere?" Dobar walked alongside Romek as they headed toward the wasp nest—a well-worn, circular opening in the ground. He envied the older Pix—now a fully fledged wasp rider. His puffy, lilac blouse and tightly-fitted, black leather trousers—set off by a wild shock of red hair between his pointed ears—emphasized Romek's jaunty gait. Next year, he too would be a wasp rider. But now, at least, he was beginning to train.

"Anywhere but the Faerie lands. Wait here, while I bring one up." Romek indicated the dirt rim of the nest. "It's dangerous down there, if you don't know what you're doing."

"Where are we going?"

"To look for the oak tree that lays eggs." Romek stepped into the sloped cave.

"That's just a child's tale."

"Maybe," Romek called over his shoulder, as he vanished into the shadow.

Dobar tipped his head. Dozens of thistle towers swayed in the gentle breeze beneath a clear, powdery blue sky. It was a good day to fly. Other Pix were beginning their morning activities at the foot of several thistles. Four dragged a legless grasshopper toward one of the fire pits. A pair of tanners stretched a gray skin onto a drying frame. A group of gatherers headed south, toward the abundant seeds of the sweetgrass field. He had been excused from his daily chore of gathering twigs for the fire, to take his first flight.

A black wasp, its antennae swaying with apparent agitation, walked from the shadow of the nest opening with Romek seated just behind its triangular head. Huge, faceted eyes stared nowhere and everywhere at once. Dobar's heart pounded. Up close, Dobar observed how the plates of its abdominal segments overlapped from front to back, and how the entire abdomen was held to its thorax by what seemed to be a quite insubstantial stalk.

"Leg!" Romek commanded. "Leg!" he shouted again, this time jerking at one of the silk harness lines. The wasp's left foreleg positioned itself as a step. "The keepers said Slug was the fastest of the lot, but he's a little stubborn." Romek lowered his left hand from the reins—tied at each end to one of Slug's mandibles—and assisted Dobar up the leg and onto a position immediately behind him. "Stay against me and grab that line that's behind your butt with your right hand. Never let go of that while we're in the air."

Dobar spread his legs and pressed his body, from crotch to chin, against Romek's back. Romek pulled Dobar's left hand under his own left arm and pressed it to his right breast.

"This will keep the wind from catching between us." He looked over his shoulder. "And it will keep my back warm," he added with a smile. A glint of white showed between his lips.

"If he's so fast, why do they call him Slug?"

"Not that kind of slug," Romek answered over his shoulder.

"What other kind is there?"

An elbow playfully poked his abdomen. "That kind."

Far across the meadow, a Pix swung a chunk of rotted mouse flesh in broad circles at the end of a rope, while he sounded a grating call from a reed whistle held in his teeth. High overhead, a vulture glided in lazy circles.

"You think he'll ever get that trained?" Dobar asked, his mouth just below Romek's left ear. "I bet it would rather eat a Pix than offer it a ride."

"I don't know," Romek answered, "but if he does train it, I'm going to fly it." With a click of his teeth and the jab of his heels, Romek urged the wasp into the air.

A deafening thrum and a breathtaking lurch lifted Slug from the ground. Dobar's grip tightened. In no time at all, they were circling above the thistle towers.

Dobar had never imagined the intensity of the acceleration and the force of the wind. Romek's red hair fluttered in his face. He pressed his cheek to Romek's neck, and closed his eyes. The subtle contraction and relaxation of Romek's muscles played in synchrony with the movements of the wasp. He opened his eyes. The morning sun stood above the horizon to his right, as they zoomed high above the grasses and shrubs, but below the branches of occasional chestnuts, poplars and oaks. Slowly, the tension slipped from his body. *I'm flying!*

"How do you know where to look?" Dobar asked.

"What?" Romek shouted.

"The tree with the eggs," he shouted back. "How do you know where to look?"

"It's supposed to be in Oldwood," Romek replied, "just beyond the bounds of Ternaria."

"We're leaving Ternaria?" Dobar had heard the stories of horrific beasts and of humans, a hundred times his size.

"Yep."

"Is it safe?"

"Nopc."

A thrill of adventure heightened his senses. "We have no weapons."

"We have Slug," Romek said through the rush of air. "We'll fly away from any danger."

After nearly an hour of flight, always heading north, Romek said, "See that creek ahead. That's Sardis Run. It's the boundary of Ternaria." Beyond the creek, an endless expanse of ancient oaks cast the ground beneath them into deep shadow.

"What are those," Dobar asked, "down on the right, just before the creek?" Below him lay five white rings, spaced evenly in a circle.

"Let's look."

The wasp abruptly descended in a spiral toward the white rings. They circled several times, then Romek brought them to the ground.

"Leg!" When Slug failed to respond, Romek jerked a harness line. "Leg!" Slug's left foreleg made a step. "He could use a little more training. You get down first."

Dobar stepped to the dirt. He found himself in a meadow of high grass that reached many times his height. Romek came up beside him. "Shouldn't you tie up Slug?"

"He'll be fine. I think it was that way." Romek pointed.

Within a few steps, a massive, milky white stone came into view among the blades of grass. Dobar climbed its ragged face and stood on the flat surface of its top. "They're just big white rocks. There's nothing but grass in the center of the ring."

"You really can't see these from down here, until you bump into them."

Dobar climbed down. "Only a human could have put them here. I thought humans couldn't come into Ternaria."

"Maybe they just reached over the boundary."

"I think it's too far, even for a human."

"Slug!" Romek shouted. The wasp flew over them and headed north. "Slug!"

A deafening hum of larger wings caused Dobar and Romek to crouch to the ground. Two fat bumblebees flew past—one ringed with green fuzz, the other with red. A winged rider sat astride the broad back of each.

"Faeries," Romek whispered. "Stay low."

"Will Slug come back?" For the first time, he saw fear in Romek's face.

"I don't know. He didn't seem to be in a very trusty disposition. We need to cut some pikes. Those bees might have been just flying by, or they could be scouting ahead for a band of Faeries on foot."

"I think there was a raspberry bramble by the creek, but it was on the other side."

"Let's go." Romek quickly moved toward Sardis Run in a crouch. Dobar followed. Half-way there, the two bumblebees returned, this time flying in the opposite direction. Once they had passed, Romek and Dobar resumed their awkward, crouching sprint toward the creek.

The water in Sardis Run flowed westward in a trickle that they crossed in a single, running leap. A short distance farther rose the thorny arcs of a bramble, replete with ripe, golden raspberries.

"There's a trail." Dobar indicated a well-worn path that crossed Sardis Run a short way further upstream and veered to the eastern edge of the bramble.

"I guess the Faerie rock haulers come by here," Romek said. He looked at the puffy sleeves of his lilac blouse, then at Dobar's tattered, green blouse. "Cut two pikes for each of us."

"Why would they haul rocks?" Dobar walked carefully beneath the bramble shafts, looking for the hard, thin spikes of last year's growth. They made the best pikes. He glanced at his own blouse, wondering if it had fabric enough to spare for yet another rip.

"They take red rocks to the humans. I don't know where the rocks come from or why the humans would want them."

Dobar shaved four spikes from a mottled brown stem with his obsidian, and dressed them with a few more strokes. These he brought out to Romek. "Be right back," he said. "I'll get a couple of berry seeds." At the end of a drooping stem, he carefully removed two back seeds from a ripe raspberry, and carried the juicy yellow globes—one in each hand—to his companion.

In simultaneous motions, both Dobar and Romek pierced the top of their respective berry seed with a newly made pike, licked the juice off the pointed end, then sucked on the oozing puncture. They smiled at one another over the curves of the golden fruit. Dobar licked his lips.

Voices in the distance startled him from the momentary pleasure. Without a word, he and Romek moved into the deeper shadows of the bramble, Romek snagging a lovely lilac sleeve in the process. They hugged the ground, the only movement being that of Romek's eyes turning to inspect the hole in his sleeve. The older Pix sighed.

A line of ten Faeries sloshed its way across Sardis Run. Between each pair dangled a milky red stone, nearly as large as a Faerie, suspended in a net of silk rope from a sagging shaft supported fore and aft on a Faerie's shoulder.

"...'wasn't my daughter,' he says to the drunk. 'That was a maggot!'"

All the Faeries in the line roared with laughter. Though the Faeries were a little shorter than Pix, their voices were deeper. Six of the Faeries wore green tunics; the other four were dressed in red. All were dirty. Sprouting from the backs of their tunics were pairs of filmy, undersized, apparently useless wings. Dobar couldn't imagine going around with wings, much less, wings that couldn't fly.

"Break!" one of them shouted.

"Break!" the others echoed, dropping their loads beside the edge of the raspberry bramble. Each of them cut a short, young spike from the bramble and his own berry seed, then proceeded to consume the juice and the sugars by repeatedly poking the seed with the spike and licking it clean.

Dobar had heard stories of the drunkenness and sexual proclivities of Faeries. The Pix drank no wines and reserved sex as the final obligation in life. And, of course, there were no daughters among the Pix—only sons and the reclusive queen. There were no parents, only brothers—older and younger. Each one cared for all those who were younger, respected all those who were older. At fourteen, Dobar shared the responsibility for nearly half the members of his community.

The Faeries, as he could plainly see, were crude, lascivious and ignorant. Even their way of consuming a raspberry seed seemed more like that of a weevil than of an intelligent being.

He watched in disbelief as they urinated alongside the path, in clear view of one another, then hefted their red stones and continued on their way. This was the first time he had seen actual Faeries. He found them—with their silly wings, ridiculous ears, and their vile habits—repulsive.

"Let's follow them," Romek whispered.

"Why? It'll take us days to walk home already."

"Ringar might want to know where they take those red rocks. And maybe we'll find the oak that lays eggs."

The Faerie haulers pitched their shelters directly in the trail itself. They had halted beside a particular shrub with leaves that naturally folded to almost a right angle along the center rib. Dobar watched as each Faerie cut his own leaf, placed it top down on the ground, then staked it with twigs to form a long tent. They apparently chose to sleep separately, since two Faeries would easily have fit side-by-side beneath a single leaf tent. Dobar had never slept alone. The notion of it made him uneasy.

Romek had backtracked to cut a gangly daisy that grew in the niggardly sunshine beside the trail. Dobar scanned his surroundings in the fading daylight for another shrub with leaves similar to the one the Faeries had called upon for their tents. He saw no other.

Carefully, and as soundlessly as he could, Dobar crept his way toward the Faerie camp. The Faeries seemed perfectly at ease in the forest of Oldwood. They posted no guard and chattered incessantly about tired backs, sore feet and foods they wished they had, while munching on uncooked grass seed. Dobar approached so close that he could smell the odor of the fungus that ordinarily served as their homes.

"Do you smell that?" a Faerie asked loudly. "Wisteria. I didn't think it grew in Oldwood. Remind me on the way back to get some for Cara."

"And what do you get in return?"

Several Faeries hooted. A playful scuffle broke out.

He gently cut off one leaf, then returned just as quietly.

"For a moment," Romek whispered, "I thought you had decided on meat with your dinner."

Dobar could only shake his head. Though surprised by the Faeries' olfactory skills, he was less impressed with their intellect. He crossed to the downwind side of the trail and pitched his leaf tent in the manner he had observed.

Romek accompanied him. "Hungry?" He held out a slice of fragrant daisy petal and the bottom of a honeysuckle blossom, filled with nectar.

Dobar accepted his share of the meal. "I don't like the idea of sleeping on the ground. You never know what's going to come along."

"Centipedes, lizards, spiders, harvestmen. Should I go on?"

"Maybe we should take turns staying awake."

"Only if you take my turns." Romek smiled and nudged Dobar several times with his elbow.

"Seriously, Romek, how far are we going to follow them?"

"Well, my friend, we are already long overdue." He sipped his nectar. "We could justify that by coming back with something useful."

"Like what?"

"Like where they take those red rocks. What are they used for? Do the humans buy them, or do they hold Faerie hostages?"

"What if they keep walking for days...or a half-month?"

"They're not going to walk in Oldwood for a half-month. It's beyond the bounds."

On the morning of their fourteenth day since crossing Sardis Run, Dobar gazed in silence at his first human. From the safety of the shadows beneath ancient oaks, he and Romek had watched as the ten Faeries, with their burden of five red rocks, marched into the dazzling sunshine. The path upon which all of them had traveled through the deep forest now crossed a vast clearing and led directly to a colossal human structure of white walls and massive, dark beams. The Faeries each waved a hand at a solitary human, clothed in a hooded brown robe as dark as the wooden beams.

"Greetings," the human boomed, lifting a dirt-smudged hand in response.

The Faeries continued along the path to a Pix-size door at the base of the building, and vanished inside. The human carefully stepped over the path and crouched at an orderly row of plants, which he appeared to be tending.

"He seems friendly," Dobar whispered.

"If he's friendly with Faeries," Romek replied, "he might not be so friendly with us." Romek picked at the numerous snags and tears in his puffy lilac sleeves.

Dobar gathered his courage and stepped out of the shadows and onto the path that led directly to the human. When he came to within twenty paces of the crouching human, he shouted, "Greetings!"

The human briefly lifted his head, then returned to plucking smaller plants from the dirt surrounding the larger, more orderly ones. Even in his crouched position, the top of the human's head reached to fifty times Dobar's height.

Dobar halved the distance separating them, then shouted again, "Greetings!"

Finally noticing Dobar, the human started to wave his hand, but stopped and leaned closer. "You're a pixie!" he said with obvious delight. He looked over his shoulder toward the building, then returned his surprised face to Dobar. "We've never had a pixie visit the abbey." His low pitched voice rumbled in a melody of sonorous vowels and explosive consonants. "I am Neruti. What can I do for you?"

"Pix. Not pixie. Just Pix."

"My apologies. We have always referred to your people as pixies." Neruti smiled. "Now I know better. So, how may I assist a visiting Pix? Two Pixes!"

Dobar turned to see Romek approaching.

"One Pix. Two Pix. Just Pix."

"Just Pix," Neruti chuckled. "Like, one sheep, two sheep!"

"I don't know about sheep," Dobar replied. "My name is Dobar and that's Romek."

"I'm pleased to meet you, Dobar and Romek."

"This is Neruti," Dobar said softly to his companion.

"What is this place?" Romek asked, his manners apparently forgotten.

"This is Moss Abbey."

"Are there more humans here?" Romek scanned the towering rows of tidy plants.

"Oh, yes. There are presently twenty-six of us, plus the Abbot...our leader."

"What do you do here?" Romek continued.

"We...um...we help to maintain the order of all Ternaria. So many questions."

"Like this?" Romek pointed to the ordered rows of plants.

Neruti smiled. "This is just our vegetable garden. We grow them for food. Here..." He reached over to a row of bright green vines and picked a flat seed pod the length of his fingernail. Delicately splitting the pod, Neruti held it toward the two Pix. "Taste it."

Dobar removed a fist-size, immature seed and bit into it, savoring its sweet, green flesh.

"That is a pea. Of course, we allow them to grow much larger for our own use."

Plucking a second seed, Dobar handed it to Romek. "It's very good."

"So, what brings you to Moss Abbey?"

"We were riding Slug to look for the oak that lays eggs," Dobar explained, "but the Faeries' bumblebees scared him away. So we decided to follow the Faeries and find out what they did with those red rocks that they're always carrying."

"You were riding a slug?"

"No, no, no. Slug is a wasp." Even though they spoke the very same language, Dobar found that communicating with Neruti was not as easy as he would have expected.

"Ah. I think I understand. Do the Faeries know that you were following them?"

Dobar leaned his head for a clear view of the door through which the Faeries had entered the abbey. "Of course not."

"I see that you're both carrying pikes. You know, fighting is not allowed here. Perhaps we should talk at the other side of the garden, rather than on the Faerie Path."

Romek now eyed the path with suspicion, stepping from it to the recently turned, black soil of the vegetable garden. "That's a long way." He pointed to the line of oaks on the far side of the garden.

"I suppose it is. And we just cultivated yesterday. Could I...um...carry you?"

Dobar and Romek looked at one another, then up at the massive bulk of the still crouching Neruti.

"If I wanted to harm you, it would not require deception," he chuckled. "Would you like a ride?" His left hand opened onto the edge of the path, palm up.

Romek made a step-cradle with his hands, and lifted Dobar high enough to climb onto the deeply creviced hand. Dobar inspected his own hand, surprised to notice similar furrows and cracks.

"Stop looking at it, and reach it down here," Romek said.

Dobar hoisted his companion to Neruti's palm. With a speed and acceleration almost matching that of their runaway wasp, Neruti whisked them across the garden to its western edge, marked by the resumption of Oldwood's ancient oaks, and deposited them onto a thick wood platform that allowed the friendly human to sit beside them.

"Now, I won't have to stoop so low, or worry about an unexpected melee. So, what do you think of the oak that lays eggs?" Neruti pointed a single finger at the massive oak that grew just behind where they sat. "That's it."

Dobar tipped his head. High in the canopy of the tree, clusters of round-lobed green leaves were speckled with a scattering of pure white acorns. "They don't really look like eggs."

"Oh," Neruti said, "it's still early in the season. Later, they will reach the size of a hen's egg. That's about this big." He separated his thumb and finger.

"Do they hatch into birds?" Romek asked.

"As you can see, they are quite high in the tree. Our tallest ladder can't reach them. When they are ready, they fall to the ground here and make a considerable mess, even on this bench. Once, one of the Brothers climbed all the way to the top of the tree, and brought down one egg. He cooked it and ate it for breakfast that very morning."

"What did it taste like?" Dobar asked.

"He said it tasted like an omelet poached in an aged red wine—like cooked egg with a rich oakiness."

"Is this the only tree that lays eggs?" Dobar was not all that certain that he should believe the silliness that he was hearing.

"This is the only one that I know of. Some years ago, a young wizard..." He stopped to glance back at the abbey. "A young wizard, named Chrysanthus, was practicing a new magical spell that caused one object to enter another and become a part of it. He would then cause the first object to come back out, just as it was before—or so he thought. He made a hen's egg pass into this tree, then brought it out again, intact. But when the egg hatched, it grew into a hen that laid only acorns."

Romek laughed.

"No, it's true. And when the acorns were planted, each of them would sprout. But they grew feathers, instead of leaves. So they would wither and die. You see, every change brought about by magic leaves in its wake other changes. It's called the counterspell. It is usually unexpected and sometimes truly dangerous."

"Do you do magic?" Dobar asked.

Neruti appeared to be uncomfortable with the question. He looked again toward the abbey. "I am not permitted to talk about that —even with trustworthy Pix."

"Is that what you use those red rocks for?" Romek asked.

Neruti smiled. "Two thousand years ago, a counterspell—many, in fact—caused Ternaria to be...mmm...different. We work to keep it...stable...in balance. The Faeries who regularly carry the red stones—sarcite—know nothing of their purpose. One Faerie priest and several of their elders know the truth of it and direct their people to bring the stones to us at great effort. Now you also know the truth. You may tell Ringar, King of the...Pix, what I have told you, and that he should avoid hampering the Faerie longhaulers in their duties."

"You know Ringar?" Romek asked, his eyes wide.

"No. But we know of him. He has been good and wise."

"Should we tell him that, too?" Romek seemed stunned by Neruti's revelations.

"It might help to compensate for failing to tether your wasp at the stone rings."

Dobar and Romek glanced at one another.

"We allowed Chrysanthus to enter within Ternaria to plant five of the acorns laid by the hen, to see if they could grow there. He marked them with rings of white stones. So far as we know, they have never germinated. But we observe them...from the abbey...from time to time."

A loud clanging noise sounded from a small cupola atop Moss Abbey.

"I must go now. The longhaulers will spend the night here, so if you head home now, you can follow the trail without worry. We keep it free of dangers." He stood, leaned a fallen branch against the seat of the wooden bench, then nodded. "Romek, Dobar." Neruti plodded away toward the abbey.

"It was incredible," Romek said, his hands representing the Pix wasps as they swooped and circled. "They had no idea we were there, until we were on top of them."

In the months since their celebrated return from Moss Abbey, Romek had acquired a reputation of precocious bravery. As a consequence, he had been given command of five pairs of scouts and the responsibility of patrolling the north-eastern corner of Pix lands for incursions by Faerie squatters.

"They were just walking along?" Dobar asked. He hadn't yet gathered the reason that Romek had attacked the Faeries.

"Just walking along? They had all their baggage and children and even their mice in tow—inside Pix lands. They were moving in!" Romek resumed his story, along with his flying hands. "So...the back rider on each wasp is going in with a cocked crossbow. We took down four Faeries on the first pass. Now, crossbow from a wasp is usually only one hit in three shots. Four out of five in one pass. Hey. Tomorrow I'm taking that reeking vulture up to the abbey to see if there are any of those eggs ready in the oak tree. Can you get away?"

Dobar shook his head. "I'm still catching up on almost a month and a half that we were gone."

"That's a shame. Well, Dobar, I've got to report to Ringar." Romek strutted toward the royal thistle.

Dobar didn't resent Romek's acclaim, nor his own near absence from the narrative that had emerged regarding the daring trip to Moss Abbey. That was just the way things worked. Romek was a wasp rider; Dobar was simply a passenger. But in a way that he could not fully explain, his doubts about the egg and the oak, and about the existence of magic in general increased with every week. All he knew for certain was that he had seen an oak with white acorns. Everything else was nothing more than words. Occasionally, he even suspected that somehow Romek had arranged the visit to the abbey in order to trick him. Neruti seemed to know too much. Romek could then elaborate to the others how big a fool Dobar had shown himself to be. He didn't really believe that—not most of the time. But at the back of his thoughts, he predicted that Romek would return from his vulture flight with an ordinary egg, and ask Dobar to sit on it until it hatched. He went back to his chore of carrying twigs to the fire pits.

The sight was truly extraordinary. Twenty Pix worked the ropes to lower an enormous, white egg from the back of the restive vulture, without cracking the shell. Romek stood beside Ringar, explaining his exploit. Dobar made his way through the gathered crowd of Pix to hear Romek's words. He felt that his friend and mentor had forgotten him entirely.

"...carried the rope to the top of the oak. When the egg was tied, Neruti lowered it to the ground, then lashed it onto the vulture. He really didn't like having all that weight on his shoulders. Neruti said that hen's eggs hatch in twenty-one days, and need to be kept warm. Since this is from an oak, he wasn't sure about either. I thought that if we..."

Dobar wandered away, almost wishing Romek would ask him to sit on the egg. It reached twice his height when lying on its side, and looked like the egg of any ordinary bird, only much larger and pure white. He hadn't really noticed any mark where it might have been attached to the acorn cap. It seemed suspicious.

Shouts drew his attention back to the vulture and the egg. Many of the Pix were throwing stones at the vulture, eventually driving it to lift off the ground. When Dobar asked what had happened, he was told that the vulture, once free of its burden, had eaten the rider in a single gulp.

Dobar pushed through the crowd toward where he had last seen Romek. The egg lay intact and surrounded by sheaves of dried grass. Romek stepped from behind the egg, shaking his head. With a vague sense that Romek didn't deserve to see him worried, Dobar turned and headed to his thistle tower. As he walked, he heard the name of the vulture's trainer as the one who had been killed.

Riding a vulture had never seemed like a good idea. Now, Romek was the only living Pix to have flown one. Surely Ringar would never allow another vulture to be trained.

It seemed to Dobar that every Pix from every village had arrived on the twenty-first day, to watch the now famous egg hatch. Merchants from all around had set up benches and offered prepared foods and beverages. No market fair had ever been better attended. New thistles had been prepared to house the visitors. Extra fire pits required extra fuel.

But now, all activities had ceased. A crack had appeared in the shell. Rather than struggle in the masses of onlookers, Dobar watched the egg from the high vantage of his thistle tower.

He had heard that, unlike songbirds, which were naked and blind at hatching, a chick from a hen's egg hatched fully developed and ready to forage. Ringar had ordered a dozen Pix, armed with pikes and crossbows, to be stationed near the egg as it hatched. If the size of the egg was any indication, the chick would stand three times Dobar's height. A variety of small seeds had been scattered around the egg. But then, if this was indeed the egg of an oak, the hatchling might be unlike anything any of them had imagined.

The hatching went on for hours. Occasionally, an observer would tear away a loose flap of shell. When finally a bedraggled, wet chick contorted its way out of the broken shell, a cheer went up. After the chick had rested, drying itself in the sun, it stood on wobbly legs. The crowd surged away from it. The chick took a few steps, then pecked at the ground, causing the spectators to step back even further.

Dobar had no special knowledge of birds, but the huge chick seemed to be quite ordinary. It was completely covered in light yellow down. There was no indication that it had come from anything other than a bird. Each time it stepped in any direction, voices would rise and the crowd would part.

Near the wasp nest, a wasp landed. Its single rider rushed into the crowd, and eventually located Ringar. Romek and his five pairs of scouts ran to the nest and shortly emerged on the backs of their six wasps. They flew off to the north-east. Dobar assumed that more Faeries had been spotted entering Pix land.

Eventually, Ringar climbed a small platform that had been erected for the occasion and gave a speech, thanking the visitors and offering various hospitalities. Then the crowds broke up and drifted toward the fire pits, leaving the unattended yellow chick to wander about, pecking at the ground.

It was just before sunset that the alarm sounded. Dobar stepped to the high door of his thistle, along with ten thistlemates, and watched from above as thirty wasps, mounted by armed riders, lifted from the nest and flew to the north-east. Dobar followed the others as they descended the thistle to learn what was happening.

At the base of the royal thistle, a small, agitated crowd had gathered. Ringar came down to them and waited for silence. "The Faeries have lured our patrol into a well-planned ambush. Only one survived and returned to tell of the deed. The other ten are dead. I have sent out a full force to find these villains and destroy them." Ringar turned to climb back into his thistle.

"Who survived?" Dobar asked.

Ringar's eyes sought out the questioner. When he saw that it was Dobar, he walked through the crowd and stopped in front of him. "Romek is dead. Only Timmik came back." He grasped Dobar's hand and patted it. "I'm sorry, Dobar. He spoke of you often, and with fondness. He felt that you should have received more recognition, despite being underage."

Dobar added more twigs to the armload he already carried. In the weeks since Romek's death, he found himself wandering farther each day, collecting twigs until his arms ached from the load. He wished that he had at least spoken to Romek, before that last flight. He still wondered if his friend had succeeded in fooling everyone with the story about the egg. Who could ever say what the hatchling of an oak should look like?

The chick had been promptly forgotten in the excitement of renewed war. Sometime during the night after it had hatched, it had simply vanished. Some said it must have just walked away. Others suggested that an owl might have swept in during the night and carried it to its own hungry chicks. Either way, it didn't add much to Romek's fading memory.

Rustling of a large animal in the brush aroused Dobar from his thoughts. He crouched, quietly lowered his burden of twigs to the ground, then extracted his obsidian shard from its green leather sheath. With a few deft swipes, he sharpened a sturdy twig into a serviceable pike. The rustling grew louder.

When the creature emerged from the brush and came into view, nothing could have surprised him more. Standing on dark, gnarled feet and rising more than ten times his height, was a huge, fat bird. Each time it pecked at the ground, it rustled like wind in the treetops. In place of feathers, it was densely clothed in the deep green, round-lobed leaves of an oak.

Dobar smiled as he cried.

CHAPTER 2—SOMETHING SUITABLE FOR A HOMELY SPINSTER

Cammia poured water from a brown clay pitcher onto the edges of a stone slab that supported her moss garden. The water quickly disappeared into the rootlets, from which sprouted dense, leafy stems rising to a height well above her head. Her square garden flourished beneath the shade of dry, woven grass, braced by a frame of wicker. The canopy concentrated a fresh, earthy fragrance of moss.

"Where are you, little bears?" Cammia pushed several stems aside. "Good morning," she said to an odd creature that munched leisurely on the edge of a leaf. It was no bigger than two of her fingers held side by side and moved about slowly on four pairs of jointless, stumpy legs that each ended in four tiny, forward facing claws, like those of a marmot. The animalcule appeared to be a miniature fragment of a caterpillar. It was nearly transparent, except for the dark green of its food passing almost straight through from one end to the other. "Where are your buddies?" She searched between the moss stems a while longer. "Here you are."

"You needed me for something, Miss Cammia?" a voice asked from behind her. His words came out individually, like dripping water.

"Yes, Yori. We need you to build canopies for the two new vats, up by the blackberry press."

Yori sighed. "Yes, Miss Cammia. When you going to need them?"

"A week is fine, Yori."

"Yes, Miss Cammia." He turned to leave, then stopped and scratched the back of his neck. Yori wore dusty, brown, bib trousers, rather than the colorful tunic worn by most other Faeries in Moonglow. "Miss Cammia?"

"Yes?"

"Those little moss bears... You sure take good care of them...like they were family."

"They're fun to watch."

He shook his head. "I just don't see it. You can hardly tell their heads from their butts."

She laughed. "See those little dark spots above the mouth?"

"Yeah."

"Those are their eyes, kind of. I don't think they see much more than light and dark."

"Then they can't really look at you."

"I suppose not. They don't care what I look like, as long as they have plenty of damp moss to eat."

"I just don't see it," he mumbled. Yori turned and slowly walked away, as though he couldn't think of anything that needed to be done.

Cammia added a little more water to the edge of the stone slab. "Bye-bye, little bears."

She walked up the grassy slope to the blackberry press, housed within a high-roof grass and wicker building. The intense aroma of raw blackberry juice filled the air. There, her younger brother, Mylis, worked at the long press arm, extracting juice from a blackberry, one seed at a time.

"Hey, Sis, have you thought about my idea of trying gooseberry wine?"

"I did, Mylis. After a few measurements, it was pretty clear that we would have to build a press so large that it wouldn't fit in here. Well, it's not so much the press as the press arm. It would need to be about five times as long as that one, and it might take two Faeries to work it."

"I guess it wasn't such a great idea." His wings drooped as he tossed another blackberry seed into the press.

"Oh, I think it's a wonderful idea. But now we know what it would require. If things go well this season, maybe Papa and Luris will be willing to set it up for next season. It would mean a new building, a new press and at least one new vat. And with all that, it may take several seasons to turn out a good wine. But that's how any of this happens."

"That's a lot of trouble and a long time."

"You ought to try a small test batch this year, say two berries. You could get enough juice for a trial without a press."

Mylis brightened. "You think they'll let me?"

"Let's just do it. If they find out, you can grovel and beg forgiveness." Cammia was about to leave when she remembered why she had come. "When Yori turns up, show him where the new canopies need to go."

Cammia walked toward the house, a roomy, two level structure, solidly constructed of woven grass and heavy wicker. The whole thing had been yellow when it was first completed, four years ago. Now it sported a stately brown patina.

Just outside the rear entry, Cammia stopped at the sound of a semi-hushed conversation coming from inside. She could see only broken silhouettes through the woven grass, but she could hear their voices plainly enough.

"But Papa, she'll never need a dowry," insisted the voice of Luris, her older brother by three years.

"Of course she will," Neelian replied. "How else will she get a mate?"

"That's my point, Papa. That chance passed her by long ago. Every Faerie in Moonglow has known for years that a third of the blackberry bramble is her dowry. That hasn't tempted anybody to overlook her appearance."

"Appearance isn't everything, Luris. She's intelligent, talented, and has a sweet disposition. She would be a wonderful mate."

"If the dowry doesn't make the difference," Luris said, "then why not just have it be the woods? That's a nice piece of land...so Mylis and I could keep the bramble in the family."

"It doesn't feel right," Neelian answered.

Cammia knew she was not pretty. Luris had teased her about her short stature, her wide, boney face and her hooked nose throughout their childhood. She had never felt attractive, and tried not to care. But to hear Luris conspiring to cheat her of her rightful share of the winery's bramble struck her as a deep betrayal. She turned and walked to her moss garden, tears spilling from her eyes. This avaricious grab, she was certain, had nothing to do with Mylis and everything to do with Luris.

"Anything need doing, Miss Cammia?" Yori asked.

"I have a favor to ask, Yori," she replied.

"I'm pretty good at favors, Miss Cammia, depending on the nature of the favor, so to speak."

"I need to go check some things in the woods west of the bramble. Could you come with me and give me your opinion?"

"My opinion, Miss Cammia?"

"If you don't mind."

"We can ride Creeper."

The two of them walked to where Yori had tied up his millipede, Creeper, and climbed onto its broad back. The ride was as smooth as resting on a garden bench. Waves of jointed legs, two pairs to each armored body segment, seemed to sweep from back to front with no perceptible jostling.

Cammia had played in the woods as a child, but it had been over a decade since she had visited. Rising through a dense undergrowth of ferns and thorns, the enormous trunks of massive oaks and chestnuts and sycamores ascended into the sky. Most were so tall that they had never been climbed.

As Cammia, seated behind Yori, rode through Neelian's Woods, a name by which it was widely know, she conducted a systematic exploration of its plants and trees, its soil and fauna. Everything she observed, she stated aloud in a running narration to Yori.

All of Neelian's Woods sloped generally to the west, though the center was incised by a pair of steep, narrow creeks that rushed down from the height of Chestnut Ridge, after first languishing in a high rhododendron bog. In the main valley, the two creeks joined to form a clear, gentle brook, on its way toward the distant river. At the juncture of the creeks, the moisture was palpable in the air. Mosses luxuriated beneath soaring ferns, to the music of burbling, clear water.

Alongside the misty juncture, a spectacular sycamore dominated the narrow valley. Guiding Creeper in a circle around its base, Yori and Cammia rode for more than a quarter hour completing its circumference. Though alive and fully leafed, its trunk revealed a bright spot of sunlight on the floor of an arched opening at its base. They dismounted and stepped inside the sycamore.

The interior floor, though littered with small forest debris, was fairly flat, its expanse far greater than the building she had described to

Mylis for his gooseberry press. At a height beyond Cammia's ability to estimate, a jagged circle of bright sky shone where the very top of the tree had once been.

"Yori, how long would it take you to build a roof across this half, about as high as the one over the blackberry press?"

Yori, stupefied by the view overhead, slowly returned his gaze to Cammia. "I've never seen such a thing, Miss Cammia. So high...the inside of a tree." He scanned the interior wall of the astonishing trunk closer to Faerie height. "Down here. Hmmm. Three weeks, maybe. I've never had wood walls to work with." He nodded. "Three weeks."

"And some steps around the wall to get to the top side of the roof?"

"You want to walk on the roof, Miss Cammia?"

"Actually, Yori, I want a small house on the roof."

"A small house on... Miss Cammia, you think of the strangest things. Moss bears, a house on a roof...inside a tree that's taller than anything anybody's ever seen. That sure would be something. And that hole at the top, up so high above the forest..." He held out both hands, palms down. "...just sucks a breeze right on through." He looked at Cammia and smiled. "Give me a month."

"I think it would be best to keep the bramble in the family," Cammia stated definitively. She sat with her father and her two brothers in the parlor of Neelian's great house. "The woods would be a better dowry for me, if you would be willing to part with it."

Relief showed on Neelian's face. Mylis seemed puzzled, but Luris looked at her with suspicion.

"Is that truly what you want?" Neelian asked, gently touching her hand.

"If that's what she prefers," Luris said with exaggerated thoughtfulness, "we should simply accept her wishes."

"But it grows no blackberries," Mylis pointed out. "It's just overgrown wasteland. Nobody could really live there."

"She says she wants it, Mylis." Luris stood as though the gathering she had requested were at an end. "I'm willing to give up the woods. You shouldn't be so selfish."

"You greedy maggot!" Mylis shouted at his brother. "You've always wanted to steal her share of the bramble."

"I'll pretend I didn't hear that, little brother." Luris walked calmly from the house.

"You're not going to let him do that, are you, Papa?"

"Mylis," she said softly, "it's alright." She turned to her father. "Then it's settled."

Neelian frowned. "What are you up to, Cammia?"

"I want to go and live there."

"We need you at the winery," Mylis said.

"It's not a suitable place to live, Cammia." Neelian stared at her thoughtfully. "You want to move there now?"

"Now, Papa."

"But Sis, what about our plans?" He glanced at his father. "You know, what we talked about?"

"Mylis, go find Yori and then you and Papa and I will ride out there on Creeper."

When Mylis left, Cammia explained to Neelian the details of her plans. Reluctantly, the old Faerie agreed that the woods should be her dowry, and that if she wished to move there now, he would allow it.

As Yori assisted Cammia and Mylis up onto Creeper's back, Neelian grumbled, "I don't trust this thing."

"It's not like she's a centipede, Master Neelian. She only eats dead plants and such."

"She? How do you know it's not a he?"

"I don't, Master Neelian, but I have to pick one or the other. Since she's of a considerate disposition, like Miss Cammia, I decided that Creeper is a she."

Cammia winked at her father. "Now come on up, Papa."

They rode Creeper into the woods, with Neelian repeatedly commenting on how decidedly comfortable it was to ride a millipede. As they scooted along the paths beneath the undergrowth, Cammia pointed out otherwise well-hidden features.

"Gooseberries are scattered over there." She knocked her knuckles on Mylis' knee. "Most are pink ones, but there is a small patch of dark red."

"That's a lot of gooseberries," Mylis exclaimed.

"You can only eat so much gooseberry," Neelian said.

"Yori, stop here for a moment."

"Yes, Miss Cammia."

"You see that huge, shaggy vine climbing into that oak? Well, look up overhead."

"That's muscadine, Baby," Neelian observed, "but it's so high you can't get to it."

"What's it taste like, Papa?" Mylis asked.

Neelian seemed to drift back to his childhood as he described it. "It's a kind of grape with a skin as tough as a beetle wing. But once you manage to cut it open, the flesh is sweet and tart, like nothing else in Ternaria. If you could harvest them, I bet it would make a wine to talk about."

Cammia turned to Mylis. She smiled and raised her eyebrows.

"You're going to try it," Mylis said.

"Maybe, if I can get to them."

"Miss Cammia does whatever she puts her mind to."

"Yes," Neelian mumbled. "I've noticed that."

Cammia saved the best part for last. At the immense sycamore, they all dismounted from Creeper. By the open arch leading into the hollow center of the tree, she stood and motioned for them to enter.

"Oh, Sis!"

"You've built yourself a winery in the woods," Neelian exclaimed.

Half of the interior floor was sheltered beneath a high-roof canopy. Within its confines stood a gigantic berry press, with a press arm that spanned the full width of the tree's interior, four large baked-clay vats and a small pottery shop with a dozen brown clay jugs already on its shelves.

"Look up there, Papa," Mylis said, pointing above the grass roof.

"And a house," Neelian said, shaking his head. "Well, I recognize the grasswork. How could you afford to do all this?"

"I couldn't pay Yori, so I offered him a share of the future profits."

"I told her I couldn't accept it, Master Neelian. I was happy just to help her with something so special. It was like a favor."

"That's an awfully big favor, Yori," Neelian said.

"Well, with all respect, Master Neelian, favors aren't big or small. They're just either a favor or not. This was."

"That's four gooseberries," Mylis said as he and Cammia released the end of the long press arm. "That's all the vat will hold."

"The last one was sweeter than the others."

"You were tasting my secret combination, Sis. The first was tart; the last was almost too ripe and the others were in between."

"Miss Cammia," Yori called from outside, "They're here."

"Oh, come help us, Mylis."

Yori guided Creeper beneath the fern canopy at the creek juncture. Behind her, she towed a grass sled onto which Yori had loaded Cammia's moss garden.

"You don't have enough moss out here already?" Mylis asked.

"It's the only way to carry the moss bears," Cammia explained. "They die quickly if they dry out. Besides, they bite if you touch them."

"You keep these things that are blind...okay, almost blind...that will bite you if you touch them!" Mylis chuckled. "Why?"

"I like them. I like to watch them."

"I just don't see it," Yori repeated.

"Where should we put it?" Mylis asked.

"I don't know. Maybe on that flat rock between the creeks."

"You know, they're going to wander away, no matter where you put them out here."

"Oh, I know."

"It's not like a dairy mouse that gets to know you."

"Well, Miss Cammia, how about if we just have Creeper drag this over to the rock and we just cut off the tow line. That grass sled is sure to rot in a month or so, and we wouldn't have to disturb those little bear things again."

"That's a perfect solution, Yori," she said.

"Because it was pretty hard to get it onto the... It is?"

"Perfect," Mylis added.

After the moss garden was positioned and Creeper was tied near a rotting deadfall, the three of them went into the great tree.

"I've decided to call this Sycamore Winery," Cammia announced.

"Good name," Mylis agreed.

"I have a favor to ask, Miss Cammia."

"Anything."

"Now that I've worked out how to peg into the walls of the sycamore, I was thinking what a glorious thing it would be to put in wicker steps all the way to the top."

"Why would you want to do that?" Mylis asked.

"Well, Master Mylis, once you can get to the top, first you could look out over all of Ternaria."

"You can do that from the mountains," Cammia pointed out.

"You can, Miss Cammia. But from the top of this sycamore, you can run a sturdy silk rope over to that oak with all the muscadines high up in the crown. Setting the rope would be the tricky part. Once that's up there, you can run a basket for going back and forth. You run another basket from the top down to here so you can bring down the fruit."

Cammia and Mylis looked at one another.

"It's a crazy idea, I know, Miss Cammia..."

Mylis entered the great tree with his right hand behind his back. "Sis, guess what I found just below the bog."

"What?"

"Guess."

"I don't have any idea, Mylis."

"Hold out your hand and close your eyes."

She did as he instructed. Something wet and slippery squished into her hand. When she opened her eyes, she saw that her hand was smeared with white mud. She was not amused. When she slowly raised the muddy hand toward her brother's face, he backed away, smiling.

"It's white clay."

"I see that."

"For jugs for the new wines."

Cammia rubbed her mucky fingers together to feel its texture. "Have you tried it?"

"Not yet."

"Oh, Mylis, look at this." She wiped her hand on a wicker post, then ushered him to the pottery. "Yori was looking for a small oak to make some pegs. This is a piece of the bark." She handed him a cylindrical piece of the bark.

"It's soft and springy."

"I thought it might work to cap the jugs, instead of a clay cap and beeswax. We can make them fit any jug, and if you drop it, it won't break."

"You know, Yori worships you."

"That's a strong word. We work well together."

"Where is he? I saw Creeper outside."

Cammia pointed up. "He ties himself to one step while he works on the next higher one. He'll be to the top within the week."

Cammia walked slowly around the inside balcony at the top of the Sycamore. The view thrilled her, accompanied by a dry breeze and the scent of far off places—so different from the damp stillness below. The thickness of the remaining trunk wall prevented her from gazing directly down, but even the thought of it made her queasy. Yori had already made the pulleys for the inside basket, but the basket itself was still unfinished.

She looked toward the oak that supported the muscadine vine. A platform had been built atop the edge of the sycamore trunk, and a like one high in the oak. Earlier, Yori had attached a silk rope to the sycamore platform and heaved it to the oak. Now he free-climbed the dizzying height of the oak to retrieve the rope and attach it to the second platform.

Cammia discovered that she worried for Yori's safety. He could, of course use his wings to slow a fall, but these heights exceeded the endurance of even the most robust Faerie. A fall from the top could well be fatal. She recognized that she cared about him. He was good and kind and generous. He was more creative than what he credited to himself. But Cammia had decided years ago that she would not subject herself to the pain of rejection. She would make her own life for herself. If no one sought to share it, then it would be their loss.

"Cammia," Mylis shouted from below.

She could not see the floor of the woods from the top of the sycamore. "I'm at the balcony," she shouted down into the darkness below.

"Papa has been hurt."

Cammia began the long descent of the wicker steps that spiraled down the inner wall. "I'm coming." The steps seemed endless. More than once, she tripped and caught herself on the wicker railing that Yori had insisted on adding. Finally reaching the bottom, she could hardly speak. She grabbed Mylis hand and began to run toward the bramble.

"A bird," Mylis said as they ran. "It tore up his arm. The healer came from Moonglow and wrapped it. It looks bad."

When they entered the house, they found Luris pacing in the parlor. "The healer is with him," he said, pointing to Neelian's bed chamber.

Cammia ran past the parlor and directly into her father's chamber. Neelian lay unconscious on his pallet, his right arm wrapped in bloody bandages. From the elbow down, his arm was missing.

"Papa?" She wiped tears from her face, still panting from the long run.

"He bled a lot," Mylis said from behind her.

She touched her father's brow, then looked up at the healer.

"I came as fast as I could," the healer said. "I think it was already too late."

As she watched, his life faded.

When the fire in the kiln had died, and the large clay bricks of its walls had cooled, Cammia watched as Mylis opened the side. The first jug he brought out had cracked, but seven others had survived the fire and the cooling. He handed a jug to Cammia. It was as white as mouse milk and so translucent that she could see the shadow of her hand when she held it against the sky.

"They're beautiful, Mylis."

"That they are, Sis, but they sure are difficult to make. Half the ones I threw on the wheel ended up back in the tub, and a third of the good ones cracked when they dried. The kiln only ate one."

"But no other wine in all of Ternaria will be in so striking a jug." She carefully stood the jug on the ground. It reached to her knee, its shape fat and cylindrical, except for a narrowing near the top. "I guess we'll need ninety or a hundred for both wines. When we seal the bark stoppers, we can use a different color beeswax for each wine: pink for gooseberry and green for muscadine."

After four trips from the kiln to the sycamore, they had all seven white jugs safely stored in the pottery.

"Come have a look, Miss Cammia," Yori called from halfway up the hollow trunk.

Mylis and Cammia stepped into the new basket suspended from the top of the tree. Mylis pulled firmly on the second rope, then unhooked two counterweights from the basket and tried again. This time, it rose easily. He continued the ascent until they reached a wicker platform in front of a new building suspended against the wall. He tied the basket at two cleats, then stepped out and assisted Cammia.

The new building, which could also be reached by the spiral of wicker steps, consisted of four separately accessible rooms, each with a single round window to the exterior, bored through the trunk wall. Yori showed them the woven grass sleeping pallets and built-in chairs and tables. Each room had a swinging wicker door and a veranda that looked into the interior of the cavernous tree.

"You really think travelers will want all the bother to stay here?" Mylis asked.

"If they don't, Master Mylis, then Miss Cammia has got a roomy guest house. It's just that simple."

"Is anyone here?" Cammia recognized Luris' voice.

"We're up here," she called. "I'll come down."

Mylis and Cammia took the basket back down. At the bottom, Mylis reattached the counterweights he had removed earlier.

"You've never come out here, Luris," Cammia said.

"Yori told me how well everything was going."

"It's going well enough. What brings you to pay a visit?"

"Oh, are those the jugs from the white clay? Very fine. And I see you've put up four vats of...gooseberry and muscadine. How are they progressing?"

"The gooseberry is slow," she replied. "The sugar is low. The muscadine has a sharp edge, but it's too early to tell how it will come out. How are your blackberry wines doing?"

"As usual. I'll just get to the point of my visit. I'm going to supervise this new operation, and put you back on the blackberry processing, which is what you're best at. I'll send some workers out to fetch your things tomorrow."

"You will not. This is my land. Papa gave it to me, not to you. You're incredible! You did everything possible to steal my share of the brambles. Now you want to take this?"

"I will bear witness," Mylis shouted. "Papa gave this to Cammia."

"Here's the problem, Cammia. Papa promised this as your dowry, though he allowed you to live here and do whatever it is you do here. Since you have not taken a mate, the land is not yours. It is mine. I have spoken with the Tribune of Moonglow. He quite agrees with me."

"You can't do this," Mylis said much softer.

"Tomorrow," Luris said as he departed.

Cammia stood in stunned silence. Fifteen years had passed since she came of age. Not one suitor had paid her even the least attention.

"I won't let him do this, Sis."

"He's right about one thing," she said. "In Moonglow, a daughter's only right is to her dowry, but only if she takes a mate. No one will have me, so the dowry is not mine."

"If Papa were alive, he would never allow this."

"You may as well go home, Mylis. There is no way to stop him that doesn't violate the laws."

"Miss Cammia, what was all that about?" Yori had finally reached the bottom by way of the steps.

"Family business. I won't be needing you tomorrow, Yori. If you could give Mylis a ride back, I'm sure he'd appreciate it."

"Yes, Miss Cammia."

When Mylis and Yori had departed on Creeper, Cammia wandered through the winery, looking at what she and Mylis and Yori had been able to accomplish. She passed her fingers over the smooth finish of a white clay jug. Cammia walked to where she could see the newly finished guest rooms overhead. At one of the vats of fermenting muscadine wine, she lifted its woven grass cover, dipped in a clean straw and let a drop fall on her tongue. She winced at the raw, unfinished taste. Cammia carefully closed the cover.

Outside, she walked to the juncture of the two creeks, breathing in the mossy air trapped beneath its canopy of ferns.

"Where are you, little bears?" She carefully pushed aside several stems, but was unable to find the oblivious little animalcules. In a place like this, she thought, they could go anywhere they chose—unlike her.

Cammia wandered back into the sycamore. She adjusted the counterweights on the basket for her small, unattractive body, and pulled the second rope until she reached the top. There, she tied the basket at two cleats and stepped onto the circular balcony. She peered out over the woods and stood motionless, watching the sun melt onto the horizon and finally vanish. A cool breeze whistled across the treetops and in her ears.

Slowly, she climbed onto the side platform for the high ropes to the muscadine. She had never mustered the courage to do that. The blackness below seemed so inviting. It would make no judgment about her. It would willingly accept her.

She gasped as two rough hands seized her hips and lifted her back onto the balcony.

"Don't do that, Miss Cammia. It would break my heart."

"Yori."

"Mylis told me what happened."

"I'm sorry. It's not something you can do anything about."

"But I can, Miss Cammia. I know I'm just a poor grass builder. I'm not smart like most other folks. But from the first day I went to work for Master Neelian—the first time I saw you—you were the prettiest girl I ever laid eyes on. You looked like a proud owlet. Those big yellow eyes. That very day, when Luris tried to give you grief, you stood your ground and turned it back on him with a smile. It was plain to see you were more clever by a long stretch. For sixteen years now, I've stayed to my station in life and never said a word about how I felt. Well, that won't do any more. If you'll have a simple Faerie as your mate...I know I'm not much of a catch, and I'm not so young as you...it's got to be at least a little better than jumping off a tree into the dark woods."

Cammia couldn't speak. Tears streamed down her cheeks.

"Now I don't know anything about dowries and such. I don't want that scoundrel brother of yours taking this from you. But what I truly want is to be with you and live with you and grow old with you. I hope I'm not too far out of line, Miss Cammia."

Luris arrived shortly before midday. Alongside him stood the Tribune of Moonglow. Six of Luris' blackberry workers waited just behind them.

Cammia met them at the entry to the Sycamore. "Why, Tribune, it's so thoughtful of you to come out."

"Get this over with," Luris grumbled.

"We'd like for you to perform the ceremony," she continued. "Yori has asked me to be his mate and I have accepted."

The tribune looked directly at Luris and said, "I would be delighted to."

"I won't allow this," Luris said. "He's nothing but a...a grass weaver." He turned to the Tribune. "I am head of the household, and I don't allow it."

The Tribune spoke to Cammia. "The law is explicit on this matter. You do not need his permission. Would you like to do the ceremony here?"

"Up there." She pointed to the disc of sky visible from within the sycamore. "Yori is there waiting, as is our witness."

"There will be repercussions, Tribune," Luris shouted as he stomped away, his workers in tow.

When the basket carrying Cammia and the Tribune reached the top balcony, Yori and Mylis were waiting.

"There is the matter of a fee," the Tribune mentioned.

Mylis held up a gleaming white jug, stoppered and sealed with pink beeswax. "It's gooseberry wine. But you can't open it until this time next year."

The Tribune frowned. "How do I know if it's any good?"

"It isn't, not yet. I just filled the jug this morning. But in a year, it will be perfect."

After the brief ceremony, Mylis departed with the Tribune. Cammia and Yori saw them off, then wandered hand in hand to the juncture of the two creeks.

"Where are you little bears?" She tilted several stems aside. "There you... Oh! Yori, look!"

Yori peered into the moss. "I see it, Miss Cammia. They've made babies. Lots of them!" Yori looked at Cammia and blushed.

CHAPTER 3—LAVENDER SCENTED THISTLEPIX

Rath knew that his tunnel into the chestnut stump was too narrow for a bee's head to fit in. But when a multi-faceted eye came into view, partially blocking the light, he froze, not sure if the bees realized that he had just stolen some of their honey. Rath tipped his head to his chest, resting his forehead against the layer of chestnut shavings that littered the floor of the tunnel. Lifting his belly and hips, he shouted between his legs.

"Pull me out!"

"What?"

"Pull...me...out!"

A hand grasped one ankle and tugged. Rath struggled and scraped backwards toward the exit of his tunnel. By the time Rath had wiggled himself completely free and stood up straight, Britt had already reached the forest floor. Rath tucked his obsidian knife, a simple shard, into a pocket stitched into the backing of his belt. Britt stared up expectantly with his large, black eyes shielded from the sun by his hand. A dense mop of black hair touched his shoulders.

"Well?" Britt asked. "How much did you get?"

"How's this?" Rath smiled. With both hands, he lifted a bulging pouch of honey from the tunnel entrance. His eyes scanned overhead for angry bees, but saw none.

"Wow! That's an awful lot of honey!" Britt shook debris from the front of his black tunic. "Lower it down on the twine."

"That's what I was about to do." Rath had not thought of using the twine. He tied a length of twine to the honey pouch and lowered it to Britt's waiting hands. He looked at his own tunic. Its original blue was masked beneath a coating of dirt and dust and rotted chestnut debris. He flicked away the largest chunks, brushed his forehead with both hands, then climbed down from the side of the tree stump. High overhead, occasional honeybees came and went.

"They don't even know the difference," Britt said, his smile reaching from one ear to the other. He looked down at the honey pouch. "How are we going to carry it home?"

Rath had not considered that. Each of the times that he had accompanied his father to get honey, they had ridden on their apis drone, Apis Pente. Now he was on foot. He looked about. "There." He pointed to a pine needle.

Rath and Britt headed for home with the honey pouch suspended from the center of the pine needle, which sagged under the weight spanned between their shoulders. Britt was nearly Rath's age. They spent most of their free time together pursuing one project after another. Rath considered this the grandest of them all. He had decided that he was old enough to have his own bee, an apis drone to carry him wherever he wished to go. With his own drone, Rath could travel beyond the familiar radius of a half-day walk from home.

"So how do we get the drone?" Britt asked.

"That's not quite as easy as getting the honey."

"I've got to rest."

They lowered the pine needle to the ground and sprawled against a milkweed stalk. "We have to watch for when the hive kicks out one of the drones."

"Why would they do that?" Britt picked sand out of his toes.

"The drones don't do any work. They just loaf around the hive and mate with the queen bee."

"Mating with a bee," Britt repeated in a pedantic tone. He extended his tongue from a gaping mouth and made a gurgling noise in his throat.

"They don't even do that very often. So when they all get tired of having the drones sitting around doing nothing, they just shove them out."

Britt turned to Rath, pressed his nose into Rath's shoulder and sniffed. "You smell like chestnut. So what do the drones do?"

Rath sniffed himself, then brushed off more debris from his tunic. "Well...they go off and die. Drones don't know how to get nectar or pollen or anything."

"So you give them honey, and they let you ride them? What if they don't want you to?"

"Stupid. You've got to train them. And it's not like they're dangerous. They don't even have a stinger."

"I know that. No need to get all gnatty about it. I was just asking."

"We'll hide the honey tonight, and then go look for a drone tomorrow. Before too long, we'll have our own drone."

"You'll have a drone."

"We'll both have to take care of it. We're partners."

"We live in different houses."

"Maybe we'll start our own house."

"We're not old enough."

"No?" Rath replied. He was not sure how old you had to be. "Sullis just tells you to start a new house, and you get to start one." At least Rath thought that was how it worked. "Whatever Sullis says is what you get to do."

Rath made certain that they approached Domes from the taller grass bounding the clearing where the boletus houses stood. Britt's home, Boletus Hepta, stood near the village margin, its cap overhanging the tall grass. Rath scanned the windows that opened from the massive fungal stem. No one seemed to be watching. He looked beyond Boletus Hepta to the rounded red cap of his own home, Boletus Pente, situated closer to the village center.

"I think we better hide it around here," Rath sighed.

"Can't we just take it to the storage?"

"Are you crazy? They'd just use it for their own drones." Not to mention, he thought, what the consequences might be for going out on their own to collect it. "Over there." Rath pointed to a tightly closed, young chamomile bud near the base of the plant's spreading branches.

Rath pried the bud open until he could fit his arms inside. Using his obsidian knife, he carved at the base of its contents, finally lifting out a mass of green with his hands.

"Okay." Rath gestured with his head. Britt lifted the honey pouch. "A little bit more." Rath grabbed the pouch with one hand and wrestled it into the hollowed chamomile bud. The stem drooped slightly under the added weight, but seemed to hold. "That should be good for a day or two."

Rath examined his blue tunic. It was filthy. Britt's tunic looked about average, he thought, for a morning spent wandering. After a brief search, Rath located a suitable spider web and launched its fist-size owner into the grass with a single swat of a twig. "Hold out your hand."

"You never clean me." Britt extended his hand while Rath wrapped it in spider silk.

"You don't get so dirty. And your mother doesn't look so close."

Britt started with Rath's hair, patting spider silk against the chestnut shavings. He patted the sticky silk against Rath's nose.

"There's nothing on my nose," Rath protested.

"You never know when a booger peeks out."

Rath jabbed a finger into Britt's chest. Britt continued, working his way down. When Britt turned Rath around to do his back, Rath lifted his wings to get them out of the way. Only once had he let Britt touch his wings with spider silk, over a year ago, and that painful memory encouraged him to lift them clear without discussion. Britt concluded with a swat on Rath's butt, then fled into the stairway of his boletus, discarding a pad of dirty spider silk along the way. Rath chased him halfheartedly, then slowed to a walk as he neared Boletus Pente.

Britt's younger sister, Bessa, approached him. "You're in big trouble, Rath Pente. Your mother's been looking all over for you." Like Britt, Bessa wore the black tunic of Boletus Hepta. Bessa seemed to follow Rath whenever she could.

"So?"

"So you're in trouble."

"I don't see any trouble."

"I do," his mother's voice called from a round window in the floor of the boletus cap high above his head. His shoulders drooped as he inclined his face upward.

"I told you," Bessa emphasized. Rath poked her arm. "Don't!"

"Go do your milking," Leela Pente called, "before that poor creature explodes." Rath could barely make out his mother's face in the deep shadow below the boletus cap.

"That's what I was about to do." Rath heard a soft utterance of skepticism from above.

"Can I come?" Bessa asked.

"No."

Bessa pinched the short sleeve of Rath's tunic and drew it to her face. "You smell like bark. No, chestnut. Really, can I come?"

Rath sniffed the front of his tunic. He smelled nothing, but wondered if his mother might notice. "Only if you hold her."

"I like holding her."

"Rath!" his father called from the base of an adjacent boletus, "Come see me when you're done."

"Okay."

"I told you," Bessa reiterated. Her wispy eyebrows raised high above her black eyes. Sparkling black hair flowed straight to her waist, and feathered at the edges in the breeze.

"You're such a pest." Rath headed to the storage puff. From inside the puffball, he retrieved the milk pouch he had washed and hung there yesterday. He also took a bucket, too porous to hold liquid, but essential for holding the pouch while he milked. He handed two seeds to Bessa, then walked to the edge of the glade, Bessa following behind.

"Can I call her?" Bessa asked.

"She won't come."

Bessa dropped the seeds and then placed her slender pinky fingers between delicate lips. At an ear-bruising volume, she whistled twice, sliding from low pitch to high. When a rustling noise approached from the surrounding brush, Bessa turned to Rath and smiled.

A mouse lumbered toward them, sniffing at the seed held out by Bessa. The bare nipples of the mouse extended beyond its fur and dangled almost to the ground. Bessa reached up and scratched its ear with her left hand while the mouse nibbled at the seed held in her right.

"Hey, baby," she whispered. "Good girl." When half the first seed was gone, she took a firm grip of the fur-covered rim of its ear near the base, still whispering soothing words. "Okay," she said.

Rath spread the pouch into his bucket, placed the bucket beneath the first teat, then began milking as he knelt. It was always easier when someone held the mouse, though he had done it single-handed many times before. "She's really full." He moved to the next nipple.

"What did you and Britt hide in the chamomile?"

"I don't know what you're talking about." Rath continued milking.

"I won't tell anybody. I'm just curious."

"Honey."

"Why did you hide honey?"

"I'm supposed to tell you?"

"I'm holding the mouse for you."

"Because you like to."

"Rath!"

"Because I'm going to get my own drone. Now you know, and you better not tell anybody."

Bessa lifted the second seed to the mouse. "I don't think that's such a good idea, Rath. You have to be older for Sullis to let you do that. And you have to start a new house and open a new boletus and everything."

"So?"

"You missed a spot," Reskith pointed out.

Rath dabbed bright yellow paint on the missed area. He had helped to paint a broad yellow band around the abdomen of the well behaved drone. His father had painted the underside while Rath stood on the back of the drone's abdomen to paint the top portion of the band. Its color matched the yellow of his father's tunic, indicating that both belonged to Boletus Hexa.

"This doesn't last very long," Rath complained.

"A month or so," his father replied, washing his brush in a bucket. "That's not too bad. But it has to be done. How else would you know if it's friendly? And how else would you know which boletus it belongs to?"

"Not mine. That's for sure."

"Alright." He tossed his brush into the bucket. "Do we have to talk about that again, Rath?"

"I'm in Pente, and here I am painting a drone for Hexa." He jumped down and washed his brush.

"Just because I moved to a different house doesn't mean I'm going to let my son go to seed. You've got responsibilities you're not going to sneak out of."

It had been months since his father had changed houses. Rath could find nothing good about the arrangement.

Reskith placed his calloused hands on Rath's shoulders. "Even if I take a new mate, you'll always be my son." Rath looked up into his father's large, black eyes. "Rath, you're letting your chores slip. You need to do them."

"I do them."

"And you need to do what's best for the whole village. You can never be respected until you see that. Some day, you'll have your own boletus with a drone to take care of. And you'll be expected to fight when the Thistlepix show up. Until then, you do what we need you to do."

Rath sighed.

"Now head on home."

Rath had just entered the spiral stairway of Boletus Pente when he heard the shouts of Britt.

"Rath! Rath!"

Rath ran toward the voice coming from beyond Boletus Hepta, Britt's home. As he approached, he saw Britt fending off a black ant with the butt of the pine needle they had used to carry the honey pouch. The ant stood half-way to Britt's knee, but its jaws could easily take off a leg. Britt, veteran of many ant encounters, faced the ant and prodded its eyes with the blunt end of the pine needle. A one-on-one confrontation like this was always a standoff, but Rath knew that an ant, no matter how small, always had more endurance than a Faerie. Few walked outside the village alone.

"He was going for the honey," Britt shouted.

"Shhh!" Rath cringed. He was sure somebody had heard. With his obsidian knife, he quickly cut a weed shaft for his own protection, and approached the ant from the rear. He jabbed the knife behind the ant's head, but it glanced off the chitin and dropped from his hand. The ant spun around, knocking Rath onto his back. The routine dispatching of an ant had now become a life-threatening, terrifying scramble. Jaws snatched at his abdomen, snagging his clothing. A rapid poke with the weed shaft drove the ant backward and tore his blue tunic.

Britt prodded from the side. The ant returned to Britt, dragging Rath as well. Rath retrieved his knife from the ground, but could not get back to his feet. For what seemed like a quarter hour they struggled, with Rath's tunic snagged on the ant's jaws, preventing his maneuvering to a kill position. Rath was tiring. As a last resort, he cut away the front of his tunic. Now on his feet, Rath decapitated the ant with a single stroke.

"Did that thing bite you?" Britt asked.

"Yeah, but only a little bit." Rath looked at the scratches on his abdomen.

"Only a little bit," Britt repeated.

"How am I going to explain this?" he said to Britt, holding a torn edge of his tunic.

Britt nodded for Rath to look over his shoulder. Rath turned. Standing behind him was his mother, a hefty cudgel in her hands. She walked directly to the drooping chamomile bud and looked inside.

"What's in the pouch, Rath Pente?" she asked. Leela wore a neatly trimmed blue tunic. The measured tone of her voice, her stiff, extended wings, and the two little furrows between her eyebrows demanded an immediate confession. While Rath considered a suitable response, Dibola, Britt's mother, accompanied by Bessa, joined the silent group.

"What if Thistlepix had found the two of you out there, nobody even knowing you were gone?" Reskith shook his head, his eyes forcing Rath's gaze to the floor. "Both of you would be roasting on a spit right now. We'd never know."

Rath had heard this before. At least his father came home for the occasion. That was something, he thought. Rath's fingers stroked the surface of a wall bench on which he sat in the family's common room.

"And *you know*, Rath, *you know* that we're short on honey," Leela added. She had tied her hair back, lending an unaccustomed severity to her face. "How could you think of adding another drone...which you had no permission to do? Sullis would be beside himself." She pulled her belt tighter, then seated herself on the edge of a wall bench opposite Rath, as if ready to pounce at the least provocation.

"But I got some honey," he pointed out. "I would have made sure I had plenty."

Reskith rolled his eyes. "Yes, for you. It's what Rath wants." He folded his thick arms across his chest as he paced.

"It's not like that," he pleaded, holding back tears.

"What it's like, Rath," Leela stated, "is that you will stay inside for the next month, when you're not doing chores."

"A month?"

"A month," Reskith confirmed, though with an uncertain glance toward Leela.

"That's not fair," Rath insisted.

"Maybe not," Leela said, rising to her feet again, "but then maybe you'll learn something from this. You can begin right now."

Rath rose from his bench and sulked his way to the stairway and up to his room near the top of Boletus Pente's hemispherical cap.

That night, as Rath lay awake on his bed, he seethed with anger. Maybe if I brought the whole honeycomb, he thought. He imagined driving a team of mice, towing a honeycomb nearly the size of the entire village of Domes. "How's that?" he would ask his mother. And he would go out and hunt for Thistlepix and kill every one he came across. *I'd sneak up on them and slit their throats before they even knew I was there.*

Rath surveyed a stand of sweetgrass for ripe heads, then cut down two mature stalks. From these he gathered a sack full of seeds, about a dozen he guessed. Britt also was allowed out to do chores, but turned away with a silent wave of his hand on the rare occasions when Rath encountered him.

"Can I help?" Bessa asked.

Rath had heard her approaching. "I'm done."

"I brought you something."

"What?"

Bessa held up a bone needle and a skein of blue silk floss. "You've gone around with that big rip in your tunic for a week."

"It doesn't matter. I'm just doing chores. Where'd you get blue?"

"I made it. And this." She pulled a square of blue fabric from her belt. "Now take off your tunic."

"Here?"

"Unless you want to get a needle poked in your belly."

"It's fine like it is."

"Rath Pente, you look like a beggar. Didn't you wear your shorts?"

"Of course I did." Rath's ears warmed.

"Then give me your tunic."

Rath sighed, then untied his belt and pulled the tunic over his head. Bessa accepted the garment.

"Your shorts are kind of raggedy too."

Rath looked down. They were more tattered than he had noticed before, and slightly small for him. He felt his cheeks blushing. Under Bessa's gaze, his torso and legs seemed scrawny.

"Oh, Rath." Bessa hovered her fingers over the linear scab on his abdomen. "That ant almost got your belly button."

"It's just a scratch." For a moment, their eyes met. Rath felt awkward and nearly naked. He pointed to the blue tunic draped over Bessa's arm.

"This is my last day," Rath announced. He continued his milking. He had learned to appreciate Bessa's company during his brief respites from isolation, since Britt had been forbidden to speak to him or see him, even after Britt's two weeks of punishment had ended.

"She still thinks you're a bad influence." Bessa's face was hidden from Rath's view by the bulk of the mouse.

"How come you can talk to me?" Rath asked as he finished the milking.

"Bye-bye, girl," Bessa said to the mouse, slapping it on the hind quarter. "She doesn't know."

"Can he talk to me tomorrow?"

"I don't know." She shrugged. "Maybe some time before he dies he'll be able to." Bessa's expression suggested her complete indifference on the issue.

"Tell him I'll see him tomorrow. I guess I'll have to apologize to your mother and everything."

"She won't believe a word of it...not again."

That evening, as Rath lay on his bed anticipating his freedom, his musings were interrupted by the thrumming of a cicada wing. *The alarm!* He sat up. *Thistlepix!* He leapt from his bed, tucked his obsidian knife into the pocket of his belt backing and followed the adults of Boletus Pente as they streamed down the stairs. *I'll show them how you kill Thistlepix.* Passing the entrance to his family's common room, Rath's arm was pulled inward.

"You stay inside, Rath," his mother commanded. She wore a quiver of nettle spikes and carried a bow.

"But I can..."

"Stay here!"

Thistlepix had attacked at dusk several months earlier. On that occasion, Britt's father had been killed, but the attackers had been driven off. Rath had been forced to stay inside during the fighting. *Not this time.* Rath waited until his mother had exited the boletus, then ran down the stairs carrying a raspberry pike. He paused at the door. In the fading daylight he counted three wasps on the ground between him and Boletus Hepta. One Thistlepix rider lay motionless on the ground, two nettle spikes protruding from its chest. The main action seemed to be in the other direction, closer to the center of the village. Two Thistlepix emerged from Boletus Hepta, one carrying the limp body of Dibola, Britt's mother. As Rath watched, Britt exploded from the doorway and, barehanded, assailed the Thistlepix carrying his mother. The other turned and fired a crossbow. Britt dropped to the ground.

"Britt!" Rath shouted. He ran full force into the attacker who carried the crossbow, while the Thistlepix attempted to reload. "He was my friend!" Rath pushed his pike deep into his opponent's chest. As the Thistlepix gasped, Rath looked into its terrified face—green eyes, tousled red hair, lightly freckled skin, gleaming white teeth, long pointed ears—above a dark, satin blouse open at the collar, all scented with wisteria. He had never seen a live Thistlepix up close. *Not much taller than a Faerie. But no wings! Strange.* Warm blood spread onto Rath's hand. He released the pike and stared at the sticky, dark liquid covering his fingers.

When Rath opened his eyes, he thought at first that they were covered, but the rushing wind soon caused his eyes to water. *I killed a Thistlepix. I killed one. It bled on me.* His head throbbed. As his thoughts cleared, he slowly assembled the information at hand. It was night—a darkly overcast night, and he was flying on what sounded like a wasp. The turbulence of the flight suggested to Rath that it had grown stormy. The silhouette of a Thistlepix rode upright in front of him, while he himself lay on his side, wrapped with rope. Occasionally, he caught the scent of lavender. *He hit me on the head.* A raindrop crashed into his face.

With some effort, Rath extracted his obsidian knife from the backing of his belt. He decided that his only hope was to cut the rope and jump off the wasp. The foul weather might mask any change in the wasp's flying as he jumped. But he had no idea where he was or how high they were flying. If he did not completely free himself from entanglement in the rope, Rath knew he would likely die from the fall. He would have to rely on his own, diminutive wings, regardless of how vulnerable that left him afterwards. He proceeded to cut the strands of rope, beginning with the ones bearing the least tension. When his hands were free, he took hold of the one rope attaching him to the main harness and cut it. With the knife still in his hand and the Thistlepix close enough to touch, Rath considered how to kill it. He recalled blood warming his hand as fear faded from the face of the Thistlepix he had slain. *It's so personal.* He stowed his knife into its pocket.

Before he could decide on the best way to roll off the back of the wasp, a high pitch chittering noise approached from the rear. *A bat!* As the Thistlepix turned its head to look behind, Rath was launched off the back of the wasp by the impact of something broad and soft.

Rath tumbled into the void. He extended his feeble wings and flapped them with all his strength. His only expectation was to break the fall. He knew he could not fly. No Faerie could actually fly. As he descended into the darkness, he thought of Britt. *If the bat came a little sooner, I'd be dead.* His strength faded. He thought of the

Thistlepix that had surely been eaten. *I should have killed it first.* He fell a bit farther, then landed on something soft that bobbed and swayed under his weight.

A dandelion! The fragrance left no doubt. *What are the chances...* The exhaustion of flight swept over him. He faded into dreamless sleep.

Rath sat up suddenly. He found himself sitting in a shallow puddle beneath a sizable cluster of dandelions. The bright overcast sky of mid-day sifted a light drizzle into his face. He shivered, extracted his knife and quickly fashioned a cape for himself from the nearest suitable leaf. Looking about, he had not the faintest idea where he was. Nothing in the distance resembled anywhere that he had ever visited.

Checking his arms and legs and body, he found no injuries. His blue tunic bore a square patch in the front, stitched by Bessa over the damage from his encounter with the ant nearly a month ago. His head throbbed. He touched a tender lump on the back of his scalp, to the left side. The act of reaching up to his head stretched a knot of strained muscle between his shoulder blades. He rotated one wing in a slow painful arc, then another. He thought again of the Thistlepix on the wasp. *I should have killed it. It was my duty.*

He conceded that he could not get his bearings without the sun shining. The only thing to do was find a safe place to wait until the weather cleared. He pulled down the corner of a leaf, took a drink of rainwater, then headed to the nearest patch of denser vegetation.

Walking on the squishy duff, he considered laying out some sort of signal, in case someone came looking for him, but abandoned the thought when he weighed the possibility of Thistlepix also searching for him. He stopped and scanned the horizon for the tall thistles used as houses by Thistlepix. There were none. Although their absence comforted him, the recognition that he was completely alone brought with it a frightening sense of exposure.

Gray sky continued to drizzle itself to the ground, drooping the grass, and casting a pall of confinement over Rath's surroundings, and a heaviness to his body as well as his spirit. He walked on, dodging puddles and overhanging vegetation, not noticing an oddly crumpled mass of purple and black until he had nearly tripped on it.

Before him lay the contorted body of a Thistlepix. *It fell from the wasp!* Rath stepped back and examined the motionless form. The fallen Thistlepix wore a light purple, satin blouse, now spattered with mud. The right arm was hidden beneath it. The other crossed over its chest. A delicate hand, with long, slender fingers extended from a full-length, puffy sleeve. The Thistlepix' face was hidden from view. Unlike a Faerie, it wore trousers, black and muddy, and shoes—tall, pointy affairs made from soft, gray animal skin. Judging from the odd shape of the left shin, Rath believed it was broken. *Serves you right.* He felt relief that the Thistlepix had not been eaten by the bat. Not even a Thistlepix deserved that. But falling to its death, Rath decided, suited it perfectly. *I should have killed it myself.* It was his duty. *Dead is dead.*

Rath walked around to the other side, keeping some distance. The Thistlepix' face appeared quite pale—eyes closed, red eyelashes, all framed in mud-spattered red hair plastered against its forehead down to its red eyebrows. Beneath a patch of faint red fuzz, its pallid lips suggested those of a sleeping child. The tip of its narrow chin was painted with a splat of mud. It appeared to be only two or three years older than Rath. *Maybe that's what their elders look like.*

The question of what to do with the dead Thistlepix troubled him. He certainly owed it no favor. *They killed Britt. The bugs can just eat it.*

A scent of lavender jogged his memory of the flight on the wasp. He bent down close to the still face and sniffed. *Lavender.* With the tip of his finger, Rath touched the cold cheek. He brushed an eyebrow. It felt much softer than its bristly appearance suggested. He noticed that the ruffled collar of the blouse extended to a hood, now crumpled behind its shoulders. He felt the smooth texture of the purple fabric. The lavender scent, the delicate symmetry of its face, the softness, the satin—all of these touched him with an inexplicable sadness.

Rath decided to bury it. He chose a spot nearby that seemed soft enough to dig, and with a quarter hour of work, using a stick and his bare hands, he managed to excavate a trench large enough for the Thistlepix. He returned to the body and stood over it, uncertain about having to get it into the trench. Gathering his courage, he grasped its left arm and dragged it slowly to its grave. When the head and torso were in place, he positioned both arms neatly over the abdomen. The trench was too short. He brought the right knee up a bit, so that its foot would fit inside the grave. When he grasped the left knee, the leg seemed much stiffer. He pulled harder. A raspy susurration drew his attention to the Thistlepix' head. Its eyes were closed, but a grimace had formed on its lips. Rath jumped back, landing on his butt beside the trench.

He leaned forward. The grimace was gone. He pushed an arm, but saw no response. Rath returned to the left leg and moved the knee while watching the face. A grimace crept over the Thistlepix' mouth. *It's alive!*

Rath drew his obsidian knife and placed its glassy edge beneath the ear of the Thistlepix. He recalled warm blood spreading over his hand. Despite the rain, blood still remained at the edges of his fingernails, forming a grizzly outline around each nail. The moment of hesitation sealed his decision. He returned the knife to his belt.

This presented a more difficult situation. He knew he could not bury it alive, not even a Thistlepix. But if he helped it, he might end up in a grave himself, if not roasted and eaten. *What if they come looking for it? I should have killed it. It'll just die anyway.*

After searching a half-hour, he discovered a newly grown morchella. He had heard of other villages living in morchellas instead of boletuses, but this towering, conical fungus seemed a most unlikely prospect. It stood ten times his height. That was fair enough. But its creamy brown, crenelated exterior was penetrated everywhere by deep, room-size caverns that ended just shy of the central stem. There was no solid mass large enough for carving a fully enclosed room. He decided to see what sort of shelter he could make of it.

Rath cut a spacious doorway into the base of the stem. Morchella seemed to cut almost as easily as boletus. His first surprise was the discovery of its hollow stem, which actually simplified the process of creating a spiral stairway leading to the cap. As he cut the stairs, Rath punctured three windows to the outside for light. Once inside the conical cap, he thumped his fist along the stem wall to locate a thinner region, then cut a door into a spacious, open-air chamber that provided an unimpeded view of the surrounding forest in that direction. *Very nice!* Rath quickly sliced a broad bench into the side wall and plopped himself down, satisfied with a mere one hour's work.

Morchella seemed considerably more fragrant than boletus—a robust, musty, homely scent. After opening chambers in two other directions, he could, with a few steps, take in a panorama of the nearby forest. If necessary, he thought, he could exit in any direction. Though the drop would be more than ideal, he could manage it. Other than its being somewhat breezy, Rath was pleased with his new quarters, even more so since he had created it himself.

He gazed out the opening to the exterior. *I did kill the wisteria one. The lavender one... It'll be dead soon enough. I have my own house. Britt is dead.* Rath sat on the floor, rested his chin on his knees and cried, blurring his view of Ternaria's drizzle-shrouded forest.

After sitting for a while, Rath descended his stairway to the ground and walked directly to the body of the Thistlepix. Kneeling, he pressed his ear firmly against the wet surface of the purple blouse, squarely in the center of its chest. A muted, rapid thump confirmed his guess that it was still alive. Rath hauled the body out of its grave. Squatting alongside, he draped both arms over his own shoulders, keeping his wings flat. Then with substantial effort, he rose to a stand, hoisting most of the Thistlepix' weight onto his back. Both its legs still dragged the ground. As he stomped back toward the morchella, bent under his burden, the head of the Thistlepix rocked beside his own. Damp, lavender-scented hair swished against his face. Across his shoulders and back, where their bodies pressed together, he sensed the warmth of life. When he finally reached the morchella, he squatted and lowered the Thistlepix to the ground against the stem. He brought both of his hands to his nose and sniffed. *Lavender.*

After a brief rest, he once again lifted the Thistlepix onto his back and climbed into the morchella, pausing every few steps to catch his breath. Uncomfortable at the thought of a Thistlepix so near, he placed it on the floor of the chamber on the opposite side of the stem. It seemed a waste of effort to carve a bench to put it on, since the floor was nearly as soft.

What to do with the injured Thistlepix was something of a mystery until he decided to do the obvious—look at the leg. He knelt to remove its trousers. After untying the belt, he was stopped by the question of whether Thistlepix wore shorts beneath their trousers. He thought of Bessa. Rath elected instead to cut off the left trouser leg, exposing an unnatural angle in the shin. The pale skin showed bruising and swelling. He knew a little about splints, but had seen Sullis put one on a broken arm only once, two years ago. Using segments of split pine needle and strips cut from the removed trouser leg, he splinted the fracture as well as his skill allowed, mostly straightening the angle. Beyond that, all that he could do was to roll up a leaf for a pillow under its head.

After dark, Rath lay on the bench of his chamber and tried to sleep. Hunger churned his stomach, but in the end, it was isolation that caused him the greater discomfort. Rath walked into the opposite chamber and curled up beside the Thistlepix. He drifted into a lavender-scented sleep.

Rath was awakened at dawn by soft moaning. The Thistlepix had rolled over to its stomach sometime during the night. Its splinted leg lay knee-down on the floor.

"Are you awake?" When Rath saw no response, he pushed on the Thistlepix' hip and shoulder, rolling it to its back. The moaning stopped.

His first priority was to get some food and water or, if he got lucky, food and nectar. His back ached from digging and dragging and carrying and, he nearly forgot, flying. He stretched his arms and extended his wings. On a whim, he jumped from the chamber to the ground, using his wings to slow his descent. "Uh. That hurts."

When he returned, he carried an armload of various seeds and the neatly trimmed bottom of a honeysuckle blossom. The seeds he dumped on the floor. Kneeling beside the pile of seeds, he gouged a conical hole into the floor and rested the cup of nectar in it. The Thistlepix remained in the position in which Rath had placed it.

"I don't suppose you're awake."

The Thistlepix opened its eyes and gasped. Rath had not expected a response. They silently stared at one another. Rath had never spoken to a Thistlepix. After a long pause, he said flatly, "I'm Rath."

"Where am I?" the Thistlepix asked in a higher pitch than Rath's voice. He screwed up his face at an attempt to reposition his splinted leg.

"I don't know. We're lost. Or at least I'm lost."

"What is this place?" His eyes remained fixed on Rath.

"It's a morchella. It's the only thing I could find."

"It smells awful."

"Can't do much about that."

"You brought me here?

"Yeah. I thought you were dead, so I was burying you. But then you moved. Good thing. So I found this..." He gestured at the walls. "...and fixed it up for shelter."

The Thistlepix retied his waist belt. The pallor of his cheeks brightened to a healthier pink. "What are you going to do?"

"About what?"

"To me?"

"I don't know." Rath had not really thought that far. *I almost killed you...twice.* "Are you thirsty?"

The Thistlepix did not answer. Rath took out his knife and lopped a chunk from the wall, which he carved into a bowl. He dipped it into the nectar and carried it to the Thistlepix. "Here."

After a pause, the Thistlepix raised himself up on his elbows, but apparently could find no comfortable way to free a hand to accept the bowl. Rath lowered the bowl to his lips. The Thistlepix swallowed until the bowl was drained.

"I got some of these." Rath placed several seeds beside him. The Thistlepix sniffed one seed, then returned it to the floor. "Well, I've got to go figure out how to get home." Rath walked to the exterior opening of the chamber and hopped off the edge, using his wings again. *Uh. That hurts.*

The Thistlepix shouted something. Rath looked up to the opening. "What?"

"Dobar. My name is Dobar."

"Why are you helping me?" Dobar asked.

The sun had set on their fourth day together. Rath lay on his back, resting his head on a pillow formed by his arms. Alongside him in the fading light, Dobar had propped himself on one elbow.

"I don't know."

"Aren't you worried I might kill you while you're sleeping?"

"No. Then you'd just die here."

"That's true." After a long silence, Dobar continued. "It's my duty to kill you."

"So...we're both supposed to kill each other."

"But you can kill me. And you haven't."

"It's not because I think you deserve to live. My friend is dead."

"My friend is dead. And you had no trouble killing him."

"This is different. Your leg is broken."

"That won't make much difference when I'm dead."

"I would feel bad if I killed somebody with a broken leg. Somebody that's helpless."

"So when my leg is better?"

"Then you won't be helpless."

That night, Rath dreamed of Bessa. In his dream, he lay in a field of sweetgrass, wearing only his tattered shorts. Bessa lay beside him with her slender arm draped across his scrawny chest, her soft breath warming his shoulder. He lifted her hand to his lips and kissed the center of her palm, then returned it to the still-warm spot over his ribs.

He opened his eyes. Predawn light brought him back to the floor of a chamber in his morchella house. Dobar's head rested against his shoulder. Dobar's arm draped across his chest.

Rath lifted the delicate hand and studied its pink, spider-like digits. *So fragile.* He replaced the hand, then covered it with his own. Turning his head toward the Thistlepix, he sniffed the hair that had spilled onto his own shoulder. The dusty, sweaty scent brought to mind the many times that he and Britt had played and wrestled and tumbled and slept together. In those distant moments, he had never considered how Britt might judge his scent or appearance or friendship. *We were young.* A hint of lavender was all that distinguished his dead friend from his living enemy. Tears burned his eyes and caused his nose to run. He turned his head away and sniffed the tears back in.

Rath slipped from under the arm without disturbing Dobar, and rose to his feet. *I'm supposed to kill you.* He descended the stairway and began another day of searching for a familiar landmark, a way back home.

After nearly three weeks, he had yet to determine the direction back to his village, despite spending half of each day walking in a straight line from the morchella, and the other half returning. Each excursion carried him in a different direction. It was near noon today. He stopped beneath a sunflower that had begun to shed its seeds. After two ineffective strokes of his obsidian blade against an impenetrable seed case, he put away his knife and sat down to consider his situation.

By now, he had concluded that his village was more than one whole day's walk from the morchella. Otherwise, he would have encountered familiar territory. The crux of the problem was not the distance, but the direction. If he knew which way to go, he could simply keep walking until he got there. *I'll never get home.*

Then there was Dobar. He could not leave him to starve. Although Dobar was now able to crawl about without too much pain, and to take care of himself within the morchella, he still could not bear weight on his left leg. Yesterday, Rath had made him a crutch, but Dobar would need time to learn how to walk with it. Even then, Rath realized, Dobar could not be expected to find his own way home on a crutch.

Each evening, when Rath returned to the morchella—he refused to think of it as home—he would describe to Dobar, at the Thistlepix' insistence, which direction he had explored that day and what he had seen. Rath carved a line representing each excursion onto the floor of the chamber they shared. Today's journey would add the last line radiating from a center point.

Dobar usually spoke to him with civility, but nothing resembling friendliness. The Thistlepix had never let slip the least expression of gratitude. Rath felt indifference on that issue. He had not helped Dobar for Dobar's benefit. He had tried to bury him when he thought Dobar was dead and clearly unable to appreciate the effort.

Father was right. It's what Rath wants. Rath did it for Rath. Now he provided for Dobar in the same spirit. Not providing for Dobar would just feel bad, he reasoned—as would be the killing of a crippled enemy. He did not care how the irritable invalid regarded the effort.

A loud crack to his left startled him. He spun around to face whatever might be there, drawing his knife as he turned. Before him loomed the massive bulk of a tortoise, lazily cracking a sunflower seed in its jaws. It hesitated just long enough to glance in Rath's direction, then returned to its meal.

Rath's heart pounded. He had never stood so close to a tortoise. Its dull, leathery skin hung in sagging folds from its shoulders to its angular head. Its coarse tongue deftly extracted fragments of seed from the broken seed case. Geometric terraces of shell plates practically invited him to climb to the summit of the placid beast. Rath slowly stepped back to the seed he had unsuccessfully tried to open. With both hands, he pushed the seed toward the tortoise, furrowing the earth as he went. The tortoise slowly rocked its head toward Rath's proffered seed and easily cracked it open in a single bite. Rath quickly removed a fist-size fragment for his lunch. Whenever the tortoise consumed a seed's contents, Rath brought it another, each time standing closer to the tortoise's head.

Altogether, the tortoise had eaten twelve entire seeds, a month's rations for himself and Dobar, before it ignored further offers. But by the thirteenth seed, Rath was able to reach behind its head and gently scratch its neck.

"You like that, don't you, nutcracker?"

The tortoise blinked.

A week later, Rath was busy painting weed sap around the base of the morchella to keep away the aphids. Nutcracker lazed beneath a nearby shrub. Rath had been surprised at how tolerant the creature was of having someone climbing about its shell. He discovered that he could sit on Nutcracker's neck, even with it pulled all the way in and the shell completely closed, though the odor was scarcely bearable. A few brisk thumps on its thick skull would cause the shell to open again. Pressing one of his toes against the large, round soft spot on the side of its head caused Nutcracker to turn in the opposite direction. Pressing on both sides at once encouraged the tortoise to begin walking.

Although Nutcracker didn't walk much faster than Rath could walk on his own, the tortoise offered a significant advantage when it came to hauling a load. Using a rope of spider silk, Rath could load food onto Nutcracker and transport it to the morchella.

Dobar emerged from the doorway of the morchella, moving smoothly on his crutch. He observed Rath for a moment, then seated himself in the shade of a nearby clover.

"Are you planning to live here forever?" Dobar asked.

"Only as long as I have to."

"What is that supposed to mean?"

Rath sighed. "You can get food and water now, so as soon as I can figure out which way to go, I'm going home."

"And Nutcracker?"

"I found him. And you don't even know how to ride him."

"I'm sure that's really difficult."

"He's mine."

An insect flew past, almost directly overhead. Rath crouched in the shadow of the morchella. *Thistlepix!* He and Dobar watched it fade into the distance. *No!* "It's a honeybee. A drone!" A quarter hour later it returned, but higher above the forest floor. *A yellow band. It's father!* Rath jumped and shouted, waving his arms, but it continued on.

"It doesn't look like they want you back," Dobar remarked.

Rath ignored him. He sat on the ground, frustrated and lonely. He missed his mother. He missed Britt. *Britt is dead! Killed by Thistlepix.* He wondered if his father had been searching for him all these weeks. *It's that way! He started from home and went back home.* "Ha!" He locked eyes with Dobar.

When Nutcracker trudged into the Domes, Rath heard several shouts of caution from mothers to their children.

"It's loaded with bundles. Look," Dibola said.

Then Rath peeped out from behind Nutcracker's head.

"Rath!" Bessa held both hands over her mouth, but came no closer.

Rath smiled and waved.

Leela ran out of Boletus Pente. "Rath Pente," she stated with surprising vehemence, "where have you been?"

Rath jumped down from Nutcracker's neck and sprinted to his mother, hugging her despite her apparent anger. "They captured me. I just now found my way home."

He saw that she was crying. "Baby, we thought you were...gone." She brushed some twigs from his hair and kissed him.

"That's a pretty big bee you got." Standing beyond his mother was Britt, his arms folded.

"Britt," Rath shouted. He couldn't believe his eyes. "They shot you!"

"Yeah, but only a little bit."

Rath laughed aloud as he drew Britt into a three-way hug. Bessa broke through the ring of arms, took Rath by the head and pressed a lingering kiss into his lips, surprising Rath and raising eyebrows around the circle. Rath pinched Bessa's shoulder, but not quite as firmly as on previous occasions.

"Rath." His father stood behind him.

Rath turned and hugged his father. "I saw the yellow band on the drone. It led me home." He began to cry, burying his face in Reskith's shoulder. "I saw the band."

He spent the afternoon explaining to his parents and others who had gathered what had happened. He had forgotten that no one had seen his encounter with the Thistlepix when they had attacked the village. He realized that, to them, he had simply disappeared. He told of killing one and of his escape from the bat. He proudly recounted his creation of a house from the morchella and of his attempts to determine the way back home. Through it all, Rath carefully avoided any mention of Dobar.

That evening, he sat before Sullis in Boletus Ena, between his mother and his father. The Elder wore the white of the first Boletus, a color echoed by a rim of white hair about his otherwise bald head. Dark curves sagged beneath his large, black eyes.

"In addition to preserving yourself," Sullis intoned, "you have brought a great resource to the tribe. You have killed Thistlepix and created a house in, of all things, a morchella. And you survived completely alone in the open forest for a month. Quite a list." He cleared his throat. "Such a distinguished accomplishment warrants recognition." Sullis extracted a square swatch of beige fabric from his sleeve and held it up in one hand.

Rath glanced back and forth from the fabric to the expectant expression on the face of his Elder. He recognized that the gesture symbolized something important, but he had no idea what it meant. He wondered what they would think if he had mentioned Dobar—if they learned that he had failed in his duty to kill him.

"Rath Pente."

"Yes, sir?"

"You have my consent to capture and train a new drone. You will, of course, need to open a new boletus and gain the support of at least two additional members for your new Boletus Octa, whose color will be sand..." He waved the fabric swatch, "to recognize your taming of a tortoise."

Rath could hardly believe what he was hearing. He looked at each of his parents. Their expressions revealed that neither was surprised by what Sullis had just announced. Sullis offered him all that he had dreamed of. He accepted the piece of fabric and studied it. Sullis, Reskith and Leela smiled at him in silence. He could just say, "thank you," and have his bee. *And go as far as I want.* But that had somehow lost its allure. He had already gone farther than he had ever wanted. He had already opened a new house, and had failed in his responsibilities. He imagined their reaction if they were to learn about Dobar after he had accepted this recognition.

"Sir," he said, returning the swatch to Sullis, "I don't think I'm ready for that."

"No?" Sullis asked.

"I've got Nutcracker to take care of." Rath looked at his father. "But I do have a...thing that I need to do. Can I fly one of the drones tomorrow, by myself, just this once?"

"What sort of thing?" Reskith asked.

"Just this once. It's just important. Something I need to finish. And it won't take very long. And I'll get to my chores right after."

Sullis scratched his chin. "I believe that would be reasonable, if your father agrees." He looked to Reskith, who nodded.

"Where are you going?"

Britt's voice in the quiet of morning startled Rath as he tightened a harness on the yellow banded drone, Apis Hexa.

"Promise you won't tell?" Rath whispered.

"I promise."

"Not even Bessa?"

"Rath!"

"I found a Thistlepix while I was out there. It's at the morchella."

Britt's eyes widened. "You're going back?"

"That's what I was about to do." Speaking those familiar words truthfully for the first time pricked his conscience.

"We're partners."

"I have to go alone."

"I know how to fight."

"I know you do. I saw you attack the Thistlepix barehanded." He hugged Britt until his friend returned the hug. "I have to do this alone."

In the end, Rath agreed to carry the pike that had belonged to Britt's father. Britt felt that it would be right for that pike to be used to get even for his father's death.

A layer of mist still shrouded the forest floor when Rath set out alone on Apis Hexa. He flew in a straight line for his morchella shelter. As he landed near the base of the conical fungus, he heard his name shouted from an opening in the cap. Dobar crutched his way out the door and directly to the drone. Rath hopped down. He saw that Dobar's eyes were red and puffy. The musty scent of morchella hovered about him.

"You came back."

"Yeah. Unfinished business."

Dobar's gaze drifted to the pike in Rath's hand, then back to Rath's eyes.

"I figured if my home is that way," Rath extended an arm in the direction from which he had come, "then your home must be that way." He pointed the pike in the opposite direction. Rath climbed onto the drone's foreleg and held out a hand.

Dobar wiped his eyes on his puffy, light purple sleeves and smiled.

CHAPTER 4—MOSQUITO PUDDING

Tatt straddled a horizontal maple branch, laughing as he watched Jardi twirling toward the ground. Dancing splashes of late afternoon sunlight dappled the branches and the leaves, as well as the ground beneath the tree. Jardi's laughter paused only briefly when the maple seed abruptly ended its flight.

"Harvestman!" Perris screamed. She turned and ran a short distance away, then hefted a fist-size stone and flung it past Jardi.

Searching through gaps between the leaves, Tatt could not see the eight-legged predator, but knew that such a warning was never a subject of humor. He looked down at Jardi.

Jardi stood, still laughing, until he lost his balance. That was half the fun. Now lying flat on his back, oblivious of the warning, he smiled up at Tatt. A moment later, all but Jardi's face was obscured by a massive, round carapace.

Even though a month had passed since poor Jardi had been killed and eaten by the harvestman, Tatt still could not drive the image from his mind. Jardi had won the draw to be the last to ride a maple seed to the ground before dinner. Tatt had shoved the seed off the branch, laughing himself breathless as Jardi spun his way down. That's why he died, Tatt thought. When the harvestman appeared, they all got out of the way. All except Jardi. He had managed two steps before losing his balance. Then it was too late. After the first bite, Jardi's whole body had trembled, then stiffened with his back arched, his teeth grinning.

"Tatt!" his father shouted, "You're daydreaming again. Turn the crystal." Foplin, standing behind another crystal, indicated the proper direction with a waving hand.

Tatt rotated the heavy tower of colorless crystal with both hands until Foplin signaled to stop. Tatt's older brother, Mipple, stood behind a third crystal. Two more crystal towers lay on their sides, unused. A waist-high stone platform stood a short distance from the arc formed by the evenly spaced crystals. The platform had been in that spot as far back as Tatt could remember. Each crystal focused a beam of sunlight onto the headless body of a medium-sized red and black ant, which lay motionless in an elongated clay dish atop the platform. The ant began to sizzle, emitting a sweet, sour aroma.

"I think we've done it," Foplin exclaimed. "Cooking without fire." Foplin's blunt wings rose with his apparent enthusiasm. "This is a day to remember."

As Tatt watched from behind his crystal, the ant burst into flame. Within a heartbeat, nothing was left of the ant but ash and a billow of sooty smoke.

"Of course, it needs some minor adjustments," Foplin said with undiminished satisfaction. "Each one of those is like six or seven shining suns, but they have to be positioned just right. Turn them out."

Tatt spread his feet and gave his crystal a firm twist, diverting its light from the platform. Mipple looked at him, then rolled his eyes, causing them both to start laughing.

"What's so funny?" their father asked.

"That!" Tatt answered through his laughter. He pointed to the smoldering ash.

Foplin raised his eyebrows. "In ancient times, the high priest would sacrifice a Faerie with fire on an altar somewhere near this spot. Some say this is the ancient altar."

Tatt's laughter evaporated. "Why would they do that?" He could almost imagine that the smoke above the platform rose from the ashes of a Faerie.

"After raising an important building, they thought it would drive away the angry wood spirits."

"How did they pick someone to burn?"

"They probably just drew straws," Mipple said.

"No. I mean, was it somebody that deserved it?"

When they had thrown sticks and rocks at the harvestman to drive it away, it had crouched its globular body down to Jardi and snatched him up in its jaws, carrying him off as it fled. Up close, Tatt thought, the harvestman looked like nothing more than a fat wood tick walking on eight stilts.

"Am I going to have to do all the work?" Perris stood with her hands on her hips.

"Oh. Sorry," Tatt replied. He and Perris were using hooked shards to excavate a root cellar into the black flesh of a truffle. Tatt carved out another chunk and stacked the edible fungus just outside the doorway.

"You don't have to help." Perris gouged at the inner wall. "I mean, if you don't want to."

"I said I would." Tatt usually enjoyed Perris' company, even if it meant helping her with her chores. He had helped Jardi with his garden the day he was killed. "Do you think Jardi knew what was happening?" Perris had been there. She had been the first to throw something at the harvestman.

"Tatt!" She stopped her work and looked at him with a pained expression. Her face softened. "I guess the first bite hurt. After that, I don't think he knew anything." She sighed. "It wasn't your fault. It just happened." She glanced at her hands, wiped them on her gray work tunic, then tucked her yellow hair back into the collar.

"He looked right at me before he fell."

"You were closest, Tatt."

"If I could find it, I'd jam a pine needle up its throat till it came out the other end."

"Captain Derina has three guards looking for it. She said they would try to snare its legs or something."

"It's been weeks," Tatt replied, resuming his excavation.

"Last week they found a couple of moths it had killed, so it's still around here somewhere."

"I wasn't the closest."

"What?"

"I was still in the tree and he looked right at me."

"I've moved the crystals a little farther away," Foplin explained, "but we need to test it on something with more juice in it than an ant."

"How about a mosquito?" Tatt suggested.

"A really fat one," Mipple added.

"Good idea," Foplin said. "You'll need to tie up an animal and wait."

"At dusk," Mipple said. "It's a full moon tonight."

"Yes. Dusk. Perfect." Foplin rubbed his hands together. "Lizard blood would be good. Or maybe one of those bluish salamanders. You'll have to work it out. I've got to go help raise the frame for the new village hall, so you boys will be on your own. Full moon or not, you get back to Elby before dark."

Captain Derina approached, her rod of office nestled in her left arm. In her right hand she held a raspberry pike. "They're waiting for us, Foplin."

"Any sign of that harvestman?" Foplin asked.

"We see signs alright, but never see the actual thing." Captain Derina shook her head. "It's like a spirit. What's really odd is that it would hunt in the day." She watched as Tatt and Mipple coiled several lengths of twine. "Don't go far from Elby."

Once Father and Captain Derina had headed off to the raising, Tatt picked up his twine and a casting net. He had never been good with a net, so he tossed it to his brother. "You think we should carry some weapons?"

"If that harvestman shows up," Mipple replied, "I'm not going to stay to duke it out."

Though Mipple was only a year older than Tatt, he had put on quite a bit of muscle. His height had reached nearly a faerielong. His brown tunic was tight at the chest and well shy of his knees, a sure sign that Tatt would soon inherit it. "No weapons. Swamp?" Tatt asked.

"Swamp."

Tatt headed east alongside his brother as they walked beneath the towering meadow grass. Beyond the meadow, they passed through open pine woods to the bog, halting beneath a rhododendron thicket. They caught a small earthworm, then set out a half dozen snares with a writhing segment of worm impaled on a stick in the center of each. After three hours of silent boredom, their patience was rewarded with a thrashing sound at one of the snares. Tatt didn't care what they had caught, so long as it contained blood.

At the snare, they found a young, black and yellow striped lizard lying motionless. It was larger than Tatt had hoped, but their spider silk twine would be strong enough to tie down its legs.

"You get the other leg," Mipple whispered, and waited for Tatt to circle around to the far side.

On Mipple's nod, each simultaneously cast a loop of twine about the lizard's front legs. It tugged against the snare, but could not escape.

"Tie it off," Mipple yelled.

They drew the lines taut. The lizard struggled momentarily, then resumed its immobile stance. Tatt was confident that the presence of even a small lizard would keep away the harvestman. Another hour passed. As dusk approached, a blanket of mosquitoes rose above the soggy duff. Each time a mosquito landed on the lizard, the reptile's sudden movement frightened it away. Tatt sat and rested his head on his hands. He knew that the mosquitoes would search for dinner from a creature larger than a Faerie.

Something bounced against Tatt's cheek. He sat up in a daze. Mipple stood across the lizard from him, pointing to a mosquito, nearly a quarter the length of the lizard upon which it fed. Mipple signaled to Tatt to wait. Moonlight from the West slanted through gaps in the thicket. They watched as the mosquito's abdomen swelled and grew dark, filling with lizard blood. While Mipple crouched with his net, Tatt checked a segment of twine to make sure its spider silk had been well dusted to prevent it from sticking to itself. He wondered how long he had slept.

"Now!" Mipple whispered, as he cast the net into a gentle spin above the mosquito. Its heavy margin stretched into a perfect circle twice the width of the mosquito's wings.

The lizard lurched, causing the mosquito to withdraw its hollow nose from the leathery back. But as the tail-heavy mosquito began its upward flight, the weight of the net brought it back down. Mipple and Tatt enfolded the mosquito in the net and lifted it clear of the agitated bait animal. Once on the ground, the folded net was staked in place.

While Mipple took care of the tricky process of untying the lizard, Tatt inserted a bight of twine into the net near the mosquito's thorax, then fed it down toward the end of its abdomen by passing it from fingertip to fingertip beneath the lattice of the net. Once there, he slipped a loop over the bulging, dark sac. At the thorax, Tatt gently drew in the twine, working the loop toward him to tie the abdomen before cutting it off. He knew that a trapped mosquito seldom struggled, but if he failed to tie the abdomen securely, all the blood that had distended it would squirt out when he made the cut, leaving only a flaccid tube. Reaching through the mesh, he laid a sack hitch over the junction with the thorax and drew it snug.

Mipple made the cut with a small shard. Bright red blood oozed from the thorax, but Tatt's hitch held tight. The front half of the mosquito tossed and tumbled as Mipple lifted away the net. Tatt laid a second hitch over the first.

"I'm ready," Tatt said, handing Mipple one of the two long ends of the twine.

"That's enough for half the Faeries in Elby," Mipple commented, as they dragged the blood-filled sac back west through the pine woods and into the meadow. The mosquito belly was heavier than usual, bigger around than Mipple and almost as long.

"How much did I sleep?" Tatt asked.

"I don't know. I fell asleep too. I think it's almost morning. The moon is ready to go down."

Their progress was slow, straining against the lines. They paused every ten faerielongs to catch their breath. The moon had abandoned them to a gray gloom. Tatt wasn't sure they could drag their burden all the way home. As the sky grew lighter, color returned to the meadow.

When Tatt first caught sight of their farm, he heard a periodic swishing of the grass behind them. Turning to look, he could see oscillating leg segments moving rapidly toward them through the drooping green blades. "The harvestman! Run!"

They dropped their tow lines and sprinted toward home, still over a hundred faerielongs away. When Tatt looked over his shoulder, expecting the harvestman to be nearly upon them, he saw no sign of it. "I think it..." he shouted between breaths, "...found the mosquito belly."

"Keep running," Mipple replied, now sprinting ahead of Tatt. "Father!" he shouted. "Father, the harvestman!"

Tatt's lungs ached. He didn't think they were close enough for Father to hear them from inside the house. Tatt looked back. He saw the legs again, lifting and falling, alternating from one side to the other.

Tatt thought of Jardi, so dizzy from spinning on the maple leaf that he couldn't run away. The vision of those huge mandibles first clamping into each side of Jardi's chest sent a wave of cold from Tatt's heart to his arms and legs. As he turned his head back toward the safety of his home, his rear foot clipped the front foot, launching him forward into the air and parallel to the ground. He flapped his wings, but not soon enough to slow his fall. The impact knocked the wind from his air-starved lungs.

Now unable to breathe, Tatt lifted himself from the surface of the meadow and ran without air, each step increasing his need to take a breath. He didn't dare look back. As his mind began to cloud, a tiny breath drew in, then a deeper breath. Far ahead of him, Mipple veered from a direct path to the house, heading instead toward a cluster of Faeries gathered by Father's crystal towers. Mipple reached them and merged into the group, which seemed to be nearly the whole village.

Tatt made out his father standing before the center of the group, motioning from behind the stone platform for Tatt to come that way. "Run faster," he seemed to shout.

Now everyone called to him to run faster. Each seemed to hold a spear or pike or knife. The sun had risen high enough to throw a band of brilliant light across the rooftop. Tatt sprinted toward the glare, hoping with each step that the increasing urgency of the villager's shouts was not an indication of how close the harvestman was to his heels. His lungs burned. Every muscle cried out with exhaustion. Now he could hear the soft crunch of the harvestman's feet as they neared.

Foplin pointed with both hands toward himself. All the Faeries, forming a semi-circle beyond the crystals, pointed and gestured toward Foplin, who remained standing immediately behind the stone cooking platform.

From the margin of his vision, Tatt became aware of barbed feet moving at a distance to either side of him. He was nearly to his father. Timing his steps, he hurdled the stone platform, but was caught in Foplin's arms and slammed onto his back atop the stone. As Tatt looked up, the huge underbody of the harvestman descended toward him. He tried to roll off the platform, but his father held him down.

"Don't move," he shouted into Tatt's face. "Don't...move!"

Tatt stared in horror. The jagged mandibles were so close that he could smell their acrid saliva. When Foplin shouted, "Now!" the harvestman's dull brown body changed to a dazzling cream color. With a crackle and a brief whistle, a gout of steam and smoke issued from its face, sending a flaming harvestman toppling away. The desiccated shell of its body thudded onto the meadow. Its eight stilt-like legs contracted toward their origins on the smoldering underbelly.

"When you didn't come home," Perris explained, "your father went to Captain Derina. She sent out most of the village to search, but your father didn't know where you decided to go."

"We fell asleep," Tatt explained.

"When the moon was overhead," Perris continued, "she called everybody back."

Foplin and Mipple approached across the meadow, dragging a new mosquito belly toward the cooking platform, which Tatt now insisted on calling "the altar."

"In the morning," Perris went on, "when they saw how big it was, your father had everyone move those crystal things closer, and they stood up two more—five of them. I didn't think the sun would come up in time." Perris grasped Tatt's hand. He squeezed it in reply. "He said that it would only work if the harvestman stopped right above the platform. You were really brave. You risked your life to lure it to the trap."

"Is that what you think I did?"

"Everybody knows that's what you did. And you evened up the score for Jardi."

Villagers now began to assemble for the celebration. In addition to completing the raising of the frame for Elby's new village hall, they had also destroyed the harvestman. Flutes began to play, Faeries began to dance, and tables were set with every variety of food the land could offer.

When the time came to eat, Foplin called everyone to gather in a circle around the altar. On a long, clay dish rested the fresh mosquito belly, this time filled with blood from a meadow mouse. Foplin had taken down the two extra crystal towers.

"In just a bit, we will all have mosquito pudding, in honor of Tatt's courage," Foplin intoned. He directed three neighbors to rotate the crystals. "This will be a day to remember."

After a momentary sizzle, the mosquito belly swelled to half again its diameter, then exploded, sending a shower of dark brown blood pudding onto all of the onlookers.

"It needs some...adjustments," Foplin mumbled, wiping the pudding from his face.

Tatt looked at Mipple, who rolled his eyes. They both looked at Perris. All the startled onlookers were splattered head to toe on whatever side had been facing the altar. Tatt scooped a finger full of pudding from Perris' forehead and licked it clean. The three of them began to laugh. The laughter spread through the assembled crowd as each Faerie wiped a finger full of mosquito pudding from a neighbor's cheek or nose or ear, and licked it clean.

CHAPTER 5—BINZO'S HIGHBUSH

Binzo kept his flail ready, in case the hummingbird decided to attack. The iridescent yellow and brown bird seemed to have a taste for blueberry blossom. So far as Binzo was concerned, it could take all the nectar it wanted, as long as it left him alone. He knew that by the time most of the berries were ready to harvest, weeks from now, the hummingbirds would lose interest. No blossom, no hummingbird.

For now, Binzo needed to work out the details of ascending to the top branches of the bush to drop those few upper berries that had ripened early. Climbing was not the problem. It was the precarious perch at the base of a fruit stem while separating it from the branch. One slip would be enough to break his leg or his arm or his neck.

He recalled his recent humiliation of twisting an ankle after a slip from a mere crocus. His deformed wings had been useless at their only purpose, breaking a fall. Binzo had considered that to be a lucky fall, since his clubfoot absorbed the impact, rather than his good right ankle. Father had chuckled that the painful sprain had actually improved Binzo's usual limp. "Now you just need to land on those wings," Father had added. Binzo recognized that Faeries could not actually fly, even with perfectly good wings. Faerie wings were just too small for anything but slowing a fall. But that didn't keep his father from frequently expressing embarrassment that Binzo's wings were curled. His ankle injury had not affected his ability to keep up with the others his age, since they had never allowed him to join them.

The hummingbird drifted backwards, hesitated a moment, then buzzed off over the adjoining meadow. Binzo's view from half-way up the highbush allowed him to scan the meadow for other possible dangers. Goldfinch heads sporadically popped into view among the dandelions as various members of their family tackled seed heads to the ground. The arrow-straight passage of a speckled kestrel high above the meadow held Binzo's attention only briefly. He knew they always hovered when they spotted prey. Binzo returned his attention to the climb ahead.

He dropped the handle of his flail into its loop below his belt in order to free both hands, remembering a surprise encounter with a silverfish the previous month when the tethered stone of his flail had slipped out of its hitch, leaving him only a blunt stick with twine dangling from its end. He had since learned to tie a fist knot, choose his stone more carefully and check it every day. Binzo leaned his head back and stared upward at the splayed branches of the highbush. Other than a gentle swaying of the leaves, nothing moved above him. He knew that this did not rule out a mantis lurking motionless, awaiting a tender Faerie for its next meal. Using the irregularities in the bark surface for fingerholds and toeholds, Binzo continued his ascent. The pointed ankle of his left foot, his clubfoot, required less effort for this sort of climbing than did the toes of his good, right foot.

A half-hour's effort brought him to the base of a top branch. He always disliked this part of a climb, because of the swaying of the thin branch and its usual paucity of surface texture for gripping. A nearby flutter and sudden jostling drew his attention to a nuthatch with a dull brown cap perched head-down at the top of an adjacent branch. At first it did not appear to notice Binzo near the base of its branch. Then its head tipped. Centered at the margin of its white face and brown cap, a beady black eye seemed to study him. This variety of nuthatch, he knew, would consume Faerie and insect alike. Worse, he knew they tended to travel in groups. He would have to drive this one off before its companions joined it. As slowly and steadily as he could manage, he moved his trembling hand to his flail. At the same time, he lowered his body to the crotch of the branch for support.

The nuthatch shuffled itself head-down toward him, then paused and tipped its head again. One more shuffle, and it came within the reach of Binzo's flail. He swung the flail upward in a sideways arc. Its stone swept just past the nuthatch's beak, causing the bird to step back and study its would-be meal more carefully.

Binzo grunted in disgust. A second nuthatch lighted at the top of Binzo's branch. The first nuthatch seemed to interpret this as a challenge to its finder's right and promptly shuffled to within pecking range of Binzo's head. A swing of the flail struck squarely on its brown-capped skull. In a chaotic flutter of wings, both birds departed. A brown feather drifted past.

As Binzo rested to allow his breathing to slow and his trembling to subside, he considered how easy it would be to gather blueberries riding on the back of a bird. Of course, it would have to be a bird that wouldn't feast on any creature it could fit into its beak. Or maybe a bird that could be trained not to eat a Faerie.

Shimmying up the slender, terminal branch took his mind off predatory birds and winged transportation. At its end dangled a cluster of five blueberries, each suspended by a stem twice the length of the berry. Since he would need the stem for a towing handle, he would have to separate the base of the stem from the branch. Swaying on the branch tip, he reached into a pocket stitched into the undersurface of his belt and extracted a glossy black shard knife. He would have time for only two trips back to Oakhaven before it grew too dark to be safe. "Two berries," he mumbled. Binzo began to work his shard knife into the base of one of the berry stems.

"Sell blueberries?" his father retorted. "Nobody's going to come all the way to Oakhaven to buy something they can pick for free anywhere."

"But they're hard to pick," Binzo pleaded.

"You go look after the ladybugs, like you were supposed to be doing yesterday. While you were out climbing that highbush, two of my ladybugs wandered off. Just wandered off." Syrick paced about the fungal balcony of their quarters partway up Hometree. He jabbed a finger toward the neatly pruned rose orchard just beyond the market stalls below. "What good does it do to clip their wings if you let them just walk away? It doesn't take two good feet to watch ladybugs."

When his father ranted like that, Binzo knew that he should just nod his head and say nothing. Syrick sighed, then descended the ladder that reached from the ground to their quarters, and beyond to the prestigious upper levels of Hometree. After waiting until his father appeared in his market stall, Binzo climbed down and hobbled his way to the woven fence that surrounded his father's rose orchard.

Father had established the first business in all of Ternaria that offered ladybugs for sale. Convincing a customer to purchase one entailed not only a recitation of their usefulness in pest control, but a demonstration of how easily they could be handled.

Through an opening in the weave, he counted twenty three ladybugs grazing on the rich supply of aphids that the roses sustained. One ladybug reached the top of a rose and spread spotted, red covers to expose its wings. As it lifted off, it simply tumbled to the ground beneath. "I know how you feel," Binzo whispered. Even the scent of rose could not lift his gloom.

With the ladybugs counted, he limped his way behind the market stalls to Hometree and dragged one of his blueberries back to the woven fence. He plunged the tip of a well-dried pine needle into the berry as far as it would reach, and then extracted it in order to lick off the sticky, purple juice. Aroma of blueberry filled the air.

"Binzo!" Syrick yelled from beside his stall. "Come help me with this." His father was wrangling one of the two ladybugs from the adjacent corral. A nearby customer laughed as he watched Syrick struggle.

Binzo scraped the last of his blue sugar into a sugar barrel, then pressed the lid closed. He looked proudly about his market stall. No more than an open-faced puffball, preserved with two coats of varnish, the completed stall had been far more spacious than Binzo actually needed for his inventory. He had carved extra shelves before applying the varnish, just in case. After setting out his stock of granulated sugar and cake sugar, he had cured its empty look by inventing what he called sugar sips, slender tubes of rolled flower petal with a thick coating of fruit sugar on the inside.

A customer approached him. "Is this the sugar place?" The stranger wore a tunic of dark blue fabric, cut in an unfamiliar style.

"Yes it is," Binzo answered with a smile, shoving the sugar barrel against the back wall, then limping to the center of the stall. "Today I have plum sugar, cherry sugar, strawberry sugar and the last of the season's blueberry sugar. I've got each of them granulated and in cakes."

The customer appeared somewhat bewildered. "What are these?" He lifted a bright red sugar sip and sniffed the opening at one end. His black eyes widened a bit and a smile spread across his face.

"You sip ordinary water though it and it comes out like fruit nectar."

"That's amazing. How do you make this stuff?"

"It's a secret method. You can have that one to take home, no charge."

"Thank you." The stranger sniffed the end of the red sugar sip again, then shook his head with a smile.

"Where are you from?" Binzo asked.

"Domes. It's about an hour west of here."

Binzo had never seen a village in that direction.

"As the bee flies. I flew here on my apis drone."

"You flew a drone? Is it here? Can I see it?"

"Sure. It's tied by your big tree.

"Hometree."

"What?"

"We call it Hometree."

As the customer walked past the other market stalls toward Hometree, Binzo limped along behind him, ignoring his father's scowl as they passed the ladybug shop, with its new red and black ladybug sign. Tethered near the base of Hometree was a large honeybee, surrounded by a dozen cautious villagers. Each time the honeybee adjusted its wings, the circle of spectators widened, only to contract again during quiescent interludes.

"What's your name?" the blue-clad Faerie asked.

"Binzo." He could hardly believe that a Faerie could ride on a bee without endangering his life.

"I'm Rath. Want to go for a ride?"

His sugar business had sprung from his accidental discovery that dried blueberry juice could be scraped from the surface of a pine needle. For that, and only that, he could thank his father, since Syrick had called him away before he had time to lick it off. The discovery had led to experiments with other fruits and other drying methods. His business thrived as word of his wonderful sugars spread from village to village. Before Rath had departed, he had placed an order for an entire week's production, and just yesterday had arrived on a gigantic tortoise to haul it west.

Conversations with Rath, and the spectacular flight on the apis drone had fueled Binzo's desire to fly. He was not about to mess with bees, but with Rath's suggestions, he thought he might be able to train a small hummingbird, if he could only figure out a safe way to catch one.

Today was his fifth attempt to lure a hummingbird with his fruit sugar. He had glued a bright red, cherry flavored sugar sip to a bladder of water and now positioned it over the top balcony of Hometree, with its sugar sip extending beyond the edge. The other colors he had tried were completely ignored by all but flies. From his vantage above Oakhaven, he could not only observe the lure, but also keep an eye on the front of his sugar shop by hiding against the raised balcony rim and watching his shop through the drain hole at the rim's base.

Binzo awoke to the buzz of wings. As he lifted his head to look at his sugar lure, an iridescent yellow and brown hummingbird shot straight up and vanished among the high branches. "Red," he said aloud, satisfied at having discovered something about a bird's behavior that had nothing to do with danger. Looking again to the lure, he noted that its bladder had lost a quarter of its volume. A meniscus of reddish water bulged from the opening of the sugar sip.

For ten mornings in a row, he climbed to the top balcony of Hometree with a fresh lure, always with a red sugar sip. After positioning the lure, he climbed all the way back down and tended his sugar shop, keeping the top balcony in sight whenever possible. Each morning, shortly before mid-day, the same iridescent yellow and brown hummingbird hovered at his lure to feed.

From the eleventh day onward, Binzo positioned the lure with its red sugar sip facing toward the balcony deck. The hummingbird, which he had decided to name Highbush, seemed skittish at first, but eventually fed from the inward facing lure as avidly as when it had projected out over the edge.

After three weeks of watching from below, Binzo decided to take the next step. Today, shortly before midday, he climbed to the top balcony of Hometree, leaned his back against the raised balcony rim and held the lure in his hands as high as he could. Right on schedule, Highbush appeared over the balcony and, after hovering above the lure much longer than usual, eventually came down to the sugar sip and fed. Binzo's trembling arms and the prickling over the back of his neck cried out for him to flee. He steadied his breathing. "Your name is Highbush," Binzo whispered. "We're going to learn to fly together." He doubted that Highbush could hear him over the deafening thrum of his wings. Their blur extended four or five times the span of Binzo's arms. Peeking around the side of the lure bladder, he watched as a slender tongue repeatedly pierced the hemisphere of sugar water, then withdrew into a narrow, black beak. *Like a pine needle in a blueberry.* The beak appeared to be longer than Binzo's entire body.

Binzo had stood beside the lure this week, each day a little farther from the lure and closer to Highbush, speaking to the hummingbird while it fed. Today, about half-way through the feeding, he reached out his hand and gently stroked its throat.

"See? That feels good, doesn't it? That's your chin." He gradually moved his stroking around to the side of its head, to a spot above its shoulders. "That's good. You're going to have to carry me."

As Binzo's fully extended arm pressed downward, he could hear a change in the thrum of its wings, while the hover held its position. He grasped the short feathers and pulled himself upward. At the moment he cast a leg over Highbush's shoulder, the hummingbird shot straight up, carrying Binzo into the canopy of Hometree.

"It's okay. It's okay. It's okay." In his fright, Binzo attempted to calm both himself and Highbush. By the time they settled to a hover, he found himself above Hometree with a panoramic view of the distant horizon. "Oh, Highbush!"

Unable to guide the hummingbird, Binzo anchored each of his hands to clusters of short shoulder feathers. His host alternated between gentle hovering and shocking acceleration as they visited dozens of blossoms scattered about the meadow. He continued to talk to Highbush. Sometimes it consisted of a running commentary of his visceral response to the abrupt ascents and dives, but mostly he spoke whatever words popped into his mind.

In what appeared to be an imminent collision with a nearly vertical branch of birch, Binzo found that his reflex attempt to turn the hummingbird's head resulted in a change of direction. Thrilled at the possibility, he turned Highbush several more times. "Ha! You've done it, Highbush. You've done it."

By the time the cooler weather had set in, there was hardly a path for him to limp within his sugar shop. The shelves were double-stacked, and columns of neatly wrapped sugar cakes stood on the floor as high as his head. Along the back, sealed tubs of various flavors of apple jelly, his latest invention, completed his stock. Having Highbush fly him directly to the best fruit had quintupled his output.

By now, Highbush depended entirely on Binzo's sugar water, since all natural sources of nectar had passed with the season. Although the other hummingbirds had migrated, Highbush returned day after day to the carefully maintained feeder at Hometree.

"One of these days," Syrick had warned him, "that bird will forget your little arrangement, and eat you for dinner."

Binzo doubted that. "Highbush is no more dangerous than those ladybugs," he had assured his father. "And he's more predictable. When was the last time one of your ladybugs came when you whistled? Maybe you should learn how to fly on them. Oh! I forgot. You clip their wings."

Binzo spent the fruitless winter months flying to neighboring Faerie villages to arrange contracts for both sales and new supplies of fruit come summer. With Highbush to carry him, Binzo no longer worried about the common dangers of woods and meadow. Though he still carried his flail, purely out of habit, he no longer felt the need to look over his shoulder for predators.

With his success, he was able to acquire the top quarters of Hometree, along with its high balcony, free and clear. He seldom needed to climb the ladder. A sharp whistle would bring Highbush to serve him. On the shoulders of the hummingbird, his clubfoot hardly mattered.

This late Spring morning, Binzo dressed himself in a stylish, new tunic. Its bright red fabric was trimmed in gold at the bottom and the sleeves. He limped out onto his high balcony and whistled for Highbush. When his hummingbird appeared, instead of hovering above the balcony deck, it maintained a noisy, agitated position beyond the balcony rim. Puzzled at Highbush's odd behavior, Binzo concluded that it must be the result of his bright, new tunic. "Red," he said aloud, slapping his forehead.

Disappointed, he decided to go back in and change his clothes. He limped across the deck. Just before reaching the door, a crushing pain enfolded his entire torso. He was lifted from his feet. Binzo tried to call the name, "Highbush," but he could not draw enough air into his lungs. He reached down to his waist and pulled against the rigid vise that held him. To his confusion, instead of the dark, smoothly curved beak of a hummingbird about his waist, he saw a thick, dull green, serrated insect leg. In his agony, Binzo's eyes followed the jointed leg to where it attached to the largest mantis he had ever seen, over twice the size of Highbush. A massive triangular head with bulging green eyes separated by a forehead as wide as the span of Binzo's arms turned on its neck to gaze at him. With pain radiating up and down his body, he drew his flail and snapped it toward the mantis' head. An empty knot of twine glided harmlessly over the green chitin. As the mantis drew Binzo toward its jagged mandibles, the crushing grip about his waist loosened, dropping him across the rim of the topmost balcony of Hometree, his legs dangling over the edge. Still unable to breathe, Binzo sunk his fingernails into the stiff fungal surface.

Highbush struck at the huge mantis, pulling off a middle leg. The mantis retreated. Again Highbush attacked, tearing a portion of wing that covered the mantis' tender abdomen. The insect staggered back along the bark. Highbush flew to where Binzo dangled from the balcony rim. Hovering beneath him, the hummingbird slowly lifted, so that he could crawl back to the deck. As he lay on his belly trying to catch his breath, the buzz of Highbush abruptly changed to a chaotic thrashing. Then there was silence.

Binzo drew in a painful breath and eased himself over to his side to look up. Where the giant mantis had been moments before, there was nothing but the furrowed bark of Hometree reaching skyward. As he stared, two short, iridescent yellow feathers floated down to the silent deck.

Shouts rose from the base of Hometree. Binzo eased himself up to the rim and looked down in time to see his father and five other villagers killing the crippled mantis. Nearby lay the still body of Highbush.

Binzo's father panted as he stepped from the ladder onto the highest balcony. He gently lifted Binzo and carried him to his bed. "Your hummingbird tore into that mantis all the way down to the ground."

"He saved my life," Binzo sobbed.

"I know." Syrick awkwardly patted him on the back of his hand. "I'll mind your shop until you're able to get about. I don't know too much about sugar and such."

"But Highbush is dead. He died for me."

"Maybe so. He didn't look so good. I've never seen a hummingbird sit on the ground. Some of the folks are seeing if he'll take some of your sugar water." Syrick inspected Binzo's injuries. "I think you've got a few broken ribs and a lot of bruises. That's not too bad for a Faerie caught by a mantis."

A resonant thrum drew Binzo's attention to the balcony deck. "Highbush!"

"Well, I'll be a cricket's ear!" Syrick muttered.

Hovering just above the balcony, Highbush gazed into the open doorway, his feathers ragged and his left foot dangling askew.

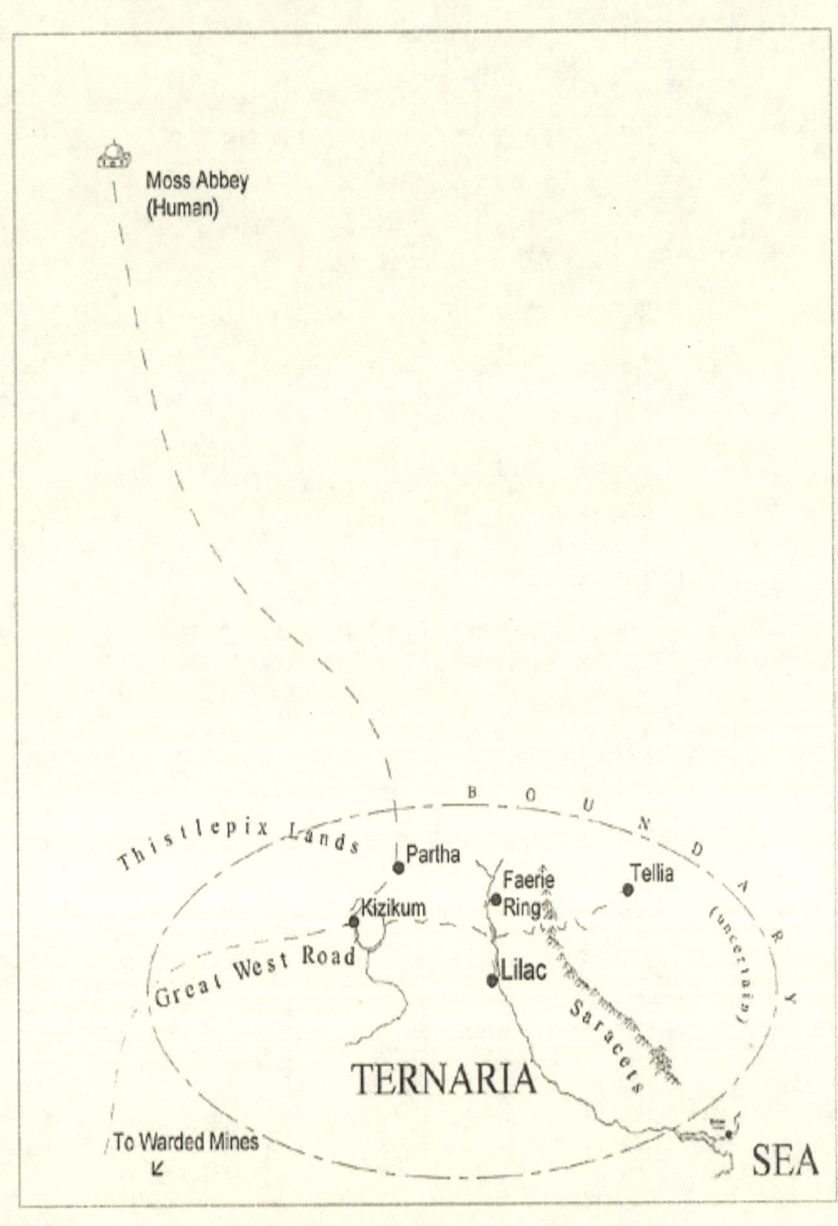

Moss Abbey
(Human)
B O U N D A R Y
(uncertain)
Thistlepix Lands
Partha
Faerie Ring
Tellia
Kizikum
Great West Road
Lilac
Saracets
TERNARIA
To Warded Mines
SEA

CHAPTER 7—BEYOND THE BOUNDS

Britt slid from beneath the leaf that had served as his shelter for the night, pulled up the stakes, and allowed it to blow away in a gust of morning air. An edge of high gray cloud approached from the West. That and the coolness of the morning suggested a rainy day ahead. From the ground where his shelter had been, he retrieved his black tunic. After shaking it, Britt opened the wide flap of the neck and stepped into it, fastening two frogs at the shoulder, just above his left wing. He tied it at the waist with a faded blue belt. His tortoise, Daisy, was still closed tight. A quick check of the cargo netting over her carapace confirmed that it was intact, and the twenty-four stones within the net, each the size of a Faerie, were all where they belonged. They formed a double ring of translucent red bumps near the carapace margin. Britt walked across the clearing in the duff and likewise inspected the other tortoise, Claw.

Beyond Claw, nothing stirred in Bennik's shelter. Britt shook his head. He wondered how someone so incompetent had been hired as a longhauler. Though taller than Britt, taller than any other Faerie he knew, Bennik's thin body and lanky arms and legs seemed barely able to coordinate a normal gait, much less perform useful work. His narrow, pointed wings, when folded, reached well below his butt, requiring him to spread them just to avoid sitting on them.

"Bennik!"

"Huh. What?" Bennik's leaf shelter tipped to one side, then blew away.

Judging from the blank expression on Bennik's face, Britt suspected he hadn't yet noticed his leaf was gone. "Nighttime is over. Get up and earn your pay."

Bennik sat up and stretched his wings while staring at his bare legs, then grasped his bunched up, yellow tunic and pulled it down from his chest to cover his gray undergarment. Bennik always seemed to sleep with his clothes on. Even draped with his tunic, his chest clearly lacked the muscles Britt had come to expect from the work of longhauling. Thick brown hair stood out from his head in several directions. Bennik's black eyes seemed too large for his slightly triangular head, broad at the top and tapering to a longish chin. The taper caused the points of his ears to diverge like the antennae of an insect. Bennik's one winning feature, Britt thought, was his bright white and very wide smile, which he had rarely seen during the two weeks they had worked together.

"Have some breakfast." Britt tossed him half a dandelion seed. It glanced off Bennik's hands and landed beside him. "It looks like rain later. We need to get across Sardis Run before it rises."

"We have to cross it today?"

"This morning, I think. The other side is beyond the bounds of Ternaria."

"Can the tortoises swim across?" Bennik spoke through a mouthful of seed.

Britt sighed. "No. A tortoise sinks like a stone and drowns. If the water is up, we have to stop and build a raft." The hauler crew that had brought Bennik to the mines had seemed so generous at the time in offering Bennik as a replacement for Britt's partner.

"Well, I guess we should hurry. I'm not so good at rafts."

"Really?" Britt added rafts to his catalog of Bennik's deficiencies.

"I built a raft before...but I can't swim...very well."

Daisy led the way down the well-traveled path, beneath high shrubs and towering hardwoods. Britt enjoyed the view from the top of the patterned carapace. Several years ago, he and his friend, Rath, had pioneered the use of reins, so they wouldn't have to sit in the stinky compartment behind a tortoise's head. All the same, they still trained every tortoise to both reins and foot pressure.

The sky was now solidly overcast and the wind had increased. Britt looked behind. Bennik and Claw were not there. He slid down to the ground, tethered Daisy to the nearest sapling, then walked back down the path. At the first turn, he found Bennik tightening the lashing on Claw's cargo net.

"What happened?"

"Oh, I was trying to loosen my foot line and I pulled the wrong one. All the stones fell out. I had to load them again"

With no more warning than a fierce gust of wind, rain began to fall.

"Hurry up," Britt shouted, as he ran back toward Daisy. "We might make it across before the water rises." When he reached Daisy, he untied her, climbed on and continued down the path. There was no hurrying a tortoise. It plodded only slightly faster than a Faerie could walk. He tried to keep to the raised edge of the trail, both to find some relief from the downpour as well as to avoid the puddles now gathering in the center. Daisy seemed to prefer the puddles, but Britt maintained steady pressure on the reins to keep to the side. "You can drink all you want when we get to Sardis Run." He looked back. Claw was drinking from a puddle. "Keep him moving," Britt shouted.

"He won't listen," Bennik shouted back, throwing his hands into the air.

Britt reached the steep, crumbled bank of Sardis Run, his tunic completely soaked. Water flowed to his left, toward the West. Though it was shallow enough for Daisy to cross, it appeared turbid. He knew it would rise soon. Rather than wait for Bennik and then attempt to cast a grapple line across, he decided to draw a line with him as he crossed. With his longest line, Britt tied the middle of it to a sturdy sapling using a slip hitch, to enable him to release the line from the other bank. He then led Daisy down into the cut and across the shallow stream. On the opposite bank, Britt tied off the standing end, wrapping the slip end loosely about a small shrub.

Bennik finally brought Claw to the south bank of Sardis Run and attempted to goad him into the rapidly rising current. Claw balked. "What do I do now?" Fear showed in Bennik's eyes.

"Just make a raft."

Bennik's shoulders slumped.

"There's a catalpa just upstream. Find some split pods."

Bennik slid down from Claw's back, looked toward the catalpa, then sat down at the top of the bank, his face in his hands. "I can't do this stuff," he muttered. "I don't know anything about making a raft big enough for a tortoise. And I can't swim...very well."

"Then what are you doing working on a longhaul?" he shouted. Britt heard the vehemence in his voice. Bennik's face remained buried in his hands. "I'll come back across." He tethered Daisy near a stand of grass. "Eat up."

At the northern bank, Britt grasped the taut segment of his line and walked his hands along it as he waded into the rushing water. A third of the way across, his feet were swept from the stream bottom. With his body now riding against the force of the flood, he walked his hands down the line until he reached footing on the south bank. The rain felt colder as the wind increased.

"Come help me get some stuff for the raft." Bennik remained seated. "Bennik?" Britt looked at the gangly, dejected Faerie. His hair and clothing were soaked. His overly long wings were splayed behind him, spattered with mud.

Britt plucked a large round leaf and carried it to Bennik. "Hold this." He offered one edge of the leaf to Bennik, then draped the opposite edge over his own shoulders as he sat down beside him. Seated shoulder to shoulder, they were shielded from the rain and wind.

"What are you doing here?" Britt asked.

"I don't know."

"No. I mean, why are you here? Why are you working as a longhauler?"

"You really want to know?"

"It doesn't seem like a job you would choose."

"Everybody thought it would toughen me, make me more normal. I wanted to go to Moss Abbey and learn how to read and how to write. I've heard the monks of the Abbey are the only humans who treat Faeries with kindness. Our Elder wouldn't give his consent unless I traveled to the abbey as a longhauler. That meant I had to go to the Warded Mines. I knew they carried sarcite to the Abbey. So here I am."

"Faeries can't read. What use would it be?"

"At home, I study flowers and plants and mushrooms. I draw pictures of them. I want to be able to say something about them. And I think about things, like why humans are so big."

"That's like asking why trees are big."

"Why Faeries have wings, but can't really fly."

"I've heard there are birds that can't fly."

"Why Faeries are smarter than insects and animals that have much bigger heads. Why I'm different from other Faeries." The last, he spoke in a whisper.

"So, you're tall and skinny. If you weren't trying to do muscle work, that wouldn't matter"

"But the things I like, the ways I feel, it's all different."

"Like what?"

Bennik abruptly turned his head to look at Britt. His chin trembled. He seemed about to reply, but instead closed his eyes. After a long pause, Bennik mumbled, "I'm just different. And I want to say it with writing. I want others to be able to read my words when I'm gone. Writing is like being able to say everything you need to say, everything you want to say. And no-one can stop you from saying it. They can only laugh after you've said it all, after you're done. Writing locks away words like treasures."

"I don't understand why you'd want to do that, Bennik, but when you talk about it, you make it sound important."

The two of them sat in silence beneath the leaf they held. Bennik straightened his slender shoulders. "So here we sit, in the rain, with the water rising and our tortoises on opposite banks. I guess you have to show me how to make a raft big enough for a tortoise."

Together, they worked in the chill rain, dragging opened catalpa pods to the crossing to serve as a floating frame for the raft. With twine and split segments of last year's pokeweed, they lashed together the deck of a raft. Britt checked each of Bennik's lashings until he was confident they were being tied properly. Bennik seemed unusually focused on the task. One end of the raft was supported on a single trestle over the water's edge, while the other rested squarely on the crumbled dirt of the embankment. Britt cast three doubled loops over the taut line that spanned the water and tied them securely to the upstream edge of the raft.

When the raft was complete, they coaxed Claw onto the deck, with Bennik in front and Britt at the rear. "No matter what happens," Britt warned, "just keep pulling the raft along the line till we get it across. And don't touch that slack line. It will untie the whole thing."

On Britt's signal, they pulled the raft off its supporting trestle and into the water. Despite having angled the deck so that the upstream side would ride higher above the water, it repeatedly dipped beneath the surface, causing Claw to rotate toward the upward slant. Tugging the raft across was slower and more difficult than Britt had expected.

When they touched the northern bank, Britt shouted, "Get up on Claw's neck and lead him off. I'll steady the raft." Bennik climbed onto the tortoise's neck and disappeared behind the mass of the carapace. Claw's back leg caught Britt's left foot and flung him into the roiling water of Sardis Run.

Britt tumbled underwater several times. When he surfaced, he faced downstream. He turned around to yell, but before he could utter a sound, he was sucked beneath a tangle of submerged branches. Forcing away his panic, he threaded himself through the branches, following the current. Britt surfaced again, gasping. Turning to face upstream, he could no longer see the raft or the tortoise. He struggled to reach the north bank, but the rushing current held him in its grip. His efforts to stay above the surface of the chilling water seemed to go on without end. He grabbed some overhanging brush, only to be dislodged by the impact of floating debris.

As the cold dulled his senses and sapped his strength, Britt lost track of time. He was vaguely aware of being trapped against a large, broken branch. His head and right arm were above the water, while the rest of him was submerged. With his strength gone and his body cold to the core, Britt closed his eyes.

He dreamed of a time when he had just turned eight. He and his closest friend, Rath, slept together, between two thick blankets of woolly mullein leaf. Their arms and legs tangled together, sharing their warmth, sharing their bond of friendship. When the sun came up they took turns playing their fingers over each other's chest, trying to imitate the feel of mites crawling over their skin. They laughed and laughed. Rath smelled of boletus mushroom and pine bark.

Britt became aware that he was shivering, but no longer in the water. He felt dry. Warmth enfolded him as he shivered. His left foot throbbed. *Claw stepped on my foot.* He opened his eyes and saw only darkness. The sound of rain pattered on a leaf above him. He drifted into sleep.

When Britt awoke, everything was bright and green and warm. He saw that he was lying beneath a leaf shelter and between two layers of mullein leaf. He ached everywhere. Raising himself onto one elbow, he noticed that he was naked. His clothes were not in the shelter. He remembered the river and the cold. When he attempted to slide out of the shelter, every muscle and joint protested. Even his wings hurt. He lay back down and closed his eyes.

"Britt. Britt."

"What?" He wasn't sure where he was.

"I warmed some chamomile soup."

"Bennik?" His mind slowly cleared.

"I thought you might want something warm to drink."

"How did I get here? Where are we?"

Bennik knelt at the open end of the shelter and handed Brit a shell of warm, fragrant liquid. He wore only his gray undergarment. "I found you caught on a broken branch that stuck out over the water. I thought you had drowned."

"Where are my clothes?"

"Oh, they're almost dry."

"You took off my clothes?"

"You were cold as a lizard and your clothes were soaked. You needed to get dry and warm."

Britt thought about the little he could remember of the previous night. "You were there...with me."

Bennik turned his eyes to the ground. "It was raining. I couldn't start a fire. I was cold, but you were really cold. You shivered most of the night."

Britt sipped his soup. He imagined Bennik undressing him. A rush of warmth prickled his ears. "I'm too beat up to do much today. Where are we?"

"Beyond the bounds...almost a quarter day west of the crossing."

"A quarter day?"

"It was nearly dusk when I found you."

Britt handed back the empty shell and slid out of the shelter. The scent of the open woodland seemed fresh and inviting. He was surprised to see Daisy and Claw munching weeds nearby. He located his black undergarment spread over a low shrub and, despite its still being damp, stepped into it, tying it at the waist. Feeling his tunic, he decided to let it dry a bit longer. He eased himself down against a stout stalk of onion grass and allowed his skin to bake in the sunlight. Britt surveyed the bruises that covered his arms and legs and torso. Bennik sat beside him, smelling smoky from the fire. It seemed odd that Bennik's thin, pale body could have enough life-giving warmth to share. "Thank you, Bennik. I would have died if you hadn't found me."

"I know." Bennik drew up his knees and wrapped his thin arms around them. "We're still two weeks away from Moss Abbey."

When sunset had passed, Bennik gathered the dry tunics and placed them in the shelter. "Can I sleep in your shelter?"

In Britt's village, only children slept together, unless they were mates. "It's actually your shelter, Bennik. I'll set up one for me."

"It's already dark. There's room...for both of us."

Britt considered his fatigue and the pain of moving his arms and legs, of bending his back. "Okay."

After Bennik had fallen asleep, Britt lay awake beside him, listening to the slow, soft breathing. His scent melded with that of the mullein leaf to remind him of chamomile, smoke and wood moss.

The following morning, Britt awoke to the boisterous chirp of a finch on a nearby bush. Pushing aside the top layer of mullein, he extracted his tunic, which lay crumpled beneath him. Still supine, he rolled it into a long whip, in case the finch decided to investigate their leaf shelter. After a short time, the chirping faded into the distance.

Britt looked at the pale form of Bennik, still asleep beside him. Bennik lay on his side, facing Britt, with a thin arm serving as a pillow. His tallowy, bare skin, with its tiny, flat nipples, seemed more like that of a child than of a fully grown Faerie. A scarcely audible whistle coincided with each breath.

He tilted, so that Bennik's head would appear right-side-up. His lips seemed so thin and so long. Bennik's eyes opened in an expressionless gaze of black. Britt wondered if Bennik was even awake. Gradually, the thin lips broadened into a white, wide smile. Britt returned the smile.

"You planning to pop me with that?" His eyes indicated the whip in Britt's hand.

"Oh. There was a...finch. It's morning."

For the remaining two weeks of their journey to Moss Abbey, Britt shared a shelter with Bennik. With each night, he grew more accustomed to the sound of Bennik's breathing and the warmth of his proximity. He wondered what it was that needed to be written—what it was that could not be spoken.

For days, they traveled northward within the deep shade of Oldwood forest, beneath massive oaks and chestnuts. Each day carried them farther from their homes in Ternaria. This morning they reached the edge of the great clearing in the center of Oldwood, where humans had raised the towering buildings of Moss Abbey. A special tortoise path of smoothly packed, black dirt led past fields of enormous, cultivated plants to double wooden doors of a size just right for a tortoise. These doors led into the back of the main building of Moss Abbey. On Britt's first and only other trip to the abbey, he had been told that no human was permitted to step on the path, which the monks carefully groomed once every week throughout the year.

By the time they had traveled the length of the path and reached the doors, a human man had squatted beside the entrance.

"Welcome, friends," the monk said, opening the double doors with his fingertips.

As low as the monk squatted, Britt still had to look nearly straight up to see his face beneath its brown cowl. "Thank you," he shouted.

Inside, white walls reached between massive structural timbers. A series of ramps allowed them to bypass wooden steps, each of which stood ten times Britt's height. The ramps led to a human-size oak door. The hall in which they now stood carried a musty scent of age, and reverberated with the murmurs of many voices behind a dozen closed doors. The door before them opened. A human man in a white robe squatted to greet them.

"I am Neruti. Come in."

They led the tortoises by their reins into a vast chamber. Built into its walls were hundreds of wooden shelves, each filled with rectangular blocks of various colors. The thousands of colored blocks each stood as tall as one wooden step in the corridor. Some were even taller. Britt had seen the strange chamber with all its shelves and blocks during his previous journey to Moss Abbey. Now he judged, from Bennik's awed expression, that he had overlooked their significance.

Britt introduced himself. Bennik seemed unaware of the conversation. "And this is Bennik. We have forty eight stones." He loosened the cargo nets on each of the tortoises and allowed the milky red stones to drop to the wooden floor.

"Wonderful," Neruti replied as he gathered them and placed them into a translucent white basin.

"What do you use them for?" Bennik asked.

"My knees are too old to squat for conversation. If you'll allow me to lift you to my desk...." He extended his huge, wrinkled hand to the floor beside the two tortoises.

Britt, with Bennik following his lead, climbed up Daisy's front foot and from there, jumped onto the hand. As Neruti carried them toward a broad expanse of oak wood, they squatted on the fleshy palm and braced themselves with their hands to avoid being swept away by the jostling, rapid movement. He delivered them to the surface, then sat in a human-size chair behind it.

"The monks of this abbey use the sarcite stones to power a special device that allows us to...maintain the balance of nature in Ternaria. Without their labors, Ternaria would cease to be the land you know. Nature is... special there. It requires... hmm... careful... continual adjustments to sustain it. I'm afraid that's not a very clear explanation, but further detail would probably make little sense to you without a deeper understanding of the nature of things and how they interact with one another. This is a subject for many years of study, and one that we do not speak of casually. I am pleased, nonetheless, that you have asked so important a question. Perhaps when you return to Ternaria, your Elder might be willing to share some of his knowledge concerning our mutual needs."

"Are those books?" Bennik asked, pointing to the shelves along the walls.

"Yes, but only a fraction of all the books in Moss Abbey. Tell me. What do you know of books?"

"Only that they preserve the words written in them. And that others can read those words."

"You are quite correct, Bennik. Some of them were written hundreds of years ago."

"And you can still read their words." Bennik sat on the oak surface, slowly turning around to survey the shelves.

"He wants to learn how to read," Britt said.

"And how to write," Bennik added, still gazing at the books.

"A Faerie has never...hmmm. Why would you want to do that? There are no Faeries who could read what you would write."

"If I knew how, I could teach them. I have...things I need to write."

Neruti looked to Britt, who could only shrug his shoulders. "Well, Bennik, I don't know how we could accomplish that. We are, after all, very different sizes."

"Will you teach me?" Bennik asked.

"I would have to discuss this with my lecturers. Excuse me for a moment." Neruti stood and left the chamber. When he returned a short time later, he sat once again behind his desk. "It can be done. You will have to create your own writing instruments and paper. We will provide the materials. You might expect two or three years of study before you acquire the skill to read even the most elementary of our books, though a Faerie may require a much longer or shorter time. We have no experience with teaching a Faerie. But I must warn you, the lives of our monks are sometimes lonely, even though they enjoy the companionship of one another. For a Faerie alone here, it might be overwhelming. For your own safety, you would have to sleep in the layover quarters that we provide for the longhaulers. And we have not even considered dietary requirements. All of our gardens yield fruits and vegetables and grains that are of quite a different scale from those that would be suitable for your needs. If you have the will, we can offer to teach you."

"I hadn't thought about all those things," Bennik said.

"Perhaps you would like to think about it on your trip back to Ternaria?"

"No," Bennik replied. He looked at Britt with anguish. "When I return to Ternaria, I will know how to read and how to write."

Britt sat beside Bennik on the floor, facing him. Their hips touched side to side. The layover quarters that the monks provided for the longhaulers consisted of an enclosed nook set into the rear wall of the abbey. Its curtained doorway opened to the tortoise ramp within the main corridor. The chamber held six Faerie-size beds and little else. Morning sunlight from a square of glass in the exterior wall rendered a golden halo to Bennik's thick, brown hair.

"I'll miss you," Bennik whispered. His head drooped. His long, thin arms lay lifeless on his knees.

Britt reached his arms around Bennik's chest and rested his head on Bennik's shoulder.

Bennik hugged him and sniffed.

"When you learn how to write," Britt said, "send me a writing."

Eight months after Britt's return to Domes, he still thought of Bennik. Last night, like so many nights, it was in the hazy time between lying down and finally fading into sleep. His chest ached at his solitude, at the silence of his chamber. He seldom dreamed about Bennik, but in those twilight moments, he could envision his smile.

Today, he watched as a pair of longhaulers passed through the village on their return trip home. Only one trip passed each month, and each month, he watched them continue without stopping. This time it was different. One of the longhaulers spoke with a neighbor, who then pointed toward Britt. Unwilling to reveal his anticipation, Britt waited. He steadied his breath and remained where he stood until the tortoise stopped, and its rider slid down and approached.

"Are you Britt?"

"Yes."

"Bennik has sent you something from Moss Abbey." He held out a small roll, tied with a single strand.

Britt could only nod his head as he accepted it. After the longhauler had mounted his tortoise, Britt asked, "Did he say anything?"

"No. Just to give you that."

Britt turned the roll over in his hands, then untied the strand. It opened to a square of what seemed to be onion skin, decorated with rows of complex, black marks. *A writing.*

He showed the remarkable square of onion skin to nearly everyone in the village. Most offered polite congratulations. Sullis, Elder of Domes, rotated it various ways, squinting his rheumy eyes and tilting his head, but could not say which way was up. He insisted that a writing had an up and a down.

Britt shaved the tenons at the ends of his fourth segment of pine needle and fitted them into the awaiting mortises of a square frame. He applied dabs of glue to the back corners and carefully laid Bennik's writing face down on top of it. He pressed two slivers into the fungal wall of his bedroom and hung the framed writing there. Since he wasn't sure which way was up, he hung it so that one of the short bits of writing that stuck out beyond the rest of the writing, one bit on either end, was at the top. He had decided that if the writing was a way for Bennik to speak to him, then one bit must be Bennik's name and the other his own name. Some day, he thought, Bennik will tell me which is the top and which the bottom.

That night, lying awake, Britt thought again of Bennik. It left him with a dull ache of emptiness in his chest. He descended from his chamber within the boletus and stood in the doorway at the base of its stem. Looking out at the dark sky, he whispered, "I miss you. Can you hear me? Do you know I'm thinking about you now? I don't know what you're saying."

Britt determined to travel to Moss Abbey as soon as he was able. Since returning with Daisy and Claw, he had declined to make another trip as a longhauler. Instead, he had spent the time helping his mother expand their herd of dairy mice. "I'll visit soon."

Britt could only sigh when he considered that three months had passed since he had received the writing from Bennik. Somehow the time just slipped away as he wrapped up his responsibilities. Now, without a tortoise, no one had noticed his approach to Moss Abbey. He let himself in the double doors and followed the ramps to the longhauler's room. When he entered through the curtained door, he found it deserted. A Faerie size desk had been added to the sparse furnishings, and a simple kitchen.

On the desk rested a Faerie-size book made of onion skin, stitched at one edge and enclosed within a cover of light green lizard jowl. Beside it, a cup held a dozen peach hairs, some blackened at the end.

Britt followed the ramp to Neruti's chamber of books. Since the massive door was closed, he slid beneath it. Neruti, now dressed in a brown robe, sat in his chair behind the huge oak desk. Britt walked to the foot of the chair and shouted, "Neruti. It's Britt."

The abbot looked down. "Master Britt, what a surprise to see you." The human seemed older than Britt had remembered.

"Bennik wasn't in the layover chamber. Can you tell me where I can find him?"

"You have not heard." Neruti frowned. "Two months ago we suffered...a sickness. Seven of our brothers were claimed by it." Neruti rubbed his hands together. "I am so sorry. Bennik also perished. We had no means to minister to him. I sent word to his family, but your villages are far apart. I should have also sent word to you. I am so sorry. He is the only Faerie buried at Moss Abbey."

A cold finality settled over Britt, making it difficult for him to breathe. "He's...dead?"

"I am so sorry. If there is anything I can offer you..."

Britt turned and walked toward the massive oak door. Halfway across the chamber, he remembered the writing Bennik had sent him. Britt returned to the desk of Neruti. He reached into his tunic and extracted a rolled square of onion skin. "Bennik sent me this writing. I..." He swallowed a sob. "...don't know what it says."

Neruti looked down at the writing and shook his head. "Bennik's writing is far too small for me to read. If you could find a way to make a larger copy..."

Britt stepped from the pine needle that lay across a huge carpet of vellum and walked the next letter onto its surface, pausing and swabbing the soles of his feet with ink whenever the footprints began to fade. He held Bennik's writing before him as a map. He had no idea what the symbols meant. He just stepped each one in ink footprints onto the vellum, each symbol nearly his own height. When he completed the vellum copy, which he had created on the corner of Neruti's desk, he cleaned his feet, then waited for the abbot. Whatever Bennik had written, Britt wanted to know its meaning.

Neruti returned to his chamber, sat in his chair and lifted the vellum to study it. Tears swelled in the man's eyes. He placed the vellum back on the desk, then sniffed, covering his face with his hands.

"What does it mean?"

"He.... He had just learned to write. It is difficult to interpret it. Perhaps you should just keep it as a symbol of your friendship."

"But what about his book? On his desk. I saw a book. His words are there."

"I did not know."

"You have to teach me how to read."

"I think that would be unwise."

"You have to teach me," Britt cried. "You have to. Maybe I could read this writing." He waved the square of onion skin. "My copy was bad. Maybe I could read his actual writing."

"I am sorry."

Britt sank to the surface of the desk and stared at the onion skin bearing Bennik's writing. "Which is the top?"

"The top? I see." Neruti held the vellum copy and indicated the top with a wrinkled finger.

Britt rotated the onion skin to match. "I won't go home until I can know what he said."

Neruti sighed and shook his head. "Please understand that I had hoped to spare you..." Neruti wiped his eyes, then lifted the vellum once more. "Britt, I...miss you. I am so...lonely here. Come...something...soon. Just a day. You...are...my only friend. Bennik"

Britt recalled the warmth that had saved his life. He thought of the months that he had proudly held Bennik's writing, not knowing what it meant. So many times he had thought to himself, Bennik must be sleeping. Now Bennik must be writing new words. Bennik is walking the paths of Oldwood forest. Bennik is reading a book. *And you were dead.*

"All that's left of him are the words in his book. No one else can read it. I could never copy a whole book. If you'll teach me...I could know the words he would never speak. Please." Britt remembered Bennik's bright white and very wide smile.

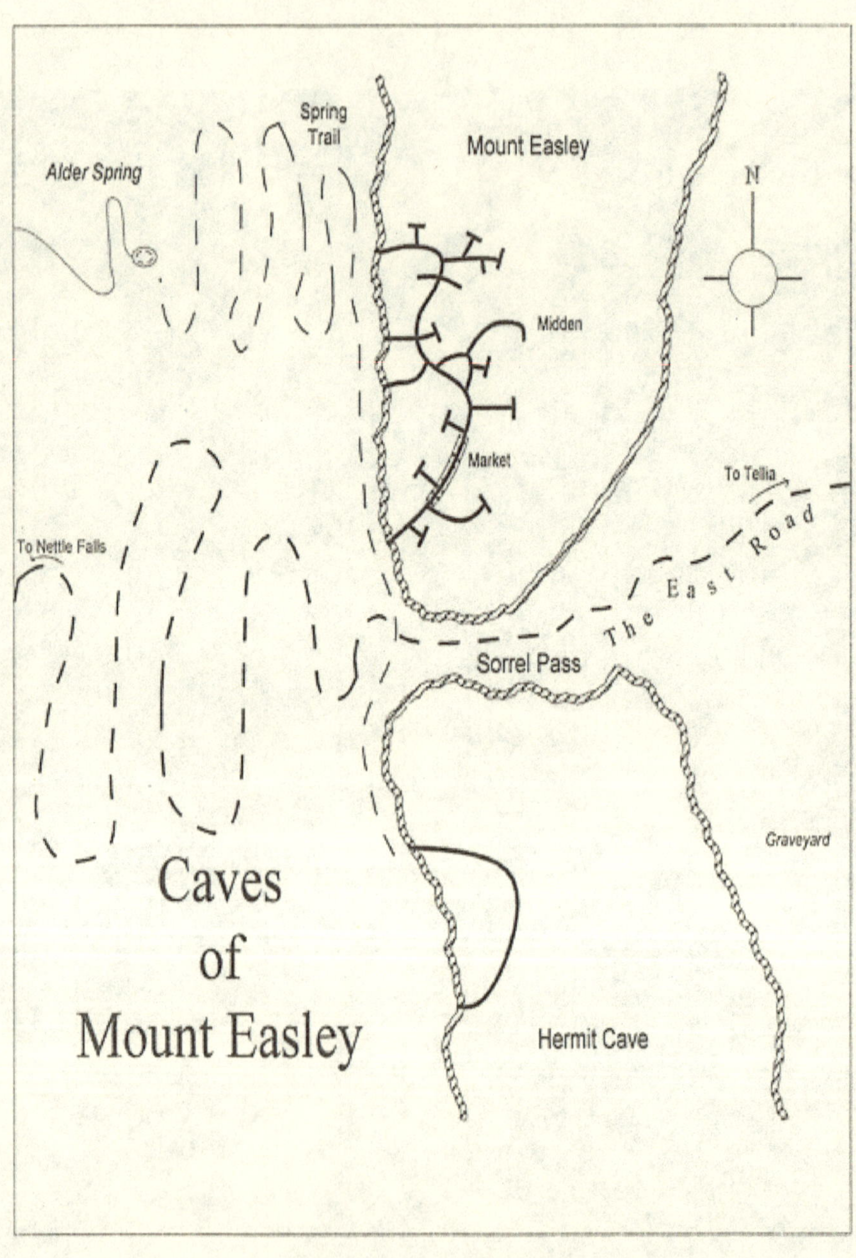
Spring
Trail
Mount Easley
Alder Spring
N
Midden
Market
To Tellia
The East Road
To Nettle Falls
Sorrel Pass
Graveyard
Caves
of
Mount Easley
Hermit Cave

CHAPTER 7—THE SWEETEST AIR TO BREATHE

"Watch out down there," Ottus shouted from high in the branches of an alder.

Pellana watched cautiously as a woody alder cone, nearly her size, glanced off several branches, thumped on the springy soil, then bounced three times before coming to rest not far from where she stood with her mother.

"That's so dangerous up there," Pellana said. "I don't like to watch while Papa cuts those things."

"Don't worry, doll," Della replied. "Ottus is too stubborn to die."

"I better go. I still have to make one more trip this morning." Pellana stooped to place a pine needle across her shoulders. A globular seed pod, filled with spring water, hung from either end.

"Oh, just wait," her mother said. "He'll be down in just a bit, and we can climb back with you."

She stooped again and allowed the pods to balance on the ground. The high ridge of Mount Easley loomed to the east. Westward, clear sky went on forever, and far below, the plain of Ternaria spread toward the horizon. Its rivers revealed themselves only as dark lines of dense vegetation. She envied those fortunate Faeries who lived beside water. A half-hour down from the caves and a half-hour back up twice each morning seemed to devour her day. "Why do we have to live so far from the water?"

"Well, doll, because that's where everybody else lives. The market's there; the hollygrapes are there. And who knows what crawls along out here at night." Della crooked her neck to watch Ottus descending the alder, then shook her head. "When you decide on a mate, you might want to visit where you'll be living, before you make up your mind."

"If you had seen Mount Easley first, would you still have gone with Papa?"

"I don't know. I was stupid with love when he showed up in Tellia. He was so handsome then."

"That was a tough one," Ottus said when he finally reached the ground. He rolled the huge alder cone toward Della. "That should last through the next batch of jam." The cone, with deep voids where its seeds had popped out the previous season, was lighter than its size would suggest.

Della grasped one end of the cone while Ottus took hold of the other. In tandem, they began the half hour ascent up the rocky, winding path. Pellana stooped once again to lift the water and followed.

As Pellana cleared the stillness of the alders that shielded the area about the spring, she followed her parents climbing through a narrow band of aspen, waving constantly in the unending breeze high on the mountain. Above them, fir trees replaced the damp forest smells with a rich fragrance of balsam, until the trees became smaller and disfigured by the increasing wind and elevation. Just before the trees gave out completely, the four openings to Mount Easley's cave village offered the Faeries a welcomed shelter from the sharp wind. Immediately to the south of the caves, the main road up from Nettle Falls, three days west, crossed the ferocious gusts of a saddle at Sorrel Pass, and descended the more gentle, though much drier eastern face of the mountain ridge to Tellia, another three days off.

The village itself was a collection of a little over forty families sparsely distributed within a remarkable network of natural solution caves that penetrated an isolated stratum of limestone. With no openings on the eastern face of the ridge, the caves tamed the steady west winds into a gentle circulation that lifted the smoke of their fires up and out through yet other vents higher on the western face.

They greeted other Faeries who passed them in the curving main tunnel, then turned at the third branch to the left, a short passage that they shared with one other family.

"Hey, Pellana." Sorlin stood in his doorway, opposite Pellana's house. "Want to go over to the other side with me?" Sorlin sometimes went alone over the pass to gather snakeweed on the eastern slope in the few days before market, while his parents were busy preparing and wrapping it for sale.

"No. I still have one more trip to the spring. You could help me," she said, knowing his response. He seemed to think that they had been courting over the past year, but she couldn't imagine where he had gotten that idea.

"Pellana," he replied, "that's girls' work. Guess I'll see you later." He disappeared into his house.

Pellana's house had no door, but instead, its walls of fir needle lath were staggered in such a way that she could walk right in with her water still over her shoulders. She lowered the pods to the floor and poured their contents into a large clay pot.

"That Sorlin is one worthless boy," Della mumbled.

"He's honest and works hard," Ottus said.

"Works hard at not working," Della added. "You know, Ottus, we ought to try to get to that hollygrape we saw up the rock slide."

"He'd make a good mate," Ottus said to Della, but clearly directed at Pellana. "That old snaggled shrew hunts in that rockslide."

"I'm not interested in a mate, Papa."

"You will be soon enough," he continued, "and he comes from a family you've known all your life. You need to be thinking about such things."

She sighed irritably and exited with the empty water pods. She had been given the chore of fetching the water when she had turned thirteen. Now seventeen, she estimated that she had made the trip well over two thousand times. Only two or three days each winter was the snow deep enough to give her a respite. Usually there were other girls to gossip with, there and back. Today, she had waited to go down with her parents, since they needed more fuel to do the batch of jam. Now she walked alone.

She descended the winding trail through the firs and into the aspens.

Pellana sensed that she was being carried. When she opened her eyes, she couldn't focus. She tried to speak, but her mouth wouldn't cooperate. For a moment, she thought she saw the face of Willi, the strange hermit who lived south of the pass.

"Hey there, sugar," he said.

She awakened with a terrible headache. She lay on her bed.

"Are you feeling alright, doll?" her mother asked.

"My head hurts."

"I expect it does."

"What happened?" Pellana asked.

"Sorlin said you fell and hit your head on the rocks down by the spring. Don't you remember?"

"No. I just...Sorlin?"

"He carried you up here." She sat at the fire, stirring a clay pot.

"Sorlin carried...I don't remember...I was passing the aspens. Nobody was there. That's the last thing I remember...except somebody carrying me. Sorlin? I thought it was Willi."

"Sorlin brought you in here. He didn't say anything about Willi. And you keep away from that Willi. He's not right in the head."

"Where's Sorlin?"

"Oh, he finally went over to the other side."

"I don't think he even knows where the spring is."

"Well, doll, you didn't fly up here. Your head is still a bit scrambled."

After a half hour, her head felt better. "I'm going to go get those water pods."

"Are you sure you feel okay?" She lifted a spoon from the pot and watched as the boiling jam slid from its surface. "Almost ready."

"I'm fine." She walked out of the house, and turned into the main tunnel. As she stepped onto the trail that contoured south below the four cave entrances on its way to the main road, she turned north to return to the spring. There, at the head of the spring trail, sat her water pods, filled with water, their pine needle resting alongside them.

She couldn't remember much about what happened earlier, but one thing was certain. Sorlin would never have made a second trip to the spring to bring up her water. She left the water where it stood and headed in the opposite direction, toward the pass.

Just south of the last cave entrance, the wind picked up. She fought her way through the strong gusts that rose with the afternoon sun's heat on the western face and gushed through the saddle to the cool, dry slope of the east. The wind usually made the journey over the pass eastward an almost self-propelled walk, by just opening her diminutive wings. Today, rather than go over the pass, she cut directly across the wind's path to the continuation of the ridge further south. The trail narrowed. The winds slowed.

She had always been forbidden to go where she now stood. Just ahead was the single, perfectly round entrance to the hermit's cave. A little more than a stone's throw beyond, another cave opening appeared as an elongated frown above a sheer drop, as though it regretted that it could not be used. Here, the scent of balsam, gathered by the wind from the expansive stands of fir that reached almost to the plain below, unalloyed with spruce or deciduous interruption, suffused the air she breathed with intoxicating magic.

"Hey there, sugar," a voice said from behind, startling her. "Isn't this just the sweetest air to breathe?"

She turned to see a smile on the face of a Faerie she had often spied from a distance, and often been cautioned to avoid. "Yes. I've never smelled balsam so...so..."

"Sweet."

"Yes, so sweet."

"Not too many folks come over here," he said, still smiling, "except rascally boys trying to see which of them is strong enough to throw the biggest rock up to my back door." His brown jacket and trousers were ragged, but spotlessly clean. His wings were tipped with streaks of balsam.

"That big frown connects?"

"It's not so convenient for going in and out, but it has completely different air. In the afternoon it catches wind from up that ravine and brings the smells of the plain right up past, and over that big notch above." His eyes twinkled. "Once or twice each year, in the spring, I can smell the lilacs, but only for a moment and only from my back door—never from the front."

"I've never smelled lilacs."

"That's because they're days away. The town of Lilac has a big grove of them."

"I've heard of that. That's way out in the plain and down the river."

"Are you looking for something, or just taking a stroll where Ottus and Della warned you not to go?" The expression on his face reminded her of Papa when he would ask a rhetorical question.

She felt a momentary embarrassment. "You carried me up from the spring, this morning."

Willi simply nodded.

"What happened? I don't remember anything."

"That last turn before you reach the spring. Your feet just went out and you cracked your head on a rock. 'Thock.' I heard it like that. 'Thock.'"

"And you carried me back up."

He nodded.

"How did Sorlin carry me in?"

"Well, sugar, when I reached the cave, your boyfriend was walking out. He looked so shocked to see me carrying you, that I just put you in his arms, said you hit your head on a rock by the spring, and went on my way."

"No. You went back and brought my water up. And he's not my boyfriend, just...my neighbor."

He nodded again. "I've never seen that boy down at the spring, ever. So I took care of the water."

"You were kind to do all that."

"Anybody would have done the same... except maybe your... neighbor."

"I guess I should go. I just wanted to thank you."

He nodded. When Pellana turned to head back across the windy saddle, Willi said, "Would you like to see something no other Faerie in all Ternaria has ever seen?"

Pellana looked into his kind eyes and saw an almost parental joy. "Yes."

He looked across the plain at the late sun. "We'll have to hurry, or we'll miss it." He took her hand and helped her up to the cave, his "front door." They hurried along the smooth, curved tunnel.

Inside, Pellana saw no house walls. Only some willow furniture and a kitchen area. The floor rose gently until they reached the brilliant sky at the wide, frowning opening she had seen from below.

Willi stood behind her, turning her by her shoulders until she faced directly toward the sun, which had almost reached the horizon.

"There's only about ten days every summer when you can see this."

"It's pretty." The surprising scent of oak and maple and chestnut rose in the warm breeze.

"No. It hasn't happened yet. You just watch right there."

She gasped. "There's another sun!" Below the sun, an equally bright, orange-yellow sun dazzled her eyes. She squinted at the glare, then it was gone. "What was that?"

"That's a reflection off Lake Willow, on the far side of Ternaria. It would take you a week to get there from here. Half-way there, you'd have to cross the river on a barge below Nettle Falls. But here we stand. Some years, you can see the full moon do that, just before dawn. This summer, there's no full moon during that special ten days, but there will be next summer. If you're still here, you need to see that."

"Why wouldn't I be?"

"You're of an age to find a mate. Somebody's going to show up who's more to your liking than your neighbor boy, Sorlin. Then your common sense will turn to mush, and you'll follow him to who knows where. That's just the way things happen."

Her cheeks warmed. "Did you ever have a mate?"

Willi smiled briefly. "I almost did. I was so in love. I worked to earn a little more, and fix up this special place, but somebody came and stole her heart. I guess I never had the resilience to find somebody else. Instead, I live where I can breathe the air I choose to breathe, look out on the view I want to see, and only deal with the Faeries I care to run into. I decide every day to be happy."

Pellana sat at a willow bench, beside nine clay jars of hollygrape jam. She always took an early spot at the end of the market closest to her home, so she wouldn't have to drag everything so far. Everybody knew where to find her. For the last two years, she handled it all. Twice every month, she would clear the bench of whatever had accumulated on it—usually clothes that needed washing, flip it over and nest jars of jam in its basket-like underside. Then she would drag it or carry it out to the market. Most market days, only the empty bench went back home.

Every month or two, a trader from some other village or town might bring in unique items, but for the most part, market day was a chance for all the families of Mount Easley to come together, gossip and exchange their local products. There was snakeweed rootstock, sliced and toasted, huckleberries, salsify, sorrel leaf, baskets, wall panels, water pods, balsam, various seeds and jams.

Pellana sold out early, delighted at the chance to wander. About half-way down the market a Faerie lad of about thirteen sat beside three small Faerie dolls exquisitely carved from what he said was mouse ivory. On each, the hair had been polished with bright yellow beeswax, in contrast to milk white skin.

"Do you make those?" she asked.

"My father does, but he's teaching me."

Near the far end, at the cave entrance closest to the pass, a gangly stranger struggled up the entry slope with a two wheel cart filled with a collection of different items. When he saw Pellana approaching, he slipped, caught himself, then rolled the cart alongside the first vendor.

"I hope I'm not too late," he said to her. His dark brown hair was clipped close, emphasizing his thin, dusty neck. He was like a handsome hollygrape—a blush of color on his cheeks—but not quite ripe. He appeared to be about Pellana's age. His green eyes caught her attention. The faded blue fabric of his tunic looked as though he had slept in it for a few days. He smelled of wood moss and flinty road dust.

"No," she replied, "It should go another hour or so."

"Oh." His demeanor sagged with his thin shoulders.

"How far did you come?"

"From Westbog," he said glumly.

"I don't know where that is."

"It's six days west, out by Lake Willow."

She immediately felt his disappointment. "What did you bring?"

"Salt, salt minnow—that's a fish, fish sauce and three willow footstools. I tried to get here sooner, but I had trouble pushing the cart up that last part of the road. If it hadn't been for an old Faerie that helped me, I'd still be down there."

"Raggedy brown trousers and a brown jacket?"

"Yes. You know him?"

"That's Willi. He's a hermit." And chooses to be happy every day, she thought. "So, what do you do with fish sauce?"

"Oh, it's wonderful on foods that don't have a lot of flavor on their own. Faeries buy it all over Ternaria. And here..." He opened a pack of salt minnow and broke off a flake. "Taste this."

It smelled odd, but exploded with flavor in her mouth. "That's wonderful."

"So, how does everybody usually do this...you know...sell things here?"

She studied his goods. "Turn your cart around and set the stools down on the floor. Open that one pack of minnow and break off little pieces for everybody to taste, open one jar of fish sauce, and give me one copper."

"What for?"

"Something to taste with the sauce."

He reluctantly opened the strings of his purse and lifted out one copper with his slender fingers. "I only have two."

"Don't worry. You'll have plenty. I'll be right back." She walked down the market, until she came to Sorlin's table. "I'd like two bundles of toasted snakeweed."

"You hate snakeweed, Pellana." Sorlin laughed. "Did you forget?"

"I hate it because it has less flavor than a chip of alderwood." She put down the copper and snatched two bundles. "Bye."

Pellana returned to the stranger's cart and handed him the snakeweed. "Spread all of these out next to the fish sauce." She turned toward the body of the market and shouted, "New things! New things here." She took a toasted slice of snakeweed and dipped it in the fish sauce. When she placed it in her mouth, all she could do was smile and nod at the young, brown-haired, green-eyed vendor from Westbog.

His eyes widened. When she looked behind her, nearly every Faerie in Mount Easley was walking toward her. She stepped back and watched as the goods in the cart dwindled. She found the boy's confident yet awkward manner somehow charming.

When the market ended at mid-afternoon, all that was left was one small willow footstool. "You're amazing," he said. "I don't know your name." His cheeks blushed.

"I don't know yours either."

"I'm Wallis."

"And she's my girl," Sorlin said, approaching with his shoulders back, his wings held high. "So don't bother to wash the dirt off your neck."

"Oh," Wallis replied.

Pellana could hardly believe Sorlin's audacity. "What he means to say is that I'm his neighbor, and that's all he can claim. Wallis, this is my *neighbor*, Sorlin. Sorlin, this is Wallis, who walked a week to come to this market, and is entitled to our hospitality."

"Well, don't get too comfortable, *Wallis*, or I'll show you my hospitality."

"Pleased to meet you," Wallis said weakly, holding out a hand.

Sorlin looked at the hand, then at Pellana. He shook his head as he stomped off.

"My name is Pellana."

Wallis smiled, then looked at his feet.

"Aren't you pleased to meet *me*?"

"You saved my hide. I don't know what I was thinking when I decided to go trading. I almost ran out of money, with inns and river crossings. Then I almost couldn't get up the mountain, and almost missed the market. The next one is when? Two weeks?"

"Two weeks."

"I'd have starved. I don't know how to thank you...Pellana."

"I'll think of something. In the meantime, you can use your cart to carry my market bench back home, and I'll show you who takes borders."

They headed north up the main tunnel. Half-way through the rapidly dismantling market, the sculptor's son was wrapping his three Faerie dolls of mouse ivory.

"You didn't sell any?" Pellana asked as they passed.

"No. They sell better at the inns down at Nettle Falls, with all the pilgrims going through. But then it's three more days there and six more to get back to Tellia."

"How much are they?" Pellana had an idea.

"Four coppers each. Sometimes, when the innkeepers buy them at the Falls, they sell them to their guests at eight."

"How about ten for all three, and you can head home?" She watched Wallis as the concept settled on his mind.

Wallis opened his plump purse and counted ten coppers. "And if they sell in Nettle Falls, I'll buy more when I come back in a month."

"Agreed. You turned this into a much better day."

"Pellana has a way of doing that," Wallis said. "I'm Wallis." He held out his hand.

"Pyxis...from Tellia." He shook the hand.

"Good to do business with you, Pyxis. This is Pellana. She lives here. I live in Westbog, by Lake Willow."

"That's the other side of Ternaria," Pyxis exclaimed. "Hi, Pellana."

Pellana smiled and nodded. Once the dolls were wrapped and carefully placed into Wallis' cart, they continued toward her home. Along the way, she pointed out the boarding house.

"It's too bad I got up here so late. I never saw what anybody else had to sell."

"Most things you can get just about anywhere. I'd say that huckleberry jam and hollygrape jam and balsam would sell. Everybody usually has more than they take to market. Oh, and sage leaf mattresses. You should take one and show it to the innkeepers at the Falls. They're soft as can be and smell wonderful. I'll take you around."

"It looks like there aren't any ripe ones," Ottus complained.

Pellana stood with her parents on the eastern slope of the mountain ridge. The three of them could usually manage to roll two hollygrapes back through the pass and into the cave. A little farther north, the solitary Willi wrestled with bringing down a leaf of mountain sage. Beside him were several sage leaves that had been speared onto a spruce needle, ready to be carried through the windy pass. As always, Willi kept to himself.

"There's two, just a little ways up the rockslide," Della pointed out.

"But that snaggletooth shrew still hunts up there," Ottus cautioned.

"It's just a little way," she insisted. "Shrews have bad eyes, poor hearing, a weak nose, and they can't jump."

Sorlin came through the pass. "Morning." He saw the hollygrapes they were looking at. "I saw that snaggle shrew up there yesterday."

"Where was it, Sorlin?" Ottus asked.

"Up by the top."

"You see, Ottus." Della had begun to climb the rocks. "You just holler if old snaggle pokes his nose out."

Ottus grumbled and followed a short distance behind.

Pellana had seen a shrew kill a mouse half again its size. "Sorlin, could you wait up here until they come back down? I'm worried."

"I'm hardly going to scare off a shrew with my obsidian blade."

"Just stay."

"Since you ask me so sweetly. You forget about that skinny boy from Lake Willow already?"

"As a matter of fact, it's none of your business." She thought of Wallis constantly.

"I don't see you asking him to fight off a very large shrew with a little obsidian."

But, she thought, Wallis would swallow hard and give it a try. "He's a trader, dummy. He left the next day."

She looked up. Her mother braced her feet against a rock and used her hands to roll a hollygrape free of its stem. Ottus climbed toward her. The hollygrape gave way with a soft pop, and bounced down the slope. Della lost her balance and followed the hollygrape, tumbling down the rocks. "Mama!" As Pellana moved to climb toward her mother, Sorlin grasped her arm and restrained her.

"There's a shrew in those rocks. And your father is right there."

Pellana slapped Sorlin as hard as she could on the side of his head, then began to climb toward her mother. Ottus had just reached her.

"Oh. She's...oh, Della. She's hurt really bad." Ottus patted her hand, then drew her into his arms. He rocked her back and forth, moaning her name.

Behind her father, much farther up the rockslide, something moved. Pellana stopped and stared. A snaggletooth shrew walked rapidly down the rocks, directly toward her parents. "Papa, the shrew!"

Ottus ignored everything but Della, pleading with her not to leave him.

Pellana picked up the largest rock she could manage and continued climbing toward her father, calling to get his attention. The shrew moved more quickly and more nimbly over and around the rocks of the slope. She could see that it would reach her father before her. As she prepared to heave her rock, a dull green object swept in front of her face, blocking her view.

Willi surged past her carrying a spruce needle on which several sage leaves were impaled. The shrew turned toward the waving sage leaves, each as long as Willi himself. At the shrew's first attack, Willi maneuvered the pointed end of the spruce needle directly onto the tip of the shrew's long nose, which overhung its mouth by half and arm's length. The shrew backed off. Willi waved the leaves from side to side as he backed down the rocks toward Ottus, who still knelt with the unconscious Della in his arms. "Take them down from here!" he shouted at Pellana.

The shrew lunged again, this time biting at Willi's chest, but getting only a mouthful of the wagging sage leaf. Pellana helped her father lift the limp body of her mother, and begin the short climb down the rocks. She looked back to see the shrew bite the front of Willi's neck, then begin to consume him.

In a gently sloping pitch of desiccated land south of the pass, but on the eastern slope of the ridge, Pellana said goodbye to her mother. Her body lay wrapped in alder leaf on a carpet of aspen leaf, surrounded by a ring of stones. Dozens of carefully aligned mounds of stones trailed down the slope in perfectly spaced rows. Only the grasses of the high mountain were allowed to grow here. Every Faerie in Mount Easley stood around. She recounted aloud an amusing anecdote about her mother, tears clinging to her cheeks. When she finished, Ottus spoke.

"Della was always a good wife to me, and a good mother to Pellana. She was faithful and hardworking. I suppose my only complaint would be that I never could admit to her that I prefer huckleberry jam to hollygrape." He smiled as he wept. "But I lost two folks that I loved yesterday. Those of you who are old enough, know that Willi was my brother, older by seven years."

Pellana looked at her father, but he spoke down to Della's grave. She had never heard about the things her father was saying.

"He fell in love with Della before I stole her away. He forgave us both, a long time ago, but we never could speak to him after that. I was too ashamed, I suppose. He lived his strange ways because of me. But his love for us both, and for Pellana, led him, without even needing to think about it, to trade his life for ours.

"Willi will have no grave, but it doesn't matter. We don't mark our graves, because, once you pass on from this life, it doesn't matter what Faeries used to call you. Your name only lives in the hearts of those who care, until they too pass on. So we'll have to count Della's grave as belonging to them both."

When he finished speaking, each Faerie, one by one, placed a large rock onto the grave and expressed their sympathies. Only one very old Faerie mentioned Willi, and only to Pellana.

"Willi was good and kind. I always felt you ought to know he was your uncle. But he didn't want you to be embarrassed over him." The old Faerie had rheumy eyes and no teeth. He patted Pellana's hand. "You know, he always watched after you. If there was critters down by the spring, and he knew you'd be coming, he'd chase them away before you got down there. I wasn't surprised to hear he took on that shrew." Then he whispered in her ear, "He'd saved up a lot of money before he decided to go off and live by himself. You need to go up there today." He patted her hand again, and then turned to her father. "You did the right thing, Ottus, and finally said what needed saying."

Pellana climbed the last bit of trail on her return from the spring. Water pods swung gently from the pine needle across her shoulders.

Tomorrow was market day. Tomorrow Wallis would be back, if he came back. She had fantasized about his return, that he would ask her to be his mate. She knew that her recent wish to be anywhere but Mount Easley had colored her thinking. Her recollection of his face was something of a blur, but she clearly recalled his thin arms and thin neck and thin fingers. His hair was brown and cut close. But he was considerate and seemed to have a happy outlook on things. Of course, he might have somebody waiting in Westbog. Maybe he was just appreciative of her help and nothing more. He was so polite, maybe she just couldn't tell the difference. He might not even find her attractive.

"There, she's coming right now." Papa stood with someone in front of their home.

As she came closer, she realized that it was Wallis standing with her father. She was so surprised that no words came to her.

"I didn't want to be late this time," Wallis said. He took the water from her shoulders and carried it to the house. "My cart's at the boarding house. It's fuller than last time." They strolled out of the cave. "Your father told me about your mother and your uncle. I'm really sorry."

"I was just thinking about you, wondering if you'd be back."

Wallis stopped. A scent of balsam wafted up from the sunny slope below them. "I haven't thought of anything else since I left a month ago. You know, I sold everything on the way back."

"That's good." She was transfixed by his green eyes. His words almost didn't matter.

"I saved almost half the money, and spent the rest to fill up the cart. I even loaded it with peat bales to push up a steep hill twice every day—practice, so I wouldn't have trouble getting up the mountain."

"Your shoulders look...thicker than I remember." He wore a fresh, blue tunic, its creases still showing where it had been carefully folded.

"Really?" His cheeks blushed. "I wanted to ask you...if you ever gave any thought to...um...living somewhere else. I know it's beautiful here. It's one of the most beautiful places I've ever..."

Pellana placed her hands on his cheeks and kissed his lips. His cheeks, his lips, his fair skin were all softer than she had imagined.

"I'm so glad you came back. And yes, I've thought about living somewhere else. Why did you want to know?"

"I don't want to be trading forever. I was thinking that if I could save up, say for a year, and build a place—a really nice place on the lake—you might come and be...my mate...I mean, if...if...if you might be interested in that...in me...you know...in that way."

She understood what he was saying, but its reality seeped in slowly. "What would you do, if you're not trading?" His hair was a little longer.

"I could get a boat and trap minnows. That's what I did for years. That way I could always be there for...you...and help with...to have...to raise a family." He blushed again. "I love you Pellana. Will you wait for me?"

"Take me with you when the market is done."

Wallis was startled. "You mean now?"

"Yes. When Uncle Willi died, he left some money. Papa won't take it. He says it should be for when I start my own home. Take me with you when you go back." Pellana thought of the second sun reflecting from Lake Willow on the far side of Ternaria.

"My father died when I was little." They walked side by side, Wallis pulling his cart from within the limbs, Pellana outside to his right.

The morning sun warmed her wings and shoulders, and cast a magical shadow of the two of them together. She watched the shadow couple as she walked, occasionally turning her head to watch her mate speak of the past and of his dreams. They were two days out of Mount Easley, and would stop tonight at one of the inns at Nettle Falls.

"He was out over the deep water when a storm swept the lake. We never saw him again. I don't really remember him. Mama died last year of the bruises. It just showed up and took her in a month. They said there was nothing to be done."

"That's so sad."

"It was hard for a while, and then one day I just decided I wasn't going to feel bad every day."

On the evening of their third day, they reached the Buttercup Inn, a small establishment at the base of the magnificent Nettle Falls. There Wallis sold half the mouse ivory dolls, sage leaf mattresses and jams that they had bought at Mount Easley. Pellana stood on the small deck behind the inn, watching the waterfall and the river until it was too dark to see.

The following morning, a roped barge took them, with their cart, across the river to the Earwig Inn, situated on the west bank, directly across from the Buttercup. A north-south road followed the river on either side. After selling the remainder of their merchandise, the cart was so light, with only a few of Pellana's belongings, she insisted on taking turns with Wallis in pulling it.

In three days, they would reach Lake Willow. She could hardly imagine actually living on a lake. The Great West Road meandered through lowlands and across occasional low rocky bluffs. They slept in meadows each night. Pellana could not recall a happier time in her life. Wildflowers and rich grasses towered overhead, adding their perfume to the heady mix of fertile soil and sun-warmed roots.

Pellana and Wallis began their final descent toward Westbog when an overpowering stench assaulted her senses. "What's that awful smell?"

"Oh. That's from the saucers making fish sauce."

"Where do they do that?"

"In Westbog."

She stopped in the road. "Do they make it every day?"

"They do, but...I'm sorry. I should have said something about it."

Pellana began to cry. All of her fantasies and expectations collapsed into a jumble of exhaustion and confusion. They continued walking. To the left, a dreary peat bog extended as far as she could see. To the right, massive rhododendrons spread into the sky, completely blocking out the sun. The reeking of the saucers grew more intense.

"Pellana. You once turned my day around." He placed his arm over her shoulder. "Will you let me do that for you?"

"I don't know how you could."

"I do." The road plunged into the rhododendrons. They continued toward a distant line of sunlight. "Look up."

When, Pellana turned her head toward the dense canopy, she suddenly realized that they were already in the town. Countless houses with verandas were built high overhead, among the branches of the rhododendrons. One or two ladders extended from each.

"And I've already picked out a place for a house." They broke out from beneath the canopy and stood near the edge of the water in a fresh, steady breeze off the lake. "It takes two days just to sail across the lake by boat. But..." He turned around and faced the rhododendrons. "That one. I'm going to build up there, in the first one. It will have a veranda, so you can look out over the lake every morning. And it's always upwind of the saucers. The view is...well...you see the view. I picked it because I knew you would like it. It just has the sweetest air to breathe."

She took a deep breath. Crisp lake air carried the scent of willows, rich humus, cattails and the slightest hint of sun-baked limestone. The late sun formed a rippling puddle of brilliant yellow across the vast expanse of water.

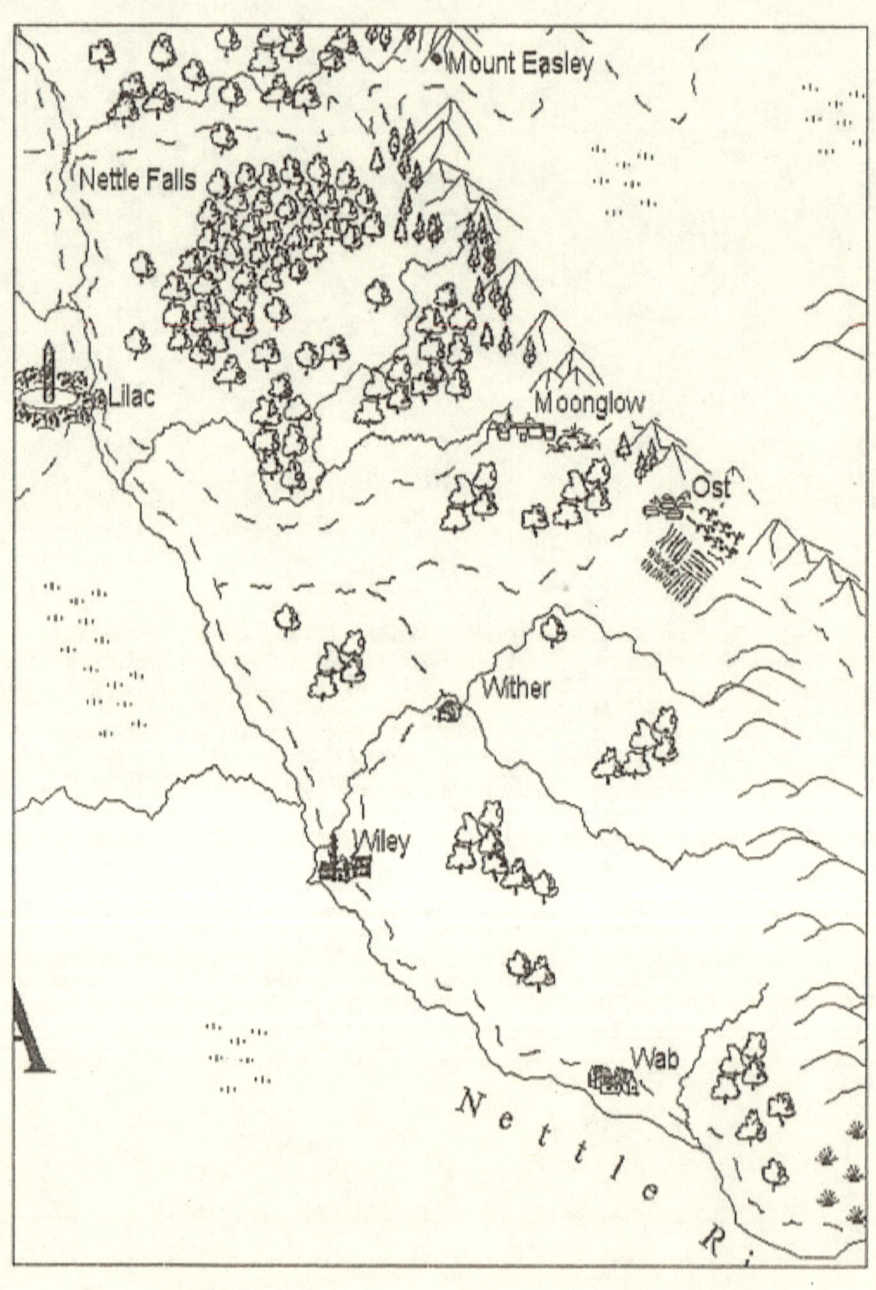
Mount Easley
Nettle Falls
Lilac
Moonglow
Ost
Wither
Wiley
Wab
Nettle Ri

CHAPTER 8—JUST A GIFT OF LIFE

Yori had been struggling to guide Twitcher, his millipede, along the poorly maintained and seldom traveled trail that wound in and out of every hollow on its way from Moonglow to Sorrel Pass at Mount Easley, when they came upon the dead Thistlepix. Behind Yori sat Cammia, his love, and his mate of four years. Lashed behind her, to Twitcher's annoyance, were eighteen large jugs of wine: nine of muscadine and nine of gooseberry, in large, translucent white, fired clay jugs. Yori decided to stop and investigate.

Since their Sycamore Winery had finally begun to produce more wine than they could sell in Moonglow and to the few traders who ventured out to that remote town, Cammia had decided to take some of their output to the market at Mount Easley, and on east, over the pass to Tellia. She had figured that five days on this miserable, forested mountain trail would be a better route than the eight days by road into the valley and back up to the spine of the mountain.

"Why are we stopping?" Cammia asked. Now four days out of Moonglow, she had become more irritable than he had ever seen her.

"I think we've got a dead Thistlepix, Miss Cammia. Over there."

"Huh. There's what's left of its wasp, a little down the slope."

Yori climbed off Twitcher's smooth back and offered Cammia a hand.

"So what are you going to do? Bury it?"

"I was thinking to, Miss Cammia."

She approached the dead Thistlepix. "It's all shriveled up. It's probably been out here for months. I guess even a Thistlepix deserves a burial. Get the camp shovel and I'll find a spot to dig a hole. You know, Yori, it'll be time to stop for the night in an hour anyway. You may as well unload everything, and we can set up...over there by that little creek."

"Yes, miss Cammia." Yori knew that Cammia was smarter than he ever was or ever would be. Following her instructions was always the easiest way to the best outcome. He started unloading Twitcher for the night.

"Look down there," she said. "There are two cargo bags below that wasp."

Yori shuffled down the steep slope to where Cammia had knelt near the head and thorax of a wasp. Its legs extended in an unnatural rigor from the empty thorax. The abdomen was missing completely. "You're not going to open that, are you, Miss Cammia? You don't know what might be in there."

"How else am I going to find out? Check that other one."

Yori untied one of the fabric cargo bags. Inside were four transparent lilac-colored stones, each as long and as thick as his thigh. "These are pretty things, Miss Cammia. Look. They must be worth something." When he turned to his mate, she was wiping her hands on the surrounding duff. "What is it?"

"This one's full of some kind of curly, gray metal, but it's stained the palms of my hands all black."

"Well, don't be touching it any more, Miss Cammia. You can go wash up at the creek."

"Bring that bag. We'll just leave this one, whatever it is."

By the time they had buried the shriveled Thistlepix, set up camp, and eaten dinner, the sun had set, and a half-moon had appeared overhead. Yori nestled beside Cammia, where she reclined against the slope, and slipped his arm around her. She looked at the palms of her hands in the moonlight.

"That never did wash off." She sighed. "I guess it'll just have to wear off. At least it doesn't rub off on anything else. Let me see one of those stones you brought up."

"They're heavy, Miss Cammia." He lifted one and handed it to her.

She accepted it with both hands and held it over her eyes. "You have to look at the moon through one, Yori."

He lifted another of the six-sided, lilac stones and held it over his eyes. "They're prettier at night than the day." He put his down and wriggled his head between Cammia's stone and her face, shadowing her eyes from the lilac moonlight. He kissed her lips. "Day or night, Miss Cammia," he whispered, "you're always the prettiest."

"Look at that, Yori," Cammia said from behind him, as Twitcher approached the first indications of habitation, south of Sorrel Pass.

"That cave?" The air was filled with the scent of evergreens.

"No, love. Right in front of your face."

Yori then noticed Cammia's hands to either side of his face. "Well, I'll be. That black stuff did wash off, Miss Cammia."

"No. It just went away on its own. I hadn't really thought about it until now. Unless it rubbed off on your back." She tugged at the collar of his tunic. He felt her warm breath swoosh down the back of his neck and between his wings. "Not there. Not anywhere."

"Should we stop here and ask where the inn is for Mount Easley, Miss Cammia?"

"I think that is the inn, Yori. A trader who came up to Moonglow last spring, the one with all that willow furniture, said it's the cave on the south of the pass."

"An inn in a cave? Who ever heard of such a thing, Miss Cammia?"

"Who ever heard of a winery inside a hollow sycamore?"

"I guess if we can be inside a tree, they can be inside a mountain."

"He said it was the sweetest air in all of Ternaria."

"Sweeter than the top of the sycamore?"

"He's been to both."

"We'll just have to see about that, Miss Cammia."

He tied up Twitcher below the cave entrance and escorted Cammia into its wide, circular mouth. Inside, five separate wicker rooms, woven of brown fir needles, stood against the curve of the eastern wall.

"Hello!" Cammia called.

No one responded. They walked farther, following the curve and gentle upslope of the cave, eventually coming to a second opening, too high above the trail to be used as an entrance.

"You can almost smell Moonglow from here, Miss Cammia." The great plain of Ternaria unfolded beneath him. A dark green, wiggling line of vegetation marked out what he assumed was the meandering course of the Nettle River, on its journey from the far north to the far south. A thin layer of brilliant white cloud extended from the western horizon, shadowing the western third of the plain. "Isn't that something."

"Here's somebody." Cammia tugged gently at his wing.

"Are you hoping to stay for the night?" A young adult Faerie with short brown hair and a yellow silk tunic smiled. "We do have one empty room. Only three coppers for the night." His smile persisted.

"You appear," Cammia said, with an equally insincere smile, "to have five empty rooms."

The Faerie shrugged. "Okay, one is my own."

"Then four empty rooms."

"And one is the kitchen." His smile finally began to fade, but not by much.

"We'll pay your three coppers, but for two nights." Cammia's unblinking yellow eyes were never hard to misjudge.

"Agreed. Welcome to Sorrel Inn. I'm Sorlin. I'll help you unload your...centipede."

"If that was a centipede," Yori said, "you'd have been his dinner. Twitcher is a millipede. Just eats plants."

"Of course, my mistake. Are those jugs going to the market tomorrow?"

"Some of them," Cammia answered. "The rest are going on to Tellia."

"What's in them?" Sorlin asked, as they headed down the gentle slope from the cave entrance.

"The best wine in all of Ternaria," Yori replied. "Gooseberry and muscadine."

"That's a lot of wine. You'll need to open one tomorrow for folks to taste. Then it's only three more days to Tellia, and you can use the same open one. I've got a market bench and ten clay cups you can use."

"For a price?" Cammia asked.

"For a taste."

Yori dipped a water bag at the spring, amid towering alders. The market had not gone as well as he had hoped. Although they had sold three jugs of wine, nearly half the large, open jug of muscadine wine had somehow been consumed by too few potential buyers. He did sell one of the transparent lilac stones for as much as a jug of wine.

"Next time you come," Sorlin said with overflowing enthusiasm, "everybody will be waiting to buy some."

Sorlin had graciously offered to escort them down to the spring and help carry their water back up to the inn. Yori suspected that the young innkeeper might have consumed more than his share of the sample muscadine wine. He couldn't help feeling that Sorlin's presence at their market bench had caused some of those who approached to merely nod politely and pass them by. He knew from his experience at Sycamore Winery that free wine is not often declined.

"We'll be leaving for Tellia at sunrise," Cammia said to Sorlin, "so an early breakfast would be helpful."

"No problem," Sorlin answered brightly.

"If your bags are full, Yori, just go on back up and make sure that millipede is situated where he can eat something tonight. I'll be done in just a bit."

"I think I'll wait for you, Miss Cammia."

"Yori, I won't get lost, I promise." She waved him on with her free hand.

Yori looked at Sorlin, who smiled fatuously. "Yes, Miss Cammia."

He trudged back up through the aspens and the fir with his filled water bags. After dropping them at their wicker room in the cave, he went out and untied Twitcher.

"Well," he said to the oblivious millipede, "we've got a lot farther to go, but with a lighter load. What do you want for dinner tonight?" He led Twitcher to a fresh spot of dead vegetation and tied him to a twig. "You get your rest tonight."

After a quarter hour, when Cammia had still not returned, Yori walked below the windy pass and beyond the four entrances of the main cave of Mount Easley, then headed down the steep trail to the spring. He descended through the fir and aspens. By the time he reached the alders that surrounded the spring, the light was fading.

In the pond beneath the spring, Cammia stood naked, bathing herself in the clear, cold water. He looked about and saw no one else.

"Miss Cammia?"

Cammia looked up, her eyes reddened and wide, then turned away from him, hiding her breasts beneath her arms.

"Are you alright, Miss Cammia?" She had never hidden herself in his presence. "Come out and dry off. It's getting dark and we'll get lost going back up that trail. Miss Cammia?"

"Just leave me alone for once."

"I will not, Miss Cammia. You sent me up that trail contrary to my will, and look at you now. Tell me what's wrong."

She silently waded out of the water and pulled her clothes onto her wet body. Without glancing at Yori, she headed up the trail in the twilight. Yori located her water bags and brought them along.

"Where is that Sorlin fellow gone to?" Yori stopped her by her shoulder and turned her around. "Did he hurt you?"

She pulled her shoulder away from his hand and continued up the trail. "I want to leave here tonight."

"You want to head off to Tellia at night?"

"No. I want to go home tonight." She sniffed.

"Back to Moonglow? Miss Cammia, did that young fellow do something. Did he...force himself on you?"

"Forget about him and take me home...please."

When they reached the entrance to the Sorrel Inn cave, it was completely dark. No lamps had been lit. Yori put down the water and stood facing his mate. "I will take you home, Miss Cammia, if that's what you want. But nobody's going anywhere until you tell me what happened. I deserve that much."

Cammia lowered her head in the darkness. "It was my fault. I knew he was drunk, but he looked so foolish and harmless. I sent you away." She sobbed. "I'm sorry."

Anger pounded within his head. "Did he...mate you?"

"I'm sorry. I tried to stop him. I'm so sorry. Take me home now."

Yori left her standing there in the dark. He ran toward the main cave of Mount Easley and into the first entrance. His ears rang as he tried to catch his breath. His hands and feet prickled. He stopped the first Faerie he came to.

"Where is Sorlin?" he demanded.

The startled Faerie stepped back and pointed further into the cave.

Yori ran and stopped over a dozen times until a Faerie told him that Sorlin had gone down the passage to the midden, and that he didn't look well.

As he ran into the midden passage, the rank odor of rotted garbage grew stronger. With the cave well lit by oil lamps, Yori had no trouble finding Sorlin, who sat against the wall just short of where the floor abruptly dove into a fathomless darkness. When Sorlin saw Yori coming, he scrambled to his feet, and stepped onto the garbage strewn edge.

"She..." was all he said before his eyes widened and his feet slipped from under him. In an instant, he vanished down the pit.

Confused, Yori carefully approached the edge, bracing his hand on the side wall, and looked down into the darkness. Only then did he hear the distant, damp thud of Sorlin striking the bottom. He wondered what Sorlin had wanted to say. From the little he knew of Sorlin, he was certain that the innkeeper was about to excuse his actions. Yori had wanted to pound him senseless, but he felt no pity that the drunken Faerie had ended up with the rest of Mount Easley's garbage.

He retraced his steps out of the midden cave and stopped the first Faerie he encountered. "Your innkeeper fell down the midden," he said calmly. Then he walked back out of the main cave, crossed beneath the windy pass, and found Cammia tying the last of the cargo onto Twitcher's back.

"I got everything. Now let's go."

"I would have helped, Miss Cammia."

"You didn't hurt that drunken boy, did you?"

"He's not a boy, Miss Cammia. I didn't hurt him, but I think he's dead."

Yori stood beneath arching ferns at the branch of the two creeks near Sycamore Winery's great hollow tree. He watched little moss bears munch at moss leaves. Mylis, Cammia's younger brother, stood nearby, listening silently as Yori recounted the events that occurred at Mount Easley two weeks earlier. Mylis had expected them to be gone for at least eighteen days, and had been surprised to discover them at the winery today.

"I'd like to talk to her, Yori."

"You can try, Master Mylis, but she's hardly said a thing to me. Not for the whole trip back. And not since we got back four days ago. She sleeps up in one of the high guest rooms. She won't even come out when I take food to her. She just says to leave it at the door. It's just not like her, Master Mylis. She's always so cheerful. She always knows how to handle things. This has really got her."

"Maybe I'll give her a few more days."

Yori nodded. "That's probably best."

"Do you think you'll have to go back to explain what happened?"

"I don't know. It's been two weeks. They knew we came up from Moonglow."

"Let me know if I can help, Yori."

"Thank you, Master Mylis."

Yori watched as Mylis hiked out the trail. The surrounding woods, which towered to staggering heights all around him, had been known for decades as Neelian's Woods, named after Cammia's father, but in just the four years of the winery's existence, it had come to be called, at least in Moonglow, the Sycamore Woods. Everything had seemed perfect, before the trip to Mount Easley. Now, with Cammia in such a sad state, he found it difficult to accomplish even the simplest chore.

He wanted to be strong for Cammia, but she had always been his strength. Sorlin had taken something from her that he didn't know how to restore. Cammia had accepted his explanation of what happened to cause Sorlin's death, but then, he had never lied to her or to anyone. Yori had always considered himself not smart enough to lie without being caught at it. So he always took the simplest approach and told the truth as he understood it.

Without much thought, he pulled a few coils of soaked reed from the soaking bucket and began to weave a basket for carrying one of their wine jugs. It seemed so simple an idea, he wondered why no one had thought of a jug basket before. An hour later, he slipped an empty jug into it and made a few adjustments. He removed the jug and added a hinged wicker lid that swung between the two twisted arms of the shoulder-length handle. Winery customers might easily pay a copper for a basket to safely carry the wine away. He hung it to dry outside the entry to the hollow sycamore. As he did so, he wondered when Cammia would care enough to even look at it.

Although he wasn't hungry, he stepped inside to prepare some food for Cammia. They hadn't restocked their food since returning from Mount Easley. He sliced a seed of sweetgrass, then added a dab of freshly prepared mustard paste to the side of the brown clay dish. In the center, he placed a dollop of shredded, fermented kale. As he turned with the dish, he was startled to see Mylis standing in the doorway motioning to him. He set down the dish and went outside to see what had brought Mylis back so soon.

"I have bad news, Yori. The Tribune of Moonglow came out to see Luris. He said that innkeeper's family hired a searcher from Mount Easley to look for you. They want you to return with him to explain what happened to him. Everyone in Mount Easley believes you murdered him, because you left so suddenly."

"I left because your sister wanted to come home right then."

"So I explained to the Tribune what you told me. Luris became incensed. He said that Cammia has dishonored the family—that he would be shamed for as long as she lives. I think he means to kill her. I know it's hard to believe all this, but I think you should take Cammia away from here, before Luris comes."

"And go where," Yori asked, "and for how long?" He was numbed by what he was hearing. "He would kill his own sister because someone hurt her?"

"I think you should get out of here, at least until Luris calms down."

"How much time do we have?"

"He's probably on his way, so a quarter hour."

"Bring Twitcher around to here, Master Mylis, and I'll load up some things."

Yori rushed inside and climbed to their house above the winery ceiling. There, he grabbed the bags of clothing and gear that had been abandoned, still packed, at their return. He took them down and handed them to Mylis to lash to the millipede. He carried his new jug basket, still damp, to the kitchen and filled it with any foods that would not spoil. He passed that to Mylis, then hauled himself in the rope basket up to the guest rooms.

He found Cammia sleeping. Her hair disheveled, her clothes a wrinkled mess, he lifted her in his arms and out to the rope basket.

"What are you doing," she asked, still half-asleep.

"We have to go right now, Miss Cammia. No questions until we get moving."

"What do you mean?"

"No questions!" he barked.

At the entry, Mylis hugged her.

"Do you know what's going on, Mylis?"

"Be careful, Sis. Yori will have to explain it. Now go, and stay off the road...and don't talk."

Yori guided Twitcher up the ravine to the rhododendron bog, then swept along the western edge of the escarpment, heading south and passing east of Luris' blackberry bramble. All he knew was that many days away, maybe a week, the remote village of Ost, perched on the slope below the high mountain ridge, would be their next comfortable stop.

There was no road—not even a trail, other than the random runs of mice and shrews. He knew that even Ost itself connected to the rest of Ternaria with only a rude trail.

Once underway, Yori explained what Mylis had told him. He expected her to protest or insist that they go back, or even to tell him where they ought to go and what they ought to plan. Instead, she sat silently behind him, occasionally bumping his wings—his only indication that his mate had not fallen off.

The ride on Twitcher had never been more uncomfortable. With no trail to follow, the millipede went up and over every twig and pine needle, or followed a tedious, tortuous path around them. Each day merged into the next. Yori sometimes thought aloud about where they were, what they encountered, what they would have for their next meal.

The western slope of the high ridge gradually thinned its vast stands of pines, giving up its grand beauty for a scrubbier, somewhat sparser forest of shorter pines and junipers that reflected the transition in the smaller plants to those less dependent on frequent rains. When the drizzle did come, they rode on, as they would on any other day, allowing the raindrops to bathe them.

"Grackles," Cammia said one afternoon, as they sat on a needle of the endless pine duff, eating lunch. It was the first word she had uttered all day.

"What's that you say, Miss Cammia?"

She pointed to the blue sky north of them. "Grackles."

He looked up to see a flock of a hundred or more black birds swirling and landing one by one in the distance, only to erupt into the air once more and swirl as a single living thing, closer with each landing to where they sat. He shoved Cammia into a gap in the needles and dove in after her.

"Dig deeper, Miss Cammia," he whispered.

The pine duff became more compressed the farther into it they crawled—the needles less springy and the gaps between them smaller. At two faerielongs beneath the surface, they stopped and waited, struggling to breath in the ample air, redolent with pine oils. Yori's eyes watered. Since he could see nothing so far down, he closed his eyes, listened and waited.

Soon, a deafening flutter of wings enveloped them. The weight of a bird pressed from above, as the fluttering abruptly ceased. Sudden jostles, he assumed, were pecking movements, as the grackle above them located and consumed small morsels—Faerie-sized morsels. Just as suddenly, the deafening flutter resumed, the weight lifted from them, and all became quiet.

When Yori could no longer endure the fumes, he tugged at Cammia and climbed the jumble of needles to the surface. He gasped for air, and then pulled Cammia's head clear of the duff. She inhaled deeply, then looked back and forth at the clear sky. He helped her climb out.

"I think Twitcher twitched his last," she said.

Yori's relief at hearing Cammia speaking, was crushed when he looked at his millipede. He climbed over the randomly strewn needles to the fractured remnants of Twitcher, partly curled, partly broken open. His thorax, the only segments with single instead of double legs, was completely hollow, his head missing. The belongings that had been lashed to his forty abdominal segments were strewn about, but seemed to be intact.

"I guess," Cammia said, "the grackles were too excited to bother with our things."

"I shouldn't have tied him up out here, Miss Cammia. Millipedes are night creatures."

"There wasn't anywhere that a hundred hungry birds wouldn't discover, love."

"Now what do we do?" Yori wept.

"We just go on, Yori. We just go on." She put her arms about his chest.

"How do I know you have any notion about grapes?" Asif asked. He looked over Yori and Cammia, all their possessions on the ground beside them. A vineyard of white grapes—two vines—luxuriated in the rich soil of Asif's hollow. The middle-age Faerie wore the simple, brown tunic common to farmers.

Cammia, who had just descended with Yori through the steep slopes above the vineyard, reached her hand into the soil. "You plant your grapes here, instead of up on those slate hills, because they grow better and mature more predictably down here. It makes a sweet wine. But you're not happy with it, because it has very little flavor. If you grew them up in that slate, they'd be difficult to cultivate, they'd just barely ripen most years, but it would soak up the flavor of the slate. The wine would have a crispier taste and more body. You wouldn't have just wine. You'd have great wine—wine that others would want to buy."

"Is that so?" Asif said, now showing more interest.

"But we're not interested in planting and growing your grapes," she continued. "We can design and build you a small winery and pottery, with a grape cutter and a press, vats, potter's wheel and a kiln, all under a wicker roof, so you can produce enough to pay for your costs and all the wine you keep for yourself. To make a real profit, you'd need to plant more vines."

"Where have you come from?" Asif asked.

Yori touched Cammia's shoulder and took the question. "A family member threatened her life. As her mate, I felt it my duty to take her to safety and travel until it all gets straightened out. I'm sorry, Master Asif, but I'd rather we keep our past unspoken."

Asif stood silently for a moment. "Well, I suppose you could have said you came from just about anywhere, and I would never know the difference. So I have to thank you for your honesty. Your mate knows her grapes. A grower to the south of Ost told me the same thing about the slate five years ago—maybe six now. How long to build it all? I've got two months until harvest."

"Six weeks," Yori and Cammia said simultaneously. Yori looked at Cammia and smiled. "Or a little less," he added.

Asif provided a corner in his barn for them to call home. While Yori explored sources for wicker and clay, Cammia worked at building the wheel and kiln. The real challenge was designing a grape cutter that could slice a grape—of nearly her own height—in a single movement of the cutter arm, and in such a manner that very little of its juice would be lost in the transfer to the press. Her solution was to build a two storey building, with the slicer on the upper floor, the press directly below it. The structure would stand against the slope, so that a grape could be rolled in directly to the slicer through a rear door, or hoisted with ropes to a side door. Once a grape was sliced, the floor of the slicing bin would swing down.

"What is this, Yori?" she asked one day, holding up the battered jug basket. "We've been carrying stuff in it for weeks, and it occurred to me only today that I didn't know how we ended up with it."

"Back at the Sycamore, I thought it might be something we could sell for carrying a wine jug." He sighed. "I never got a chance to tell you about it, Miss Cammia."

"I like it." She placed the twisted bail over her shoulder. "If we finish the winery early, maybe Asif would buy some."

Yori nodded. "I guess that's better than moping about not putting our own wines in them."

"Much better, love."

The new winery, which Asif named Slate Hill, in the expectation of expanding the plantings up the slope, was completed in five weeks. Yori and Cammia stayed on for the harvest and the first trials of her new designs. They filled the days with the manufacture of jugs and jug baskets. Yori did the wicker work, while Cammia threw the jugs and fired them. The light brown clay that Yori had located fired into a deep green jug.

For these work-filled months, Cammia had seemed to Yori to have regained her laughter and her creative excitement. But with the harvest complete, she lapsed into a despondent state, like a sycamore shedding its leaves.

Yori walked with her beside the new winery, as the last of the grapes were hoisted, one at a time, up to the side door of the slicer, and rolled in.

"Isn't that something, Miss Cammia?"

"What?"

"All those big green grapes and all. It works just like you thought. I don't know anybody who could come up with that. You're always a wonder, Miss Cammia."

"I'm going to have a baby."

For four years, they had thought that they were just getting a little too old. They had tried, but no babies had come. "That's the nicest thing I could imagine, Miss Cammia." The suddenness of the news left him in a confusion of joy and wonderment. But as he looked at Cammia's sad, yellow eyes, he remembered what had happened at Mount Easley. "Aren't you happy, Miss Cammia?"

"I want to be, Yori, but it reminds me of something I want to forget. It might not be your baby."

"But it's your baby for sure. Because I love you, it'll be our baby. A little baby doesn't pick its parents. It just comes out into a world of danger and trusts its mama and papa love it. And we will."

"What if it looks like Sorlin?

"That Sorlin fellow was an ornery, selfish fool. But he was a good looking fool. Miss Cammia, I don't give a gnat's ear what that baby looks like. And you shouldn't either."

"Yori, I don't think I could get through life without you."

He touched her cheek. "When do you expect to...you know...have it?"

"In five or six months. I'm not sure."

"Five or six... We'll have to get some things ready, baby things and all."

"Yori," Asif called out, running up to them. "There was a fellow came into Ost today. He's asking for you. Name's Luris. Too many folks in town know you've been out here doing the winery. I told him you used to be here, but you left to go out to the Scrub. That's out southeast, in the dry parts. Get your things and go south from the vineyard for four days—there's a faint trail, but you can follow it—then head due west another four days. That will take you to Wither. Now, two days south of here the trail branches east to go to the Scrub. Don't take that one."

Yori felt bewildered. He wanted to think about a new baby. "Is he coming up here?"

"I'd be surprised if he didn't. You get packed up and I'll bring the rest of your payment. I wish I could recommend you, but I guess that would be useless now." Asif headed back to his house.

"Why don't we just talk to Luris, Yori?"

"Miss Cammia, I don't want to hurt your brother, but if he raises a hand to you, I swear, he'll never raise it again."

"It's hard to believe that he's stayed away from Moonglow for so long. He's never really trusted Mylis to run things."

"Where there's enough hate... He never forgave you for keeping your dowry."

"So you want to run for the rest of our lives?"

"Of course I don't, Miss Cammia. But we need to clear this up at a time and a place of our choosing, not when he's waiting to pounce on us."

"Okay, Yori. But in a few months, I really won't be able to pack up and run away at the snap of a finger."

"Miss Cammia, look what I bought in Wiley, yesterday." Yori held up a tiny, light green blanket.

Cammia looked up from her pottery wheel, her hands glistening golden brown with mud. Yori had recently raised the wheelhead and added a kick wheel, so she could sit more comfortably with her enlarged abdomen. She smiled. "Did you ask about the midwife?"

"I talked to her. I don't know if she'll come this far out."

They had built a small home an hour south of the trail that connected Wither and Wiley—about half-way in between them.

Though Wiley was a modest village on the main road that ran along the Nettle River, Wither could hardly be called more than a monthly market square. Every two weeks, he carried wicker furniture and home pottery—dishes, bowls and cups—to one market or the other. His small two-wheel cart could easily carry as much as would likely sell. At either market, he seldom spoke with anyone other than customers, and then only about the current transaction. When pressed to give a location of his home, he would vaguely point in a random direction and say, "a couple of days out that way." Initially, he spent two days going and two days returning for each trip. The past month, he would leave at sunset and return by sunrise the day after, rushing along with his cart and doing without sleep until his return.

During Yori's last two journeys to market, his belly and back had caused him pain. He was certain it was from hauling the cart so fast and with so little sleep and food. He said nothing to Cammia about it.

"What are we going to do, Yori? You don't know how to help with birthing."

Yori sat on a stool and folded the tiny green blanket in his lap. "I don't know, Miss Cammia." He felt the softness of the fluffy blanket and touched it to his cheek. "I'm afraid to leave you now, with the baby so close. What if it came while I was away? There'd be nobody at all to help."

"Tomorrow morning," she said, "after you've rested up, I'm going to climb into that cart and we'll take two days and go to Wiley. We'll take a room, and stay there until the baby comes."

"I worry about too many eyes, Miss Cammia."

"It can't be helped. I'm not going to have a wicker weaver birthing our baby. Next thing I'd see would be you putting the poor thing in a jug basket." She laughed. "My mind is made up."

"Yes, Miss Cammia."

Yori sat outside the door of the rooming house in Wiley, leaning against the mud wall, struggling to not cry out in pain. His lower back and his belly hurt more than he could bear. The pain above his navel reached out to the left. He had eaten little the past few days of waiting for the baby to come. Now, as he could hardly think, Cammia was with the midwife, enduring her own pain.

The midwife had told him that the baby would be quite small, but attributed that to Cammia's unusually small size. He couldn't help but think that things would have been so different had they been at home, inside the hollow sycamore at Moonglow. He thought of Sorlin. He wondered if the wastrel could have ever understood the grief he caused. And Luris, her own brother... Cammia called out. Her voice echoed the pain of whatever malady had taken hold of him.

After a short while, he heard a tiny voice crying—smaller than the voice of any Faerie baby he had ever heard. Yori folded over in pain, then forced himself to stand. His legs no longer commanded the strength that had carried him through more than four decades. The bib trousers he had worn since they fled from Moonglow now hung loosely about his dwindling frame. He closed his eyes and willed the pain to loosen its grip, if only for a moment.

"Yori?" The midwife stood in front of him. "Are you alright?"

He nodded and forced a smile.

"You have a son."

The discomfort in her demeanor told him that something was wrong. He waited for her to continue.

"He seems healthy...but he's very small...and his hair is white..."

"I don't care what color his hair is."

"...and he doesn't...he's got no wings. None at all."

Yori had never heard of a Faerie born without wings. "Why? What causes that?" The shame, he thought. It was caused by the shame of his conception.

"Cammia is resting, but you can come in and see your son now."

He walked as naturally as he could manage, his head held high, a smile on his face as he entered the chamber.

"I'm sorry, Yori," Cammia said.

He knelt beside her, the baby between them, wrapped in a light green blanket. "Why is that, Miss Cammia?"

"He's not perfect. You deserve perfect."

Yori unwrapped the blanket. The pitiful little creature before him was half the size of a normal baby. Its full head of hair and its eyebrows were as white as snow. "I count ten fingers and ten toes, Miss Cammia."

"He's got no wings, Yori." She began to cry. "They'll laugh at him all his life."

"What good have wings ever done for even one Faerie? You can't fly with them. They're just like decorations."

The baby opened his eyes. Their faint, red glow startled Yori.

"What should we name him, Miss Cammia?"

"I don't know."

"How about if we call him little Neelian, after your papa?"

She smiled through her tears and nodded.

The midwife wrapped little Neelian, nestled him in Cammia's arm, then escorted Yori back outside. "Cammia's got no milk. I'm going to get you some mouse milk, and come right back."

As soon as she had headed toward the center of Wiley, Yori sat again, leaning on the cool mud wall. His pain hovered in the background of everything he did, occasionally striking out at him with greater vehemence. The thought of the two day trip back home—after a week, the midwife had said—seemed an impossible task.

A Faerie whom he recognized from the market approached him. "Pardon. There's a fellow from Moonglow asking after you and your mate."

Not now, he thought. Not again. "What did you tell him?"

"I told him you were in a boarding house, but I didn't know which one. You want me to go tell him you're here?"

"No need. I'll go find him in just a bit. Thank you."

Once the midwife returned with a bag of mouse milk and departed for the evening, Yori brought the cart around to the door. While Cammia slept, he loaded their gear, put the bag of mouse milk inside his tattered jug basket, then lifted Cammia and little Neelian in his arms. He paused to catch his breath.

"What are you doing, love?" Cammia asked, still sleepy.

"We have to go now, Miss Cammia."

"Oh, Yori. I can't travel like this."

He made certain each of his feet stepped solidly onto the ground, and carried her and the baby, step by painful step, out to the waiting cart.

"I can't protect you here, Miss Cammia. I've come down with a weakness. That Luris would just shove me aside."

"Can't we just talk to him?"

"He wants to kill you, Miss Cammia. To kill you."

She began to cry. He placed them gently in the cart, then walked around to stand between the limbs. "There's mouse milk in the jug basket." Yori strained to get the cart moving, but once it began to roll, he never allowed it to slow.

Yori pulled the cart southward, along the remote river road, resting only long enough to catch his breath and fight off bouts of pain in his back and his belly. Whenever little Neelian would cry, Cammia fed him drops of mouse milk from her fingertip. Yori lost count of the days after five or six.

Two days after they had passed the fishing village of Wab, Cammia developed a fever. Her eyes and skin had taken on a dark bronzed color. She had not gotten up from the cart for over a day. Now she complained that her arms hurt too much to lift little Neelian when he needed to be fed.

Yori found a gentle slope in the bank of the Nettle River and rolled the cart close to the water. For two hours, he dabbed a wet cloth onto Cammia's forehead and arms and legs, hoping to drive off the fever.

"Yori, I think I'm dying."

"You're not going to die, Miss Cammia." Tears came to his eyes. "I promised you I'd always take care of you."

"I know you did, love. I know. Now you have to take care of little Neelian when I'm gone."

"Don't talk like that, Miss Cammia."

"My arms and my legs hurt too much to ever move them. The mouse milk has started to go bad. Hold him up, so I can see him."

Yori lifted the tiny, white-haired baby.

"He smiled," Cammia said, returning a weak smile. She closed her eyes and died.

"Miss Cammia? Oh, Miss Cammia." He took the baby to his shoulder and gently patted him on the back. "Your mama saw you smile." He sobbed.

Unable to move the cart back up the slope, Yori carried Cammia's body a short way above the river bank and dug a grave with a thin, flat stone. Over the grave, he transplanted a scraggly sycamore sapling.

With the mouse milk gone, he bundled little Neelian into his light green, fluffy blanket and tucked him into the jug basket. The pain in his belly grew more intense. His mind wandered, as he walked southward, just east of the river road. He found a ripe raspberry and fed some of its sweet juice to Neelian, along with a little water.

As the sun set, a full moon rose, allowing him to keep moving through the night. He had no idea where he was headed, or even if there were any more villages south of Wab. But sorting things out was no longer possible. Pain, grief and exhaustion had deprived him of any forethought. He just walked, the jug basket over one shoulder, a water bag over the other.

Yori stopped and blinked his eyes. The lowland woods had abruptly changed. Before him, sprouting from a barren gravel plain, a crop of dark pointed knives, each fifty times his height, grew in menacing clusters. He looked behind him: nothing but ordinary, open woodland. His mind reeled. He felt that he could go no further, but if he stopped, little Neelian would die. He looked again at the bizarre plants. To his right, he heard weeping. He headed toward it.

Now twenty paces from him, a female Faerie sat alone on a rock that rested between the woodland and the plain of knife plants. Her face rested in both her hands, her head slumping to her knees. Yori was not certain he could reach her. He slipped the water bag off his shoulder and let it down to the ground. Wracked with pain, he staggered forward.

When he neared the weeping Faerie, he carefully lowered the jug basket to the ground. He whispered goodbye to little Neelian beneath the full moon, then turned back the way he had come.

A short way into the woods, he heard Neelian's tiny cry. It soon stopped, replaced by the sweet sound of a soft lullaby.

"Yori, wake up. Yori, it's Mylis."

Yori opened his eyes. Every part of his body ached. His tongue was thick with thirst. Mylis knelt over him. He poured a bit of water into his mouth. He had difficulty understanding Mylis' words. That it was Mylis who leaned over him confused him as well.

"I looked for you in Wiley..."

"Luris?" he uttered past dry lips.

"He disappeared...dry lands...maybe Saracets killed him."

Yori had never heard of such a thing as a Saracet. Was Luris dead? He wasn't sure if he had understood.

"...other girls...Sorlin...believe your explanation..."

He thought of the gravel plain of giant knife plants. It felt as though his body had been tossed onto one of the pointed blades. He became aware that he had been panting—short little gasps that seemed to offer no air.

"...Cammia...midwife..." Mylis had been talking.

Yori wanted to tell Mylis that his sister had died, and where he had buried her. And of little Neelian. *He smiled for her. A lullaby. The weeping Faerie sang him a lullaby.* Yori grasped Mylis hand, took one last breath, then closed his eyes.

CHAPTER 9—NECTAR OF JESSAMINE

Alek awakened to a pricking in his side. He squinted upward to see the silhouette of his new classmate, Caluño, against a dazzling sunrise over the monastery garden.

"I think it's ready," Caluño mumbled. Though thick and muscular, the boy's shoulders slumped; his head always slightly in front of him. "They said three true leaves."

Alek grasped the stem of the chamomile under which he had slept and hoisted himself to his feet. A short distance away, three delicate leaves, green lace, stood atop stems reaching more than five times his height. The seed for this sacred carrot had been carried to the New Life Monastery by Father Britt himself, all the way from Moss Abbey, from the garden of humans. "Three it is." Alek lifted the long rod they had brought with them the previous night. "We need the biggest rock you can find."

"What for?"

"A fulcrum. I'll show you."

Caluño hefted an angular rock from the far side of the garden. "Where do I...put it?" he grunted.

"The Book says 'the greater the burden, the nearer the fulcrum.'" He guessed at a suitable spot near the carrot, then pointed. "Right there."

After wrapping silk twine around the base of the carrot leaves, he lashed it to the near end of the rod. "We put it on the fulcrum at this end, then pull down the other end." The far end of the rod now loomed above his head. He jumped and grasped the rod in both hands, but the carrot held firm in the sandy soil.

With Alek hanging by his hands, his feet suspended above the ground, Caluño strolled to a position just below Alek's face. The younger boy spoke softly, in the measured pace of a grandparent retelling the days of his youth. "In Lilac—that's where I grew up, in Lilac—we didn't say 'fulcrum.' We called all this a 'lever over a rock.' Your rod and fulcrum looks like it's stuck. Did you need some help?"

Alek replied with a smirk.

Caluño reached his left hand to the rod, below Alek's, and grinning triumphantly, flexed his substantial left arm. With a soft tearing sound, Alek's feet returned to the ground and a pale orange cone as thick as Alek's thigh lifted partway from the sandy soil.

"After completing the writing of his great book, Bennik departed this world and descended to that below." Father Britt paced back and forth on the courtyard steps, his long black robe swishing with each step, his wings drooping. Occasionally he paused to adjust the hood that draped over his back, or to tighten the white rope at his waist. "By observing each requirement according to the Book, we will enable him to live again in this world. He stopped his pacing and stood erect, as he always did when quoting from the Book, and solemnly spoke the words:

Not among the Faeries
Where no kindness grew,
But within these queries
My life is born new.

"The growing of a carrot has now brought us one step..." His eyes fell directly on Alek. "What are you writing?"

Alek's face warmed. "Just...some thoughts."

Brother Quartrik paused from his endless work of mending the pebble wall to purse his lips at Alek in a jesting scold, then returned to his task. Though older than Father Britt, Quartrik was the least tenured of the four monks at New Life Monastery.

"Show me the...thoughts...that were more important than the lesson." Father Britt extended his hand. Once the writing slate was delivered, he sent Alek back to his seat on the ground, beside Caluño. He read it aloud, struggling to sound out the words:

Brother Quartrik finds a rock
To place upon the wall,
Wondering why a tiny knock
Should cause the thing to fall.

Faeries never built with rock,
So it is no surprise
Making all the pebbles lock
Requires so many tries.

Father Britt shook his head. "Are you mocking the Book of Bennik?"

The question stunned Alek. "No sir. I was...It's the words...the sounds. I was trying to make them bounce. Like...like the feet of a spider."

"It has a certain quality," Quartrik offered with a chuckle.

Britt silenced the older monk with a stare. "What is the message that you deliver with your...spider feet?"

"No message. Not truly. It was more like an exercise."

"The writing of words carries a power that must be respected." Father Britt's voice trembled slightly as he spoke. His face always reflected more worries than Alek expected to see on a Faerie of Britt's modest age. Now, the vehemence of his words seemed to erupt from some deeper place. "The message! The meaning of the words is what matters, not the measured dance you put them through. If you have no message to bring, who can care how it is delivered?" After a silence, he flipped his hood onto his head with one hand, pivoted, then vanished through the wood-framed doorway, carrying the writing slate with him.

Caluño looked to Alek and shrugged. By the wall, Brother Quartrik made a shooing motion with his hands that seemed to indicate to Alek that he and his fellow student should take full advantage of the opportunity to depart.

"Remain." Brother Tercerik stepped from the shadow of the doorway. A nod of his head redirected Quartrik's attention to mending the pebble wall. He surveyed the two boys. Tercerik, a hovering kestrel of a monk, might strike at any moment—eyes focused and implacable, voice carefully measured and well aimed. "Pey, ehr—only this pair of letters—pey, ehr. Repeat them until your slates are filled, perfectly aligned. Perfectly!"

At the snap of Tercerik's fingers, Brother Secundik shuffled through the doorway, maintaining a position of safety behind his nominal junior. He held forth a new writing slate. Alek scrambled to his feet, past the looming Tercerik, and accepted the slate from the simple, pious, powerless Secundik. Of the four monks, Brother Secundik alone revealed no trace of guile, though perhaps more than a trace of open-hearted gluttony. His menial task accomplished, Secundik bowed to no one in particular, gathered the hem of his black robe, then stepped backwards into the monastery.

"When you have successfully completed this assignment, to Brother Quartrik's satisfaction..." At Quartrik's show of surprise, he added, "...who will later present them to me for *careful* examination, you may go."

An hour later, following several brief sessions of mutual critique, Alek and Caluño handed their slates to Brother Quartrik for inspection. Quartrik shook his head and clicked his teeth. His hand gestured for a stick of chalk. Delicately erasing several strokes with the edge of his little finger, he carefully amended the letters. He viewed his corrections as arm's length, then added two smudges with the tip of his thumb.

"Hmmm. I believe your work is perfectly aligned. Perfectly!" He winked. "Enjoy this beautiful afternoon." As Alek and Caluño fled toward the gate, Brother Quartrik added, "Don't be late for supper."

Outside the gate, they passed the wood statue of Bennik, ridiculously tall and thin in his monk's robe. One long-fingered hand held a scroll, the other, a stylus. Exaggerated wings rose well above his head.

"Father Britt says this is what Bennik really looked like. I think it's just that the piece of wood was too narrow."

"Did Father Britt know him?" Caluño asked.

"Secundik told me that Father Britt was Bennik's only friend. Bennik saved Britt from drowning...or something like that."

Once beyond the grounds of the monastery, Caluño seemed to stand more erect, though still not quite equaling Alek's height. The blue sky, with its sculpted white clouds, promptly erased from Alek's consciousness the oddity of Father Britt's reaction to word play and the predictable harshness of Brother Tercerik.

"We should walk to Faerie Ring," Alek said. "I think it's still the market fair."

"They said we shouldn't go there."

"When you've been at the monastery longer, Caluño, you'll learn to distinguish 'it is forbidden' from 'it is discouraged.' The first gets you in serious trouble if you ignore it. With the second, it's just an earful."

"How long have you been there?" His head tilted back toward the monastery.

Alek didn't often dwell on that issue. "A few years."

"Are your parents dead too?"

"Yeah. Killed by Thistlepix when I was about ten. My little sister too." Alek reflected on the one day that not only took away his family, but also forced him to leave his only friends. "Father Britt has been okay. So are Secundik and Quartrik. If Tercerik wasn't there, it wouldn't be too bad a place." Alek walked on in silence, until they approached Faerie Ring.

"I've never seen boletuses in a circle," Caluño said. "How do they do that?"

"Quartrik told me that instead of moving the village when the boletuses start to fail, they store the spores and plant them in a circle with a secret potion that starts them growing. He said that Father Britt built the monastery where it is because Faerie Ring is a Faerie village that stays put." Alek looked at Caluño's white robe and then at his own. "Maybe we should leave these here until we're done in the village." Alek untied his robe and stashed it, rolled in a ball, behind a thistle. His tan tunic seemed a bit short and tight. Caluño followed Alek's example.

A flute could be heard above a cacophony of voices. Alek guessed that there were more than thirty market stalls, selling everything from seeds and pots of nectar to tools and weapons. One booth sold nothing but coils of dusted spider silk in a variety of twists and braids. Another offered fabrics in thirteen different colors. One stall displayed containers of granular fruit sugar made from berries.

Since Alek had nothing to exchange, he wandered toward the sound of the flute, to a small fenced area in which eight Faeries were dancing. About twenty others sat on the fence, watching the dancers. From the diversity of clothing, Alek gathered that folks had come from many other villages to attend the fair.

"She's a pretty one," Caluño whispered. "There, on the other side."

Alek scanned the faces of the girls on the opposite side of the dance area. All were quite pretty, some with garlands in their hair. When he saw her, his breathing stopped. When he finally took a breath, he grasped Caluño's muscular shoulder. "She's the most beautiful thing I've ever seen. Her golden hair shimmers like sunrise on the dew. And see how she moves!"

"I just said she was pretty."

"Oh no! She is exquisite! And in the first flower of fertility." Alek's thoughts stumbled as he sought the words to describe the singular vision that had transfixed him. "I think I'm in love."

"That's stupid. You don't even know her. She may be a maggot monger or a scrub girl."

"Look at those delicate fingers. They have never toiled, never touched a stone or a thistle. That perfect chin. And her eyes! Oh, they pierce me! I think she looked at me!"

"So...go talk to her."

"I...I'm afraid somebody will recognize that I'm from the monastery."

"Is that bad?"

"Here, in Faerie Ring, it's bad. They don't like us very much. They think we work magic with vegetables."

"Maybe she's from somewhere else."

Alek looked again across the dance area, but she had vanished. "She's gone!" He thumped his chest. "I think I may die."

"Will you dance with me before you die?" a fragile voice asked from nearby.

Alek spun around. There she stood, an arm's length away, even more beautiful, more perfect. Her diaphanous wings sparkled in the sunlight. The fragrance of honeysuckle drifted about her.

"Is your friend ill?" she asked Caluño, a coy smile slowly revealing a hint of dazzling white.

"Yes," Alek answered.

She raised her eyebrows.

"Yes, I will dance with you before I die."

"We have to go over there." A slender finger pointed toward the fenced area. "The gate is this way." She grasped his hand and led him to the center.

The music had changed from flute to lyre, though still at a lively pace. Silently, he followed her steps as she moved to the rhythm of the plucked strings. Benumbed by the hypnotic motions of their bodies and the enchantment which flowed from the touch of her hands, his mind could assemble no coherent thoughts. Her eyes and the evanescent flash of a smile absorbed his focus. Now flute, now lyre, now both. He danced, intoxicated by her proximity.

"Alek," Caluño half-whispered from a distance.

When Alek had located his friend outside the fence, he saw that he was pointing toward the sun, which now stood only two fingers above the horizon. "I have to go," he said. "I don't know your name."

"Daiella. And your name is Alek."

"Yes. My name is Alek. What village are you from?"

She pointed to a nearby boletus. "That's where I live. And you?"

Alek swallowed. "The...I live at the monastery."

Distress flashed across Daiella's face. "Are you a monk?"

"No. I...Caluño and I...That's Caluño. We live there. My parents died. So did his. So we live there and study."

Tenderness showed in her eyes. She grasped his hand briefly. "I have to go too."

"Can I see you again?"

"Maybe."

Alek rapped hesitantly on the wooden door to Father Britt's private chamber. The summons had been delivered by Secundik in his usual dull manner, so there was no hint as to why.

"Enter," responded Father Britt's voice from behind the door.

As Alek opened it, he was surprised to see how small a chamber it was. "You sent for me?"

"Sit." Father Britt gestured toward a padded stool.

Alek sat and looked about the chamber. On the walls hung dozens of lovely, colored drawings of vegetables, seed pods, fruit, pea vine, barley, loquat, blueberry. A shelf held a collection of small clay jars, each sealed with wax and labeled with a square of vellum: clover honey, radish seed, dandelion seed, nectar of jessamine, and many more—each different and each ordered on the shelf by the first letter of its label. On the table before Father Britt rested a thick book bound in the pale green skin of a lizard's jowl.

"Yes," Father Britt answered to Alek's unasked question. "That is the Book of Bennik. It is why this monastery exists."

"That's a lot of writing."

"The quantity challenges the length of one's life. Understanding its message, even a small portion of it, challenges ones wisdom and insight."

"Have you read it all?"

"I have read it twice. The first time required three years, the second, two years."

Such spans of time spent at a single task seemed unimaginable to Alek. "And you still read it?"

"I continue the struggle every day. And the brothers each study one page over a week, attempting to clarify its message. Our lives are devoted to that task."

"It sounds difficult."

"That is one of the reasons I've called you here."

"You want me to read it?" The thought of such dull labor raised a wave of dread within him.

Father Britt lifted a writing slate, which Alek recognized as his own, and read from it aloud:

Brother Quartrik finds a rock
To place upon the wall,
Wondering why a tiny knock
Should cause the thing to fall.

"And so forth. You recognize this, of course."

"Yes sir."

"I, and the brothers as well, learned to read words as adults. We struggle with individual words. I fear that the meaning of the whole passage is lost with the effort. You, Alek, learned to read letters and words as a child. It is now part of your nature. Written words flow like a clean stream through your mind. Let me show you a page from the Book of Bennik that also bounces 'like the feet of a spider.'" He lovingly opened the green book to a place marked by a strip of dried grass, then slid the book to the edge of the table so that Alek could see the clumsily written text. With the strip of grass, Father Britt pointed to a section. "Can you read this for me?"

Alek scanned the section, then read it fluently, emphasizing the meter and the rhyme of its lines:

The pea, if left to grow as nature should,
And ripen to its fullness on the vine,
Will yield a pod as hard as wood
That carries fruit, however good,
So huge, on each a hundred Faeries dine.
Instead the pod is cut when blossom fades,
Of length to match a Faerie, head to feet.
It's flavor of a thousand shades
Each morsel of its flesh pervades,
One fruit one Faerie for a meal may eat.

"Can you find its meaning?"

"It's a reminder to pick peas before they grow too large."

"But, the meaning of 'a hundred Faeries' and 'a thousand shades?'

"They don't have much meaning. They just make the words bounce nicely." He looked over the passage again. "It says, if you let peas grow to their full size, you can't eat the pod, and each fruit inside will be too big to manage. If you cut it from the vine right after it's formed, the pod tastes good and each fruit is small enough to handle. The bouncing of the words, like dancing to a flute or lyre..." He thought of Daiella. "...and the way the lines end with matching sounds makes it easy to memorize, so you'll be sure to harvest peas at the right time."

Father Britt sat motionless, staring at the words. After a moment, he lifted his gaze to the drawing of a pea vine and placed his hand over his mouth. He looked again at the text, nodding his head to its rhythm, then lowered his hand. "It's so simple." He turned to Alek.

"You have a gift, a calling. Up until now, only the brothers have been permitted to read from the Book. I would like you to spend a portion of your study time each day reading it. You may write your understanding of each passage in this pad of vellum." He handed Alek what appeared to be a small book bound in rectangles of dragonfly wing.

"I'll try," Alek replied. As he stood to leave, Father Britt touched his arm.

"And, Alek, I must discourage you from visiting the girls in Faerie Ring. The folks there are...not happy...with our presence."

When Daiella stepped from the doorway of her boletus, Alek made a hissing noise. Failing to get her attention, he called her name softly. When she spotted him, he motioned for her to join him in the shadow of a massive sow thistle.

"You're not supposed to be here," she said.

"Why not?"

"When Papa heard about us dancing, he insisted on knowing where you were from. Then he went out to the monastery and told them not to let you come back to Faerie Ring."

"Who did he talk to?"

"A monk...Tercerik, I think."

He could hardly believe his misfortune. Secundik would have just passed the message to Father Britt. And Quartrik might have convinced Daiella's father that his visiting would cause no harm. But Tercerik...Tercerik had not only told Father Britt, but would also store the knowledge like a weapon for use at a later date. Alek put the thought aside. "Can I read something I wrote for you?"

"I don't understand."

"I wrote some words about you..." He extracted a rectangle of vellum from the sleeve of his robe and showed it to her. "...and now I can read the words aloud."

"Those are words?" She pointed at the dark purple marks on the vellum.

"Yes."

"And they're about me?"

"Yes. Let me read them aloud:

"Just as sunrise shimmers on the dew
Daiella's golden hair, her radiant face
Cast lambent rays of joy across the sky.
At that fleeting sight of her I knew
That nothing yet to happen could erase
So sweet an instant 'till the hour I die."

"What does that mean?"

"Should I read it again?"

"No. I think I understand it."

"It means that my first sight of you changed me forever."

"A good change?" Daiella placed her hands on his chest and looked up into his eyes.

"Painfully good." The soft fragrance of honeysuckle and the warmth of her breath drew his lips to hers. Her delicate fingers touched his cheeks.

"Daiella!" a booming voice shouted from the nearby boletus.

"It's Papa!" she gasped. "You have to go."

"One more kiss." His ears throbbed with heat.

Daiella grasped his head and pressed a ferocious kiss against his lips, her wings held high and rigid. Then she turned and ran toward her home. "Here I am, Papa."

As Alek crept away, confusing thoughts spun around his head.

"Is someone there?" her father asked.

"Just me," a fragile voice replied.

For three weeks, Alek labored over the Book of Bennik, several hours each day. Twice more he stole away to Faerie Ring to meet with Daiella secretly—once at the river below the village and once at the raspberry bramble. Each time he read to her new words—words about her and words about his love for her. He found no other use for the blank vellum book bound in dragonfly wing.

The Book of Bennik, which he had now read in its entirety, seemed to contain no mysteries, no prophecies, no obscure notions at all. The only aspect that seemed unusual to him was that a number of pages, perhaps twenty or thirty, had been cleanly cut from scattered locations throughout the book, though none of these missing pages interrupted the flow of the existing content of the Book. Although it occasionally expressed Bennik's profound loneliness, the remainder seemed merely to describe plants and explain the intricacies of growing vegetables in a manner useful to Faeries. He had learned gardening from the humans at Moss Abbey and had modified their techniques.

During those same three weeks, Father Britt had been away. On returning, he again summoned Alek to his private chamber.

"I traveled to Moss Abbey and read your bouncing words about Brother Quartrik to Maha Neruti, their abbot, their leader. I did so because of its similarity with certain portions of the Book. He tells me that you are what they call a natural poet, and that such writing is called poetry among humans. Each writing is called a poem. He advises that we encourage such writing."

This meant very little to Alek. He wrote what he wrote because it felt right. He wondered if Father Britt would encourage his writing—his poems—to Daiella.

"Have you made much progress in reading the Book?" he asked with a cheerful countenance.

"Yes. I finished it yesterday."

Father Britt frowned. "You've read it all? Is that possible in so brief a time?"

Alek stepped back at the veiled accusation. "I have read it all," he stated flatly.

"You must show me your comments on each section this evening. I'm eager to see them."

"I...only noted what was not clear."

"Yes. Of course." Irritation and disappointment formed a mask over Father Britt's face. "One thing more." He placed on the table all three of the poems Alek had written to Daiella, each on a leaf cut from the dragonfly book. "Brother Tercerik found these among your belongings. These may be poetry, but their message is worrisome. I forbid you to visit Faerie Ring or the girl you mention, until I decide what should be done. Her father, Dailik, will tolerate it no more."

That evening, Alek took no supper. Instead, he stared at the blank dragonfly book, trying to decide what to write. Anger flooded his thoughts. He wondered what hatred seethed within Tercerik, hardly a brother, to commit so vicious an act. What had he gained from it? It was all nonsense—Father Britt, the monastery, the mystical Book that was not mystical at all.

Alek dipped a hummingbird quill into a small bottle of poke berry ink and wrote a simple assessment of Bennik's writing on the top leaf of the dragonfly book, blotted it dry, then slammed it shut.

As he walked to Father Britt's chamber, he formulated what he would say in his own defense. He concluded that he didn't care what Father Britt thought or said. Alek resolved to leave the monastery that night.

When Alek entered the chamber, he found Father Britt sitting at his table, staring at the closed cover of the Book of Bennik.

"Just leave it here and come to speak with me before breakfast tomorrow." Father Britt never looked up at him.

After an awkward silence, Alek simply left the chamber and closed the door behind him. Fatigue swept over him. One more night in the monastery couldn't make a difference now.

Before going to sleep, he gathered the few belongings that he cherished and placed them in a sack by his bed.

Caluño, with whom he shared a small chamber, watched him from his bed. "You're leaving?"

"Tomorrow."

Without another word, Caluño turned toward the wall. Alek wanted to say something, but no words came.

After a fitful night, Alek arose early while Caluño still slept, and walked to Father Britt's chamber. He was too tired to care what might transpire. He rapped on the door. There was no answer. He opened it slowly and peeked inside. On the floor lay the contorted figure of Father Britt, motionless. He touched the hand of the Master of New Life Monastery and found it cold and stiff.

The Book of Bennik lay open on the table; beside it, an empty clay jar labeled, "nectar of jessamine." He recognized Bennik's peculiar poem written on the open page:

Honey of clover is seen
To sweeten maidens' breath.
But if from jessamine,
Will end in certain death.

At the end of the table, Alek's dragonfly book lay opened to the top page. There, in all their anger and candor, he saw the words he had written the previous night. "Bennik had no true friends. He reveals deep loneliness and despair. The remainder of his book is nothing more than a useful guide to plants and the growing of vegetables. A number of pages have been removed."

Alek wept.

Brother Quartrik spoke as he continued digging the grave with Alek. "I understand." He heaved a spade of sandy soil over his shoulder. "You are, in a way...responsible to some extent. I believe...you presented him with...with the truth."

"I don't know...if it was the truth." He and Quartrik worked knee deep in the grave, digging with their backs to one another. Secundik and Caluño rested nearby in the expansive shade of the pea vine. Each pair dug a quarter hour, then rested while the other pair dug.

"Your anger simply increased...your candor. Your words were...unkind—not an unheard of response to...frustration in someone of your age—but were...nonetheless honest. Father Britt was unable...to face the truth. You mentioned...the missing pages. I too...had noticed. This morning...I located thirty-four pages...in Bennik's hand...that had been cut...from the book." Quartrik placed his spade beside the grave.

"What was on them?" Alek asked absently, while continuing to dig.

Quartrik lowered his voice. "They spoke with startling candor—perhaps indecent candor—of Bennik's love for Britt. Time for rest," he said loudly.

"They were lovers?" Alek stopped digging. He had never heard of such a thing among Faeries.

Quartrik shrugged. "Come rest." As he stepped from the grave, he signaled to the others to wait in the shade, then guided Alek there by the shoulder. All four of them had cast aside their robes earlier, working more comfortably in their tunics. Quartrik's bare arms rippled with the strength of a mender of walls.

Quartrik lifted a writing slate and chalk. "The grave must be as deep and as long as I am tall."

"How much more time do we have?" Caluño asked.

"The burial will be tomorrow morning. Because we dig in sandy soil, we will need to brace the sides." He drew a diagram on the slate. "After Father Britt is laid in the grave, we pull these two supports..." He pointed to the drawing. "...and the soil will spill down and mostly fill the grave. If you should..." Brother Quartrik placed his hand on the top of Caluño's head and rotated it to face him. "If you should disturb the supports prematurely, the grave will fill, and we will start over." He gestured to Secundik that he had finished talking.

"Quartrik," Alek said.

"Yes?"

"If the Book of Bennik is not what you thought it was, and all the gardening was just to make food, what will you do now? What will happen to the monastery?"

"I suspect it will continue much as it has. I have never been inclined toward mysticism, but I do love this garden, and mending walls."

"What will you do with Bennik's missing pages?"

"Bennik wrote them with the knowledge that no other Faerie in all of Ternaria could read. I'm sure he never imagined that they would ever be seen, even by Britt." Quartrik heaved his shoulders in a deep sigh. "When the grave is complete, I will hide them beneath the soil at the bottom. Such private words should be kept between the two of them. The other brothers—the monastery—can go on without a hint of their existence."

"Who will be the new master?"

"Secundik was Father Britt's first follower, but he is just that, a follower. Tercerik, then, would lead." Quartrik's face revealed no hint of how he felt about such an outcome.

For Alek, Tercerik's succession made his decision to leave the monastery an even clearer choice. He thought of distant places that he could go with Daiella. *Daiella!* Alek knew she would not be eager to leave her family. He thought of various things he might do to earn an invitation to live in Faerie Ring—perhaps grow vegetables or teach others to write words. If he learned to play the lyre, he could sing his poems.

After a supper of pea and chamomile seed, eaten in uncharacteristic silence, Alek left the others and walked out to the courtyard. In the cool evening air, he strolled out the gate toward the wood statue of Bennik. He wondered if Bennik had had any notion of how other Faeries might interpret his sad book. He must have felt completely alone just to have chosen to live among the humans at Moss Abbey. His plants and vegetables provided his only companionship. "Did you ever love someone?"

"I trust you are not on your way to Faerie Ring." The voice of Tercerik from the courtyard shattered the moment.

"No, sir"

Tercerik walked out of the gate and joined him in the fading light. "I have learned something that may clarify your thoughts."

"My thoughts are clear enough."

"So you believe. I spoke today to Dailik, Daiella's father."

Alek felt a pang of violation to hear her name on his lips. But his self-assurance crumbled.

"He has solved her disobedience and your recalcitrance by giving her as mate to a successful merchant living...let us say...far from Faerie Ring. So the matter is settled. Your bleating words will need to be directed elsewhere."

A buzzing echo rumbled in his ears. Cold gripped his hands and feet. "That can't be true!"

"Apparently the girl was willing to escape her father's control by whatever means at hand. It seems you were not essential to attaining that end."

"I don't believe you!"

"You have a choice to make as we stand here. You may remain at the monastery—my monastery—and follow the rules—my rules, or you may retrieve that sack of meager belongings that I found beside your bed and go off as a vagrant orphan, begging your meals."

Alek turned and ran. What he had just been told made no sense with what he knew of Daiella. At first, he had no destination as he ran, just the catharsis of exertion. When the moon rose, he stopped, breathless, and began to cry. Thoughts of Daiella interrupted all logic, all planning.

Without a conscious choice, Alek arrived at Daiella's boletus in Faerie Ring. "Daiella!" he shouted in the darkness. "Daiella!"

"Go away," replied a male voice from a window high in the boletus cap. "Daiella no longer lives here." Alek was certain that it was Dailik who spoke.

"Where is she?"

"Go away before I sound an alarm and drive you away at the point of a pike."

Alek turned and walked aimlessly out of Faerie Ring. He thought about the empty clay jar which had held the nectar of jessamine. Surely there had been enough for more than one, but Father Britt had consumed it all.

When he reached the bank of the river, the same spot at which he had kissed Daiella and wrapped her in his arms, he considered jumping into the rushing water. But he recalled the story of Bennik's risking his life to save Father Britt from drowning. The awkward thought of Bennik and Britt as lovers came to his mind unbidden. *You wouldn't allow me to see the only one I love.* With a clinched jaw, he turned away from the dark water and headed back toward the monastery garden.

Once there, he erased the slate bearing the diagram of the bracing for the grave, took up a chalk and sat on the sandy soil in the moonlight. Words spilled out of him, an uncontrolled vomit of anguish.

Just as the wounded face cries out from gibbous moon
While honeysuckle scented breeze unnoticed fades,
So love unanswered fills the night with baleful sobs.
Can pledge of love unending dissipate so soon?
A Faerie mind decays to doom of dusty shades,
When dark deceit its will to go on living robs.

Despair washed over him—a wave that crushed without mercy, without hope. He did not read the words he had written. With his final poem, Alek descended the ladder to the bottom of the freshly dug grave. He removed the ladder from the wall, which rose well above his head, and placed it carefully along the bottom. Lying on his back, with his poem on his chest, and Bennik's missing pages covered in the soil beneath him, he reached to his sides and grasped the two main supports for the bracing. As he looked out of the dark pit, the moon crept its brilliance into view. He studied every feature of its increasingly visible face as it moved over the grave.

"What a lonely vision you are," he whispered. He thought of Daiella and closed his eyes.

"Here he is." The voice was that of Brother Secundik.

Alek squinted against the bright sky, the air redolent of garden soil. For a moment, he could not understand where he was. His arms ached. He felt his fingers gripping the rigid supports for the bracing. "I forgot to die," he mumbled to himself.

Brother Quartrik's face appeared above the grave. Alarm showed in his eyes, once he had viewed the precarious situation. "You have been tricked. You are the victim of conspiracy and deceit."

"I know."

"No. You don't understand. Daiella has been locked away at her uncle's boletus on the far side of Faerie Ring. She has not taken a mate."

"But Brother Tercerik told me..."

"He lied to you. Secundik spoke to me last night. He overheard a conversation between Tercerik and Daiella's father. They invented the story. We have been looking for you all night—in the village, on the roads."

Alek simply didn't believe what he was hearing. He wanted to believe it, but he felt so tired and hurt.

"She is coming here. I sent Caluño to fetch her a short while ago."

At those words, Alek released his hands from the supports and sat up. The slate with his poem slid to the floor of the grave. "She's truly coming?"

"Yes."

"Now?"

"Yes. Come up and brush off your tunic."

Alek carefully stood the ladder against the end wall and climbed out. By the time he had brushed the sandy dirt off of himself, Daiella ran through the garden gate, with Caluño following close behind.

"They told me they were looking for you all night," she said. She stood an arm's length from Alek, as she had when they first met. Her diaphanous wings sparkled in the sunlight. The fragrance of honeysuckle drifted about her. As she looked past him to the grave, concern grew in her eyes.

He reached out and gently touched her cheek. "You're here."

"This is intolerable!" shouted a voice from the garden gate.

"Papa! Let me live my life!"

Dailik stomped across the garden. He grabbed her arm. "We are going."

"No!" she shouted, pulling her arm away from his grip. Daiella fell backwards into the grave. Her diminutive wings flared to break the fall, but her arms struck the two supports. The moment she landed softly on her side in the floor of the grave, the sandy soil flowed with a fatal susurration, pressing her fragile breast against Alek's poem and filling the grave nearly to the top.

Alek fell to his knees and began to heave the soil to the side with his hands. "Dig!" he shouted.

Caluño ran for the spades while the others joined Alek, digging by hand. After a quarter hour of frantic work, only a third of the soil had been cleared away.

Brother Quartrik stopped. He pressed his hands onto those of Dailik and whispered, "She is gone. We should not disturb her grave any further. You must go back to Faerie Ring now and inform the Elder so that he can arrange a ceremony. Brother Secundik will go with you." He nodded to Secundik.

When Secundik departed with Daiella's dumbstruck father, Tercerik passed them at the garden gate. "What has happened here?"

Alek rose to his feet with murder in his heart. Quartrik threw his massive arms around him to restrain him.

"You must not," Quartrik said. "Caluño, hold onto him." Quartrik approached Tercerik. "The girl fell by accident into the grave and has died. She will remain there."

"She will not. This is to be the grave of Father Britt. A female does not belong here." Tercerik turned without waiting for a response and strode toward the garden gate.

Quartrik was on him in an instant. He snatched Tercerik's right arm and twisted it under his wings. With a mighty shove, he tossed Tercerik through the gate, spilling him onto the ground. "If you ever set foot within these grounds again, I promise you I will break your neck without regret and leave your carcass for the ants."

Five months had passed since the deaths of Father Britt and Daiella. The outer walls of pebbles radiated the warmth of the midday sun. Low clouds of white puff raced their shadows across the meadow in endless succession. Alek steadied a ladder at one side of the new gateway to the courtyard, while Caluño did the same with the ladder at the opposite side.

"That's perfect," Secundik said, clapping his hands in delight.

"This end is secure," Quartrik stated from atop Caluño's ladder.

"As is this one," Dailik replied from above Alek.

Quartrik and Dailik descended to the ground. The ladders were laid on either side of the gateway.

Secundik turned around and addressed the visitors, scores of them, from Faerie Ring and all the surrounding villages. "I know that the letters above the gate have no meaning to you, but soon your sons and your daughters will be able to read the words, 'Daiella School of Reading and Writing.'" The spectators applauded. "You may now enjoy the celebrations."

Flute and lyre began together. Tables offered up an array of succulent vegetable morsels, seeds of every kind, mosquito pudding, nectars, honey and clay cups of blackberry wine. Some of the young, and the not so young, danced to the music as they ate. Others sang together the lyrics of the folk tunes.

Alek wrestled with the bitter-sweet weight of commemoration. Daiella was forever gone, but her name and her memory would live on beyond his own life. He stood before the wood statue of Bennik, studying the new plaque at its base: "Bennik, Founder of Horticultural Methods." He looked up again at the gateway. An inconspicuous sign to the side of the post read: "School of Gardening." A tiny arrow pointed toward the garden gate.

Quartrik came up behind him and placed his hands on Alek's shoulders. "Bennik would have been pleased to know that someone was teaching the true meaning of his life's work."

Caluño took Alek's hand and shook it vigorously. "Congratulations, Master of Gardening."

Alek smiled politely as he looked beyond Caluño to the dazzling yellow flowers of his newly planted vines creeping up the outer walls by either side of the garden gate—to the right, honeysuckle, to the left, jessamine.

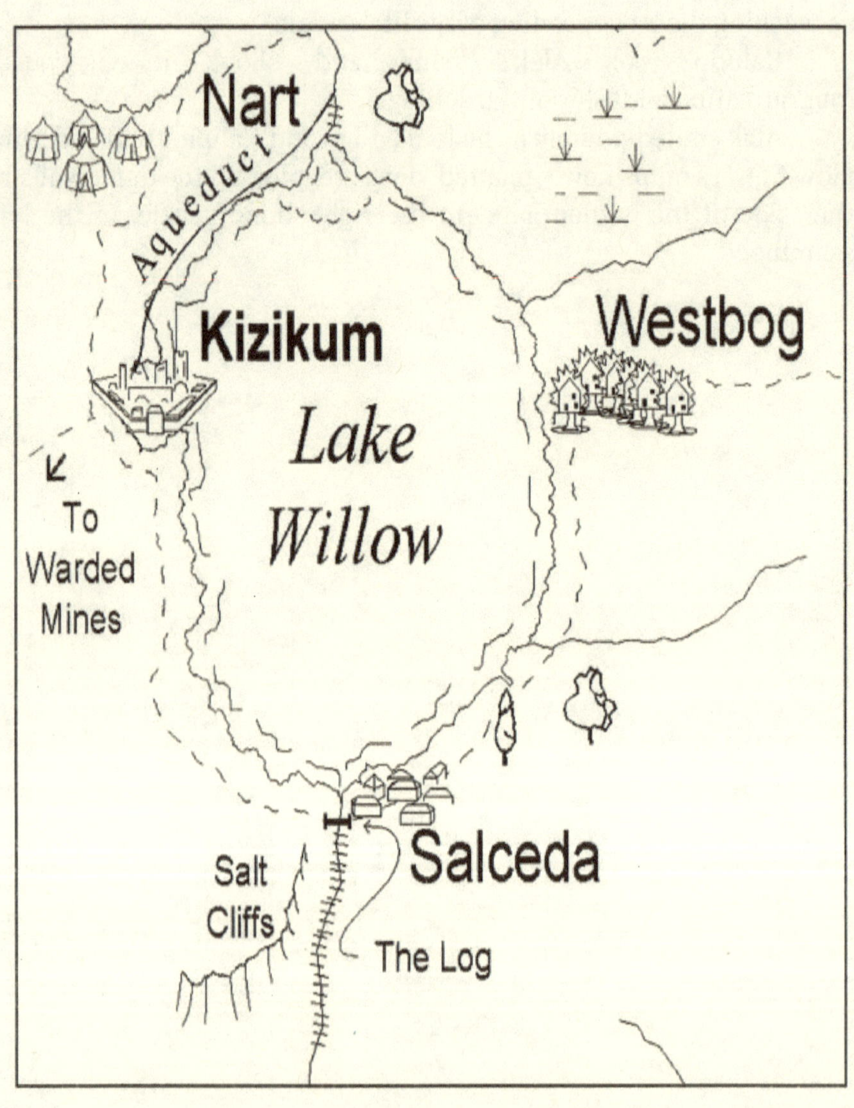
Nart
Aqueduct
Kizikum
Lake
Willow
Westbog
To
Warded
Mines
Salt
Cliffs
Salceda
The Log

CHAPTER 10—FAERIE LORD OF KIZIKUM

After a three day journey since their overnight in the Earwig Inn, back at Nettle Falls, Nebridio looked forward to a decent place to sleep, until the afternoon breeze carried a foul stench his way.

"Tell me that smell is not coming from where I think it is," said Alfrito.

"Would I take my only brother to somewhere that reeks of dead fish?" Nebridio asked.

"You just might." Though two years younger than Nebridio, Alfrito's height equaled that of his unusually tall brother.

"I told you it was a fishing village."

"There's fishing, then there's rotting. That smell is not fishing."

Nebridio laughed. "They make your favorite fish sauce. It's not a very fragrant process, I'm told. It's sold all over Ternaria."

"When a smell like that gets into your wings, it lasts for weeks. You can't wash it off."

The Great West Road began its gradual descent into the rhododendron and peat bogs on the eastern shore of Lake Willow, the largest body of water in Ternaria. Before reaching the village of Westbog, the road followed the boundary between the high-arching rhododendrons to the south and the relatively barren peat bog to the north. It was here that Nebridio heard the pleading of a male voice. A short distance into the peat bog, a group of about a dozen Faeries stood in a circle.

"There are only two of us," Alfrito pointed out.

"But we are armed. We should at least see what's going on."

"Is something amiss?" Nebridio asked as he and Alfrito approached the group.

"This is official business," a stout Faerie in the group replied. They all bore the vile odor that had greeted Nebridio a quarter hour earlier.

The group surrounded a deep rectangular trench, from which blocks of peat had been removed. At the bottom, pinioned by forks of wood branches at the elbows and knees, and further restrained by a lath of sticks, a weeping Faerie implored the others not to proceed.

"I'm Elder of Westbog, Dunedek. This wastrel is guilty of forcing his uninvited attentions on another's mate. This is his penalty." Dunedek motioned to the others.

Each of the Faeries surrounding the pit heaved an armful of peat onto the squirming, pleading Faerie. This they repeated, until the voice had ceased and the pit had been transformed into a slight mound.

Their official business concluded, Dunedek turned again to Nebridio and Alfrito. "If you are heading into Westbog, I could show you to the inn. Sorry about this nasty business, but these things come up from time to time. An unfortunate burden of office."

"Actually," Nebridio replied, "I believe it was you who sent for us."

Dunedek frowned as he examined the two of them. "You're from Lilac?"

"Yes," Alfrito said.

"This is the military assistance I requested?"

"The council felt that we should come and examine the...situation," Nebridio explained. "Perhaps speak with the Faerie Lord, in the hope of resolving your disagreement without resorting to violence. Kizikum is, after all, the Land Seat of West Ternaria. The Faerie Lord is your suzerain."

Dunedek irritably escorted them toward Westbog. "Don't they understand? Lord Ruprecht has committed acts of war. We have declared war on Kizikum. What is not clear about that?"

"That much I already know," Nebridio continued. "But with a better knowledge of the details, we could try to negotiate a mutually agreeable outcome."

"I ask for soldiers and they send me two boys."

"We have been on the road for six days, Elder. Perhaps you could show us the inn and we could discuss all that's happened in the morning. I am Nebridio, aide to the Third Tribune of Lilac. This is my brother, Alfrito."

"Welcome to Westbog, aide to the Third Tribune...and his brother," Dunedek grumbled. "The inn is the twelfth ladder." He turned and stomped off.

"That went well, Nebbie," Alfrito said with a broad smile.

As they entered the tunnels of arching rhododendron, Nebridio discovered that the village had been built entirely among the branches of the rhododendrons, high overhead. Only the docks by the lakeshore were anchored in the boggy soil. The dense canopy of huge leaves concentrated the stench of rotting fish. At the twelfth ladder, Nebridio looked up to see a veranda of tightly woven willow. He climbed the willow ladder, three times his height, followed by Alfrito. The inn, built of the same material as the veranda, stood three stories above him. From the veranda, scores of other structures could be seen at the same elevation and in all directions.

"That's a big inn for such a small village at the ass end of the road," Alfrito commented.

"This is the road that the longhaulers use to reach the Warded Mines," Nebridio said. "They probably get twenty travelers a week, in bunches."

"I'll bet they don't stay long."

"If we can't get this silly argument cleared up, nobody will be able to get through for a long time."

In the morning, Nebridio left Alfrito at breakfast. A quick bowl of tea would have to carry him through the morning. He took along a slice of cranberry. Once down on the ground, he realized he had forgotten to ask directions to the Elder. He looked about. The only activity seemed to be that of the minnowers at the lakefront, so he walked out from beneath the high canopy of the rhododendrons and across the mudflat.

"Who are you?" a lad of about seven asked.

"Don't be rude, Willi," a beautiful, dark-haired mother scolded. "Go help your father."

"I'm Nebridio. I have a meeting with Dunedek this morning, but I'm not sure where I would find him."

She held the hand of a boy of about four. With her free hand, she pointed to a structure with a ladder at each end, in the rhododendrons. She smiled.

Nebridio noticed the older boy assisting his father in placing willow minnow traps into a weathered acorn cap boat that floated beside the dock. "Thank you. I don't know your name."

She glanced at the minnower, then said softly, "Pellana."

"Thank you, Pellana."

"This is Pippi, and that's my mate, Wallis...and Willi. Where did you come from?"

"Lilac."

She sighed with a distant stare. "I hope you're not going any farther than Salceda, because The Log is blocked."

"The Log?"

"Salceda is south, along the lake. After Salceda, The Log crosses above the cataracts. The Faerie Lord blocked the end of it, so nobody can go across."

"Do you know why?"

"They're arguing about taxes or the price of peat or something. Everything is a mess. The salt people in Salceda can't get across to the salt cliff, so the saucers can't make fish sauce in Westbog. The price of fish is down here. And the poor peat cutters can't send their peat to Kizikum, so it's piling up by the bale, and they can't buy fish oil for their lamps. The oil makers in Salceda have stopped buying fish from their minnowers, because they have hundreds of jugs of oil they can't..." Pellana put her hand over her mouth. "I didn't mean to go on like that."

"Well, Pellana...and Pippi, thank you again."

Pippi looked up at his mother, slightly embarrassed.

Nebridio offered Pippi the slice of cranberry. The boy snatched it and ate it in three greedy bites.

"Say thank you."

Pippi mumbled something through a mouthful of cranberry.

Nebridio walked to the house that Pellana had indicated and ascended the ladder at the nearest end.

"You're late," Dunedek complained.

"Do forgive me, Elder."

"What do you plan to do, aide to the Third Tribune?"

"Nebridio is sufficient, Elder."

"Well, Nebridio?"

"Have I missed anything, Dunedek?" A well built Faerie of middle age entered the house.

"This is the assistant to the...this is Nebridio. The council at Lilac sent him, with his brother, to solve all our problems."

"I'm Rhodek, Constable of this fish camp."

"Rhodek had hoped to take command of the troops sent from Lilac."

"That was you hoping, Dunedek. I'd rather watch it all at a great distance."

"I would be pleased," Nebridio said as politely as he could manage, "if you could start from the beginning and explain the sequence of events that changed what was once peace into a prospect of war."

"Kizikum put a toll pike at their end of The Log," Dunedek stated. "That so called Faerie Lord refused to lift the toll. We declared war. It's simple, really."

"Do we know why the Faerie Lord imposed the toll?"

Dunedek threw a withering glance at Rhodek, who rolled his eyes.

"We taxed the dried peat that goes over to Kizikum," Rhodek admitted. "They're answer was a toll on The Log."

"The cost of fish and salt grew too high," Dunedek said. "We had to do something."

"And you buy those from Kizikum?"

"Absolutely not," the Elder continued. "They've tried to sell us minnows cheaper, but we have to support our own minnowers and those of Salceda. Kizikum uses nets in the deep water. That's just unfair."

"So, you sell them peat, but you buy nothing from them. What do they do with the peat in Kizikum?"

"They burn rock," Rhodek said. "It helps them build with stone."

Nebridio rubbed his head. "I will go to Kizikum and speak with the Faerie Lord." He hoped that Ruprecht could at least present the situation in an understandable way.

"But we are at war!" Dunedek shouted.

"Has there been any fighting?" Nebridio asked.

Rhodek shook his head. "We're at war, because we said so."

"Then I will go."

"But you are *our* emissary from Lilac," the Elder insisted. "I won't allow it. Send your brother. I don't want to risk sending you."

"You want my brother to go because there is a risk?"

"Not technically. No. There's no risk. But you must stay on our side. I will allow only your brother to go."

"Alright. I will go with Alfrito to negotiate a talk truce at the toll pike, then he will travel to Kizikum and speak with the Faerie Lord. How do we find The Log?"

Rhodek escorted Nebridio to the veranda and pointed. "Go south along the lake for two days. That will bring you to Salceda. The Log crosses the outlet at the bottom of the lake there. From The Log, it's two more days north along the opposite shore of the lake to Kizikum."

Nebridio felt grateful that the prevailing wind on Lake Willow was a west wind. As soon as he and Alfrito moved south of Westbog, the foul stench of its saucers was replaced by a vague scent of sun-baked limestone coming off the deep, open waters. Stone cliffs were barely visible on the far side of the lake, but Kizikum, which he was told lay directly across the lake from Westbog, could not be seen. As they moved south, he observed a persistent, solitary and oddly linear cloud streaming across the lake from a source that Nebridio assumed was the city of the Faerie Lord.

Throughout their two day journey to Salceda, Nebridio's mind returned to the beauty of dark-haired Pellana. He had never struggled so intensely as from his repeated attempts to block her from his mind.

"You had better watch where you put your feet, Nebbie, or you'll end up in the water."

"I can't stop thinking about Pellana."

"Who is she? That pretty one who waved to you by the docks?"

"That's her."

"Well, you could do worse."

"She has a mate, Alfrito, and two small boys."

"Ooo. Take care that you don't end up staked at the bottom of the bog. The folks here seem to take that sort of dalliance with very little humor. Besides, if you see her again before you get downwind of the village, she may just remind you of my favorite fish sauce, spilled in a latrine."

"Has anyone ever told you that you have a gift for words?"

"I don't believe anyone has."

"I didn't think so."

A ragged Faerie approached them from the south, pulling a two wheel cart packed with skinned, salted minnows. "Are they buying yet in Westbog?" the carter asked.

"I don't think anything has changed there for the past two weeks," Nebridio answered.

The carter continued on his way. "Now I've got to take this all the way to Nettle Falls," he complained over his shoulder.

Their approach to Salceda once again assaulted their senses with the nature of local industry. Rather than the rotting odors of Westbog's saucers, Salceda reeked simply of fish. On their left, just outside the village, Nebridio saw hundreds of amphorae stacked carefully on their sides.

"That must be all the lamp oil they can't sell," he pointed out to Alfrito.

"What's it made from? Wait. Fish?"

"You amaze me, Alfrito. Seriously, this declaration of war has practically halted all trade. The fat politicians, like Dunedek, don't have to worry about having enough food. But everybody else is worrying about feeding their children."

In Salceda, they met the Alcalde, a timid Faerie named Riverto, and Spall, their Saltmaster. They stood near the western edge of town, where a huge log spanned the chasm between the rocky cliffs on either side of Lake Willow's outlet into the cataracts.

"With the toll, they made each salt miner pay going to the cliff and then pay again returning to Salceda," Spall explained. "It's not such a burden to the longhaulers. They may not cross The Log more than once a month. But two trips a week to the salt cliff is four tolls a week. It's just not possible to pay it. Of course, with Dunedek's new war, we can't cross at all. We have four salt miners stuck on the other side."

A smooth, broad ramp climbed to the upper surface of The Log. At the top of the ramp, a forlorn Faerie sat on a small willow stool.

"That's our Constable," Riverto said proudly. "He's guarding our end of The Log."

"What would he do if an army from Kizikum tried to cross the bridge," Alfrito asked, winking at his brother.

"They wouldn't do that," Riverto insisted, with sudden understanding in his eyes, "would they?"

"I don't know," Nebridio replied. "Do they have an army?"

"Indeed they do," Spall said. "Lewek is their General. I've heard the army is about four hundred. And the navy. Don't forget the navy. They have a lot of those long canoes they make from catalpa pods. Each one can hold fifteen Faeries. Almirant Tordian commands them. They've chased some of our minnowers from the deeper waters."

The following morning, Nebridio and Alfrito climbed up to the top surface of The Log, both unarmed. They greeted the constable, then walked a quarter hour to reach the western end.

As they approached the lowered toll pike, two Faeries, each wearing a bronze helmet and bronze breastplate rose to meet them. Nebridio realized that each wore a bronze sword at the waist, though they did not draw them. Just beyond the end of The Log, four dust covered Faeries lounged beside two carts of salt rock.

"Good morning. I am Nebridio and this is Alfrito. We are emissaries of the council of Lilac. Alfrito must go, by safety of a talk truce, to discuss important matters with the Faerie Lord in Kizikum. He is unarmed, as am I, so I'm certain that you will allow him to pass on his diplomatic mission."

"What about you?" one of them asked.

"That's a more difficult matter. Those poor fellows stranded over there," Nebridio pointed to the salt miners, "should probably not be left behind this important guard post, since one of you, I'm sure, will want to accompany Alfrito to the Faerie Lord, and perhaps be acknowledged for your excellent judgment. I would suggest that you might allow them to return to their wretched homes in Salceda."

The two guards whispered to one another, then one insisted on being the escort for Alfrito. "Their carts stay, and they still have to pay the toll."

"How much is that?" Nebridio asked, lifting his purse from his belt, making certain that it jingled as he did so.

"Four coppers," one guard said.

"Each," the other added.

"That's a little more than I had hoped." Nebridio opened the drawstring of the purse and pretended to count his coins with a frown. "Perhaps we could agree at two coppers each. That would be four. They are, after all, just salt miners."

"Four it is." The guard held out his hand.

"With their carts...unless, of course, you have need of some broken rock here at your post."

"Take them."

While one guard went to fetch the salt miners, Nebridio spoke softly to his brother. "Remember, agree to nothing. We need to learn the best terms Ruprecht is willing to accept in order to end this nonsense. And be careful. Kizikum is two days away. I will wait for one week in Salceda, so you'll have three days to negotiate. And speak well to Ruprecht of the guard who accompanies you." Nebridio clasped his brother's arm and hugged him.

Nebridio chatted with the Saltmaster of Salceda while touring the salt works. Spall apologized repeatedly for the much slowed production that resulted from the political crisis.

"We usually have fifteen crushing the salt rock," he explained, pointing to three Faeries wielding stone mallets to reduce the salt to a coarse powder. "It is shipped all across Ternaria. Not just the saucers in Westbog, but everybody in every village will soon run out of salt."

Other Faeries raked the crushed salt, which was then sifted through bowls of woven, dried grass by still others. Finally, two Faeries shoveled the finished salt into tightly woven baskets of willow leaf.

"We have about two week's more salt rock, even at this pace, then everything stops."

"Has anyone in Salceda visited Kizikum in the last year?" Nebridio asked.

"I was there just two months ago for a large sale, which has now been canceled." Spall shook his head.

"Do all of the Faerie Lord's troops wear bronze armor and carry swords of bronze?"

"All those I saw were equipped that way. When the rock burning oven is not making building lime, they mix copper with something else and make the bronze. The city is a strange place, with its stone walls and stone towers and... You know, they bring water into the city over a great stone bridge that takes it from high above the cascades, north of Lake Willow. It runs directly into many of their houses. They don't even have to dip it out of the lake. Some of the water turns a wheel that pounds the limestone into a powder."

"I saw the stockpile of oil east of town. Is there an oil master?"

"Not any longer. Only Faeries that live on the lake will use the fish oil for their lamps. No one else in Ternaria will buy it. It smells like fish."

"Does it burn well?"

"It's a bit difficult to light, but once lit, it burns slowly and with a hot flame. That's why it's kept outside the village."

"If an army should threaten Salceda, you could dig a trench across the road in the soil leading up to The Log and burn an oil flame to prevent their crossing."

"There's not going to actually be a war, do you think?"

"I hope not. But it seems that Dunedek has made no preparations for the war he declared. Have any of the Faeries of Salceda ever trained for battle, or fought in battle?"

"Only the Faerie Lord's army has fought against the Thistlepix. They never come down here."

"Are there any other crossings at this end of the lake, other than The Log?"

"The closest suitable spot is four days south, to get past the cataracts. On the north of the lake, Ruprecht's stone bridge for the water is a half day north of the lake—that's two and a half days from Westbog. You can't cross there, but you can another half day further north. The stone bridge picks up water on the west side."

"And it runs straight to the city?"

"Yes. You know, Kizikum is on an island. A wood causeway connects it to the land. But the water bridge goes right over to the island, high above the roofs."

"If you will agree to sell your dried peat at the old price for one year—that is, with no tax," Alfrito explained to Dunedek, "then at one quarter copper of tax for each raft during the following year, then the Faerie Lord will remove the toll now and open The Log."

"That's unacceptable!" Dunedek shouted.

"And," Alfrito continued, "if you fail to agree, The Log will remain closed."

"You will have to go back and present him with *my* terms."

"One other point, Elder. If he should learn that you are mobilizing an army, he will march on Salceda and Westbog and destroy them both. He asked me to remind you that he is not an equal to be threatened, but your Faerie Lord, and that his patience is becoming short."

"Here are my terms, Alfrito, my final terms. You will take them to him."

"Elder," Nebridio interrupted. "The Faerie Lord has a large army with bronze armor and bronze weapons. You can not stand against him with minnowers and saucers and peat cutters. He commands a navy with faster vessels than your acorn boats."

"He will be surprised to see the true spirit of Westbog. We can mobilize an even greater number than those rock burners."

"I don't think we can win such a fight," Rhodek said from the far corner. The Constable gave a pleading look to Nebridio.

"You can be easily replaced, Rhodek. Here are *my* final terms. I will cut the tax by half, but the toll must go."

"Elder," Nebridio said firmly. "I will not allow Alfrito to return to the Faerie Lord with those terms. We will offer to reduce the tax on peat by half, in exchange for his reducing the toll by a like amount, and allowing the salt miners to pay one small fee each year for free passage. Alfrito will insist on nothing, and he will accept the best terms he can manage." He looked over to Alfrito, who shrugged and nodded.

"But I..."

"And, Elder, you will abide by those terms."

"I have to think about it."

"No. You will agree now and Alfrito will travel again to Kizikum, or he and I will return immediately to Lilac and recommend to the council that you be removed from your post."

Nebridio and Alfrito departed from Dunedek with his grudging agreement to Nebridio's scenario. At the waterfront, Alfrito pointed directly across the lake.

"The smudge in the air is the smoke of Kizikum's great clay oven. They never let it go out."

"Did you examine the water bridge up close?" Nebridio asked.

"Yes. Ruprecht is proud of it. He took me up there. They call it an aqueduct. None of the stone buildings rise to its height; only a narrow stairway climbs to it from the city. The water seems to be about waist deep and flows fairly slowly. Are you thinking about war plans?"

"I have to, with that mad elder prodding the Faerie Lord. And these folks couldn't fight an angry caterpillar, much less battle hardened troops in bronze."

"This is all a pity," Alfrito said. "They have created some wonderful things in Kizikum. With their building lime, they can put two stones together at any angle, and when the lime hardens, the two stones are like one. They can't be separated."

"Then why do you think they make their great oven of clay, instead of stone?"

"The fire. The clay resists fire. The fire is so hot, it would split stones apart. Well, Nebbie, I had better get started. Kizikum is four days away."

"Do you want me to go with you?"

"No need. They were a lot more civil than Dunedek."

"You accept anything Ruprecht offers. I'm not even sure you should mention the terms we discussed. Just agree with him, then get yourself out of there." Nebridio watched as Pellana washed clothes at the edge of the water. "The most important thing is to be careful. This is an unpredictable situation."

Alfrito glanced at Pellana. "Should I repeat what you just said?"

"Be safe, Alfrito." He clasped his brother's forearm and hugged him.

Once Alfrito was on the road south, Nebridio walked to the water's edge. "That looks like a lot of work," he said to Pellana.

"Oh, it's so close I can actually keep those boys clean most of the time." She pointed to the first rhododendron from the lakeshore. "I live right there. It's nice. The wind almost always blows in from the lake, so I only have to put up with that awful smell if I go further into the village."

"Do you like it here?"

"Wallis' work is here. I grew up at Mount Easley."

"That's a long way."

"Wallis was there doing some trading eight years ago. Westbog took a while to get used to. But we do alright. Even when there's no money, there's always minnow and cress to eat. Sometimes we get a clam. North of the bog, there are acorns. Of course you have to pound it and wash it forever, but then it cooks up a nice cake with fish sauce."

"I never see you with any of the other Faeries."

"I've lived here for eight years, but most folks still think of me as a foreigner. The children keep me occupied."

"You just seem lonely here."

"I've got to go." Pellana gathered an armload of child's clothing and walked quickly toward her home.

"I'm sorry. I didn't mean to upset you."

For two days, Nebridio traveled about Westbog, evaluating everything he encountered for its military potential. Much of the willow furniture and structures could be cut into effective shields and barriers. A raspberry bramble southeast of the village would supply a limitless quantity of pikes. Of particular interest was the vast supply of dried peat, stacked in bales on elevated racks. Peat soaked in fish oil could offer a reasonably safe, though temporary defense for a damp village like Westbog. He guessed that, between Salceda and Westbog, he could raise a force of about four hundred Faeries.

Throughout those two days, his mind drifted to Pellana. She had succeeded in making herself invisible. Sometimes he saw the two boys, but never their mother. Her mate, Wallis, returned each night from tending his minnow traps.

Early on the third day after Alfrito's departure, Nebridio became aware of large gatherings of Faeries who fell silent whenever he approached. In mid-afternoon, he encountered one of the four salt miners he had retrieved from the Faerie Lord's guards.

"Why have you come up to Westbog?"

"I can't really talk about that."

"Why not?"

The salt miner glanced in all directions, then whispered, "I'm not supposed to. Riverto said not to talk to you or that other tall fellow that was with you."

Nebridio allowed the frightened Faerie to go. He sensed an unmistakable yet unspoken tension and anticipation among the gathered Faeries. He also felt the barrier that marked him off as somehow untrustworthy. Clearly, the leaders of Salceda and Westbog had made decisions that intentionally excluded the representative from the council of Lilac.

He pondered whether to question Dunedek at the point of a pike, but decided that whatever the Elder said could not be taken as the truth. Instead, he would attempt to complete his understanding of the key military elements of their location in the six days remaining before Alfrito's return. Nebridio gathered his travel gear from the inn and, with a small supply of food, set out north along the lake. Spall had indicated that the crossing above the cascades was three days from Westbog. Nebridio pressed hard to make the six day round trip in four.

The nearly trackless bog east of the lake slowed him more than he had hoped, so once he reached more solid ground, he increased his stride, resting only a quarter hour every three. He recognized that it would be foolish for the Faerie Lord to attack Westbog from the north, an approach that would force his troops to fight from the bog. An attack, if it came, would be across The Log and through Salceda. He could hardly imagine that the Almirant's long canoes could alone hold sufficient troops for an effective force on land, though they might easily subdue the defenders at Salceda who attempted to block passage of The Log with a fire of fish oil.

Toward evening, Nebridio sighted smoke some distance ahead and slightly east of his course. With time pressing, he continued north. As he passed closest to the smoke, he saw that a small group of Faeries had surrounded a caracol with a circle of burning peat bales. Unable to flee, the caracol could only withdraw its eye stalks and wait while its fire-heated spiral shell roasted its body in its own juices.

Nebridio continued walking into the evening, so long as there was enough light to allow him to see where to place his feet. Thoughts of Pellana filled the twilight walk, and filled his dreams when he finally stopped to sleep.

By mid-morning of the next day, the Faerie Lord's great stone aqueduct came into view across the cascades. Improbable stone arches of increasing height carried the nearly level stone bridge south toward Kizikum. At mid-day, Nebridio stood directly across from the aqueduct's entrance, which allowed a small fraction of the cascade's turbulent flow to stream gently toward the city. As best he could determine from the opposite side of the cascades, water within the open aqueduct ran no more than waist deep. This potential road directly into the city of Kizikum was protected by no one. Nor was there any visible sign of a recent guard post or encampment that might suggest that the Faerie Lord considered the aqueduct a possible weakness.

Just before sunset, Nebridio found the river crossing above the cascades. Here, the river widened considerably, dropping its burden of silt and sand and small stones before narrowing abruptly and quickening in a rocky froth as it plunged in long, jagged steps toward Lake Willow, a day to the south. He waded, knee deep, to the opposite bank, then returned, to sleep before his forced, two-day return to Westbog.

As he ate his meager supper of salt minnow and dried cattail shoot, he worried about his younger brother. Alfrito would reach Kizikum this same evening. With political tensions increasing, Nebridio felt less comfortable about the reception that Alfrito might encounter from Ruprecht this time. Although the Faerie Lord had been quite correct in demanding that his vassal village of Westbog rescind their irresponsible tax, Ruprecht had also shown his contempt and willingness to resort to precipitate violence. He knew that Alfrito would remain neutral and accommodating, but events beyond his control might trump all.

"Mama, here he is," young Willi shouted as Nebridio arrived at the northern edge of Westbog. "Mama."

Along the lakeshore, over a hundred Faeries, each holding a raspberry pike, milled about in groups of five or ten. Under the late afternoon sun, some pointed across the lake. None seemed to notice Nebridio except Willi.

"What's happening," he asked the dark-haired boy.

"Mama's looking for you. Papa's missing."

Nebridio took the boy's slender hand and waded into the crowds to find Pellana. Before he saw her, he heard her voice calling his name. She stood beneath the rhododendron that supported her home. Pippi clung to her neck.

"Wallis told me that Dunedek was sending him to Kizikum with a message. It's two days there and two back. He should have come back this afternoon."

"That would get him there about the same time as Alfrito. What was the message?"

"Wallis said that he couldn't talk about it. But that crossing is dangerous in an acorn boat. The deep water holds things big enough to swallow it. If he were coming tonight before dark, we could see him by now."

"Do you know where Dunedek is now?"

"I do," Willi said. "He's teaching some Faeries to be soldiers." He grasped Nebridio's hand. "I'll take you there."

"I'll wait here," Pellana said, brushing her fingers in Willi's hair.

Willi tugged at Nebridio's arm, leading him in the direction of the raspberry bramble southeast of the village. Shortly, they came upon Dunedek incompetently demonstrating a lunge with a pike before a group of bored Faeries. Nebridio strode up to him and snatched away the pike.

"This is the proper lunge that will not tempt your opponent to lop off your head with his bronze sword." Nebridio lunged forward on one leg, his elbows extended in front of his ears. He returned to a defensive stance. "You." He pointed to a bright looking Faerie. "Can you show me?"

The Faerie lunged. Nebridio adjusted the angle of the pike. "Again. Excellent. Now you teach the rest of them."

He grabbed Dunedek by the back of his arm and escorted him beyond earshot of the others. "What message did you send to Kizikum?"

"I am not answerable to you, aide to the third..."

His reply was interrupted by Nebridio's hand at his throat. "The message."

"I simply wanted to improve our bargaining position."

Nebridio tightened his grip of Dunedek's neck, while still holding Willi's small hand. "Are you going to force me to send this lad away? I wouldn't want him to see what is about to happen."

"Let...how can I...Alright! I sent word that I am mobilizing my forces. If Ruprecht does not agree to my terms, I will attack."

Nebridio released the Elder. In a calm voice he said, "If my brother, or this boy's father, comes to grief, I will come for you."

As he walked back with Willi, awful possibilities passed through his mind. The Faerie Lord had stated clearly that if Westbog mobilized, he would destroy both it and Salceda, and he had the forces to accomplish that with little difficulty. More worrisome was Alfrito's fate and that of Wallis, Willi's father. Pellana's mate. Everything seemed to be turning out badly.

"Tell me what else has happened here the last few days, Willi."

"I don't know. Just lots of Faeries that don't live here." He wiped his nose with his free hand. "Some of them said you were a spy. Is that something bad?"

"A spy is someone who tells your enemy what you're planning and what you're doing."

"Isn't that what the Elder did?"

"Yes, it is."

"So he wasn't supposed to do that?"

"No."

"But Papa did the same thing. Was he a spy?"

Nebridio knelt and spoke directly into Willi's face. "No. Your papa was ordered by the Elder to carry a message. He was expected to do that, no matter what the message was. He did the right thing." He continued to stare at the boy until he saw a smile, then they continued through the village.

"Oh, oh...the oil! A lot of carts came up from Salceda with oil."

"How many carts?"

"Wow...I can't count that many. But I've never seen so much oil."

Nebridio sat by the lakeshore with Pellana and the two boys until it was too dark to see anything on the water. He walked them back to their home.

"I don't think it's safe for you at the inn, Nebridio." Pellana's voice sounded genuinely concerned. "You could stay here tonight. They were saying terrible things about you."

He glanced at the ladder and up into the darkness above it.

"Please stay," Willi urged him, pulling at his hand.

"That might be dangerous for the three of you. I'll come by early tomorrow." He turned and left, his heart pounding.

The village did not smell as foul as usual. Nebridio guessed that the making of fish sauce had been suspended for lack of salt. He climbed the ladder to the inn, but found its rooms as well as its veranda filled with guests. Near the lakeshore, Nebridio climbed to the first crotch of a rhododendron that grew near Pellana's home and slept as best he could.

Nebridio awoke at sunrise and climbed down from the shrub. At the deserted water's edge, he stood and searched the water in the direction of Kizikum. He thought he saw a speck in the distance, but couldn't be sure. As he stared westward, he caught a glint of reflected sunlight from the horizon just south of Kizikum. He watched longer. It seemed to be multiple points of light stretched out over what must be a considerable length. *Bronze!* With frightening realization, he understood that the Faerie Lord was on the march. They would reach Salceda tomorrow evening.

The speck on the water reappeared. Some sort of vessel was approaching from the direction of Kizikum. It might be an hour or two before it was close enough to identify.

Faeries began to descend from their homes and lodgings. He spotted the salt miner he had encountered days earlier and called to him. With obvious reluctance, the Faerie approached Nebridio.

"Look on the far cliffs, just south of Kizikum, and tell me what you see."

"I don't see anything. Ah! There are tiny lights! I've never noticed that."

"What you see is the bronze armor of the Faerie Lord's army reflecting the morning sun."

The miner looked with alarm at Nebridio.

"Go to Salceda now, as fast as you can, and tell Spall that they will arrive tomorrow night. He knows what to do."

"But the Alcalde sent us here. He said you were helping the Faerie Lord."

Nebridio pointed again to the glint in the distance. "Let your eyes judge."

"I'll go."

As others gathered at the shore, their attention was on the vessel that approached, still unidentifiable.

"Is he coming?" Pellana's voice asked from behind him. She held Pippi at her hip. Willi stood beside her.

"Something is coming. A single vessel."

"That can't be one of ours," a Faerie said. "It's coming in too fast. It's one of the Faerie Lord's canoes."

"I don't think so," another said. "See how small it is."

"It's coming straight at us," the first explained. "That's why it looks so small. It's too fast for an acorn cap."

Soon enough, it became obvious to all watching that it was a catalpa pod canoe with seven Faeries paddling on each side. At a safe distance from the shore, the canoe came about and dumped two naked Faerie bodies into the water. The canoe then headed back toward Kizikum.

"Take the boys back home," Nebridio said to Pellana. The horror he saw on her lovely face was matched by his own. He had no doubt whose bodies had been tossed into the lake.

Nebridio waded out with several other Faeries. The bodies had sunk immediately to the bottom, but the water was only neck deep.

The first to be brought up was that of Wallis. His arms and legs had been broken and his abdomen opened. No intestine remained. He wept as he accepted the body of his brother from others. Alfrito had been similarly tortured and slain.

The sun was setting as Nebridio carried a small oil lamp into the shallow water. Each of two acorn caps had been filled with dried peat, soaked in oil. One bore the carefully dressed body of Wallis, the other, that of Alfrito wearing Wallis' remaining tunic. With the touch of a flame, each very slowly began to burn. Nebridio pushed them out into the lake and stood there in the water watching the flames grow in the still evening air.

The custom in Westbog was to bury the dead beneath the peat bog, but Nebridio would not allow his brother to share the fate of their common criminals, and in a place that Alfrito loathed. Pellana had agreed.

Dunedek had gone into hiding at the news of the deaths, and had yet to be located. At the Constable's insistence, Nebridio took charge of the war preparations.

The Faeries from Salceda recognized that, though they could delay the Faerie Lord at The Log, there was no hope of saving Salceda if Ruprecht decided to destroy it. Most agreed that Riverto would send their families to safety in the expansive wilderness southeast of Salceda. Those few who were not so confident of the Alcalde's wisdom had already rushed south at the news.

Nebridio had counted nearly five hundred Faeries willing to fight. He had gathered them at mid-day and instructed them to collect their weapons and enough food for eight days. Now, with the faint glow of the pyres drifting further into the darkness, he returned to the shore, his face illuminated by the small lamp.

"It is my intention to leave two hundred of you here, to defend Westbog. Rhodek will select you and will command here. With the aid of fire, you should be able to hold off the Faerie Lord's army until he returns to Kizikum."

"Why would he do that?" a voice asked from the darkness.

"Fifty of you will go to Kizikum by acorn boat, carrying peat and oil. You will circle the perimeter of the lake, to the north. Two hundred fifty will march with me to the north. Of every five Faeries, one will carry five pikes, two will each carry an amphora of fish oil and two will each carry a bale of dried peat. When we reach Kizikum, we will destroy it, along with everything and everyone there, like roasting a caracol. We leave at sunrise.

In the late evening of their second day's march, Nebridio saw, even from the distance of the river crossing above the cascades, a glow of fire at the southern horizon. He knew it could only be Salceda. He had no way of knowing if the glow came from their defensive fire or from the destruction of the village. The Faerie Lord would have first reached The Log the previous evening.

"If they can delay the Faerie Lord until tomorrow morning," he said to the Faeries who looked on with him, "then Westbog might be saved."

Most of the Faeries who marched with Nebridio were astounded at their first sight of the great stone arches that carried the aqueduct away from the cascades. They were even more stunned when they learned that they would be walking for two days in the water of the aqueduct, directly into the heart of Kizikum.

When Nebridio climbed onto the sluiceway, he was delighted to discover that the water flowed like a gentle creek, and only knee deep. It was clear enough to see the occasional stone that had washed in from the cascades. Directly above each massive pillar, the sidewalls widened with spillways to drain excess flow over the side. The spillways were wide enough for ten Faeries to sit and rest on each side. He instructed the first twenty to reach a pillar to rest until all the others had passed. In that way, every Faerie could rest about every thirteen pillars that were traversed.

He also left three Faeries behind at the head of the aqueduct with instructions to block the flow of the water completely at mid-day tomorrow, then open it again at midnight. Nebridio had no way of knowing how many hours the water spent in its journey from the head to the city. His plan was for the city to be dry when he arrived early tomorrow evening. The water would then reappear just before dawn.

"Nebridio, look!" one of his soldiers shouted, the afternoon of their first day in the aqueduct.

Nebridio looked down from its eastern face and saw Westbog's acorn boats moving below them along the western shore of Lake Willow. "They keep pace with us."

As he watched, a Faerie standing on the spillway of the previous pillar fell from the edge. The unfortunate soldier's wings flared and flapped to break the fall, but the great height exceeded his endurance. Shortly after his amphora of fish oil smashed to the ground below, the Faerie's wings fluttered above his head, dropping him onto the same spot. Nebridio saw no movement of the splayed body.

With a little more caution, Nebridio's army continued their march, knee deep in water, some with a tied bundle of pikes, some carrying amphorae on their backs, some with a dark bale of dried peat balanced above their heads. As their first night in the aqueduct approached, Nebridio realized that he had failed to consider how they would sleep. At dusk, he gave orders to each successive resting group to stop for the night and tie themselves to one another to prevent anyone from rolling off the edge while they slept.

That night, Nebridio watched for a glow of fire in the direction of Westbog. If the glow appeared, then the Faerie Lord had not been held a day at Salceda, and Westbog would be lost. Nebridio slept little. Most of the night he sat at the edge of the gently flowing water, allowing his feet and boots to dry.

He missed his brother. Never again would they joke and squabble. He blamed himself for having allowed him to go alone to the Faerie Lord that second time. Nebridio considered that, if he were to die at Kizikum, at least he wouldn't have to stand before his father in Lilac and admit his failure to protect his younger brother. But then his father would never know what happened. Perhaps, he concluded, that would be best after all. *Pellana might tell him.*

He had told Pellana to flee to Lilac if the Faerie Lord came to Westbog, and to call on his father for his hospitality. She had not agreed to do that. He saw no glow of fire to the east.

By late afternoon of the next day, the flow of water in the aqueduct noticeably diminished. The stone towers and walls of Kizikum could be seen rising from the island. The approach of Nebridio and his soldiers was completely blocked by the aqueduct from the view of those inhabitants of Kizikum who had remained after the army departed. Soon they might notice the flow of their water cease.

As they crossed over the sound that separated the island from the mainland, now walking along an empty aqueduct, Nebridio studied buildings and the layout of Kizikum. He tried to block from his mind the obvious predominance of mothers and the very old and very young who remained in the city. They would share the penalty for Alfrito's torture and death. And with a degree of luck, Ruprecht himself would also pay that price.

From directly above the city, he identified a fountain that had stopped flowing. Old Faeries stood about it in discussion. One pointed to a stone cistern as high as the aqueduct, still nearly full of water. It seemed to feed a large, wooden wheel which turned a crank that repeatedly lifted and dropped a huge mallet. It crushed large chunks of limestone that spilled slowly down a steep stone slope, then dropped as powder into a heap below. Beyond the cistern and below it stood the whitewashed clay dome of the great oven. A tall stack emitted the plume of gray that Nebridio had seen with Alfrito from the south of the lake. Even the departure of the army had not caused them to allow the great oven's fire to die. Nearby the furnace stood stack after stack of peat bales, hundreds of them waiting to be consumed by the furnace.

Nearly every structure within Kizikum was built, like its walls, from stones held in place by their building lime. There were some smaller wood structures, including the causeway to the mainland. An incomplete stone version of it stood alongside the wood one, which was guarded by only two soldiers.

Nebridio wanted the causeway to burn before the inhabitants realized that they needed to flee. Then he would roast the caracol.

The end of the aqueduct, which split into six branches of square, slate conduits, each of which dropped steeply toward a different section of the city, was supported by six flying buttresses—one for each branch. One of the buttresses also provided a narrow, stone stairway, apparently for maintenance. Although each of the buttresses could be descended by a Faerie with empty hands, or perhaps a single pike, only the stairway would allow them to carry their burdens down.

Nebridio didn't dare show his presence in the daylight. If they began their operation at sunset, he guessed that he would have about six hours before the water flowed again. He decided to take a chance with sending two of his soldiers onto the top of each slate conduit, hoping that they might be seen as workers—a perception that might explain the cutoff of the water flow. It would also allow them to sabotage the precarious branches of the system in daylight.

The twelve who were to appear as laborers were directed to each find a rock that had washed into the aqueduct and that could serve as a hammer. Once they had found their hammers, or pried one from the aqueduct itself, Nebridio sent them out onto the exposed buttresses to do their work. All of the bales and amphorae that they had carried were carefully collected against the inside walls at the end of the aqueduct.

"Hey!" a voice called from the street. A soldier looked up from the paving below. "Who sent you up there?"

Nebridio shook his head and moved his hand over his ear, hoping to convey to his "workers" that they can not hear.

"You, up there!" the soldier called again. He then began to climb the long series of steps, periodically shouting to them. When he finally reached the top, facing the workers he shouted, "Are you deaf?"

At that moment he wrinkled his nose and turned toward Nebridio and the invaders, but before he could retreat, he was pulled into the aqueduct by many hands and slain by Nebridio's pike through his neck. Nebridio removed the soldier's sword belt and bronze sword, then said, "Pass him back to the rear. Don't take the breast plate, or you may be mistaken for one of them."

Below the aqueduct, no one took notice of the missing soldier. Nebridio had planned to send two of his Faeries down the steps to the great oven, but the soldier they had slain seemed to have smelled them before he saw them. After four days of marching, a river crossing and sloshing down the entire length of the aqueduct, he and his troops apparently still reeked of Westbog.

After sunset, several of his Faeries were sent to the causeway. Others were assigned to go to the great oven and disperse its vast supply of peat bales to critical locations. One by one, the bales on the aqueduct were tossed down against the eastern wall of the city and against the nearby buildings. Outside the east wall, those who had sailed around the lake in their acorn boats were expected to be doing the same.

The timing of various actions would determine the survival of those Faeries who carried them out. Any errors or mix-ups and some of his soldiers would be trapped.

Nebridio, still atop the end of the main aqueduct with most of his Faeries, took out his tinder kit and sparked a glow onto a shred of dried bark. Cupping it in his hand, he puffed on it until it lit the wick of a small oil lamp. He held the lamp high and moved it side to side. It was the signal to begin the destruction of Kizikum. Only then did he see the glow of fires across the lake in the direction of Westbog.

In the dark city, a small fire began at the wooden causeway and spread rapidly over its length, indicating to him that his Faeries had been able to dispatch the two guards and dowse the wood with their amphora of fish oil. His soldiers at the great oven would wait for those from the causeway to pass before starting their task.

Farther back on the main aqueduct, where it crossed over the sound, a small chunk of burning peat was dropped to the water far below. Shortly after that signal, fires began to appear outside the eastern wall.

As an alarm sounded in the dark city, Nebridio heard the wet crunch of clay amphorae smashing near the great oven. Shouts of panic rose from the stone streets, now illuminated by gouts of sooty flames belching from the open doors of the great oven.

Nebridio counted the returning Faeries as they climbed off the stone steps at the top of the aqueduct. One was missing. He waited a short while longer, then gave the order to cast all the remaining amphorae of oil off the aqueduct into every section of the city they could reach. Screams from below filled the night.

As they all turned to run back up the aqueduct, the missing Faerie topped the steps and joined them. They stopped when they were beyond the last pillar that rose from within the walls. All of Kizikum burned in the hot fires of oil and peat. Fires also burned outside the eastern wall, facing the lake. At times, tongues of flame reached high above the wall, as new supplies of wood and other combustibles were touched by the spreading fires. For six hours, the burning of Kizikum lit the night sky. Then the aqueduct began to flow once again.

All of the slate conduit branches had been breached on their upper surfaces, so that the restored flow of water would spray forcefully out over the stone walls and buildings. At first, Nebridio heard only hissing, as the initial spray of water touched the heated stones. Then the loud crack of splitting rocks echoed in the darkness. Finally, with shuddering crashes that shook even the aqueduct, the high walls of Kizikum began to crumble. Screams from the city had ceased hours earlier. Episodically, the collapse of a building could be heard from one section of the city, then another.

As the first light of dawn revealed the utter destruction of Kizikum, Nebridio could see water, which continued to rush off the destroyed end of the aqueduct, spilling out of the ruined city through cracks in what remained of the blackened walls.

On the lake, forty long canoes approached the charred city from the direction of Westbog. As they disembarked beside the burned docks, one of the passengers, whose bronze helmet was decorated with large purple plumes, looked up and saw Nebridio and his army peering over the edge of the ruined aqueduct. He walked to a spot on the shore below where Nebridio stood, drew his bronze sword and broke it over his knee.

"I am Ruprecht, Faerie Lord of...Kizikum. Tell Dunedek," he shouted, "that we are done. I accede to all his terms. We are done." He walked back to his men, tossing the broken sword into Lake Willow, and wrenching the plumes from his helmet. When he reached the burned dock, he sat and buried his face in his hands.

"The canoes landed to the north of Westbog and their soldiers killed many of the women and children who had sought refuge in the peat bog, before we could drive them back." Constable Rhodek's hair was singed nearly to the scalp. "Some...could not be recognized. All were buried together the following day in the bog."

"And you know nothing of Pellana and her children?" Nebridio asked.

"I knew you would want news of them, but no one has been able to say."

Nebridio stood at the lakeshore of Westbog, near the line of the main battle. All the nearby rhododendrons, including Pellana's, had burned down to the damp soil. Somehow, the fires had purged the village of its stench. "Dunedek?"

"Two witnesses saw him carried into an ant nest the morning after the battle. They couldn't tell if he was still alive. He had been hiding east of the village while we fought and died to defend it."

Nebridio felt no joy at his victory. His effort to avenge Alfrito's undeserved death left him only with a sense of shame. He had lashed out at a city and its lord, but had slain only the helpless, and in the most horrific way. He vowed to always wear the captured bronze sword into battle, and never to draw it. It would serve as a reminder to show mercy.

He left for Lilac that evening and walked through the night and all the next day, before collapsing in exhaustion. At sunset the following day, he reached Nettle Falls. The last time he had stopped here, over six weeks ago, Alfrito had been alive. Many Faeries now dead had then been alive.

Passing the entrance to the Earwig Inn, he turned down the west river road that would carry him, in three more days, to his home in Lilac. But only a short distance down the road, he was stopped by the balding innkeeper, who had run after him.

"Nebridio, isn't it?"

"Yes."

"I have been told that you are not a spy."

"What?"

"Nearly a week ago, a very young guest informed me that if I see you, I should know that you are not a spy."

Nebridio's heart raced. "A dark-haired mother with two boys?"

"Yes."

"Where were they headed?"

"To Lilac."

CHAPTER 11—THE INNS AT NETTLE FALLS

While Herrik waited for his load of pokewood, he pointed out to his young assistant the Faeries on the high ropes, splitting the green, growing poke stems vertically, for next season's harvest. The hot sun of Ternaria baked the sweat from his brow as soon as it formed.

"It would take forever to cut into planks," he explained to Joshi, "if they waited until after it hardened."

"But cutting it only stinks when it's green," Joshi observed.

"Who have you brought with you?" asked Ginto, who managed the mill.

"This is Walto's boy," Herrik replied. "Runs the crossing barge below the falls."

"I'm Joshero, but everybody just calls me Joshi."

"No doubt, Joshi, you'll earn your keep," Ginto said, winking at Herrik. "Are those two old fools still at it?"

Herrik shook his head. "First Blit adds a new room, then Kallian has to add a bigger one. I guess I should be glad for the business, but it's hard to come out ahead, when half the load has to be barged across the river no matter which road I take."

"Don't they pay for the barging?"

"If I don't pay it myself, they'll buy from someone else."

"Can't that marmot swim across?" He gestured toward Herrik's albino marmot that munched happily at the tall grass nearby.

"Oh, Mookie can swim it alright, but not with a load on her back."

"So, which one of them gets free barging?"

"One trip I cross to the road along the west of the river; the next time I take the east road. Most of what I earn from the one customer I lose on the other."

After lashing the pokewood high on Mookie's back, Herrik and Joshi climbed on, just behind the head of the shaggy, white marmot. Herrik dug in his heels. Mookie slowly turned her head to look at

Herrik, then began her leisurely waddle out of Faerie Ring and toward the ford across the Nettle.

The river was running clear and low enough for Herrik to see the rocky bottom of the crossing. "Jump in and cool off," Herrik suggested, offering Joshi a hand down.

"See you on the other side," Joshi shouted, before disappearing beneath the water, just downstream from the ford.

Herrik rocked along on Mookie's broad shoulders, watching the boy skillfully swim a diagonal line toward the west bank. It was plain to see that Joshi had grown up on the river. On the far bank, a bit downstream, Herrik hoisted the soaked lad back onto Mookie for the short trip to the falls. The marmot completed in two hours a journey that occupied the better part of two days for a Faerie on foot.

"Looks like Blit gets his pokewood first today."

"I think you should charge them more," Joshi suggested.

"It's an odd situation. Blit wants to build some new addition whenever Kallian is getting more guests. So it's when he really can't afford it. Once Blit's new improvement attracts more guests, then Kallian wants to build more. Just about the time one expense begins to pay for itself, it's time to spend more. They've been doing that for years."

"Why don't they just call a truce and they both could stop."

"Too old and too stubborn."

"What will you be building this time?" Herrik stood beneath a hanging sign of an earwig, its rear pincers held menacingly into the air, while Joshi began untying part of the load of pokewood.

"Ahh. Go look at what the Buttercup's done." The aging Faerie still wore a black apron from serving beverages to his current guests. The apron accentuated his short, sagging body.

Herrik walked to the north side of the Earwig Inn and looked east toward the river. Before him, to the left, Nettle Falls cascaded from its heights, plunging into a roiling pool just upstream from the rear of Earwig. Across the river, through the mist that always rose from the bottom of the falls, a new deck extended from the back of the Buttercup Inn to the very edge of the river.

"Visitors can just sit there and watch the falls," Blit grumbled. "I don't know why I never thought of that."

"So, you're going to build a deck?" Joshi asked.

Blit frowned at the quantity of pokewood left tied to Mookie. "Maybe. Is all that going to *him*?" He thrust his thumb toward the Buttercup.

Herrik nodded.

"What's he planning now?"

"I don't know." Herrik always endured the same questions from whichever innkeeper received the first half of the delivery.

"He just doesn't know when to stop," Blit moaned. "He's driving me out of business. It's no wonder I've lost my hair." He passed his hand over his bald scalp.

"Why don't you cross over and talk to him?" Herrik suggested.

"Ahh. The last time I tried, he walked away."

"The last time you tried," Herrik quipped, "you probably had a full head of hair."

"But some things don't change. He's just stubborn. He'll keep this up until I'm ruined."

After his stop at Earwig Inn, Herrik guided Mookie down to the river's edge, where Walto, Joshi's father, waited to load his barge with the cargo that would go to the Buttercup.

"Don't be under foot," Walto snapped. Joshi had begun to move the cargo from Mookie's back to the barge platform. Walto took Joshi's place assisting Herrik.

Joshi stepped back and folded his arms. Once the barge was loaded, he untied the line, jumped to the barge and sat on the stack of pokewood. When Herrik, unasked, lent Walto a hand at walking the crossrope from front to back, in order to pull the barge to the dock at the opposite bank, Joshi helped as well. Espiria, Joshi's mother, stood at the dock on the far shore watching.

At about the halfway point, Herrik held his arm straight overhead, then brought his hand down to his face. Mookie slipped her bulk into the water and swam toward them, keeping only her head above the surface.

Without warning, Walto lunged at Joshi from behind, sprawling the boy onto the platform. The next instant, with nothing more than a soft grunt, Walto lifted into the air in the piercing mandibles of a dragonfly.

"Papa!" Joshi cried out.

Espiria stared into the sky, both hands covering her mouth.

"How's the boy doing?" Ginto asked, as he supervised the loading of yet another shipment of pokewood onto Mookie's back.

"Alright, I guess," Herrik replied. "You know, there hasn't been a dragonfly attack at Nettle Falls in Joshi's lifetime. That's over ten years."

"Twelve years ago, at the ford above Lilac," Ginto corrected him. "Helping his mama with that barge?"

Herrik nodded. "Even with both of them, it's difficult to draw that thing across the river."

"It's good work. That barge saves four days, if you go between Mt. Easley and Westbog. And anybody coming up from Lilac who picked the wrong side of the river, why that's the only way to get across 'till the ford at Faerie Ring."

"Walto was always hard on the boy," Herrik said, "but he wasn't about to let the dragonfly get his son."

"That's it," Ginto said, when the load was tied.

This trip, Herrik took Mookie along the east road, so the Buttercup was his first stop. After descending the switchbacks that took the east road from the top of Nettle Falls down to the bottom, he tied Mookie near the large painted sign of a buttercup.

Kallian awaited his arrival outside the front door. He wore a sober, black tunic over his tall, lean frame. His dyed black hair was pomaded and combed to either side, leaving a white line over the middle.

"I don't know if I can keep this up," Kallian said. "Blit has lost his mind. Come see." Kallian led Herrik into the door, through the inn and out the back, to his newly widened river deck. "Can you believe that?"

Across the river, emerging from the back of the Earwig was not only a river deck, but an extension, supported by a pokewood tower that cantilevered the extension out over the water. On the extension deck, bathed in the mist of the falls, three Faeries stood, looking up at the cascading river.

"Word has already reached Lilac that the west road is best, because of his new deck. I'm losing business."

"Are you planning to build one like it?" Herrik asked.

"No. You brought the silk rope?"

"I have it."

"I'm going to build something safer than that."

Herrik took care of business at the Buttercup, then rode Mookie down to the barge dock on the east side. Joshi hopped from the barge and, after feeding Mookie a handful of slivered cattail shoots, one-by-one, began transferring her load onto the barge. Meanwhile, Herrik carried an orange cube, the size of his head, to Espiria, who sat on the dirt above the dock, watching her son doing the work of her dead mate.

"I brought you this from Faerie Ring."

"What is it," she asked.

"It's a piece of vegetable," Herrik answered. "They said it's called carrot. You can eat it or cook it then eat it."

"What does it taste like?"

He cut off a slice and handed it to her. "Sweet and crunchy."

She accepted the orange stick and bit into it. Her eyebrows rose. She took another bite. "Joshi, stop and come taste this."

Herrik stopped Mookie at the Faerie Ring ford and watched the horizon to the north. Far in the distance, tall, black clouds moved slowly from west to east. Even in the bright sunlight, the lightning flashed repeatedly. He turned Mookie onto the east road and began the jarring waddle toward Nettle Falls. Today, he carried only a half load, with the hope that Kallian might buy it. Blit had informed him on his last trip that his resources were used up. He could no longer afford to keep up with Kallian's "wild" schemes.

About halfway to his destination, Herrik noticed that the river level was rising. He had encountered no rain. To the north, the black clouds had moved beyond the far eastern ridge. Yet the water continued to rise. He looked at his half load of silk rope and pokewood. It represented all of his own assets, though the profit would be better this trip. With a sigh, he unlashed his cargo and allowed it to drop onto the road.

He dug his heels into Mookie. She turned her head to look back at him, then resumed her waddle. Again he prodded her until, at last, she sprang into a jolting, high canter. Whenever she slowed, he urged her on. Beside him, the river level was rising faster than Mookie could carry him.

At the point where the east road began its winding descent toward the Buttercup, he could see Faeries on the two long and precarious deck extensions fleeing to either side of the river. Huge chunks of debris and shafts of shrubbery launched themselves from the angry falls and dropped frighteningly close to the spectators running for their lives from the swaying decks.

As Herrik descended further, the eastern barge dock came into view. Espiria stood high on the bank, screaming at Joshi, who struggled on the barge to offload a two wheel cart to the nearly submerged dock.

The heavy crossrope tore loose from its mooring post. The barge, with Joshi aboard, still hanging on to the cart, spun around once, then sped downriver. Herrik rode past the Buttercup, pushing the exhausted Mookie. He held up one hand to Espiria as he rode past. Sometimes Mookie would gain a little on Joshi's barge, then she would fall behind again when the fatigue was just too much. Travelers along the road scrambled out of their way.

At first, the barge slammed into whatever stood in its path, knocking Joshi about. After a quarter hour, Joshi broke apart the cart, providing him with the flat of one side attached to one limb. With the makeshift paddle, he gained some control, steering around the larger obstacles.

After an hour and a half, the river level crested and began to recede. Herrik felt confident that Joshi could control the barge well enough to bring it to a stop at Lilac, where the shallows provided the first ford south of Nettle Falls. He halted Mookie and allowed her to rest and graze.

Herrik dismounted and scratched her cheek. "You were wonderful. I don't know what we'll do now, but at least *your* food is free."

When he finally caught up with Joshi, the barge was tied up on the east bank, across from Lilac, a town famous for its circular grove of lilac trees. A good portion of the traffic through the inns at Nettle Falls came from pilgrims visiting the grove from Faerie Ring. On their journey south, they would stay at either the Earwig or the Buttercup, depending on which side of the Nettle River they traveled. There, they could see the other inn across the river and decide which road to take on their return trip. The ford at Lilac was a three day walk from Nettle Falls. Mookie usually completed it in about half a day. Today, she had covered the distance in a little over two hours.

"What took you so long," Joshi asked, a glorious smile on his face. He sat on the river bank, munching some seeds that had been part of his cargo.

"You look like you're still in one piece." He tied up Mookie in a stand of sweetgrass.

"I don't know how we'll replace the lost cargo."

"Offer the owner free river crossings at Nettle Falls forever."

"Forever. That's an idea. That's a great idea." Joshi tilted the soaked sack of seeds toward Herrik. "Want some, before I dump it out?"

"No. We've got to figure out how to get the barge back upriver."

"You have some silk rope?"

"I left it along the road not far from Faerie Ring."

"Maybe we could get some in Lilac."

"I have nothing to exchange. I think I'm out of business."

"Maybe we could do some bargaining."

In Lilac, Herrik looked for someone who was not a pilgrim, and found a Tribune, named Caluño, patrolling the promenade. He explained to the Tribune their situation.

"You plan to tow the barge up to Nettle Falls?" Caluño asked.

"If we can get some silk rope," Herrik answered, "but we have nothing to exchange."

"How long is the trip?"

"Only three or four hours with the marmot," Joshi chimed in.

Caluño seemed surprised. "We have wealthy pilgrims who seldom look forward to the five day walk back to Faerie Ring. I'll see what we can arrange, and meet you at the ford in the morning."

Herrik and Joshi walked back to the barge. Herrik guessed that three or four passengers might be willing to pitch in and buy a coil of rope in exchange for the transportation.

"Do you think the docks washed away?" Joshi asked.

"I saw one of them float downriver."

"Good. I hate that barge crossing—back and forth all day. What about those decks they built out from the inns?"

"They were swaying, but still standing when I left. They're so long, I can't imagine what keeps them standing out there in the air."

"Oh," Joshi laughed, "lots of pokewood. They just made the towers bigger and reinforced everything. By the time they were done, the workers on one side could stand at the end and talk to the workers on the other side. But those two old farts still wouldn't say hello to each other."

Joshi slept on the barge, but the rocking and the lapping of the water was too much for Herrik. Instead, he bedded down beside his white marmot.

"Well, Mookie, if we get a rope, it should be an easy walk for you tomorrow."

Herrik awakened to voices. Down by the barge, Joshi was loading two huge, ripe cherries and two fat blueberries onto the four corners of the barge. Three well dressed adult couples, each with a lovely daughter, nearly of age, stood patiently nearby. He recognized Caluño in the distance, returning to Lilac.

"Here's the rope," Joshi shouted at Herrik. "It shouldn't take much longer," he said to the others.

Herrik walked down to the barge. "How many are passengers?" he asked softly.

"All of them."

With the nine passengers seated cross-leg on the floor of the barge, and Joshi standing at the stern with his makeshift rudder—now lashed in place, Herrik climbed onto Mookie's shoulders and began to tow the clumsy craft upriver. At only five places during the voyage did Mookie have to briefly leave the road and slip in and out of the river to go around tall vegetation. A little over three hours later, they arrived at the Buttercup. Joshi unloaded the fruit directly onto the riverbank, while Herrik escorted the passengers to the inn.

Kallian seemed flustered. "I have room for only three more guests tonight."

"Perhaps you could take us to the other inn," one of the fathers suggested to Herrik.

"Kallian, if you could get them some dinner, I'll see what we can do to carry them across."

The process of assisting guests to stay at his rival's inn seemed to disturb the old Faerie. He wrung his hands. "Yes. Dinner. Come in."

Herrik went down to Joshi at the riverbank. The mooring posts for the crossrope were gone, as were both docks. "The guests could cross on Mookie, one or two at a time," Herrik said, "but they would get soaked." He looked at the fruit resting on the bank. The blueberries were each an armful, the cherries even larger. "How are they going to carry those all the way to Faerie Ring?"

"They're not. The fruit is ours. Part of the fee." Joshi returned to the barge and brought back a small sack. "Here's the rest of the fee." He poured twenty coppers onto the ground. "Half of it is yours...and so is half the fruit."

"But the rope?"

"Just part of the deal. They were so glad not to have to walk the whole way, we probably could have gotten more. It might not be a bad business to get into."

"So we can sell the fruit to the inns. Hmmm. But we still need to get the extra guests across to the Earwig today. I guess Mookie could swim a rope across, then tow the barge to the other side."

"I have a better idea. How long would it take you to go back upriver and get the pokewood you dropped?"

"If it's still there, two hours."

"I'll meet you at the Buttercup when you get back."

"And do what?"

"I'll show you when you get back."

Herrik wasn't sure what inspiration had taken possession of Joshi, but one crisis after another seemed to bring out an unshakable optimism. He walked to Joshi's small pokewood cottage below the Buttercup. It stood back a short way from the riverbank. His justification was to assure Espiria that Joshi was safe, but he knew she had already spoken with him when they arrived. She stepped out to meet Herrik.

"I was scared to death," she said. "You've been so good to Joshi."

"I like him. He's a bright boy, full of ideas. Walto would have been proud to see him take control of that barge. Most others would have frozen in panic."

"Will you stay for some dinner? It's not much."

"I have to go back upriver to pick up cargo I left by the road."

"Oh." Espiria's wings slumped.

"Come with me."

"But Joshi..."

"He's fine. He's more than fine. Come with me. It will be a relaxing ride. And besides, Mookie likes you."

"Mookie?"

"Yeah." Herrik smiled. "Mookie."

"What...what are you doing?" Kallian asked, as two laborers assisted Joshi and Herrik in carrying pokewood beams through the Buttercup and out the back to the deck.

"We're fixing a problem out on the deck," Joshi explained.

"But I..." He lowered his voice. "I can't pay for any repairs now."

"It's already paid for—ten coppers." Joshi said, as he continued out to the long deck extension.

Kallian looked to Herrik, who shrugged. "I'm not sure what he's up to."

"You really don't know?" Espiria whispered.

"Not the slightest idea."

Out at the end of the swaying deck extension, which reached nearly to the center point of the falls, two joiners had already removed the end rail, and were busy cutting mortises into the side beams. Herrik's eyes followed a rope that had been tied to the top of the tower behind him. It led across the heart-stopping gap to the tower supporting the swaying deck that projected from the Earwig, on the opposite bank of the river. "You're going to swing the guests across to the other side?" he asked Joshi, who was busy explaining something to the joiners.

Joshi smiled. "Nope."

The joiners laid out the two longest pokewood beams. To the center of each, they joined a shorter, vertical post, then diagonals from the top of the center posts to the ends of the beams. As each was finished, it was hoisted onto the high rope and pulled across toward the Earwig deck. It was then that Herrik noticed three workers on the other side of the gap removing the end rail of the Earwig's deck.

Blit stomped out to his end, shouting imprecations at the workers, who pointed across the gap to Joshi.

"You must tell me what you are up to," Kallian shouted from behind Herrik.

"Kallian," Herrik said, "it looks like Joshi's connecting the two decks."

"He can't do that. You can't do that!" Kallian stood erect when he realized that Blit, from the opposite side, had simultaneously shouted the very same words.

Kallian and Blit stared silently at one another. Both shrugged helplessly as the flooring planks were cautiously laid and pegged over the new intervening span.

Herrik noted that the worrisome swaying of the deck extensions had ceased as soon as the spans were joined and the flooring placed. At the pegging of the final plank, the joiners shook hands, then backed away.

The pilgrims from Lilac had wandered out toward the commotion. When the dumbfounded Kallian noticed them, he looked across once more to Blit, then escorted the supernumerary guests across the solid span. "You have six more guests for the Earwig tonight," he said to Blit.

Blit welcomed them, then approached Kallian with tears in his eyes. "I've missed you, old friend."

"And I've missed you, old fool." Kallian wrapped his arms around Blit, then kissed his bald head. "We built a bridge to each other."

"We just didn't know it."

Joshi walked out to the center of the bridge, where the two old Faeries stood arm-in-arm, and shouted, "Nettle Falls Bridge is now open! Free river crossings forever!"

CHAPTER 12—PRAYER OF A SARACET SLAVE

Kurash lowered his gaze, as a corpulent Faerie shuffled her way into the healer's consultation chamber and seated herself on the treatment bench. He did his best to be merely part of the furnishings.

"Archon, what brings you?" the healer asked.

"Does...that have to be in here?" she asked, tilting her head toward Kurash.

"Just ignore him. He keeps a record for me. Very handy."

"It's hard to ignore a Saracet in a Faerie town, Ostrik. Are you sure it's safe? I mean, can you trust it?"

"Come now. I've had him nearly a year. So...are you not feeling well?"

The Archon hesitated. "My legs. They're swollen."

Kurash glanced up from his small desk to see Ostrik press his fingertip against her shin. Daylight filtered through the translucent white stone walls.

"Yes," the healer said. "I need to listen to your breast. May I?"

"Go ahead." She straightened her yellow tunic at the shoulders.

Ostrik placed his ear against the center of her chest. "Yes." He turned to Kurash. "Nepata, Archon of Tellia, suffers from dropsy."

Kurash dipped a quill and recorded the information on a square of vellum.

"I will send Kurash to get the medicine. You can come by tomorrow morning for it."

"Dropsy? Is that bad?" she asked.

"No one comes to me for something good, Archon. But the medicine will help invigorate your humors and reduce the swelling. It would be wise for you to eat a bit less as well."

Once the Archon departed, Ostrik said, pointing to the vellum, "Digitalis leaf. Do you know the plant?"

Kurash carefully spelled the word on the vellum. "Foxglove flower?"

"Yes. The purple one. Gather only the mature leaves from a plant that has just flowered. Dry them separately in the sun. Bring them to me tonight."

As Kurash left the chamber, he stooped to clear the lintel. At fifteen, he was already taller by a third than the Faeries of Tellia. In the street, he tried to avoid making eye contact with the Faeries that walked past him, though most crossed to the opposite side of the way to avoid him. If his height weren't enough to appear threatening, his dark skin and the twin black horns on his forehead usually accomplished that.

One and two level buildings lined both sides of the street. All were built of finely dressed, translucent white stone, found nowhere else in Ternaria. He had been told that Tellia was unique in its construction.

"Good morning, Kurash." A Faerie with glistening blonde hair to her waist smiled from a white stone doorway.

"Good morning, Darissa," he replied. Darissa was one of the few citizens of Tellia who spoke kindly with him.

"Going to the woods again?" She tipped her head up to look at his face.

"Yes. Not much else north of town."

"Ostrik says you're a big help. He's getting old, you know. You be careful out there alone."

"I will." His face felt different when he smiled. It happened so seldom that it almost ached.

Kurash walked a half hour into the woods, until he reached a rocky, treeless ridge. There he located the digitalis plant. He selected the perfect specimen and carefully removed two leaves. Wrapping them over his shoulders, he carried them to his drying rock, a slab of exposed white stone just northeast of the town. After laying out the two leaves to dry in the sun, he walked to his nearby garden, a secret he kept from Ostrik. Once the living digitalis went to seed, he would bring one of its seeds to the garden and plant it among the borage, marigold, coltsfoot, yarrow, nightshade and other medicines that he identified in the woods.

He looked overhead to the position of the sun. It was time to pray. He knelt on the soft dirt and lowered his face to the ground, speaking the ritual mid-day prayer from the Usharashada. Then he added his own words.

"Great Lord Dianthus, you have taken everything from me and given me a new life among a foreign people. Give me the wisdom to find a path to your truth."

"That is a tooth from a mighty large mouse," Pyxis said as he accepted it from Kurash.

"It was hard to get from the bone," Kurash pointed out.

"Okay. But I can still only pay two coppers."

"What are you working on?

Pyxis lifted a partly finished doll of a Faerie child, shaped from a chunk of milky white stone as long as his forearm. "Like it?" He stood it on the bench to grind a bit from the foot with an obsidian stick. A little cloud of white dust billowed into the air when he puffed at it.

"I do."

A Faerie lad of about ten and with an unmistakable shade of blond hair entered the shop. Kurash recognized him as Darissa's son, but had never spoken with him. His tunic was a well-fitted green, and very clean. The boy frowned when he saw Kurash.

"I want to get a gift for my mother," he said to Pyxis.

"What sort of gift?"

"Next week is her thirtieth year. Something for that."

"Thirtieth year. A special year. How much did you want to spend?"

The boy hesitated. "I only have one copper."

"So, something small."

"As big as I can get for one copper. And pretty."

Kurash knew that Pyxis sold nothing for so low a price. "Maybe a likeness of yourself in mouse ivory?"

Pyxis looked up at him with surprise. Kurash just nodded his head.

"That sounds alright."

Pyxis showed five fingers below the bench. Kurash nodded again.

"Let me make a drawing." Pyxis rapidly sketched on the floor with a stick of charcoal. "Turn sideways." He sketched again. "Pay me now, and come back in five days."

The boy handed the sculptor his copper and left.

Pyxis held out an empty hand to Kurash, who dropped two coppers into it. "You know," Pyxis said, "that's Alketas, Darissa's boy."

"I didn't know his name."

"She's the whore. She sleeps with anybody who pays the price."

"Is that worse than selling a sculpture to anybody who pays the price?"

Pyxis thought for a moment. "I suppose not, when you put it that way. You're more noticing of unfairness than Faeries. But I guess you would be, the way folks treat you here."

"Unkindness is never surprising from a stranger."

"Why do you wear that band on your arm, if you're not a slave?"

Kurash looked at the thin copper band high on his right arm. "Ostrik says that Faeries are less afraid of me if they believe I'm a slave. I think he's right. I don't really have much to be free about, so it doesn't matter either way to me. Once, all Saracets were slaves."

He stooped through the doorway and into the street of perfectly aligned buildings. The mat weaver was just two buildings down and across the street. Partway there, he remembered that he had not only given away the mouse ivory, but had also spent two of the coppers he had.

Faeries stood in groups, completely ignoring him. There seemed to be some excitement about a discovery in the quarry—something about copper. He returned to the healer's.

"No. Nothing right now."

"I'll be in my house," Kurash said, by which he meant the one room cell that stood separate from the back of the healer's two level building.

Kurash sat on his stool and opened a scroll. He thought of a portion of the Usharashada that he recalled fairly completely, but had not yet recorded. Once the opening sentence came to him, he began to write in rich, black soot ink. Ancient Shadhana flowed into the first blank section of the scroll. He had studied, read and written the language of the Usharashada all his life, at least until he ran away. It discomforted him that he was uncertain of the sequence of all the sections he had recalled, but he did his best to honor Dianthus, his god.

He paused and looked up at the small statue of Dianthus that Pyxis had carved for him of mouse tooth. The sculptor had initially sketched a likeness of Kurash, horns and all, only with wings added, but Kurash had told him that Dianthus looked more like a Faerie, but with much larger wings. So his statue vaguely resembled Ostrik with huge wings. At the time, he had spent every copper he had saved to make it. Now he could look at it and smile and trust that Dianthus looked down on him with at least kindness, if not a smile. Dianthus had brought them out of the house of bondage.

That the statue resembled Ostrik made sense as well. The healer had been searching for a medicine when he found him wandering alone, lost in the wilderness. He had brought him to this new home and fed him and sheltered him and clothed him. The hostile stares of the Faeries couldn't compare to what he had endured at the hands of his fellow Saracets.

No. Dianthus had blessed him—had saved him through Ostrik. If only he could find what Dianthus intended for him, he could be at peace.

"Kurash," Ostrik called.

He put down his quill and his scroll and stooped to look out the doorway. The healer stood at a window. "I am here."

"They've found something unexpected at the quarry, a vast chamber filled with copper and brass. Everyone is talking about it."

"Then the quarrymistress is wealthy."

"The Archon says it belongs to all."

Kurash knew that "all" did not include a dark-skinned Saracet.

"The Ephor will hear the arguments in a week."

In his secret garden, Kurash knelt on his new grass mat and prayed to Dianthus. As he stood to leave, he changed his mind and knelt once more. With his horns touching the ground, he added, "All I ask is a sign. Give me the wisdom to recognize it and understand the true meaning of your power and your will." He rose once again.

"What was that about?"

Kurash, startled, turned to find Alketas seated on the drying rock. "I was praying to god."

"Oh. Because you do that a lot," the blonde Faerie boy stated.

"How would you know that?"

"I've seen you come out here every day. I followed you a few times."

"Why?"

"Well, you're kind of...strange. I thought you might eat bugs or something."

"Saracets eat only plants."

"Oh."

"How did your mother like her gift? I saw it when Pyxis finished it. It looked a great deal like you. He even dyed some beeswax a light yellow to match your hair."

"She liked it. I thought it was going to be all of me, but it was just a head and shoulders and a little edge of wings."

"It would have been unrecognizable if he fit all of you on one tooth."

"Um. Pyxis told me you helped pay for it."

"Your mother has been kind to me."

"What do you mean?"

"Most of the Faeries in Tellia won't even talk to me."

Alketas grimaced. "She didn't...you know...sleep with you, did she?"

Kurash had not expected a question on such a topic from a ten year old. He lowered his head and sat beside Alketas. "No."

"I don't even know if Saracets...even do that."

Tears came to his eyes. "Yes. Saracets mate—the ones that can."

"What do you mean?"

He took a deep breath. "Each year, all the males who have reached thirteen that year are...judged...by the chief. The one who is selected is left alone. All the rest are emasculated." He began to weep.

"I don't know what that means."

Kurash looked into Alketas eyes and shouted, "They castrated me. Now I'm nothing." The alarm on the boy's face caused him to immediately regret having said anything about it. "Don't tell anyone," he said between sobs. "Not even the healer knows."

"The letters are Shadhana, but they each make a sound," Kurash explained, sitting beside Alketas, "so I can write 'Alketas' like this." He wrote the letters, pronouncing them as he went.

"But why go to all the bother when you can just say it?"

"The Usharashada was written over a thousand years ago. Even though those who spoke the words then have been dead a long time, I can still hear their words by reading them. And I write a record for the healer—one for every Faerie. Five years from now, he will be able to see what treatments he has given."

"Can he read your records?"

"No. But I can read it back to him. Or you could read it to him."

"We should go to the court. The Ephor is going to judge on the stuff they found at the quarry."

"It doesn't really have much to do with me."

"But it might to me and my mother."

In the street, everyone in the town seemed to be going to the court. When they arrived near the end of the line, they followed the crowd into a semi-circle of stone benches, built row after row, like steps. Kurash took a seat in the center of the very last row, even though two entirely empty rows remained in front of him. Alketas sat with him.

"Gordion, Ephor of Tellia," a Faerie announced from the front, "will now hear and judge arguments over the treasures found at the quarry."

The Ephor entered from the bottom level of the court, wearing a white robe with red trim. He seated himself on the one chair of the rostrum.

The Archon began her argument for why she believed the treasure should be shared. Though still as stout as ever, she seemed to stand and walk more comfortably than when he had first seen her at the healer's. She pointed out to the Ephor that the quarry did not belong to the quarrymistress any more than the woods belonged to the healer. The treasure should therefore be shared.

When Andra, the quarrymistress, stood, Kurash was struck by her solid muscularity. She cited the long tradition in Tellia that allowed the finder of anything from a common ground to take possession or use of what was found. The quarry's stone served as her most forceful example. Since she and her workers took possession of all the stone they cut, it was only natural that the treasure should be treated likewise.

"What do you estimate the treasure to be worth?" Gordion asked of Andra.

"There is brass that is decorative and formed into huge pieces, which we gladly offer to the town. The copper seems to be about 60,000."

"And Archon, how do you value the treasure?"

"The quarrymistress and I made the estimate together. So, the same."

"And there is nothing else of significant value that either the quarrymistress or the town claim?"

The quarrymistress and the Archon both answered in the negative.

"Listen now to my final judgment. I agree with much of both arguments. Because of the vast sum of the value, I rule that the town shall have two thirds of the copper and all of the brass. The quarrymistress shall receive one third of the copper. The town's share shall be divided equally to all Faeries, young or old, living within Tellia or its surrounds to a limit of a quarter hour walk from the center of town, measured from this court. This share will not go to the quarrymistress or her workers. The last count of Tellia arrived at 973. So each Faerie shall receive about forty coppers, the exact amount to be determined by and distributed by the Archon."

The audience cheered. Once the Ephor had regained their attention, he continued.

"Of the remaining 20,000, seven thousand will go to the quarrymistress and one thousand coppers to each of her thirteen workers. The quarrymistress shall make that distribution. In the unlikely event of any further discoveries, it shall, with this notice, go entirely to the finder or finders, and shall not be further judged by this court. This judgment is final." With that remark, the Ephor stood and departed.

Alketas leaned close to Kurash. "That last part, about any other treasure, must be the Ephor trying to keep somebody working at the quarry."

"A thousand coppers is about three years of pay for working in the quarry," Kurash said as they exited the court. "They'll spend it in less than a year, but I doubt they'll go back to work before then."

"See," Alketas said. "Nobody's working."

Kurash stood with Alketas at the edge of the quarry. "I guess when the price of stone climbs high enough, a new quarrymaster will get it going again." He followed Alketas to the opening where the treasure had been discovered. "How do they cut the stone?"

"They used this stuff." Alketas carefully lifted a coil of silk rope coated with pulverized obsidian. "Instead of dusting the spider silk, they roll it in obsidian. A Faerie holds each end and they pull it back and forth. Then they hammer these wedges to break it loose."

The opening was taller than Kurash. He stepped to the edge and looked in. A spot of light from the mid-day sun illuminated a floor far below. A new, very long series of ladders led to the bottom. He looked to either side of the vast chamber. The walls appeared to be carved in low relief and painted in bright colors. He could make out a Faerie with huge wings. "What is this place?"

"Everything is pretty big. Maybe humans dug this a long time ago. Let's go in." Alketas climbed down the ladders. From the floor far below, he shouted, "You coming?"

Kurash reluctantly followed. The floor was littered with fresh shavings of copper, left after all the larger objects of copper had been cut into pieces small enough to haul away. Gigantic urns and bowls of brass stood among other huge brass objects whose purpose was a mystery to Kurash. The bright spot of sunlight on the floor made it difficult to see the walls clearly, but they were covered from halfway up to the ceiling with paintings. And words. "Look at that." He pointed to the winged figure that he had mistaken for a picture of a Faerie. "It says 'Magic King,' oh, 'Mage King.' It says Mage King. It is a picture of a Mage King. There are words all over, but I can't see them well. We have to come back with a candle or an oil lamp."

"Humans didn't dig this here," Alketas said. "Look at the seams."

Long vertical and horizontal seems delimited perfectly rectangular blocks of stone—enormous blocks. "They built this," Kurash said. He was beginning to understand the nature of the quarry. "The stone is not a natural part of the land. Faeries have been quarrying the corner of a huge building all these years."

"There's an entrance way over there. It's all collapsed."

"How could they discover this and only care about how much copper they could get? The building tells a story, and the paintings tell a story."

"And the words. What do they say?"

"The letters are shaped oddly, but I think it's Shadhana. I'll make up a new scroll. When we come back, I'll copy the words and... You know, Pyxis should see this, with all the carving."

"My mother should see this. And she told me not to go to the quarry."

"I've used up half of my share of the treasure buying all this reed paper from Faerie Ring," Pyxis complained as he hung another sketch to an interior wall of his shop. Each sketch represented the huge painting of one wall of the treasure chamber.

"What I don't understand," Darissa said, "is how this big building got underground."

"In the Usharashada," Kurash explained, "there are stories about things that happened over eighty generations ago. That may have been built two thousand years ago."

"But did they build it in a hole?"

"Two thousand years is a long time," Pyxis said. "Imagine how much dust accumulates on your floor if you don't sweep for a week or two. Two thousand years of dirt...there could be a whole city of giant buildings under the hills here."

Darissa shook her head. "Time happens so slow for something that's so long."

"I don't know what that means." Pyxis climbed down from a stool. "But it sounds like you said something important. I'm sure Alketas would agree that time happens slow."

"Alright." Darissa stared at one of the sketches. "He's probably learned as much of a lesson as he ever will. But I told him not to go there. I'll let him go back, but only if someone is with him. You know, those soldiers that come from wasps..." She pointed to the sketch. "...look like Thistlepix."

"But see those trees," Kurash observed, "they're not really the right size, but the soldiers are probably human size. And the wasps are little, but they become much bigger as soldiers. Thistlepix are small enough to ride on wasps."

Pyxis, Darissa and Kurash looked at one another, then at the sketch. The army of soldiers that had come from wasps was all male, except for a single queen soldier.

"No one has ever seen a female Thistlepix," Pyxis said. "Look at these dark soldiers." He pointed to a different sketch. "These could be Saracets. And see, this one in the rear of them, it definitely has horns. I'm sure none of the others did. The trees here show the dark soldiers are taller than the wasp soldiers."

"Saracet soldiers are always female," Kurash mumbled as he stared at the sketch. The others looked at his rather diminutive horns. "Really. Always. You know, I didn't see the Saracets with the actual painting in front of me."

"The wall paintings are too large to grasp with the mind. It's only when I copy them to the reed paper that I have a full notion of what is there. Even then, each sketch is so large that I can hardly afford the paper."

Darissa turned to a third sketch. "So, are these big Faeries? We have big Thistlepix and big Saracets."

"Their wings are three times those of a Faerie," Kurash observed. "It shows them flying—actually flying."

"But see," Pyxis interrupted, "This...Mage King...makes them from humans. It's like he took humans and gave them huge wings so they could fly."

They all turned to the fourth panel. The Mage King transforms a lizard to give it wings and a breath of fire. They are small enough for him to hold one in his hands.

"What are those?" Darissa asked.

Kurash looked at Pyxis. The both shrugged.

"How long will it take?" Alketas asked.

Kurash hunched over his new scroll containing, in black ink, all the sections of text he had copied from the treasure chamber. Above a small number of words, his translation was written in a dark purple. "It's not really Shadhana. I've figured out all the letters from the words I recognize. So now I'm left with a lot of words that I can read, but I don't know what they mean. Sometimes if I see the same word in two different places, it suddenly makes sense, like the flash of a firefly. The more words I recognize, the faster it goes."

"I guess that means a long time."

"Mage King...wasp...army...against..." I don't know what this means. It reads 'Ternara.' And see, here it is again, 'Ternara.'"

"It's a place, like Ternaria."

"Of course, 'city of Ternara.' Yes. And there's 'from Tel.' That might have been where the name Tellia comes from. So the Mage King is from Tel and makes the wasp soldiers to fight against Ternara."

"Remember, I was the one who figured it out. Where's the Ternara word? Ah! I can read that. And the one you're pointing at is ta epis lam—Tel."

"That's very good. But you see what I mean about the odd shape of some of the letters." Kurash rolled the scroll and stood. "I'm going out to the garden."

"I'll meet you at Pyxis shop."

Kurash felt that he was teetering on the edge of understanding something important. As he walked to his secret garden, he carried a sack over his shoulder with a seed from a digitalis flower. While he planted it, he felt that the sketches had planted something in his mind, but he couldn't avoid a disquiet that came with it. There was something missing.

"Oh Great Dianthus," he uttered after the ritual mid-day prayer, "help me to see what I have not seen—to understand the truth, to know how I should serve you."

When he stood, he looked directly at his drying rock and saw it, for the first time, for what it was, "a city of giant buildings under the hills." Judging from the quarry, he would need to dig a hole over twenty times his height to reach the first horizontal seam. Kurash climbed up on the drying rock and looked about in all directions. In the distance, he identified three other hills of equal height with at least some exposed white stone. *This is Tel.* He wondered how much lay hidden beneath the ground.

But the thought of wealth reminded him of the impact of the recent treasure distribution. Everyone had more to spend, so the cost of everything rose accordingly.

He returned to the town, seeing more suspicious hills along the way. The town itself seemed to be one of those hills. The streets cried out to him. None of them was paved in separate stones. They were all a continuous slab of well-worn white stone. He wondered if anyone had ever bothered to notice. Perhaps Dianthus was answering his prayer.

Kurash stooped as he entered the sculptor's shop. Pyxis glanced at him, then returned his gaze to the sketch of the possible Saracets. "I see what you mean."

"Part of it's missing," Alketas said to Kurash. "See how the other ones show that Mage guy with the big wings making one thing out of another? He turns the wasps into those soldiers in that one. He turns those humans into giant Faeries with really big wings. There he changes lizards into those little fire lizard things with wings. Well, he's not even in this sketch."

"I copied it all," Pyxis insisted."

"No you didn't," the boy replied. "It's on the block of stone they cut away when they discovered the room."

"Of course!" Pyxis said. "We have to find it."

The three of them set out for the quarry. Although Kurash assumed that the stories in all the paintings were myth, learning what the Saracets came from seemed important, even if only a myth. He saw more suspicious hills along the way.

At the edge of the quarry, only one block near the bottom appeared to be the one that had been cut from the treasure chamber. It had apparently been simply toppled out of the way in their hurry to get into the chamber. Alketas climbed down into the vast pit. Kurash and Pyxis followed. The gouge marks in the talus indicated that the block had slid down on its outer surface, then flipped over near the bottom, leaving the painted side down when it came to rest at an angle.

Alketas lay on his back and shuffled beneath the block. "It's here!" he shouted. "It's so big and so close to my face, I can't tell what I'm looking at." He shuffled his way back out.

The block of stone was as tall and as thick as Kurash's height, and twice as long. He studied the slope of dust and white stone fragments that supported the stone in its present position. "It would take about ten workers with ropes to move this anywhere, maybe more."

"Maybe," Pyxis suggested, "if we dug a wide trench just down slope from it, we could get it to stand up or flip over."

"What if it moves while we're digging the trench?" Alketas asked.

"What if it doesn't move after we dig the trench?" Pyxis added.

"Maybe we could pay the quarry workers to help us?"

"You forget, Alketas, that they are all wealthy," Pyxis replied.

Kurash walked up the slope and shoved the stone with his hands. It did not move. "I guess we dig the trench."

"That will take days," Alketas complained.

"Wait," Pyxis said. "The image of the Mage King on the other walls was ten times the size of this block. It made sense, looking at my sketch, but the actual paintings are twenty times bigger than my sketches. I feel stupid."

"So it can't be under there," Kurash said.

"Then where is it?" Alketas asked.

"The pictures on these two walls are complete," Kurash said, pointing to sketches on opposite walls of the sculpture shop. "I can read most of the words. This one says the Mage King used magic to make the wasps into soldiers, to send an army against Ternara. This one says he used powerful magic to give wings to the human army of Tel, to send against Ternara."

Darissa, Pyxis and Alketas sat on the work bench as he spoke. None of them seemed impressed by what he had said.

"The other two walls, opposite each other," he continued, "each show only part of a picture. None of the figures is cut off, but the words on this side stop halfway through a statement. On the other side, the words are only the end of a statement. These two walls are longer than what we've seen. 'The Mage King used magic to give reptiles wings and...' But on the other wall it says, '...to send against the forces of Ternara.' The wall with the winged humans is a door. There must be another room where the pictures continue."

"I would like to help," Pyxis said, "but I need to spend more time in my shop. I'm losing business."

Darissa appeared uncomfortable. "Me too."

"Mama," Alketas said, almost inaudibly, "I still have treasure."

She put her arm around her son. "That won't last much longer."

He squirmed from her arm. "It'll last a little longer."

Her hand covered her mouth as she nodded. "Okay, sweetie."

Kurash studied the wall that he guessed to be a door. The late day sun illuminated it. Its edges were slightly rounded where it met the side walls, leaving a deep crease on either edge.

Darissa had brought a broom, as well as a small oil lamp. "It needs a good sweeping," she said. Her first stroke of the broom against the debris accumulated at the base of the "door" wall sank beneath it. More carefully, she swept away the dust and fragments from the corner all the way to the middle of the wall. Then she pushed the broom beneath the wall in sweeps that pulled debris from under that section.

"Mama. I can get under there."

"Let me sweep it one more time." When fully half the length of the wall's base had been cleared, she stopped. "There's a post in the middle."

"The whole wall must turn on the post." Kurash looked up at the full height of the door. "There is no way we will ever move that."

The door towered well over eighty times Kurash's height and spanned an equal width.

Without waiting any longer, Alketas scooted beneath it. "There's a big chamber," his muffled voice said, "as big as the first one. It's pretty dark."

Kurash squeezed his way beneath the door. The distance he crawled seemed to be about five times his height, before he was able to stand again.

"There's a lot of stuff in here," Alketas said.

"I can hear you, but I can't see you."

"When you get used to it, you can kind of see things."

A band of light wavered near the floor as Darissa came through with her oil lamp. When she stood with her lamp, she gasped.

On the far side of the room, on a stone slab that rose toward the head, lay a human-size skeleton in a state of crumbling. Its tumbled feet faced them. Much of it was hidden by the mass of the slab. The far wall, behind the skeleton, was hung with human-size weapons of every sort, most decorated in gold and mounted with translucent green stones and green stone handles.

To either side of the skeleton's slab stood huge golden pots and pitchers. What appeared to be the crumbled remains of a wood box spilled massive disks of gold onto the floor. Alketas stepped up onto one of the disks, as thick as the span of his hand, and of a diameter equal to his height.

"It's a human coin," the boy said. "It has writing around it, with somebody's face in the center. Oh! Look at those." Among the coins and urns to the side of the slab, a deformed, skeletal wing lay in large fragments. "It must have broken off that skeleton."

Kurash walked to the other side of the slab. "Here's the other one." He climbed the handle of an urn to view more of the skeleton. "It has no teeth. It must have been an old man...or old woman...when it died."

The light changed as Darissa walked closer to the continuation of the wall that depicted the fire lizards. It showed them over a huge city besieged by all of the armies created by the Mage King. This was followed by an image in which the Mage King holds a sword from which a beam of light shines on the fire lizards. The lizards are now shown in an enormous size, with a vast wingspan, over the same city, gouts of fire belching from their mouths. All the other besiegers have vanished.

Kurash opened his scroll and recorded the words stretching beneath the images. When he had finished, they turned with the lamp to the back side of the great swivel door. On it was a map with two cities depicted, one labeled Ternara, shown in ruins, the other identified as Tel.

"This is Ternaria," Kurash said. "Look at the rivers."

"And Tel," Darissa observed, "must be where Tellia now stands."

"This tomb is part of Tel." Kurash explained his secret observations. "All the hills around here are the buildings of Tel, buried under two thousand years of dirt."

They turned with the lamp to the remaining wall, a continuation of the depiction of what appeared to be Saracets. There, the Mage King transforms a herd of hornless black cattle, all cows, save for one thick shouldered bull, with horns that spread well above its proud head. Kurash had no difficulty reading the text beneath it.

"The Ephor and the Archon have agreed to divide the treasure five ways," Alketas said. He sat beside Kurash on his bed within his tiny house.

Kurash had little interest in the treasure. The Faeries had been justified in looking down on him all this time. He was nothing more than the spawn of cattle.

"The Archon will figure out how to cut it all up," Alketas continued, "and hand it out. Then each of the four of us gets one fifth of it."

"The text that I copied," Kurash mumbled while staring at the floor, "said that when the Mage King used magic to make the fire lizards increase to a great size—he called them 'Dragomin'—it consumed the life of all his other armies. He made us the size we are now, but thought he destroyed us. I guess he didn't really care, as long as he could destroy Ternara with his Dragomin."

"Oh, and Pyxis made this for you." Alketas handed Kurash a square of reed paper. "He said we missed it when we were there. It was at the base of that big slab with the broken down skeleton."

Kurash accepted the paper and read it aloud. "Dianthus, Mage King of Tel." He wept.

"What's wrong?"

"I prayed to Dianthus that he would show me a sign, that he would help me find the truth. Now I've found the truth. The truth is that my god was the Mage King who made us from cattle. We were slaves to the Mage King. My god was the Mage King who did all these terrible things in order to destroy a city. The truth is that he was human." Then in a sob, he shouted, "The truth is that my god is dead!"

"But he answered your prayer."

CHAPTER 13—DANCING ROUND THE LILAC STONE

The circular promenade within the lilac grove was crowded with pilgrims, nearly a hundred Faeries, mostly parents accompanying their pubescent daughters, when the attack came. Caluño had plenty of experience driving off the troublesome insects that occasionally intruded on the pilgrimage. That was his duty. But it was not insects that he saw today. Four battle shrews swept below the ring of trees on the far side of his position. Lashed to the back of each shrew, an armored turret carried three dark-skinned Saracets. One guided the vicious mount with sharpened prods, one wielded heavy thorn spears, while the third handled the casting nets.

"Climb the trees!" he shouted, knowing that few could hear him above their screams of panic.

Faeries who opposed the shrews were eaten alive or killed by the thorn spears, then eaten.

Caluño waited until the nearest shrew came within range of his raspberry pike, then heaved it at the turret. A Saracet netter toppled onto the ground. Before some of the Faeries in the promenade understood what was happening, the shrews were gone, together with five young Faeries that the Saracets had captured in their nets.

Berenguer lifted his rod of office to silence the council. "You implore me to take on the mantle of Dictator." He pulled at his white beard. "You relinquish all debate. If that is what you believe is required in this crisis, then I lay aside my office as Elder and accept your calling." Berenguer unfolded a scarlet sash and tied it over his white tunic diagonally, shoulder to waist. "I declare myself Dictator." He turned to Caluño. "As First Tribune, it will fall upon you to slay anyone who questions my word."

Caluño was not expecting such a responsibility. He scanned the faces of the council. Each nodded in turn. "I will do it." Caluño was not at all certain that he would carry out a summary execution, if it came to that.

"Nebridio," Berenguer continued, "Since you have seen more war than any of us, I name you Strategus. You will assemble and command, to my will, whatever forces you require." From a small sack, the Dictator lifted a silk cord, at the center of which was attached a small, transparent lilac prism. He handed it to Nebridio. "Your stone of command."

"Yes, Dictator," he replied. Nebridio tied the lilac prism about his neck. Though younger than Berenguer, age was beginning to show on the tall, vigorous Faerie. "I would select Vifredo as my lieutenant."

"So be it," Berenguer intoned. He passed a similar, though colorless prism necklace to Vifredo. "Seventeen are dead and five have been carried away, including my granddaughter, Riquilda. We will discover where the Saracets call home, and we will wage war upon them. They have, no doubt, taken captives in other villages, so allies will be plentiful and eager for retribution. I will continue as Dictator until I have decided the crisis is over. Caluño, you have traveled Ternaria. What do you know about these creatures?"

"I know very little about them," Caluño answered. "They are thought to live somewhere far to the south."

"They are a dark race of Thistlepix," Vifredo stated.

"I understand," Caluño said, "that they are neither Faerie nor Thistlepix, but a more primitive animal. As you saw from the one we killed, their bodies are much taller, but with a small head. I have heard that they trade with the Thistlepix, but I have no idea what they trade."

"So you know more than 'very little' about them, Tribune." The Dictator frowned at Caluño. "And their strength of arms?"

Caluño knew nothing more, other than that the dead one had only the sort of teeth that grass eaters possessed. He deferred to Nebridio.

The new Strategus rose to his feet in the soft soil of the now-deserted promenade. With a twig, he drew a gentle arc, open to the south. He positioned his feet at the center of the arc. "I have spoken with the ambassadors. If I stand where we now meet, at Lilac, then all the villages that have been attacked fall on this curve or farther south. We are the most distant from where the Saracets live. We must assume that the four battle shrews represent a mere fraction of their full strength. Though the villages to the south of us were attacked just as we were, they have mustered neither the will nor the courage to resist. I am certain they will join our effort, but we will need to recruit stronger allies from the north."

"Send messengers," Berenguer ordered.

Caluño marched beside Vifredo, as the young lieutenant led a reconnaissance of twenty lightly armed Faerie skirmishers. Information from the villages they passed during the previous two weeks directed them to the south-east in their pursuit of the Saracet's home.

Vifredo picked slender, barbed seeds, each the length of his little finger, from the lower edges of his lilac tunic and flicked them away. "Cursed little things!" The black hems of his garment indicated his office as Third Tribune, an office which continued, despite being named lieutenant.

"Do they weigh too much?" Caluño chuckled.

"You might tend to your own hoary tunic," he replied, pointing to the seed-speckled white border of Caluño's lilac tunic. "Have you seen Nebridio's bronze sword?"

"Yes. He always wears it during times of war."

"How does an old Faerie come by a bronze sword?"

"Nebridio never speaks of it, but some have said that it was presented to him by the Faerie Lord of Kizikum, after Nebridio destroyed the great stone city."

The terrain was becoming more arid. The trees were less frequent, less luxuriant in their foliage, and concentrated mainly in the cuts of dry stream beds. Brown grasses and aromatic thorn bushes predominated over rocky hills. Vifredo skillfully led them through the meandering low areas, maintaining only two well-concealed advance scouts on the higher ground to either side. Though the younger Vifredo, as Third Tribune, was subordinate to Caluño in all civic matters, their relationship was reversed on this military excursion.

One of the scouts returned at a jog. Drawing up before Vifredo, he thumped his right fist to his chest, in salute. "A patrol of two battle shrews moves slowly toward us in the next valley to the east. Far beyond, I see smoke rising." The scout described the lay of the land

and the route of the shrews, drawing in the desiccated soil with the butt of his raspberry pike.

"We will take them here," Vifredo said, pointing to a narrow cut through which they would likely pass, "as we have trained. Caluño, deploy the forces with the required gear."

"Perhaps we should hide and let them pass."

"I want a prisoner to question. Only two shrews is our good fortune. We will take them."

Vifredo accompanied the scout to his vantage point. Caluño sent a messenger to the other advance scout to apprise him of the plan, then set about organizing the ambush. Once all the non-essentials had been stashed, he deployed the Faeries, who carried only their pikes or bow and quiver, along with four long silk ropes. At the selected spot, Caluño supervised the placement and concealment of four snares as well as the positioning of his forces. There they waited.

After half an hour, Vifredo returned. "They stopped for a rest," he panted, "but they've started again. The shrews are bigger than the ones that attacked Lilac."

"Will our ropes hold," Caluño asked.

"Hold or not, we will take them. With sixteen on the ropes, that leaves only the two of us against six Saracets, until the ropes are tied."

"Hopefully, surprise will work in our favor." Caluño readied his bow.

As the two shrews approached, each nearly triple Caluño's height, they became restive, apparently sensing the presence of the hidden Faeries, but their drivers simply prodded them more aggressively with their pikes. The other two riders in each turret paid no attention to the shrews or their surroundings.

Caluño released his arrow, then made a high pitched "kee", attempting to imitate the sound of a bird of prey in the distance. One passenger from the second shrew slumped into the turret.

At the sound, both shrews froze and looked up at the sky. Loops of rope rose from beneath a thin layer of dirt, ensnaring each of the front legs of the lead shrew. Its legs suddenly moved apart, as four Faeries to either side of the trail passed their ropes around sturdy shrubs, then pulled the far ends back toward the shrew. When its feet were spread enough so that its razor teeth could not reach the ropes, they tied them off, took up their weapons and converged on the enemy. The thrashing of the shrew had thrown its occupants to the ground empty handed. An arrow from Vifredo dropped one Saracet. They easily dispatched the other two with their pikes. Nine Faeries then attempted to kill the panic stricken, though still deadly shrew.

Simultaneous with the snaring of the lead shrew, the hidden ropes were pulled to ensnare the second beast. The loop beneath its left front leg, the one closest to Caluño, closed and held, but the right leg escaped its snare. The surprised shrew dumped its three riders, one already dead or wounded, then turned toward the four Faeries pulling the rope on its left leg.

"Wrap it twice!" Caluño shouted.

The shrew ran so much faster than the Faeries, that it nearly caught them before the rope, looping twice around one shrub somersaulted the creature in its pursuit of its tormentors.

"Tie it!"

The four Faeries with the unsuccessful snare ran to help their comrades. By taunting the tethered shrew with pricks of their pikes, they distracted it from chewing at the one rope that held it.

With obsidian shards, both front legs of the lead shrew were slashed just above the ropes which held them. Blood pumped in rapid spurts, until its thrashing abruptly ceased.

When Caluño turned to the remaining Saracets, one had fled in the direction from which it had come. The other was running toward Caluño with a heavy pike half again as long as the Faerie's raspberry pikes. With his opponent closing fast on him, preventing him from nocking an arrow, he turned to run toward his troops. Instead, he tripped over a taught rope and landed on his side, bruising his wing.

He rolled over to see the dark skin of the looming Saracet blossom in a patch of blood. It plucked an arrow from its chest, then another. A final arrow through its right eye brought it down.

Vifredo hoisted Caluño to his feet. He pointed to the last shrew, still tethered by one leg, but still holding off the attempts of sixteen Faeries to subdue it. "Arrows can't penetrate well."

Caluño painfully rotated his wings. "One escaped."

"We have to kill this thing before it breaks free."

At the standoff, Caluño positioned eight Faeries on either side of the shrew, while he and Vifredo approached its head, taunting it, to keep the rope tight. At his signal, the two lines of Faeries pressed their pikes into its chest from opposite sides. Unable to recoil, the shrew shuddered as sixteen pikes entered its body. In a moment it was over.

"I had hoped to capture one of the Saracets alive," Vifredo said. "Now, one has run back to warn them of our presence."

"The next ambush may not be ours."

"But we can not return to Lilac without learning the whereabouts of the captives. Berenguer will not stop while Riquilda is still held."

"Perhaps a larger force would have a better chance of success." Caluño shouted orders to retrieve all the gear and reassemble. "This was only two shrews and six Saracets. And surprise was with us."

"Nebridio felt that a small force was more likely to make it past their defenses without risking a full battle, before we understand our enemy."

The eighteen Faeries marched on in the direction from which the Saracet patrol had come. Caluño felt confident that the two advance scouts would remain ahead of them. That evening, they stopped for the night at a seep spring, since the terrain was becoming drier and rockier the farther they ventured.

As they ate their breakfast of seeds, one of the advance scouts stumbled into camp, exhausted and covered in reddish dust. He immediately sought out Vifredo, who stood with Caluño. They conjectured on the reason for his return.

"Vifredo," he said, fatigue in his voice, "I have located the Saracets. I tracked the one who escaped the ambush all the way to their home. Once it was clear where he was headed, I killed him and hid the body. You will have to look at their defenses for yourself. Only your own eyes will convince you of what I saw."

The Dictator listened impatiently as his Strategus, Nebridio, presented to the council of Lilac all that had been learned about their enemy and the captives.

"Mount Gumush is a low mountain with a ridge that runs north to south." Nebridio used his forearm, held vertically, to represent the mountain ridge, pointing with his finger to indicate the geography. "Its east face is an unapproachable cliff. A great city, Seraz, is perched on its western slope. South of the city, but higher up the slope, are mines that pierce the mountain. It is there that we believe the captives are held."

"Then we send a force only to the mines," Berenguer interjected.

"If I may continue, Dictator?"

"Of course. Go on."

"All of this—the ridge of the mountain, the city, the mines—as well as the fields and pastures, is surrounded by a high wall of stone, ten faerielongs high. Along that wall, within bow's-shot of one another, are forty stone towers—forty, standing higher than the walls. There are four gates that pass into the city. Each gate is defended by two additional towers."

Caluño shook his head at the recollection of having viewed Seraz with Vifredo. Before the council meeting, he had expressed to Nebridio his opinion that no Faerie force could hope to conquer such a place. The Strategus had told him that Berenguer held two objectives beyond discussion: the rescue of Riquilda and a return of paying pilgrims to Lilac's grove.

"The Saracets do not guard the mines themselves. Instead, at each entrance are kept toads which devour anyone who attempts to pass."

"How do the Saracets pass?" Berenguer asked.

"That is not known," Nebridio replied. "They have as many as one hundred battle shrews." A gasp spread among the council members. "It seems that the attacks on villages are as important for feeding their shrews as for acquiring captives. In addition, the population of Seraz is said to be counted at ten thousand." Whispers began.

"So what is it they dig from the mines?" a council member asked.

Nebridio appeared puzzled. He gestured to Caluño.

"Silver metal. They trade it to the Thistlepix," Caluño answered.

The Dictator's attention revived. "But silver metal is poisonous."

"Only to Faeries," Caluño said.

"The captives are Faeries. How can they mine it without being poisoned?" Berenguer asked, fear showing on his wrinkled face.

"I don't know Dictator. I'm sorry."

"Strategus, you must find a way to rescue my granddaughter. To rescue all the captives, of course."

Nebridio continued. "Many villages have offered what forces they have, and are willing to serve at my command. But we will not succeed by strength. Only by subterfuge."

"Succeed any way you choose, but you must succeed."

"Yes, Dictator."

The allied Faerie army assembled before the great stone walls of Seraz. A thousand Faeries stood in ranks before the main western gate. Among them were not only foot soldiers, but also archers from Domes, mounted on apis drones, a contingent of huge, black bombi and a small strike force on humming birds from Oakhaven. A train of mice carried all the supplies, while tortoises hauled dozens of scaling ladders that had been assembled in Lilac. On their approach, the Saracets had withdrawn behind their massive, well supplied fortifications, leaving the Faerie host in the barren wasteland beyond the walls.

Nebridio, wearing a bronze sword at his side, spoke privately with Caluño and Vifredo. "Berenguer meddles in too many matters that he does not understand. He rides here on the back of a mouse, like an old spinster, and then supersedes my orders with a whim."

"We are sworn to obey him, so long as he is Dictator," Vifredo reminded his superior.

"I don't know how to succeed without violating that oath."

"Then we need to carry out plans that work...along side...his plans" Caluño suggested. "We allow his hopeless frontal assault to serve as a diversion for us."

Vifredo looked at him expectantly. "Do we have our own plans?"

"We can not take this city by force," the Strategus said again. "We may be able to bring out some or all of the captives if the attention of the Saracets is directed elsewhere."

"If we can sneak in and out to rescue captives," Vifredo pointed out, "we can sneak in and take their leader as a hostage."

Nebridio paused for a moment. "Vifredo, develop a plan to do that. Caluño, plan a way to release the captives. Both of you come to me in the morning with your ideas. Meanwhile, I have to find a way not to throw away our lives and those of our allies, simply to please the Dictator."

"Strategus, with respect," Vifredo retorted, a didactic tone in his voice, "Berenguer did not ask to be named Dictator. It is we who chose him as Dictator. It is we who surrendered all debate to him."

Caluño placed a hand on Vifredo's shoulder. "Take care with your words, my friend."

"You may go, Lieutenant. First Tribune, remain."

After Vifredo departed, Nebridio spoke softly to Caluño. "We are doomed. If we can not succeed, Berenguer will never relinquish the dictatorship. If we do succeed, the prestige and power will intoxicate him with delusions of his own importance. I fear that Vifredo has sensed that path to power. He has no more confidence in the old fool's decisions than you or I do. It is absolute power that he supports."

"Vifredo is skilled and dedicated, if a bit rash," Caluño replied. "His youth and enthusiasm do him no favors. Maybe the course of events will show him a more reasonable path."

Early the following morning, after explaining to Nebridio his plan to rescue the captives, and receiving his tacit approval, Caluño set out alone to circle to the southernmost extent of the great wall, keeping well beyond the sight of the Saracet eyes in the towers. Armed with only a raspberry pike and an obsidian shard, he moved along the shadows of the low hills and scrub-filled gullies. A trickle of water flowed from the direction of the southern wall, at the point where the stonework began its steep ascent toward the ridge of Mount Gumush.

He had pointed out to the Strategus that the land which supported the wall on the southern side of the city lay slightly lower than that of the north. Since they had learned that there were springs within the city, Caluño assumed that the water must somehow flow beneath the wall to the south. He crept along the rivulet toward the wall, keeping beneath the increasingly verdant vegetation. So far as Caluño could tell, the Saracets had not bothered to clear even those shrubs immediately adjacent to the wall. *They are overconfident!*

A stone arch, nearly twice the width of his body, but only knee high, marked the source of the water. A dark grid over the opening allowed only water to pass. Caluño grasped the grid with his hands, to see if it could be loosened, but it was firmly attached to the wall. A dot of light shined at the far end of the tunnel.

When he released the grid, Caluño recoiled at the appearance of his hands. Every skin surface that had touched the grid had changed to black. He immediately submerged his hands in the rivulet, but the black would not wash off. *Silver metal.*

Any noise might draw the attention of the Saracets, but somehow he needed to get past the silver grid. He tested the edge of his obsidian shard against the metal. A bright silver gouge appeared. By stroking the shard across the metal at a specific angle, it caused small metal shavings to drop away. After an hour of tedious effort, Caluño had cut through all the rods at one side of the grid, which then bent easily to open the passage. He crawled on his elbows through the tunnel, scraping green algae onto his wings for the entire distance.

When Caluño finally emerged into the daylight inside the southern wall, he was dumbfounded at the sight. The sun was just now rising above the ridge to the east, lighting up the distant circuit of towers in a golden white brilliance of stone pickets. Within the wide plain enclosed by the walls stood immense groves of cherries ripe with fruit, loquats, date palms, apricots, almonds, cashews and other fruit and nut trees that he could not identify. Wide gardens were planted with blueberries, blackberries, raspberries and sweet greens of every sort.

Most surprising was to see all these tended by hundreds of Faeries. They moved about freely, with no apparent supervision. A small herd of dairy mice munched at baskets of seeds, carelessly watched by several Faeries who appeared to be passing the sunny morning telling tales to one another. Other Faeries walked leisurely along the well tended paths that led up to the city. What struck Caluño as truly odd was that none of these Faeries seemed at all aware that an opposing army stood just outside the gates.

Caluño moved into the shadows that still clung to the western slope of Mount Gumush. The only Saracets that he could see were those patrolling the top of the wall, and a few visible in the windows of the stone towers. He realized that he and the council of Lilac had based their decisions on incorrect information. But for now, his mission remained that of locating and freeing the captives.

From his location, he could identify two paths leading up from the city to two dark openings in the face of the mountain slope. Occasionally, a cart pulled by a Faerie entered or exited each of the openings. As with the Faeries in the fields and groves, these Faeries appeared to be under no duress. He began the steep ascent, doing his best to remain hidden by rocks, shadows and vegetation. If the Saracets intended a sortie against the Faeries, it would be at this time of day, when the sun over Mount Gumush was at their backs and in the eyes of the besiegers, but as he climbed higher, he could see no preparations for action. The high walls and towers were guarded by Saracets; the Faeries within those walls went about their daily business. Caluño formed some new notions about the real situation in Seraz, but he needed to reach the captives to verify his suspicions. He continued climbing through the rocks.

At the path entering the nearest mine entrance, Caluño, First Tribune of Lilac, with his hands now blackened and his wings smeared by the green slime of the tunnel beneath the great wall, waited in the shadows until the path was clear, then slipped into the dark entrance. Thirty paces beyond, he sighted the silhouettes of two great toads, one on either side of the mine tunnel. Sooty flames guttered and glowed on the tunnel walls further in. Pressing himself against the wall, he advanced, holding his raspberry pike ready.

The nearer he crept to the toads, the larger they appeared. He guessed their height to be over three times his own. They squatted motionless, facing each other, with just enough space between them for one of the carts to pass. He could see a chain holding the nearest toad close against the tunnel wall. He wondered if they were alive.

A rumbling sound from within the tunnel sent Caluño crouching into a deep crevice in the wall. A Faerie, one of the contented ones, walked slowly toward the toads, pulling a two-wheel cart by its limbs. At the moment that it passed between the closed mouths of the toads, the Faerie positioned his back close to the body of the cart. Together, cart and Faerie appeared as a single, large object, passing safely. Caluño could see within the cart piles of curled, blackened silver.

Close behind the cart, a second Faerie, covered with filth, wings blackened, hesitated momentarily between the toads, his eyes wide with terror. The instant that he lurched forward to catch up with the cart, two broad tongues, sparkling with moisture, silently lashed out from opposite directions. Each tongue took half of the doomed Faerie and disappeared into the toads' mouths.

Bile rose into Caluño's throat. He would somehow have to kill one or both of the toads in order for all but the most agile to pass. The blackened Faerie had verified that there were captives within the mine, and that at least some made attempts to escape. After assuring himself that the nearest toad was chained by both legs, preventing it from turning, he shuffled against the wall to a spot nearly behind the dull brown, lumpy creature. By climbing to a precarious outcrop, barely large enough for him to sit with legs dangling, he positioned himself above the wide, warty back of the deadly sentry.

With a leap, Caluño drove his raspberry pike into its neck, just at the base of its skull. The pike punctured the tough skin and slid easily into its head. The toad trembled slightly, but otherwise seemed unaffected by the wound. With his feet now on the toad's back, he swiveled the pike back and forth within the toad's skull. Uncertain of what he had accomplished, he withdrew the now bloody pike and touched its tip to the toad's eye. No response. He poked the tip firmly into the edge of the eye. Although the toad occasionally breathed, it was otherwise oblivious.

Caluño jumped down on the far side of the disabled toad and studied the other. He saw no way to safely reach a position above it. Judging from the distance between the mouths of the two toads, a Faerie could pass close to the mouth of one while remaining beyond the reach of the other's tongue. With the pike, he prodded the unresponsive toad on its jaw, took a deep breath, and walked between them, staying as far from the still deadly one as he could. The healthy toad made no effort. He passed between them again, this time more confident, and headed deeper into the mine.

Widely spaced torches, alternating on either side of the tunnel walls, led his way, as did the foul fumes that emanated from whatever kept them burning. Well into the mine, he noticed that the smoke seemed to be blowing away from a cleft in the upper wall and out toward the mine entrance. Although the cleft was dark, it clearly opened to the outside. The opening admitted him, and the climbing was fairly easy. His only doubt that this might serve as a route of escape was his knowledge that a Faerie would have still risked the passage between the toads.

A quarter hour of following the freshening breeze upward brought him toward light and a leveling of the grade of the passage. At a sharp turn, he was startled to find himself in a bright forest of angular, lilac stones. Far overhead, an unreachable opening admitted sunlight which scattered in a spectacular array of bright dots and lines onto the walls of the chamber. The massive lilac stones, rising as six-sided towers, some vertical, many standing at angles, others broken and lying on the floor, echoed the sun like light through frozen lilac water. Most ended in a sharp bevel or in a perfect, six-sided point. With the movement of the sun, the light diminished, but the breath-taking beauty remained. He headed back down the way he came.

Deep within the mine, he arrived at a deserted side chamber that appeared to be a sleeping area for the captives. In the distance, he heard the dull clack of stone axes. Caluño walked cautiously toward the sound. At the furthest extent of the mine, a bedraggled group of about thirty Faeries harvested large curls of silver metal from the floor and walls, tossing the liberated chunks into a pile behind them. Each of the miners was unmistakably a Faerie, but with black skin and pitiful black wings. He recognized none of them.

"Is Riquilda here?"

One by one the miners stopped their labor and turned to stare blankly at Caluño. He could now see that all of them were young, the oldest barely of age.

"If they catch you not working," said a male youth with a hoarse voice, "they won't let you eat." He and the others returned to their task of mining silver metal.

A younger boy squinted at him. "He carries a pike."

"I am Caluño, First Tribune of Lilac. We have an army of a thousand Faeries standing at the walls of Seraz. Come with me now."

"But there is a second mine, Dictator," Caluño repeated.

"How do we know Riquilda is there? Maybe she is being kept as a special hostage." Berenguer fumed as he paced beneath a palm frond that had been erected as his traveling council chamber and headquarters. "My granddaughter would be of great value to them for bargaining."

"The Saracets may not know nor care about her identity," the Strategus pointed out. "We will of course make another effort."

"In the future, Nebridio, you will inform me, in advance, of any...plans...that you invent."

The Strategus' right hand moved to the pommel of his bronze sword. Instead, he lifted the lilac prism from around his neck and offered it to the Dictator. "I am not worthy of the office. I resign. I will fight as a common soldier."

"Don't be ridiculous. I don't allow you to resign." Berenguer turned his back on his Strategus. "Now go get ready for the assault."

"But, Dictator," Caluño interjected, "the situation is so different from what we had thought."

"Are you questioning my decision, Tribune?"

"Of course not, Dictator, but we may not have to take the walls."

"Our victory will be all the easier. Your assignment is to go back and find Riquilda. And the others."

"Yes, Dictator," Caluño replied.

"Now both of you," he shooed them with his hands, "go do your duty."

Nebridio spoke softly to Caluño as they walked away from the headquarters. "I see you avoided telling him that all the captives have been blackened by the silver metal. That was wise." He looked up at the early afternoon sun. "You have about three hours before the sun is in our favor and that ignorant old buffoon orders the assault."

"Any word from Vifredo?"

"Nothing." Nebridio stopped to place the prism of office around his neck. "If you are unable to locate Riquilda with the remaining miners, bring them out before you look further."

"I will do that, Strategus."

"Tell me your impression of the free Faeries you saw. Do you believe they are complicit in the crimes of the Saracets, or are they victims as well?"

"Perhaps both. You should speak with the captives."

Nebridio nodded. As Caluño turned to head back to the mines, the Strategus touched his shoulder. "Caluño, my friend, take care. They are probably aware of the escape by now. And I'm afraid I may need your support for another difficult task, once we have finished here and returned to Lilac."

Caluño knew he could only mean the Dictator and his growing hunger for power.

Poor Riquilda—her fair skin poisoned with silver metal, her lovely wings shriveled and blackened like fireblight—was among the fifty captives Caluño found. The second mine was still unguarded when he entered. He had been able to pith the brains of both toads and make it to the miners at the far end of the tunnel. He tried to comfort the Dictator's granddaughter, but her feeble sobs continued. He hurried the captives out of the mine, toward the water drain at the base of the south wall, but from his vantage as they passed the entrance of the first mine, he saw two Saracets direct Faeries to block the waterway with stones. They were trapped.

"We will have to hide for now." He turned them around and led them into the first mine. Caluño explained to them that only the toad on their right was safe. Passing so close that he brushed against the mouth of the right toad, he led them past, with Riquilda's shoulders pressed to his chest. At the sound of gasps, he turned to see black Faerie wings protruding from the mouth of the other toad. It chewed twice, then the wings vanished.

"Stay to the side," he said, louder than he had intended.

Several of those near the back of the line fled at the horror, and ran out of the mine. Just then a dull roar of voices and the screams of distant battle drifted into the mine. The assault had begun.

The First Tribune of Lilac led the captives up into the chamber of lilac stones. With their many hands, he quickly had the passage blocked behind them with whatever stones they could find. All they could do now was await the outcome of the battle.

With the passage blocked, no outside sounds, other than the wind at the opening high above his head, penetrated into the chamber. Riquilda was in no condition to talk, so he spoke with some of the others about the Saracets and the free Faeries within the walls.

"One of the carters told me that his parents, when they were children, were among the last Faeries allowed outside the gates," an older boy explained. "That was when the Saracets came."

"Do you know how many Saracets there are?" Caluño asked.

"No. But not very many. They're the only ones with weapons. And they have those shrews."

Caluño gathered what information he could. But the captives, most too young to know much beyond their own villages, could add very little. Hours passed.

All of them wanted to know when they would eat next, and how they could clean away the black stains from their skin. He understood that it was likely permanent, but he kept that from them.

Gradually, the light faded, leaving them in total darkness. Caluño spoke softly and encouraged them to sleep while they could. He dozed off.

When Caluño awoke, the chamber seemed to be illuminated by a faint lilac glow. Above his head, moonlight shined on the upper edge of the wall. With so small an opening to the sky, the moon could actually be seen to move. He shifted his position so that he could look at the face of the moon through a transparent lilac pillar that stood at an angle.

The moon had never appeared so beautiful. More beautiful still was the sight of one of his hands. Where the moonlight had passed through the lilac stone before striking his hand, the skin, with a slight tingling, had been cleansed of the black stain of silver poison. He compared the palms of his two hands, then held the other in the lilac glow. In an instant, the black vanished.

Excited, he awakened Riquilda and brought her to the stone before the moon passed beyond the aperture. He held her facing the moonlight. To his amazement, her once-blackened wings took on a sparkling silvery glow.

When the girl saw that her hands had been cured of the poison, she removed all of her ragged clothing and danced in the lilac moonlight. "Oh, Caluño, you've done it!"

Caluño walked beside Vifredo as they passed beneath the main western gate of Seraz, escorting a now-clothed Riquilda to rejoin her grandfather. One of the free Faeries of the city had offered her finest gown.

"If one of them hadn't told us you hid in the mine," Vifredo said, "I don't know if we would have found you."

"What have you done with the shrews?" Caluño asked.

"The Faeries who tended them said that if they don't eat, they die within two days. We left them in their cages."

"I still don't understand about the uprising."

"I couldn't locate the Saracet leader," Vifredo explained, "He must have been in one of the towers. So I found the oldest Faeries and had them spread the word about the army outside the gates. The moment Berenguer's assault began, the Faeries inside the walls, almost eight thousand of them, took up whatever tools they could lay their hands on and killed every Saracet they found. They went up into the towers and swarmed the walls. I don't think we killed more than fifty of them ourselves."

"How many Saracets were there?"

"About two hundred. It's no wonder they didn't attempt a sortie. The shrews numbered about fifty." Vifredo laughed. "I'll bet the Dictator was disappointed."

Caluño directed the teams of Faeries holding the ropes that stretched from the massive lilac column, still lying on its ramp, all the way across the circular promenade in the center of the lilac grove. As they pulled, the base of the column tipped into his carefully designed pit at the very center of the promenade. Other ropes, pulled in the opposite direction, stabilized the great lilac stone, as it assumed a perfect vertical upon a flat base of sandstone. When it stopped rocking, the ropes were loosed and all those present, workers and spectators alike, cheered and clapped their hands.

Early that evening, the Dictator called a meeting of the council. Caluño assumed that the gathering had been convened so that Berenguer could relinquish the dictatorship.

"I have decided," the Dictator announced, "that we will reassemble the great Faerie army and finally stop the Thistlepix from threatening the lives of Faeries throughout Ternaria."

Most of those present sat in stunned silence. Only Vifredo seemed to have expected the decision. "It is true," the Third Tribune added, "that no single village has the strength to move offensively against them."

Nebridio stood, removed his prism of office as Strategus and forced it into Berenguer's hand. "I will not be a part of it."

"Are you questioning me?" the Dictator asked.

"There is no question," Nebridio spat. "The crisis is over. We have no need of a Dictator. I have no need of a Dictator. I'm done with it."

"You go too far!" Berenguer shouted, his wrinkled face turning red behind his white beard. "Tribune," he looked directly at Caluño, "he has broken his oath. You must do your duty. Now!"

As Caluño stood, he drew his obsidian shard from his belt. Walking to the unmoving Nebridio, whose bronze sword rested untouched in its scabbard, he placed his free hand on the older man's shoulder. "Nebridio is wise and he is my friend. I agree with him. You may choose now, Dictator, to give up your powers and live to see your granddaughter again, or I will spill your blood here in the council."

"This is treason!" the Dictator sputtered.

"Yes it is, of a sort," Caluño agreed. "Which will you choose?"

"Vifredo," Berenguer pleaded, "surely you have not been party to this conspiracy!"

Vifredo stood, also drawing his obsidian shard. He studied Nebridio and Caluño, as well as the silent members of the council, then looked at the frightened old man. "I am not a party to this conspiracy, but they speak what is in the minds of all those seated here. You may live and become a legend among the Faeries, or die on this spot a shameful death.

Caluño looked on as nearly eighty former captives, still blackened by the poison of the mines, held hands and circled the transparent lilac monolith in the warm night air. As the moon showed its face above the lilac grove, they released their hands, removed all their garments, and then danced in a moving circle. As the moonlight filtered through the stone column and illuminated each passing Faerie, the stains vanished, and his or her wings glowed sparkling silver against the shadows of the grove.

"See, grandfather," Riquilda said. "That's exactly what happened."

Beyond the sparkling wings of Riquilda, Berenguer turned to Caluño. "Perhaps, for a fee, we could expose the wings of pilgrims to silver metal, and then have them transformed by the lilac stone. What do you think?"

CHAPTER 14—THE JEWELERS OF SHIBAM

"So when were you going to tell me, Joshi?" Pippi was furious. "When I stepped into our boat?" Pippi paced about the common chamber of his house, while Joshi sat, apparently unperturbed by his tirade. "Oh, by the way, your half of the boat is really only a quarter of it."

"If you'd let me finish..." Joshi ran a tow barge between Lilac and Nettle Falls, but had finally been able to hire employees to take over much of the repetitious work.

"And sorry, Pippi, the politicians would like a bit more room for their elbows, so you'll have to sit this one out."

"Pippi!" Joshi rose to his feet. "It's twice the size we planned and has a mast that folds up or down."

"Meaning what?" Pippi had traveled more than anyone he knew, but almost all of it on foot.

"Meaning your lazy butt can sail back up river, instead of having to row back the whole way."

"Really?"

"And the council didn't actually buy half the boat. It's still completely ours when we get back."

"Still, you should have told me before you agreed. We had a business deal."

"I really didn't have a choice, and I would have wasted a day coming down here."

"So I guess we've traded rowing back for spending several weeks in close company with a Councilor and the First Tribune."

"It won't be so bad, Pippi. Caluño went to that school of yours, up in Faerie Ring."

"Yeah. When I was still in nappies. Then there's Ramún. Too bad Riquilda isn't coming, instead of her father. He's the most boring Faerie I know."

"He never lets her out of his sight. He'll probably lock Riquilda in the house with her mother while he's gone." Joshi raised his eyebrows. "You sure you don't want to get left behind?"

"Don't distract me, Joshi. You have to admit that you were a slug for not telling me about the changes."

"I, Joshi, am a slug. Now can we get past this?"

"Hello, Joshi." Pellana, Pippi's mother, entered the chamber.

"Hello, Ma'am."

"I'm glad I caught you both together," she said, taking a seat on a stool. "I wanted to say something about this expedition."

"Yes, Mama, we'll be careful."

"That's reassuring, Pippi. But this is a little more specific. I realize that you are both adults, and probably don't want to hear this, but just let me say my piece, then you can go back to being tireless explorers."

Joshi glanced at Pippi, then obediently sat down.

"I know that Ramún is going to be there, but still, you...both of you, Joshi, need to show consideration and respect. When you return, I want to hear only tales I can be proud of. And I want Ramún's opinion of you to be even higher than it is now. Remember that she's only sixteen."

"Mama," Pippi said, "I don't know what you're talking about."

Pellana's wings drooped. She covered a surprised smile with her fingertips. "You haven't heard. I wondered why you two were still arguing."

"Heard?" Pippi always found it annoying when his mother wallowed in cleverness.

"The council won't allow Caluño to be gone for so long, so Ramún has decided to take Riquilda along, instead."

"The best knowledge we have," Pippi explained to Ramún, "is that there are no falls bellow Nettle Falls, and that the river ends near a Faerie town called Tewesh." He and the Councilor sat across from one another at the two aft rowlocks, each leisurely rowing the boat downstream in synchrony, to give just enough headway for Joshi to steer it with the stern tiller.

"How can it just end?" Riquilda asked. She sat facing astern on the bench for the empty fore rowlock in front of Pippi. Her pure white hair fluttered over her shoulders in the gentle, westerly breeze.

"Of course it goes somewhere, Riqui," her father said.

"We think it flows south into a great sea," Pippi added, "but all of our information is passed along through four or five traders before it gets up to Lilac. Across the river from Tewesh, they say there is a human town."

"So the Nettle is the boundary of Ternaria there?" Ramún asked.

"That would seem so."

"The Nettle is in the middle of Ternaria at Lilac and Faerie Ring." Riquilda had studied at Faerie Ring for five seasons, and, unlike her father, could read and write. "Where does it start being the boundary?"

"I don't know," Pippi admitted. "When you go northwest to Moss Abbey, the only thing that looks different is that there are humans and human size buildings...and a lot of very large animals. If there's a boundary in the middle of nowhere, I don't know how you'd tell the difference."

"Don't the monks there know the boundaries of Ternaria?" Ramún had momentarily lifted his oar, causing the boat to veer slightly.

"Steady rowing, Councilor," Joshi reminded him.

"They must know," Pippi said. "But when I was there, they wouldn't talk about it. They use the sarcite stones our longhaulers bring to them to work some kind of magic that sustains the boundaries. The monks take turns tending to it day and night. I guess that's the best argument that Ternaria is not natural. It's not how things are supposed to be."

The Nettle River flowed largely to the south, through open grasslands and past occasional tributaries that sprouted stands of cattails partway into the main channel. Joshi's boat rode well on the water. The hold was completely decked over, accessible through a main hatch amid ship and a smaller hatch near the stern. In addition to the four rowing benches—each extending only a third of the way to the centerline—he had built a shallow bench beneath the gunwales on each side, reaching from the stern around to the bowsprit. His folding mast, with its single boom, lay across the midline from its hinge box at mid-ship to its support bracket on the transom, just above the rudder. He had loaded most of their supplies and some of their trade goods below, to provide ballast. The remaining trade items were lashed above deck to either side of the folded mast and forward of its hinge box. The deck was far enough above the waterline that Joshi had installed scuppers to drain away any water that might fall on it.

"We'll land for midday at the next handy spot," Joshi said.

Ramún seemed surprised. "Why stop?"

Joshi nodded toward Riquilda.

"Oh," the Councilor responded. "Of course. Good idea. Stop at midday. We can stretch our legs."

"Dragonfly!" Riquilda shouted. She squatted on the deck and raised the point of her raspberry pike.

Ramún and Pippi shipped their oars and did likewise. Joshi simply rolled under his stern bench, leaving one arm up to hold the tiller. The dragonfly zoomed in from up river and hovered above the drifting boat for a while, then moved out of sight down river.

When Pippi sat up on the bench again, they were headed directly for a small sand spit that protruded a short way into the western side of the Nettle, where the river entered a bend to the west. "That looks good to me."

"Agreed," Joshi said, slipping the bow straight onto the sand. "I guess we should always have at least one of us facing each direction."

"I wouldn't mind rowing backwards," Ramún said as he stepped off the bow with a mooring line.

Riquilda hopped on the sand carrying her pike, and vanished into the brush.

"Stretching her legs," Joshi said with a smile.

Ramún shrugged. "I forgot."

Pippi brought down his chart cylinder and carefully unsealed the cap. He sat on a rock, opened his small drawing satchel and began updating his map of Ternaria. He had meticulously copied it from his original. "How far walking would you guess we've come this morning, Joshi?"

"Maybe a day and a quarter?"

"What's that curved line down there?" Ramún stood over Pippi's shoulder and pointed to an arc near the south east corner of the map.

"Last year, I asked the southern traders in Lilac to find out how far each of the traders traveled, from one trade off to the next, all the way to Tewesh. Once they had passed the word along, and the numbers came back, it tallied to something between twenty and twenty-six days from Tewesh to Lilac walking. This arc represents twenty-three days from Lilac. We don't know how the lower river turns, so Tewesh could be anywhere along the arc. These dotted arcs are a day apart. So I figure our directions from the sun, and..." He placed a small circle and a brief note beside it. "...I mark where we've reached and where the river goes."

"That's very clever, Pippi," the Councilor said. "Did they teach you that up in Faerie Ring?"

"No. But they teach mathematics. I'm just putting it to use. Nobody has ever mapped all of Ternaria."

"I don't think they were teaching that when Caluño was there. At least he never mentioned mathematics. So what will you do with it when you're done?"

"Papa," Riquilda said, appearing from the undergrowth with a huge strip of bright orange nasturtium blossom draped over her shoulder and four of its seeds in her arms. "You are so thick sometimes. I'll bet not a day passes that you don't draw a map in the dirt to show pilgrims different roads in Lilac. Think of what it might mean to traders and travelers to have a map of Ternaria."

"If it increases trade, then I guess it's worth all the trouble. Are you going to share that, Riqui, or eat it all yourself?"

She dropped the seeds onto the sand and handed the blossom strip to her father to hold while she cut it into four sizeable portions with her obsidian blade. "You didn't think I was going to eat those awful grass seeds the whole trip, did you, Papa?"

"I brought fish sauce," Joshi pointed out.

"Why don't we try to catch a real fish, since we're out on the river all day?" Riquilda twisted a small strip of orange into a ball around her fingertip and popped it into her mouth.

Pippi and Ramún looked at Joshi.

"Okay," he said. "Whoever is not rowing can fish. You'll have to make up some gear. I've got plenty of silk line in the hold."

While Pippi made his final map entries for the day, Joshi turned the spit over the fire. It held Riquilda's trout, nearly a third of her weight. The aroma of the trout roasting over coals was spectacular. Pippi sealed his map cylinder and then stood downwind of the fire, just to enjoy it.

"I figure," Ramún said, "that if we sell just the four jugs of lilac water, it should pay all the costs of the trip."

"That's if anybody out in this wilderness cares a gnat's ear about lilac water, Papa." She sat reading her copy of *Bennik's Gardening*.

"And we've got those mouse ivory carvings, and the willow chairs and stools. We'll do alright. But what I really want to do, Riqui, is find some new things from somewhere and set up some trade deals for the future. Lilac is too dependent on pilgrims coming to the grove. What if blight or something killed the lilacs? Where would we be?"

"I'm sure we'll find some interesting new things before we get back." As the light faded, Riquilda's wings began to sparkle and glow. She looked over her shoulder. "I guess these are pretty noticeable out here."

Pippi recalled that she had been poisoned by silver metal three years ago, when the Saracets had captured her and sent her to the mines. He had been traveling at the time, but knew well of the miraculous cure brought about by moonlight shining through a lilac stone, like the transparent monolith that now stood in the center of their lilac grove. Caluño had discovered its effect. Riquilda's grandfather had led the Faerie army all the way to Seraz to get her back from the Saracets. Pippi's stepfather, Nebridio, had occasionally spoken about the campaign, though only when begged to do so. For this journey, Nebridio had insisted that Pippi take along a bronze sword—one which Nebridio had brought back from the battle of Kizikum, two decades ago. Pippi had stowed it in the hold of the boat.

Initially, moonlight through the lilac stone had restored her blackened flesh to its former beauty, though her wings began to glow at night. Riquilda's hair eventually turned completely white, as had the hair of all the captive Faeries who had been exposed to silver metal and cured by the moonlight. Now, in the twilight, her white hair, white tunic and glowing wings created an aura about her—a sparkling halo that marked her as truly beautiful and unique. She could read and write and was always brimming with ideas. Ramún was right to guard her closely. At sixteen, she would soon be taking a mate.

He looked at Joshi and noticed that he was transfixed by the sight of her. He couldn't recall that Joshi had ever seen her at night. "Don't burn the trout."

A firefly more than half her size approached and hovered beside her, flashing twice.

"I can't do that, sweetheart," she said to the firefly. "They never go out."

It flashed twice more, then drifted away.

"Since I was thirteen," she said to Pippi, "I've never been in the dark. I kind of miss it, sometimes."

"But you can never get lost," Joshi said.

"Just because you can see what you look at, doesn't mean you're not lost." She closed her book. "It's not bright enough to read by. But everything out there that I can't see can see me."

Once they had all gorged themselves on trout, they settled in for the night beneath tarps aboard the gently rocking boat. Joshi and Pippi stretched out on either side of the huge jugs of lilac water lashed amid ship, Ramún and Riquilda on either side of the bow.

"There are some travelers ahead," Ramún said, "over to the east." He had spent the morning of their fourth day on the river unsuccessfully fishing in the bow, since his daughter had insisted on rowing. "Maybe we should go ashore and talk to them."

"Too many of them," Joshi said from his bench at the tiller.

"What difference does that make?" the Councilor asked.

"They may not be as friendly as you'd like," Pippi said.

The six strangers sighted the boat coming their way and ran to a barge tied at the shore. Many of them waved for them to come over.

"There are mothers with babies," Riquilda shouted. "They're on the other side."

Pippi could see the mothers gesturing for them to go to the Faeries at the barge. All of them appeared to be desperate, rather than threatening. "Joshi, what do you think?"

"Riquilda cheated," Joshi said, as he pulled the tiller hard to the right, guiding the boat toward the eastern bank and the strangers on the barge. "Everybody knows thieves and scoundrels never have families. Councilor, you might want to trade your fish line for a pike."

"Everybody knows that," Pippi echoed facetiously.

"Everybody does," Riquilda stated more emphatically, "don't they, Papa?"

Ramún shooed his daughter from the oar and took her place for the more strenuous rowing required to come about. "Let's hope they know that."

The strangers wore simple, undyed tunics and carried no weapons. All of them had black hair and the sun-bronzed skin of those who labor in the field. The barge was moored to a sturdy post at a small dock. A similar dock and post stood on the opposite bank.

"It's a crossing barge," Joshi observed. "The cross rope is gone."

Riquilda tossed the waiting Faeries a bow line. They wrapped it to the post and hauled the boat to the dock.

"You are so kind to stop," an older Faerie said. "I am Vanivoort. We have just been robbed. Not an hour ago, pirates came and took all of our money."

"How many were there?" Ramún asked, as he stepped onto the dock.

"Eight. They stole almost two hundred coppers. They went downriver in a six-oar boat, lower and shorter than yours."

"Do you have a village nearby?" Pippi asked.

"Chive Crossing," Vanivoort said. "It's just a short way. We manage the crossing barge when somebody comes to cross."

The other Faeries worked at splicing an extension to the severed rope. Across the river, the mothers and children stood watching.

"You had two hundred coppers from working the barge?" Joshi asked. "That's a lot of traffic."

"Oh, no," Vanivoort answered. "We trade chives and sisal furniture."

"And pickled clover blossom," another added.

To the northeast, Pippi could see the stupendous, dagger-like spikes of sisal rising skyward in the distance. On the opposite bank, a veritable forest of chives obscured the view of the plain.

"How can we help you?" Ramún asked. "Can we run your rope across?"

"We can swim it across. But the money. It was everything."

"We will do what we can," the Councilor said in a manner befitting a politician. "But as you can see, there are only four of us."

"What about the boy?" another Faerie asked.

"We shouldn't trouble them with that."

"What about a boy?" Riquilda asked.

"He's just an orphan...deformed. They took him to keep us from following."

"You don't want to rescue him?" Indignation smoldered in her voice. "What does he look like?"

"As I said," Vanivoort continued, "he is deformed. He's runty. About this high..." He indicated the middle of his chest. "...he has white hair, like yours, but no color in his skin. He can't work in the sun without burning. And...he was born with no wings. He has no wings." Vanivoort shook his head. "He was actually a foundling. He was rightly exposed at birth, but in the light of the full moon, he was found and taken in by a mother who had just lost an infant. Since she died, we have all helped to feed him. He goes by 'Gedzik.' He will likely have died in the sun by the time you could find him."

"We will be coming back up river in a week or so," Ramún said. "If we can get your money back, we will return it." He glanced at his daughter. "We'll see what turns up about the boy. And if you have trade items when we return, we may be able to do some business."

Vanivoort spoke to one of his companions, who ran off with another toward the village. "If you can wait for a moment, we have a gift for you." Shortly, the two villagers returned carrying an obviously heavy cask. "Please accept this. It is pickled clover blossom. For your journey."

Ramún studied the cask. It appeared to be made of thick, woven fibers that had been completely sealed with wax. "Is there liquid in here?"

"Yes. The brine."

"What is this cask made from?"

"We make it from sisal, then coat it, inside and out, with beeswax. It can be used over, many times."

"If this doesn't leak," Ramún said, as he untied the boat and hopped into the bow, "I'll buy all the empty casks I can carry, when we come back."

Vanivoort waved. "Don't forget about the money."

"Can you believe how callous he was?" Riquilda said as they got underway.

"Don't be too harsh, Riqui. It sounds like the deformed boy was a burden, and couldn't do the things that needed doing there."

"He has a name, Papa. Gedzik."

The river continued its gentle course. That afternoon, it made a definite turn almost due east. It was then that Pippi saw, far in the distance, a low, six-oar boat at the south bank. "So...what do we do about the eight pirates?"

"I'd say we stay well upriver from them," Joshi suggested. "If they pull to the shore, then we pull in and wait. They've set off again now."

"We have four pikes," Ramún said, "and Nebridio's bronze sword. We might be able to defend the boat, but not attack them."

"I have a pod of lamp oil in the hold," Joshi added.

"There's a little boy with them," Riquilda said.

"Well," Joshi replied, "we could use it to threaten them if they attack...and not really use it."

"If we can rescue the boy and the money," she grumbled, "we should just give the money to the boy and take him somewhere else to live."

Ramún turned from his rowing bench and offered an admonishing expression to his daughter. "Trade is built on trust, Riqui."

Riquilda walked forward and sat on the bow bench. "A little boy is not a trade item, Papa."

"Should we pull over and get more pikes?" Pippi asked.

"As long as we can keep our distance," Joshi replied, "we can wait until we stop for the day. Then we can look for a bramble."

"And we can open up those pickle things and see how they taste," Ramún added. "Are we going to have trout tonight, Riqui?"

She did not answer.

"Well," the Councilor continued, "if we find a bramble, we can get a raspberry."

"Out of season," Pippi said.

That evening, Riquilda ate nothing and sat apart from everyone. When her father approached her, raving about the pickled clover blossoms, she simply moved to a different spot. Each of them had taken four new pikes and trimmed them into shape. Riquilda kept hers beside her.

Pippi sat with Joshi near the boat. "Your boat has been riding well. How's the steering?"

"It's touchy. I think the rudder may be a bit too large."

"Can you cut it down?"

"Yeah, but we'd have to haul it up on the sand. I don't think we'd want to do that without unloading all the cargo first. Maybe after we unload at Tewesh. Another seed?"

Pippi smiled. "I'll wait for tomorrow's trout."

As the light faded, Riquilda took her five pikes to the stern of the deck and curled up beside them, beneath the tiller bench. She didn't bother to set a tarp.

"I think I'll sleep out here tonight," Pippi said softly.

"If we don't find that boy," Joshi whispered, "it's going to be a long trip."

"If we do find him, it may be a very short trip."

"Wake up, Pippi," Joshi shouted. "The boat's gone!"

When Pippi rolled over, half of him landed in water. "The river's up!"

"Get the Councilor. I'm going to run down and try to catch sight of it."

"Riquilda's on the boat!"

"I know." Joshi carried two pikes and dashed off into the brush along the flooded river.

Pippi shook Ramún, quickly explained the essentials to the bleary-eyed Councilor, then chased after Joshi with four of his five pikes. The river did not seem particularly violent in the predawn light, but it had risen enough to top its banks and flood into the adjacent scrub, requiring Pippi to detour inland to stay on dry land. When he could no longer run, he walked until he caught his breath, then ran once again.

About mid-day, under a perfectly clear sky, he briefly caught sight of Joshi, far in the distance. He called to him, but doubted that his voice would carry over the roiling sounds of the river flowing through grasses and shrubs. He rested for a short time and, seeing no sign of Ramún, continued on. He never once saw the boat.

From the look of the river, he guessed that it was carrying the boat at least three times as fast as he was traveling. His only relief was to have not found it wrecked. Though Riquilda had no experience controlling a boat, he was confident that, once awake, she could steer it clear of large obstacles and perhaps even find a place to pull into the shallows.

By sunset, Pippi had yet to see Joshi again, the boat, or the Councilor. He had jettisoned all but one pike along the way. He didn't feel entirely safe sleeping alone on the ground, so he located a sow thistle, climbed to the first leaf, and curled up in the deep pocket beside the stem. His exhaustion enveloped him.

At first light, he climbed down, aching in every joint and muscle. The air seemed drier, the river quieter. "Joshi!" he called out.

"What?" Not ten paces away, Joshi lay in the cover of a low, broad leaf.

Pippi walked over and kicked Joshi's foot. "It's morning."

"Yeah?"

"The river. The boat. The flood."

"Oh!" He sat up abruptly and blinked. "Where did you come from?"

"That sow thistle." He pointed to the plant that towered over them.

"You slept *there*?"

"I had no idea you were here."

"Where's the Councilor?"

"I woke him up yesterday. That's the last time I saw him. Did you ever see the boat?"

Joshi massaged his thighs, then stood with a groan. "I saw it right after I started chasing it. It was going sideways down the river. I think Riquilda was still asleep. I saw it off in the distance about a quarter hour later and it seemed to be under control. That's it."

"Pirates?"

"No pirates. I guess we just keep walking until we get to where she pulled in. What do we do about her father?"

"I think he would want us to find her, instead of going back for him."

Joshi smiled. "Just what I wanted to hear."

As they began walking, the first thing Pippi noticed was that the river had returned to its banks, leaving a quagmire of silt and small debris that held them away from the water. Two hours later, they found their boat resting upright in the mud, tied to a sapling.

On more solid ground nearby, Riquilda leaned against a weed stalk, eating some greens. When she saw them, she signaled for them to be quiet.

"Are you alright?" Pippi whispered.

"I'm fine. A little bored. I've been here for a day, and so have the pirates." She pointed at the river. "They're on the other bank. I don't think they know I'm here, because our boat is...well, it's not in the river. Sorry, Joshi, but it was the only place I could pull in, and it used to be water."

"What are the pirates doing?" Joshi asked.

"Hey, where's Papa?"

"He's somewhere behind us," Pippi answered.

"I think they lost most of their oars. They're tied up. All of them went off together."

"Did you see the boy?" Pippi hated to bring the matter up, but knew they would need to make some decisions about it.

"He's either not there, or he's down in the boat. How do we get this one out of the mud?"

"I have a couple of blocks to use with the ropes," Joshi answered, still in a whisper, "but I'm afraid we'll need to unload everything to move it. And we can't move it if the pirates are right across the river. You pulled it in nicely, Riquilda."

"I hope you mean that as a compliment, because it was no small deed. That tiller doesn't work very well when the boat is being pushed by the water."

"I'd like to see what the pirates are doing," Pippi said. "We can't really do much with getting the boat out if they're watching us." Pippi handed his pike to Joshi and climbed onto the boat. From just inside the small rear hatch, he retrieved the bronze sword that Nebridio had urged him to take. Its belt wrapped above his hips, where he buckled it. He then climbed back to the ground. "This will take me to the bottom, if I go into the water."

They crept through the soggy ground to the riverbank, staying well hidden among the stems of grasses and shrubs. The pirate boat floated at the opposite edge of the river, tied by its bow to a shrub. One oar was visible, as were five empty rowlocks. Although he could not see over the gunwale, to Pippi's eye, the pirate boat rode lower in the water than he would expect for an empty boat. He saw motion in the distance, well beyond the far bank of the river. Two fur-covered bipeds loped rapidly toward the river, their furry heads rocking side to side. As they neared, their enormous size became apparent. They were roughly human in shape, and at least a third the size of a human—thirty times Pippi's height. They uttered chittering sounds to one another, as they swept their furry arms through the brush, searching for something.

"I guess it's not Ternaria on the other side of the river," Riquilda whispered.

Pippi cringed at even a whisper. One of the fur beasts let out a squeal, then grabbed a hand into a shrub. The voice of a Faerie shrieked. The furry hand lifted a struggling Faerie between its thumb and forefinger. The other beast protested, but the first one rotated its hand several times to inspect the Faerie, then bit off the top of his body. It handed the remainder to its partner, which promptly ate the rest.

With some excitement, the first beast looked down into the pirate boat and reached out a hand, but as it passed over the water, it quickly withdrew it and danced in a circle, emitting noises of frustration. It reached once more, and again withdrew the hand. The other beast tried, with the same result.

"That's the boundary," Pippi whispered.

"Do you think the pirates are all dead?" Riquilda asked.

"Sneaking back to the boat didn't turn out so well for that one. Let's get our boat free, so we can get away from here as soon as the Councilor arrives."

Joshi nodded. They crept back to their boat and followed Joshi's instructions in rigging a long silk rope through both blocks and on to the stern. When they heaved together, the boat moved a little, with the sound of cracking wood.

Joshi stepped through the mud to examine the stern. "I guess I don't need to trim the rudder. We just took off the corner of it. Let's unload those four big jugs of lilac water." He loosened the bindings on the mast, then pulled it into a vertical position with its forestay. He tied the shrouds, then hoisted the boom part way up the mast. Within a quarter hour, the heavy jugs were lifted and swung over the side. Now the rope and bocks slid the boat backwards through the mud, so that it touched the water and lay at a steep enough angle to allow them to push it so only the bow remained on land. They muscled the jugs over to the boat and then reloaded them with the boom. Joshi then lowered the folding mast back to its resting bracket on the transom.

Riquilda stood on the mast's hinge box and looked across the water to the pirate boat. "I think there's somebody inside that boat. And those fur people are gone."

"I think if we stay off the river bank on that side, it should be safe," Pippi said. "We can row over there and then land a little further down when we cross back to wait for your father."

Joshi and Pippi rowed across, with Riquilda at the tiller, and tied onto the stern of the pirate boat. In the floor of the boat lay a motionless, wingless Faerie boy wearing only shorts. His pure white hair, matted and sprinkled with debris, reached to his shoulders. All of his exposed skin appeared to be badly burned. Beside him lay sacks and wicker boxes.

Riquilda stepped into the pirate boat and knelt over the boy. "He's breathing."

"So what do you think we should do with all the money," Ramún asked as he rowed opposite Pippi.

"You better not give that Vanivoort one copper more than his precious two hundred," Riquilda said from beneath the tarp that they had lashed over the bow of the deck. All day, she had sprinkled water into Gedzik's mouth, and gently smoothed aloe sap onto his swollen face and arms and legs. His torso had not burned as badly, but she treated that as well. Even the scalp beneath his white hair was reddened.

"That still leaves about two thousand coppers and twenty rings of gold."

"The only village we know of is Chive Crossing," Pippi pointed out, "so I doubt we could find the other owners even if we tried." He had, with some relief, returned Nebridio's bronze sword to the hold.

"I guess it's ours, then," the Councilor concluded.

"It was next to Gedzik," Riquilda said. "It should be his."

"Do you think he'll pull through this, Riqui?"

"He might, and he might not. But if he does, I say it's his."

"From what Vanivoort said, we may have to pay some kind folks to care of him."

"I'll do it for nothing," Riquilda replied.

Ramún looked over at Pippi and sighed, shaking his head.

"Papa," she continued, "when we stop tonight, I need one of your extra tunics for him."

"One of yours might be closer to his size."

"I'm going to take it in so it has long sleeves and reaches almost to the ground. I'll use the leftover to make a hood."

"Yes ma'am," Ramún answered.

Pippi had been able to determine fairly well the point on the river at which their left bank marked the boundary of Ternaria. During the day today, they had sighted a number of large animals grazing, though none was able to come into the river. "If large animals and humans could get into Ternaria, I don't think Faeries would last very long."

"If the monks at Moss Abbey keep up the boundary," Joshi said from his bench at the tiller, "it makes you wonder how it all began. Did Faeries come here from somewhere else and the monks decide to help them out, or did the monks set up Ternaria and then put in Faeries and Thistlepix?"

"And Saracets," Ramún added.

"Maybe," Riquilda said, "Faeries lived everywhere, and the humans came from somewhere else."

"There is land everywhere beyond the boundaries," Pippi pointed out, "but we have no idea how much or where any of their towns are. And I don't know how a Faerie could survive if he went out to explore it. It could go on forever. We'll never be able to map anything but Ternaria."

When they came in for the night, Joshi pulled up a fish trap that he had fashioned from one of the pirate's wicker boxes. He had baited it with bits of seed and dangled it off the stern of the boat. In it, he found seven little fish that neither he nor Pippi could name.

"I know what you call those," Ramún said. "Dinner."

Riquilda ate some of the roasted fish and greens, then resumed her vigil beside Gedzik, while she reworked one of her father's lavender tunics to fit the pitifully burned Faerie boy with no wings. With a nettle bristle as a needle, and silk thread pulled from the tunic itself, she labored, hunched beneath the bow tarp, illuminated by the glow of her wings.

When Pippi awakened at dawn, stiff from sleeping on the deck and still aching from the run the previous day, he sat up to find the white-haired boy looking back at him, seated in raggedy shorts beside the sleeping Riquilda. His face appeared less swollen, though still spackled with aloe sap. The boy looked at Riquilda, touched her white hair with his fingertip, then looked at the two other sleeping Faeries. He crawled gingerly from beneath the bow tarp, stood on wobbly legs, then leaned over the side and peed into the river. His thin back and shoulders revealed not the slightest hint of wings.

Pippi looked beside him for a water pod. "Pssst. Are you thirsty?" he whispered.

Gedzik sat near Pippi, beneath the aft tarp and drank. "Who are you?"

"I'm Pippi and you're Gedzik. We stopped at Chive Crossing and heard about the pirates."

"Where are they?"

"I think they're all dead. They went onto land in a bad place."

"Yes. I saw the boundary."

"What do you mean?"

"When you get close to the boundary, it looks like...sisal fibers...that shimmer. Nobody else sees it, but I do. I guess it's something else wrong with me. I can see it now along that bank of the river."

Gedzik sounded more eloquent than Pippi expected from a boy who looked to be about eight or nine. "How old are you, Gedzik?"

"Sixteen." When he saw Pippi's surprise, he added, "I'm just not very big. Who is that girl with the white hair?"

"That's Riquilda. She's been taking care of you. Last night she made a long tunic for you...that light purple one." He pointed to the tunic beside her. "I don't know if it's done. That's her father, Ramún, on the other side, and Joshi is under that bench."

"What are you going to do with me?" he whispered.

"Whatever you want to do. We're going to the end of the river, to Tewesh. Then we'll sail the boat back up to Lilac. That's where we started."

"Toe Wash. It's not Tewesh; it's Toe Wash. They say the river goes up and down with the moon. When it's up, you're supposed to be able to sit in the doorways of the houses and wash your toes."

"Toe Wash." Pippi chuckled. "Do you want to go back to Chive Crossing?"

"Not in a thousand years. The sun will be up soon. I'm going to try that tunic." He crawled beneath the fore tarp and lifted the lavender tunic. Something fell from it. He held up a pair of matching, lavender shorts. He stood again between the tarps, his legs still wobbly, and after a quick glance toward Riquilda, removed his shorts, exposing skin as white as his hair, and stepped into the new ones, tying the cord at his waist. He tossed his tattered shorts into the river. When he pulled the new tunic over his head, its hem fell to just above his ankles. It's sleeves extended to his first knuckles. He noticed the hood and pulled it over his head. A stiffened cowl hung out over his red face.

Gedzik smiled slightly, ten winced, reaching up with a sunburned hand to touch his blistered lips. "I've never had a tunic."

"What did you wear at Chive Crossing?"

In his new cowled tunic and with no wings, Gedzik resembled the human monks of Moss Abbey, only much, much smaller. His eyes glowed slightly red in light reflected from the river. "Just those shorts. They never let me go outside in the day."

By sixteen, Pippi had seen nearly half of Ternaria. "Well, Gedzik, it's time you saw what's out there. Are you hungry?"

"Not really. I feel like the fever."

"One other thing. You're wealthy. The pirates left all their money in the boat."

"Oh. They stole that from Chive Crossing," he whispered.

"That was only two hundred coppers. There were two thousand more, plus twenty rings of gold, and it's yours."

Toe wash was a village built on stilts nearly ten faerielongs high. Causeways connected the houses and shops. Beyond it, the Nettle River opened onto a vast, seemingly endless expanse of surging water to the east. More remarkable to Pippi was the opposite bank of the river, which had become more distant from the near bank for the past hour of travel. On its edge stood the colossal structures of a human town. An immense ship with two masts and seven sails moved away from the town and out into the sea.

"Do you know the name of that, Gedzik?" Pippi asked.

Gedzik had spent much of the day sitting cross-leg beneath the bow tarp beside Riquilda, who was using her copy of *Bennik's Gardening* to teach Gedzik how to read. The boy may or may not have been interested in learning to read, but he sat close to Riquilda, their hips touching. He looked out. "That's Shibam. The boundary is about in the middle of the river."

At their approach to the main dock of Toc Wash, a villager waved to get their attention. "Walk the rope up the ladder and tie it up here, or the tide will sink your boat this evening."

Pippi had once again buckled Nebridio's bronze sword to his hip. "I'll stand around the deck, so everybody can notice the sword, then I'll sleep on the boat."

"I think I want to sleep on the boat too." Gedzik said from beneath his cowl. He looked with concern at the high ladder.

Riquilda knelt in front of the boy, lifted the front hem of his long tunic and tucked it into the waist cord of his shorts. "There. I'll follow you. You want to sleep on something softer than a boat deck tonight."

Pippi knew that Gedzik was accustomed to being seen in only his shorts, but the boy's blush was visible even beneath his hood. He suspected that Riquilda had not asked Gedzik his age. "I could use an extra set of eyes down here."

Gedzik looked at Pippi, then at Riquilda. He seemed to wait for one of them to decide for him.

"Okay," Riquilda conceded, "but you'll have to put the aloe on him before he goes to sleep."

"Get yourself one of those pikes," Pippi said. "I hear there are pirates on the river."

Gedzik straightened the front of his tunic, and watched from the bottom of the ladder as Riquilda followed Joshi and Ramún up to the dock. He stepped to the collection of pikes lying beneath the recumbent mast and selected one. "I don't know how to use this, but you already know that." He sat on a side bench near Pippi, but didn't look up.

"Are you afraid of the long ladder?"

"Yeah."

"Well, I think you should climb it anyway. Maybe later, when it's not so long." He paused for a moment, uncertain as to how to approach a delicate subject. The boy had clearly been deprived of any normal relationships with other Faeries, and seemed to crave the kind interaction and the physical contact he'd found. "Riquilda thinks you're a child."

"I am."

"No, Gedzik, you're nearly an adult."

"I guess. I don't feel like it."

"She was going to sleep with you tonight. She was going to cuddle up with you, to comfort you."

"I'd like that."

"But you're both the same age. She would believe you tricked her when she found out. And Ramún would be so furious, he'd put you off the boat immediately. I know you've had a tough time, and you don't really know what anybody expects of you."

"All of you have treated me like a real Faerie, instead of a freak." His body seemed to shrink within his long, lavender tunic. He sniffed, then wiped his nose on his hand.

Pippi sat on the bench beside him and reached his arm around him, drawing the boy against his chest. "You are a real Faerie." He brushed back the lavender hood and pressed his cheek against the top of Gedzik's head. His hair smelled of aloe and sweat. "I will do my best to help you figure things out. You are handsome and intelligent and healthy—sunburned, but healthy. Now you have several Faeries who care about you. That's as many as any of us can ever claim."

Gedzik sobbed.

"You nourish those friends by always being honest with them and respecting them. The first thing we should do is cut your hair like an adult. Then you need to take a bath so you don't smell like week old sweat. Tomorrow, we'll start you with some exercises to build your strength. We'll have a sartor in Toe Wash make up another tunic like this one, and more shorts, so you can always have clean clothes to wear."

Gedzik tipped his head back to look up into Pippi's face. His reddish eyes brimmed with tears. "No one has ever talked to me like this."

"That's because you never had an older brother, until now." Pippi thought of his older brother, Willi, and of all the love and support he had received from his mother and Willi and his stepfather, Nebridio. He could hardly imagine growing up with none of it—of simply being a burden and an outcast.

Gedzik's arms slipped around Pippi's waist and hugged him tightly, as his body convulsed with sobs. After a short while, he sat upright and said, "Let's cut my hair."

"We need to take care of something first." He motioned to a Faerie lad sitting at the dock, which now seemed a bit closer, to come down the ladder. "Take off your shorts, Gedzik."

"Why?"

"So you won't have to stand around naked while your clothes dry." To the local lad, he handed ten coppers from one of the pirate boxes. "I want you to go to the sartor and buy a pair of shorts...this size." He handed him Gedzik's lavender shorts. "The color doesn't matter. And we need him to make four more the same size. Bring back what he has, and ask him to send the others as soon as they're done. There will be two coppers for you."

The lad disappeared up the ladder. The deck of the boat stood in the long afternoon shadows cast by shrubs near the dock. Pippi opened the rear hatch and pulled out the small jib sail.

Gedzik sat in the shadow on an aft rowing bench, dressed only in the jib sail that he had wrapped about his waist, while Pippi trimmed his white hair with an obsidian blade. Having no wings to sight as a reference, Pippi estimated the length currently fashionable in Lilac, leaving it just touching the tops of his ears and tapering halfway down his neck. By the time he was done, Pippi thought the boy looked at least a few years older. A new pair of black shorts arrived.

"Can you swim?"

"I never tried."

"I'll teach you, but not today." He carried two water pods to the bow. There he rigged a corner of the tarp out to the bowsprit. "You'll have to bathe here. There's plenty more water if you run out. Wash these first..." He tossed him his lavender tunic and shorts. "...and I'll hang them out. Use that jib sail to scrub your back. Don't forget to do behind your ears. We can see them now." With a smile, he recalled his mother saying those same words, and how he would always forget.

When Gedzik returned to the stern of the boat, wearing his new black shorts, Pippi handed him a pod containing the aloe sap that Riquilda had collected. "Put this everywhere that's sunburned."

Gedzik set down the aloe and leaned over the gunwale to look at himself. He reached up and touched his white hair. He looked at his sunburned arms and legs, and then gently smeared the aloe onto his skin, starting with his face. When he was done, Pippi applied it to his back and shoulders, noting how truly little flesh held his bones together. All cleaned and trimmed, the boy appeared more fragile than before.

Pippi rinsed his hands in the river, then drew the bronze sword at his hip. As he moved through the first pattern exercise, he named each position and held it momentarily. "I've never fought in war, but this is how I started sword training."

Gedzik's eyes widened. He looked at his hands, then washed away the aloe sap in the river. "Can I really hold it?"

"The first pattern begins in the scabbard. Watch your toes. If you drop this, you will lose them." He unbuckled its belt and wrapped it about Gedzik's narrow hips. After a second wrap, he buckled it.

"It's heavy."

"That's why it strikes fear in an opponent. When you practice, don't try to bring it to a stop. Always keep it moving."

A diminutive hand grasped the hilt, another, the scabbard. Gedzik took a deep breath and tugged. Nothing moved.

"That's where it begins."

Pippi awakened to voices on the dock high above him. The morning sun stood an hour from the horizon. Above the ladder, now even taller than on the previous afternoon, a lavender hood fluttered in the sea breeze. Nebridio's sword rested in its scabbard beside the bench.

"Yes," Ramún said. "We'll be back this evening."

"Because I ordered some things," Gedzik said.

"I see. Well, if what they say is true, we'll be going back and forth for at least a few days."

"You can go down," Gedzik said. "I'll do the rope."

"It's tricky," Joshi said, "when there's this much rope."

"I watched the other boat leave this morning."

"Okay."

Riquilda, followed by Ramún and Joshi descended to the boat. Gedzik drew a bight of the rope beneath the dock, then untied it. As he came down the ladder, he took up the slack, keeping the boat directly beneath the ladder. After jumping onto the deck, he brought in the rope, leaving it in a tidy coil.

"Did you teach him that?" Joshi asked Pippi.

"He saw it for the first time this morning. Gedzik may be odd, but he remembers everything he sees."

"He is odd. He woke us up at the inn to tell us that he was sixteen and hadn't meant to trick anyone."

"How did Riquilda take it?"

"Not very well. I think she was hoping to take care of a child."

"So, what are we doing, Councilor," Pippi asked.

"Some of the Faeries in...Toe Wash...trade at the human town. There are three jewelers where it is safe. They have built a tunnel directly to their shops. Today we can speak with them and see what they have to trade."

"What about trading at Toe Wash?" Pippi had yet to even see the village.

"They have discs of pearl cut from clam shells, sea salt, smoked clam meat, a lovely purple dye and...what else, Joshi?"

"Sauce made from hot pepper pods. There are two sartors, so you can have fancy clothes made at a good price. There is a sail maker. Oh, and a tinker who makes cooking pots of iron and lines the inside with tin. Those might sell in Lilac."

"Are we going to row?" Gedzik asked.

"We may as well set the mast and sail across," Joshi replied. "It's a long way."

Within a half hour, the boat was rigged and the triangular mainsail set. Joshi turned the helm over to Gedzik and played with the ropes, his first chance to do so on truly open water.

"Crossing the boundary," Gedzik called out about half-way across.

Pippi sat beside Riquilda at the bow. Her enthusiasm seemed to have deflated.

"You know Gedzik needs you."

"Doesn't seem like it, 'brother.'"

"He said you were the kindest Faerie in his whole life. He needed someone to help with things like, 'cut your hair,' 'take a bath,' 'wash your clothes,' 'make your muscles stronger.' That's what I'm doing. He really likes you, but in a mixed up way. And he never learned how to...interact with other Faeries. They always ridiculed him and convinced him he was abnormal and worthless. He needs to know we're not going to cast him away like everyone else has. I don't think anyone has hugged him since he was a toddler."

"It's just so awkward. He's my age. I can't just be hugging him."

"You saved his life. And...he has never had a tunic until you made him one. You made him feel like a real Faerie, instead of a freak. He told me so."

Riquilda stood, kissed Pippi on the shoulder and went aft to join Gedzik on the tiller bench.

"Do you remember the letters?"

"Ah bey vey geh deh..." Gedzik recited all twenty eight, in perfect order. He turned his head toward Riquilda. A smile glistened from the deep shadow of his cowl.

"Head west of the big dock," Ramún called out. "Aim for that stone spire. There's a Faerie dock there."

Joshi gradually reduced the sail and then took the helm. He slapped Gedzik's knee. "You're a quick study. Watch how I bring her about. Pippi, prepare to cast a line." He brought her in beside a Faerie boat with twin masts, a hull half again as long, and just about as wide abeam. It mounted rowlocks for four on each side. "Cast your line! I wonder where that sails from. I'll stay with the boat."

Just in from the dock, a single, Faerie-size wooden door opened to a covered stairway, illuminated by skylights spaced at even intervals along the way. At the top of the stairs, the corridor continued for a quarter hour, ending in a wider vestibule into which three doors opened.

"What is that?" Gedzik asked, pointing to a strangely shaped character painted in the center of the door. Each door bore a different glyph.

"I can't read it," Riquilda replied.

"It's some kind of foreign letters," Pippi concluded. "Which one are we supposed to use?"

"They said that each one leads to a different jeweler," Ramún said. "I think we should stay together until we know the situation." He pointed emphatically to the door on the right.

Beyond the right door, a corridor led to the right, opening into a beautifully decorated chamber furnished with Faerie-size tables and padded chairs. Thick weavings and knot work hung about three walls. Where the fourth wall would have been, a finely polished wood railing, made of symmetrically carved knobs and spindles, overlooked a stupendous human-size shop filled with shelves and racks of jewelry in every precious metal. Golden chains and necklaces and bracelets sparkled with jewels of a dozen colors. The ceiling was hung with a thousand prisms interspersed with squat candles, whose flickering gave it all the appearance of a living, breathing mass. In the center of the shop, three humans sat around a square table amusing themselves at a game.

Pippi leaned over the wood railing. The floor was so far below him that he immediately stepped back. A sonorous clang rang out from behind him. Ramún had swung a thick rope that caused a ball of metal to strike the rim of a bronze dome suspended above it. The three humans looked up from their game. One—wearing a long white gown, his head covered with a draping, gray speckled scarf held by two coils of thick rope—stood and walked toward them. When he sat at a carved stool, his face filled the opening.

"Peace to you," he said. His dark bronze skin showed deep pits and pores. His nose was longer than Pippi's height. A pointed black beard extended from the tip of his chin, a moustache above his lip. "We have not met." His breath smelled of dark spices and toasted almond. "I am Wahid ibn Ayub al Gawahirgi Jelari, but you may call me Wahid. Just Wahid."

Ramún introduced himself as well as the others, and explained his interest in perhaps identifying items for ongoing trade with Lilac.

Wahid held up both hands. "Please. Pleasure before business." He walked beyond Pippi's view, then returned shortly wearing thick glass spectacles and carrying a Faerie-size tray on a spatula held in his thumb and finger. His bespectacled face leaned close as he delicately suspended the spatula above the table in the Faerie chamber. "I allow you to put tray. I could spill it."

Riquilda lifted the tray from the spatula and placed it on the table. Four cups of steaming, frothy brown liquid filled the air with a toasty smell. Wahid lifted a human-size cup of similar design and took a sip. "Ehweh."

Pippi sipped. Its dark, fruity aroma contrasted with its bright, sweet taste.

"People from west name ehweh 'kaffee.'" He pointed across the shop. "Wahid trades with all of towns, cities. I know of no city named Lilac."

Pippi could hardly believe that he had overlooked a map on the far wall. Nothing on it looked familiar. "Is Shibam on that map?"

"Map? Ah yes. My kharita." Wahid walked to the map and touched it at a point of a coast where a river emptied from the west. "Shibam here. Ternaria, here. Is empty. We know nothing. No man can go."

The magnitude of all the land that was not Ternaria left Pippi in awe. "I have made a map of all Ternaria."

"You bring it. You copy my kharita. I copy your kharita. Then we both know everywhere."

Ramún asked about the dark beverage. Wahid returned with a red berry the size of his thumbnail. "Ehweh fruit. From tree. You break first." He crushed the fruit, revealing two pale green seeds beneath the pulp. "Roast all green seed. Make brown seed." He held up a fragrant, slightly oily brown seed. "You make to powder. Put with hot water and sokkar." He stepped away and returned with the same spatula holding amber colored rocks the size of a Faerie fist. He tipped them onto the table. "Sokkar. Taste. Sweet."

When it came to what trade items Wahid might be interested in, the jeweler said, "Clothes. I want Faerie clothes." He pointed to a side door in the Faerie chamber. "Go in. Look"

Gedzik opened the side door and halted within the doorframe. An adjacent chamber was filled with life-size dolls of Faeries, most standing, some seated. All of them wore clothing similar to that worn in Toe Wash. "That's creepy."

"For children. They play dolls. Clothes hard to make for my big...mmm...fingers. I buy from..." He chuckled. "...Toe Wash. But different is better. To have choice." He suddenly swung his face back and forth between the two chambers to get Gedzik in the view of his spectacles. "You are not Faerie?" he asked Gedzik.

"I am a special Faerie," he replied assertively. "I am a truthseer. I can see if someone is speaking the truth or not." He tossed back his cowled hood, revealing his close-cropped white hair and sparkling red eyes.

Wahid withdrew his face a short distance. "I am pleased you bring honesty to our business agreements."

"You are not speaking the truth."

Wahid laughed, wagged a finger, then laughed again. "A businessman must keep some...mmm...advantage, or he loses money."

"That is the truth."

Wahid laughed more deeply, wagged his finger again, then laughed from his belly. "You want truth? I like you." He laughed once more. To Ramún, he said, "When you are ready to trade, I will be most happy to see you again. And bring your truthseer. His golden tongue flies him higher than Faerie wings"

When Wahid returned to his table game, Ramún said to Gedzik, "He could have taken that very badly." A roar of laughter rose from the game table in the center of the shop. "I don't think we need to wonder what that was about."

The Faeries exited the long corridor and entered the second door. This led straight ahead to a similar chamber with a balcony overlooking a jeweler's shop. Directly in front of them, three humans sat at a table playing a game. Pippi leaned over the rail. Toward the right, on the opposite wall, hung a map of all the eastern lands.

"This is the same shop," he said.

Ramún swung a rope that caused a long, tubular chime to ring out. The gray gowned jeweler who came to the open wall seemed a little younger than Wahid, though his face was mostly covered with a full black beard. His head was wrapped in a mound of white fabric that formed a flattened ball.

"Welcome. I was expecting you. I am Talata ibn Ibrim al Gawahirgi Jakari. Just Talata is fine, since that is all you will remember."

Ramún introduced himself and his companions.

"Allow me to offer you some Malagaro back tea. You will like it." He looked directly at Gedzik. "That is the truth." He laughed as he stepped away. When he returned, he brought a tray with four small cups made of glass. Thick spectacles were pinched onto the bridge of his nose. With the fingertips of his free hand, he poured an amber liquid from a Faerie-size brass pot. Allowing a fine stream to land in each cup. "Malagaro is an island a short way across the sea. This is from the dried leaves of the tea plant. If you look to my display..." He gestured to his left. "...you will see that I make furniture for the Faerie dolls."

Ramún opened the door to the adjacent three-sided room. From his seat at the tea table, Pippi could see a variety of Faerie-size furniture. Gedzik opened a second door on the opposite wall. It contained a huge empty glass bottle lying on its side. The bottle's mouth was wide enough for a Faerie to easily walk in with room to spare.

"Since I must speak the truth," Talata said with a broad smile, "that bottle is to hold a boat, floating in water. I have made a Faerie boat that floats, and a Faerie boat that will fit into the bottle, but the former will not fit the bottle, and the latter would not float."

"Our boat would fit in," Gedzik said, "and it floats."

"Ah, but the masts must be hinged to fit through the neck. It is a tricky thing."

"Where are your boats," Pippi asked, looking about the shop.

"The one that sinks was...shipwrecked...in a moment of... dissatisfaction. I dried it out and used it to boil your tea. A pity. Anger is seldom...productive. The other floats at the little dock. I am sure you passed it."

As with Wahid, they parted from Talata on friendly terms with an invitation to do business. The third door took them down a corridor to the left, and eventually, as Pippi suspected, to yet a third chamber that opened into the same jeweler's shop, but at the far end from the first. Ramún swung a padded pole into a large, circular disk of brass, causing a wavering gong to sound.

The third human stood from the game table. He was the youngest of the three. Clean shaven, he wore a light green, embroidered shirt that reached the floor. His head was covered with a small basket-like cloth cap covered in gold embroidery.

"Hello. I'm Hamsa. You're probably washing away by now, so I won't offer you anything to drink."

Ramún again performed the introductions.

"I'm not sure that I have much to offer for trade. Let me bring you a snack." His face vanished from the open wall.

Gedzik peeked into the side door. "Look at these," he exclaimed. He swung the door wide. Inside were Faerie dolls wearing jewelry of gold and gems. Some wore sword belts with long, curved scabbards, each encrusted with gems. Beyond were carvings made from enormous chunks of ivory. A Faerie doll held an iron mallet in one hand and hammered a piece of metal upon an iron anvil. A pile of metal slivers rested beside a stone oven painted to look red hot.

Hamsa returned with a dish of mashed vegetable and pieces of wheat cake. Pippi dipped a corner of wheat cake into the vegetable and took a bite. It tasted like bland, black bean.

"Wait," Hamsa said. "It needs olive oil and leymun and some black pepper." With the tip of his little finger, he flicked a drop of oil onto the bean paste. He then squeezed a corner of a bright yellow slice of fruit. Finally he dusted it with a dark powder. "Now taste it."

Pippi tried it again. It exploded with flavor. "This is fabulous!"

"Is this silver?" Gedzik asked from the adjoining chamber.

"Oh. As you see, unlike my cousins, I don't buy these from Faeries. I make it all. The silver color metal is steel—much better for tools and weapons. I don't think Faeries could make steel."

"But they could work it from small pieces?" Gedzik drew the curved sword from its scabbard.

"I suppose so."

"Why do you have three separate entrances to the same shop?" Ramún asked.

"When it comes to business, we can never agree on anything. This way, we enjoy playing games together, but all business is separate. Our fathers were brothers. They argued so much that one moved to Jakar, one to Jelar, and my father remained in Jubail. Now at least we can sit at the same table."

Hamsa looked at Riquilda. "Would you like to try on the jewelry? It's never been worn by a Faerie, only dolls."

Riquilda took one last swipe of the beans on a fragment of wheat crust, then modeled a tiara and a necklace, both of gold, with dark blue jewels. "These must be costly." She put them back on the dolls.

"The labor. Most of the cost is labor." He reached to a counter, then held up a perfectly cut, deep blue, transparent stone as large as her head. "To cut this sapphire, I discard fragments equal to what remains. Most of the fragments are of no value, because they are so tiny. The Faeries of Toe Wash have no interest in jewelry. The gold costs something, but again, it uses so very little that it is the labor that determines the cost."

On their way back to the boat, they called Joshi over to examine Talata's boat that was too big for his bottle. Joshi pointed out that many of the small details, such as the rowlocks, were not fully finished, and the battens of the two large hatches did not seal well.

"It is a substantial boat, though," he said. "With the rigging completed and full sails, that would make the trip from Lilac in just a few days. What will he sell it for?"

The journey back to Toe Wash for the night was a continuous discussion of what to trade and with whom. They agreed to have the sartors make all new clothes for each of them, so they could trade their present ones with Wahid. Gedzik refused to part with his lavender tunic that Riquilda had made for him.

"Pippi and I will stay with the boat tonight," Gedzik said when they reached the village dock. When Pippi frowned, Gedzik added, "I have to learn to swim."

"I have to copy my map anyway. How's the food at the inn?"

"Not so good as what Hamsa gave us," Ramún answered.

"Maybe you could bring us something besides seeds."

"I need a tunic from each of you," Riquilda said, "to take to the sartors."

Gedzik pulled off his lavender tunic. "Riquilda, could you have them make me four of these, exactly like this? It's perfect."

"I don't think they have the color."

"You decide." Once the others had departed up the long ladder, Gedzik sat in the shade of the reefed mainsail. "Pippi, is all that copper and gold really mine?"

"All but the two hundred from Chive Crossing."

"Do you think it would be right for me to buy a necklace for Riquilda?"

"Why are you thinking of doing that?"

"Because it suited her so well."

"It's the sort of thing someone might do if he's courting a girl."

"She wouldn't think that, would she? What if I got something for each of you?"

"That could get expensive."

"But it would be okay to give her the necklace then. Right?"

"I guess it would. How about learning to swim? Don't breathe under water." Pippi pulled off his tunic and jumped over the side. He swam on his back, on his side, on his belly and underwater. "Spread your arms and legs like this..." He showed him. "...when you jump in, and you won't go under."

Gedzik jumped in and immediately duplicated all of Pippi's strokes, and in the same sequence. When Pippi surged from the surface and pulled himself into the boat, Gedzik did the same.

"You amaze me. You see something and it all just sticks in your mind." He pressed the water from his hair with his hands.

"Show me all of the sword exercises."

"Let me catch my breath and dry off."

Pippi sat at the kaffee table in Wahid's Faerie room as he carefully copied the huge map that hung on the opposite wall. The jeweler sat at a nearby counter making an enlarged copy of Pippi's map of Ternaria, flipping various hinged lenses of his spectacles up and down as he went between the Faerie map and his own version. He paused from time to time to pronounce the place names that were written on the wall map in Sulalic. Pippi did likewise for the place names written on his map in Valish.

Ramún had made trade arrangements with him earlier. He and the others were now dealing with Talata and Hamsa. Wahid was to trade two ground kaffee seeds and a small cask of sokkar for each Faerie garment. All would be packaged for river shipment.

As he was finishing his map of all the eastern lands, Pippi saw Talata walk through the front door of the shop carrying their boat in one hand. He finished up, rolled up his new map and sealed it in his map cylinder. Then he ran down the long corridor and up the center passage to watch.

Talata slipped the boat, stern first, into his bottle, which now contained enough water to float it. Then Joshi ran into the bottle, swiveled the mast into place and began setting the rigging, the mainsail and the jib. He then set out all four oars and accepted Faerie dolls from Talata to place on board in various working positions. When Joshi was done, he stood in the adjoining chamber as Talata emptied a scoop of white powder into the bottle's water, then sealed the mouth with a large plug.

"The poison will prevent molding and rotting."

Riquilda and Gedzik had agreed that all of them would pose wearing Hamsa's accessories for some prospective customers who were to come by in the afternoon. In return, Hamsa gave casks of olive oil and a leymun. Powdered black pepper was traded for the finely carved mouse ivory. Talata offered Malagaro black tea for their willow furniture.

Before Hamsa's customers arrived, all of the Faeries went to his display chamber, where they were fitted with Hamsa's handiwork. Pippi and Gedzik buckled on curved swords—Hamsa called them sabers—in jeweled scabbards, suspended on jeweled belts. Joshi and Ramún each wore a jeweled dirk, and each of the four was armored in an elaborately engraved steel cuirass—Gedzik's made specifically for his small chest. Around Riquilda's slender neck hung the sapphire on a gold necklace, and across her brow, a sapphire tiara. Ramún decided to pose in place of the doll at the forge.

When customers began to arrive, the Faeries froze in their places. Wahid sat with an eight string oud, shaped like a pear, and began to pick an exotic melody. Talata joined in with a pair of drums made of skin over copper bowls. The customers, it turned out, were children, scores of them, with their parents. They crowded into the shop to look at the displays of dolls and their clothing, furniture and accessories. Children's faces peered into each of the display chambers. Fingers pointed and voices implored their parents, though Pippi could understand only some of it.

A pudgy finger reached in and touched Gedzik's chest, in the center of his steel cuirass. He jumped back. Gasps rose from those who saw it.

To the rhythm of the oud, Gedzik drew his saber and stepped through the first sword pattern. Children squealed. Everyone in the shop tried to get a view of the amazing spectacle. With the first pattern completed gracefully, Gedzik turned and faced Pippi, who turned toward him. Together they performed the second pattern, each complimenting the moves of the other. Their steel swords swung in large and small arcs, to either side, overhead. They kneeled, they lunged, parried. When the tenth and final pattern ended, they resumed their frozen poses. Children clapped, their parents clapped. Even Hamsa, pressed against the far corner clapped.

The oud played on, now at a livelier tempo. Riquilda turned to Joshi and named a Faerie folk dance. They danced together, weaving about the chamber, slapping their knees and clapping their hands above their heads. When they finally returned to their frozen poses, Ramún started to hammer a piece of steel that he held with tongs, keeping with the oud's rhythm.

After the impromptu performance, Wahid, Talata and Hamsa busily wrote down orders. Children pointed out specific dolls and furniture and accessories. Some parents bought human-size jewelry for themselves. Copper, silver and even gold changed hands.

Hamsa came to them after calm had returned to the shop. "I took seven orders for a little Faerie doll with white hair and no wings. We call it the 'Faerie truthseer'."

"We never make so much business in one day—in one month!" Wahid said.

"Most people in Shibam have never seen a real Faerie," Talata said. "They do not believe they are real."

"Real Faeries bring more business," Wahid stated.

"That is the truth," Gedzik said.

Wahid laughed and wagged his finger. "Our little truthseer."

When Riquilda asked Joshi to unfasten her sapphire necklace, Hamsa raised his hand. "Everything you wore for this occasion is yours to keep. I will also load the forging tools and a crate of steel filings onto your new ship."

"The ship has a name," Talata added. "On the stern, written in Sulalic, it says, 'Luli Shibami.'" That means, 'Pearl of Shibam.'"

"Papa," Riquilda said with a broad smile, "Gedzik has asked me and I have accepted."

"What? He asked you what?"

They sat amid ship, as the *Luli Shibami* sailed up river. The five crew members that Joshi hired in Toe Wash handled the sails as well as the helm, while Joshi gave orders. Pippi had overheard Gedzik's conversation with Riquilda, and now watched as she tormented her father.

"He's going to build a school in Lilac. He has asked me to be Head Mistress. Pippi will teach, and maybe his older brother, Willi."

"What will Gedzik do?"

"He wants to be the first student and the first graduate."

The *Luli Shibami* came about at Chive Crossing. While the crew untied and retied the heavy crossing cable that spanned the Nettle, Pippi and Gedzik disembarked to find Vanivoort, while Ramún purchased some of their goods. When Pippi located him, he handed over a sack of two hundred coppers.

"The pirates are dead. We recovered your money."

"We hardly hoped," the older Faerie said. "The boy, I suppose, didn't make it."

"Gedzik? As a matter of fact, he did make it. Gedzik!" he called out.

Gedzik approached in his ankle length, long sleeved, hooded lavender tunic with a jewel-handled steel saber in a jewel encrusted gold scabbard, held at his narrow waist by an equally bejeweled belt. An elaborately engraved, steel cuirass covered his chest. He cast back the hood, showing his closely clipped white hair and an implacable contempt, then handed Vanivoort a ring of gold. "That's to repay the cost of feeding me. Thank you." Without waiting to hear a response from the incredulous Vanivoort, Gedzik turned and walked back to the *Luli Shibami.*

Once underway again, Pippi sat beside Gedzik. "Somehow you've gotten wealthy, gotten even with Vanivoort, gotten a brother, gotten gifts for everyone, gotten Riquilda her necklace, and even gotten Riquilda herself, without anyone much noticing that it was you who sat at the helm—you who worked the tiller. You pulled the ropes to make these things happen. I'll bet you intentionally sent the pirates onto the land when you could clearly see the boundary and the danger."

"That is the truth."

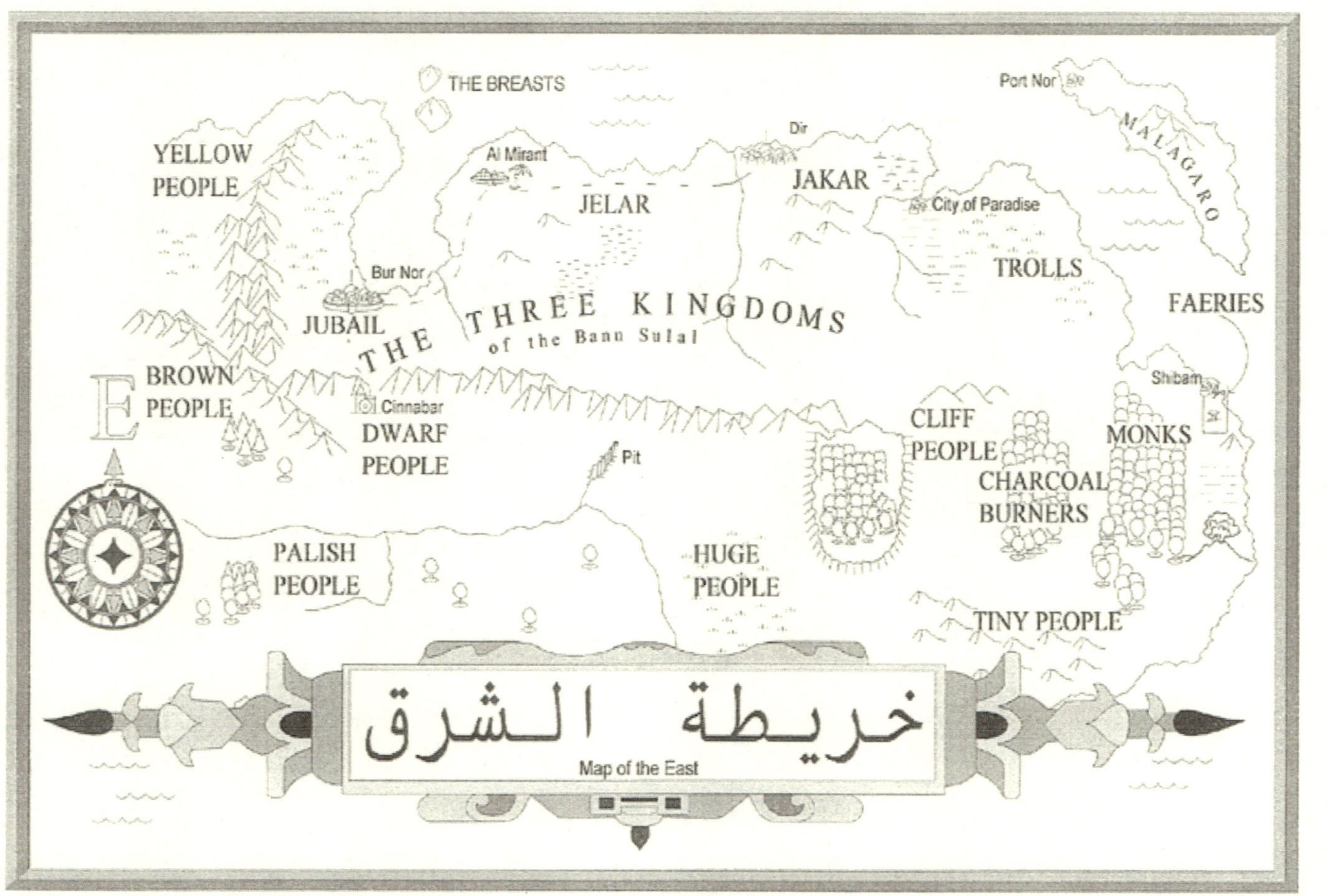
THE BREASTS
Port Nor
MALAGARO
YELLOW PEOPLE
Al Mirant
Dir
JELAR
JAKAR
City of Paradise
Bur Nor
TROLLS
FAERIES
JUBAIL
THE THREE KINGDOMS
of the Bann Sulal
E
BROWN PEOPLE
Cinnabar
DWARF PEOPLE
Pit
Shibam
CLIFF PEOPLE
MONKS
CHARCOAL BURNERS
PALISH PEOPLE
HUGE PEOPLE
TINY PEOPLE
خريطة الشرق
Map of the East

CHAPTER 15—LEGACY OF A CARELESS AGE

Kurash had just completed the record for his last patient when Alketas burst into his clinic chamber.

"All of my workers are sick," Alketas said, out of breath.

"All of them?" Kurash asked. He knew that Alketas directed a crew of about thirty laborers for his endless digging projects.

"Every last Faerie. I went down there this morning and found them all complaining of horrible headaches and stomach aches. Some have puked. You have to come."

The thought of thirty vomiting rogues crowded into his clinic was not inviting. Kurash set his quill on the small writing desk and placed the square of vellum which held his new record onto a stack of similar records at the end of a shelf of labeled clay jars. "Where are they now?"

"In the palace."

He had followed most of Alketas' excavations since the tomb of the Mage King was discovered at Tellia's quarry fifteen years ago. "Which building is the palace?" He stooped to exit the doorway.

"Kurash," Alketas scolded. He pointed to the street beneath his feet. "The one Tellia is built on."

The Faeries they passed on the street nodded with courtesy to Alketas and, after craning their necks to look into his face, with at least civility to Kurash. Now thirty, the Saracet eunuch had finally stopped growing, at a height two-thirds taller than the average Faerie. They walked east from town, then descended a serpiginous excavation that eventually led in the opposite direction. After a half hour, they reached the palace entrance, uncovered by Alketas' team after two thousand years. Kurash found it particularly ironic that its white stone roof had been exposed all along as the bedrock upon which Tellia had been built.

As they entered the narrow section of the doorway that had been unearthed, Kurash immediately smelled the sour odor of vomit, as well as the distinct aroma of proof spirit. "Were your workers celebrating last night?"

"I don't know what they would celebrate or what they would celebrate with."

Having been built by humans, the chambers of the palace, like those of the other structures they had discovered, were enormous, in area as well as height. The larger chambers supported their flat stone ceilings with multiple rows of stone columns carved in intricate geometric patterns. Alketas turned into the first chamber off the right of the atrium. There, in the near corner, thirty Faeries writhed on the floor in various degrees of discomfort.

Kurash knelt at the first one he came to, a Faerie sound asleep, with his mouth wide open and snoring contentedly. He felt at his wrist, then his forehead. He squeezed a portion of wing between his fingers. When he pressed one hand against the abdomen of the snoring Faerie, his eyes opened and attempted to focus on the healer. Kurash noticed that the eyes subtly deviated to one side again and again, before jerking back to the center.

"What's a horned damned Saracet ugly...son-of-a-whore do-o-ing here?" The Faerie asked, before dropping off again.

"Wasting his time," Kurash replied. "Alketas, this fellow, and I assume all the rest, are drunk."

"I don't know where they would find any wine in Tellia."

"I suppose you can ask your crew boss in a few hours."

"Sorry, Kurash. I worry that we'll open some ancient jug and find a surprise from the Mage King—some contagion or something."

"This is where you think he lived?"

"I'm certain of it. We've found the throne chamber and what I think was a special kitchen."

"Special?"

"Every building we've found has a kitchen for preparing food. This one has a food kitchen as well. But yesterday, we found a really odd kind of kitchen with some pretty strange things in it."

"Perhaps some wine?"

"Two thousand year old wine?"

Kurash shrugged. "Could we see it?"

"It's at the end of the building. That would be at the end of town, up there."

"I've already come all the way down here."

They walked through corridors and chambers lit with widely spaced oil lamps. Most of the chambers were completely empty.

"You've been pretty quick to remove everything, Alketas."

"This is how we found it. All the other buildings had something in them, furnishings, eating implements, something. This one was stripped bare, except for that special kitchen. It's full of stuff. I don't know if any of it is worth anything, but we'll see."

They approached an end of a long corridor. A massive stone that would have completely blocked the way stood parallel to the corridor walls, pivoted on a central post.

"Maybe whoever took everything didn't see this chamber, because of the door," Kurash suggested.

"I might have thought that, but there's another one at the other end of the corridor, and that chamber has been picked clean."

"Which side of this door faced the corridor?"

"This side." He pointed.

In the center was painted an open hand, the palm facing out. "That can't mean anything good. Maybe back then, people knew better than to go in there."

He entered. It was a small chamber, compared to most of the others in the palace. The floor stretched about one hundred times Kurash's height. "Glass!" Kurash said. "They used to blow it in Seraz, but I can't imagine a furnace that could make these things."

"Yes. And there are jugs of glass and some of fired clay. You can see that some items used to be iron." He pointed out a heap of rust.

Kurash stepped onto a newly built scaffold and saw that ropes had been used to remove a glass stopper from a glass jug. "This reeks of proof spirit. Did you open this, or did your crew show their initiative after you'd left?"

"Those slugs!" Many of the jugs still contained liquid. Their glass stoppers were sealed with wax.

"That large vessel on the bench—the one with a wick-hole out the top, likely burned either oil or proof spirit," Kurash pointed out. "Oil would leave soot on the glass."

"That must be the oldest beverage ever consumed by a Faerie."

"I suspect this is where the old fool conjured some of his potions. They're lucky they found proof spirit instead of something much worse. I would suggest you close off this room permanently."

"When I accepted election as Archon," Pyxis complained, "I had no idea what a horrid, thankless job it is." The middle-age Faerie sat on Kurash's examination bench while the healer examined his swollen knuckles.

"So many years as a sculptor has taken payment from your joints," Kurash commented.

"Back then, all I worried about was having enough money to eat. Now I have enough to eat from a golden fork, but the worries have grown beyond my endurance."

"Is it Alketas?"

"Yes, Alketas." He ran his free hand delicately over his thinning hair. "Everyone in town is afraid his excavations will cause all of Tellia to fall into a giant hole. It doesn't matter how carefully I explain that he simply exposed the entrance, that he really isn't digging beneath the town. They want me to put a stop to it. I think they're mostly fed up with the riff-raff he brings in to do the work. Every time they find more treasure, the scoundrels return to wherever they came from to squander their share, and he brings in a new bunch that's even less savory."

"You have rheumatism in your hands." From a clay jar on the shelf, Kurash scooped a gray-white powder into a folded pocket of waxed vellum. "Put a pinch of this into warm water and drink it. You do that two times each day."

"What is it?"

"It's made from the cartilage of a fish with no backbone. Comes from Lake Willow."

"Why doesn't it have a backbone?"

"You'll have to ask whatever Mage King dreamed it up."

"How long do you think Alketas will continue digging up the area?"

"You drew the map, Pyxis. This is the seventh excavation. I counted fifteen likely buildings, not considering the wall mounds, five wall towers and four gates. He spends about a year on each one. Could be a while."

The clinic shook, with a deep rumbling sound. Kurash reached out to the examination bench to steady himself. An instant later, it stopped.

A head popped into the doorway. "Archon, the south end of town has collapsed!"

Kurash recalled the special kitchen he had seen the previous day. Its ceiling had easily reached eighty times his own height—well over a hundred faerielongs. He was certain there would be deaths.

"That swivel door just sheared right off the post when we pulled the ropes." Dunthum, the crew boss, was still shaking an hour after the collapse. He stood in the shattered end of the corridor, just clear of the massive pile of fractured white stone, as he spoke with Alketas and Kurash, as well as the Archon and the aged Ephor. Sunlight streamed in for the first time in two thousand years. Three of his crew were killed immediately, and three more injured. The remainder now assisted in crawling through the rubble to remove the bodies of Faeries that had fallen all the way from the town above—so far, none of those who fell had survived. "We heard it all crack, and ran." His face, arms and wings were covered with fine white powder.

"We decided that it would be best to close the room," Alketas explained to Pyxis and Gordion, the Ephor.

"Why is that?" Gordion asked, his voice little more than a croak.

Alketas glanced at Kurash. "The workers had found a large quantity of proof spirit two nights ago, and had consumed so much that they all became ill."

"Two thousand year old spirit?" Pyxis asked.

"It was sealed very well in glass," Kurash said. "I should check the injured workers again."

"How badly are they hurt?" Gordion croaked. The tops of his wings showed the frays and wrinkles of old age.

"One broken leg, one crushed foot, and a deep cut. They should all recover." Kurash headed back toward the entrance, passing those carrying bodies of Faeries who had died in the fall. He counted seventeen dead before he stopped counting.

He recalled the paintings of the winged humans who could actually fly. The Mage King had somehow given them wings of sufficient span to lift their bodies into the air. When they were reduced to Faeries, apparently by nothing more than carelessness on the part of the Mage King, their wings became nearly useless, helpful only for softening a short fall. Those unfortunate citizens of Tellia who dropped into the hundred faerielong pit created by the collapse probably flapped their wings until their endurance was exhausted, then plummeted to their deaths. Those within buildings that fell into that abyss likely died before they had the slightest idea what was happening.

Saracets, of course, had no wings at all. "Saracet," he corrected himself. He had learned about the destruction of all the Saracets in the great city of Seraz. *I'm the last Saracet in all of Ternaria.* It hardly mattered. As a eunuch, he could never propagate his cursed race. They had brought their extinction upon their own heads.

As Kurash approached the chamber which currently served as a residence for the workers, he could hear their complaints long before he entered.

"...nothing. The whole thing is empty!"

"Now we can't even get a drink. That's all that's worth a damn in this stinking hole."

"And he sends us that horned...black-skin turd, instead of a real healer."

The conversation abruptly ceased when he entered, replaced by a background of moaning from the three who were injured. He squatted beside the Faerie with a crushed foot and gently pressed a toenail. When he released it, its pink color immediately returned. The splint he had applied earlier had obviously been untied and retied so as to be looser. He retied it properly. "If you would prefer to be crippled the rest of your life, then you may loosen it as much as you like after I've left."

He stepped to the Faerie with a laceration to his forearm. He carefully lifted the bandage and examined the cut.

"Ain't you going to sew it up or something?"

"No. It is deep and contaminated with two thousand year old dirt, dust, stone fragments, and I can't imagine what else. If I sew it, it will fester and split open again. This will heal slowly and leave a big scar, but it will heal."

The worker who had broken his thigh bone lay whimpering, paying no attention to his surroundings. Kurash checked that the toes were pink. He turned to the other workers. "I will come back shortly with some opium. I will need a length of rope and the assistance of eight of you to set the bone."

Kurash walked to the door and turned back to them. "Or, you can carry him three days to Mount Easley and take him to a real healer."

When a Faerie who resembled the one with the broken thigh bone walked into Kurash's clinic the day after his bone had been set, Kurash was stunned. Dunthum, the crew boss, came with him.

"Yes," Dunthum said. "You set that thief's leg last night."

"That's not possible." Indeed, he still wore the pokewood brace that Kurash had so laboriously fitted and wrapped and tied.

"It's some elixir they got into last night," Dunthum explained. "I don't know how much they drank, but it had them feeling so refurbished and all, they gave some to your hurt boys. Come morning, nobody felt the worse for it, and them that was hurt was up and walking around. Damnedest thing."

"They found it under all the stone that fell into the kitchen?"

"I think that's so."

Kurash examined the braced leg, then removed the bracing. "Nothing natural can do that. I would advise them to avoid drinking any more of that, or anything else from the kitchen. It may have effects that we have yet to see."

"I hope not," Dunthum said. "I might of taken a couple swigs myself."

The healer stepped back and studied the previously injured Faerie. "Your wings seem...larger than usual for a Faerie. Have they always been like that?"

"I never thought about it," the Faerie answered. "Now you mention it, they kind of ache. Only part of me that don't feel up to perfection."

"Mine ache a bit too," Dunthum added. "I thought it was on the outcome of all that commotion yesterday."

Dunthum's wings seemed to be of an average size to Kurash's eye. "Stay away from that elixir, until I can understand what it's doing."

"That might be hard," Dunthum said. "Everybody's feeling like that's all the payout they're likely to snag on this dig. Might not be another dig after the accident and all."

"I'll go back with you. I'd like to get a sample of the elixir and see what vessel it came from." He picked up a fired clay cup with a lid.

"If there's any left," the healed Faerie said.

As they headed for the excavation, Alketas approached them. "Head on down," he said to the two workers. "I need to talk with Kurash." When the others were beyond hearing, Alketas continued. "I'm in a thick soup. The Ephor just told me that everybody wants me to pay families for the folks that got killed and to pay to rebuild anything that got damaged. That's fourteen buildings and twenty three killed, not counting the three dead workers."

"That may not be your only problem. Do you remember in the tomb of the Mage King the painting that showed him making humans grow wings?"

"Yes."

"I'm afraid that he may have done that with a magic elixir. Your workers went back into the kitchen and found something that healed a broken thigh bone overnight, and I think it's making their wings change."

As Kurash and Alketas approached the descent to the entrance, two Faeries lifted into the air and flew past them. Once the flying Faeries reached a height far above the town, they began to circle it slowly. Their wings stretched to three times the wingspan of a Faerie.

After two circles, they veered west and vanished in the direction of Mount Easley.

Alketas and Kurash walked into a chamber of laughing, drinking workers, most with a pair of extraordinary wings. Those with lesser wings were doing most of the drinking.

"I need a sample of the elixir," Kurash shouted over the din.

"Get your own," someone shouted.

Dunthum slapped that Faerie in the back of the head. "Wyranic, show them where you got this stuff."

Wyranic escorted them down the full length of the building, toward the tumbled section, all the while flexing his huge wings. He climbed over the debris and pointed. "Them two."

Two glass containers stood with their glass stoppers hoisted above them. Nearby stood a drinking cup lashed with silk to a long rod. The scaffold that they had built to reach the proof spirit had been repaired and positioned by the two open containers. Kurash handed his fired clay cup to Alketas, then took the long scoop up the scaffold. He dipped it into one of the containers. With care, he poured it into his cup. Alketas pressed the lid on tightly.

Outside the dig, five broad-winged Faeries circled high over the town.

"The Ephor may allow me to repay the deaths and the damage with the wing elixir." Alketas sat on Kurash's examination bench.

"But we don't yet know if there might be ill effects. Each container is about half again my height. So I would guess that it is an amount for a single human. Human! A human is about a hundred times taller than a Faerie, so a human body weighs a thousand times more than a Faerie. Your workers have consumed among them nearly two thirds of a human dose. That should be enough for over six hundred Faeries. They've each taken twenty-five times the dose. If I'm wrong about one container being a single human dose, it only gets worse. Maybe the Mage King placed a single drop on the tongue of each human. I have to tell the Ephor not to allow this."

"You have to be reasonable about this, Kurash."

"Something about its efficacy was altered when the size of those humans was changed in the Mage King's accident—when they shrank and became Faeries. They still had wings, and all their children had wings, but none could fly. Did any try to get more elixir?"

"Maybe they couldn't get to it," Alketas suggested.

"Or maybe they did, and it didn't end well. We just don't know."

"But Kurash, you just don't understand how incredible a discovery this is. Saracets have never had wings. Faeries have always had wings, but they could never do what wings are meant to do: to fly, to really fly. Wouldn't you give anything to be able to fly?"

"I've never given it the slightest thought."

Gordion stepped into the clinic. "Healer, I just wanted to let you know I won't be needing your medicines, at least for a while." His voice rang crisp and true, as Kurash had first heard him in the court, years earlier. His wings were huge and youthful. "Alketas, I believe all of the aggrieved will happily reach an agreement on you terms." The Ephor then stepped out and rose into the air.

"It truly works wonders," Alketas said.

"How much of the elixir is there?"

"We've found three more full containers and the two that are still about two-thirds full. That's as far down as they could reach with their scoop. I have four armed guards watching it now."

"You're not planning to drink it, are you?"

"I've thought about it."

"You saw how careless the Mage King was. We know what happened to his armies. He didn't blink when he thought they had been consumed by his magic. We don't know what ever happened to those Dragomin. We don't know what happened to all the people in Tel. With magic, there was always a price to pay."

"Well, they lived long enough to build him that tomb when he died in old age."

"If he was old when he died. Maybe he conquered his enemy, then shriveled up the next day. Those wing bones were awfully deformed."

"You two better come see this." Darissa, Alketas mother, stood at the doorway.

Kurash stooped beneath the lintel. Two of the townsfolk carried the Ephor toward him. He led them into the clinic. "What happened?"

"I saw it," Darissa said. "He stepped out of your clinic, flapped his ridiculous wings, flew down the street just a little way off the ground, then seemed confused and tumbled to the stone."

Kurash examined the unconscious Gordion. His wings and skin had taken on a dusky appearance. His pulse felt thready and rapid. "How much elixir did he drink?"

"Quite a bit," Alketas admitted. "Maybe he was just too old for it."

"When did he drink it?"

"About six hours ago."

"Alketas," Darissa scolded, "I can't believe you gave that potion to him."

"Mama, he's the twenty-eighth Faerie to drink it, and the first to show any problems."

Kurash opened a container of acrid liquid and poured some of it into a clean bowl. To that, he added a small amount of the elixir from the palace and stirred it. Flakes formed in the liquid and settled to the bottom. "This elixir contains either mercury, lead or silver—all poisonous to Faeries."

"What was that?" Darissa asked.

"Vomit acid, strained and boiled down." He poured away the liquid, heated some water, added it to the flakes, then poured it off. "Lead would go into the hot water." Finally, he opened another foul smelling container. "This is essence of fermented urine." He added some to the remaining flakes, which entirely dissolved. "No mercury. This may or may not have a small amount of lead, but most if not all of this ingredient is silver. I would say there's quite a bit in that elixir. It wouldn't hurt a human, or a Saracet, for that matter, but it is poisonous to Faeries."

"Can you treat it with something?" Alketas asked.

"In Lilac, they have a treatment for silver poisoning of the skin, but I don't believe it will work for internal poisoning."

"That's more than a week away." Alketas appeared distressed.

"You've got twenty seven more Faeries that may become ill."

"Some have flown away to who knows where."

"If you can identify a young, healthy looking worker that drank the least of the elixir, send him to Lilac. He may make it there by tonight. Also send someone on foot, just to be sure."

The Ephor died the following evening. By then, his skin had darkened to black, and his huge, youthful wings had blackened and shriveled. As a result, Kurash had been offered some unpleasant comments regarding his competence as a healer. Over the following week, seven more Faeries blackened and died. Three more were ill.

Darissa ran into the clinic. "The group from Lilac is here. They're setting up a big purple stone in the side yard."

Kurash stooped through the doorway. On the clear ground south of the clinic, they positioned a transparent lavender stone of about Kurash's height.

"This is Vifredo," Darissa said, "First Tribune of Lilac. Tribune, this is our healer, Kurash."

At those words, the Tribune looked up with shock in his eyes. "A Saracet," he mumbled. The six Faeries who had accompanied him stopped what they were doing and stared in disbelief at Kurash.

"We've come to help a Saracet?" the Tribune asked.

"No, Tribune," Kurash replied. "Eight Faeries have died of silver poison, and twenty more have been exposed. They foolishly drank an elixir from an ancient building."

The Tribune's hand touched the hilt of a sword. "I'll help the Faeries who are ill," he said to Darissa, "but I want nothing to do with that black-skin butcher."

"I don't care if you're a Tribune," Darissa retorted, "or if you think that sword makes you important, but you're a fool. Kurash warned those stupid Faeries not to touch that stuff, then when they did anyway and got sick, he figured out it had silver in it. You should be ashamed."

"I'm sure," Vifredo said, "Saracets know quite a bit about silver."

Kurash turned and went back to his clinic. There, waiting inside, was the Archon, Pyxis.

"Kurash, my friend, I've been asked by the council to tell you that you must leave Tellia. They somehow blame you for all that's happened. There is a rumor that you insisted that the ancient swivel door be closed, and caused the collapse. They feel that you are withholding the elixir from them in order to have it for yourself. They believe you have caused the Ephor and the workers to die through evil intent. They're just looking for someone to blame. You are the easiest to blame. Perhaps if you could go away for a week or two, they would see their mistake."

"You are right. It is time to go. Could you ask Darissa to come in?"

Pyxis hesitated, then exited. Kurash gathered some medicines and belongings into a pack. When Darissa entered, she had tears in her eyes.

"You're not going to let them do this, are you?"

"No. I'm choosing to go. All of my share of the treasure from the tomb of the Mage King is stored in the little house out back. I've never spent any of it. I want you to take half and use it in any way you wish, and arrange for the other half to be shipped to the school in Faerie Ring. Maybe they would be interested in having a teacher of healing arts and medicinal gardening."

"I'll miss you, Kurash."

"Say goodbye to Alketas for me."

Kurash, the last Saracet in all of Ternaria, stooped through the doorway of his clinic one final time. He was well beyond Tellia by nightfall. He camped beside his medicine garden. Before going to sleep, he removed a small container from his pack and drank all of the liquid it contained. A sense of wellbeing spread through his body as he fell asleep. Perhaps, he thought, Dianthus, Mage King of Tel—his dead god—could answer one more prayer.

CHAPTER 16—THORNS OF PARTHA

Gedzik lifted a fist-size chunk of stone from its basket, carrying with it its aura of diaphanous, glowing filaments, and placed it on top of his desk. Though the stone and its aura fascinated him, his attention was centered on the face of the Moon Faerie seated across from him. Her white eyebrows lifted. "Tell me what you see, Issilla."

"A rock that glows." She sat expectantly in her long sleeve, floor length, lavender tunic, its cowled hood pushed back onto her shoulders.

"More specific, please." As master of the Lilac Academy for the past two years, he was accustomed to prodding, to encouraging his students to discover the knowledge they already possessed. For the Moon Faeries, that was a considerable body of uncategorized observations, stored in the scattered recesses of their minds.

"It's a translucent red rock...of irregular shape...that appears to emit a mesh of reddish, glowing lines from one point, that circle around to another point on the opposite side. They extend on all sides a distance similar to the thickness of the rock, and..." She hesitantly passed a finger through the glow. "...the glow has no substance."

"Have you ever been to the boundary of Ternaria, Issilla?"

"No."

Like himself, Issilla's hair was pure white and her skin without color. Though twelve years old—the first of the Moon Faeries—she appeared to be about six. Her colorless eyes revealed a glimmer of red from within. And like Gedzik, she was born without wings—considered blighted, cursed. "Thank you, Issilla. Excellent description. That will be all."

Issilla was the child of a Faerie who had been among those captured by the Saracets thirteen years ago and rescued from the silver mines of Seraz by the Great Faerie Army. Silver poisoning had been cured by moonlight passing through the transparent lilac monolith, which now stood in the center of Lilac's famous grove. Issilla, born the following year, was wingless, runted and white as mouse milk. Fifteen more of these Moon Babies had gravitated to Lilac Academy over the past seven years. Each had one parent who had been a captive in the mines. Gedzik knew of two instances where both mates had been captive. These produced only pathetic, colorless, wingless stillborns. No one knew how many live-born Moon Babies had been exposed at birth, never to be counted among the blighted.

Gedzik himself had been exposed at birth for the very same deformities, but that was twenty six years ago, long before the whole business with the silver mines and moonlight. Though the cause in his case was anybody's guess, he felt it reasonable to encourage the label of "Moon Baby," or for those beyond infancy, "Moon Faerie," as a replacement for the less considerate ascriptions of "blight baby" or merely "blighter."

"I caught you."

Gedzik turned to see Riquilda at the door. "I'm on my way to lead sword forms," he replied. "Walk with me."

Riquilda glanced at the translucent stone on his desk. "What's that?"

"It's sarcite."

"Like they use up at Moss Abbey?"

"Yes. I asked a longhauler to bring me a piece that was too small for the monks to use." He felt more complete whenever Riquilda stopped by the Academy. She had stepped down as master two years ago to accept her appointment as Third Tribune of Lilac.

"What do you see?"

"Is this a trick, Gedzik?"

"No." He nodded toward the corridor.

Riquilda walked beside him. "Um...red rock? Milky red rock? Milky red rock that probably cost a lot? What?" The black trim of her lavender tunic gave her an officious look, but her pure white hair gave away her status as one of the rescued captives. Unlike the Moon Faeries, Riquilda was of normal height—a third taller than Gedzik. Unlike the other captives, she had elected to not take a mate, despite her remarkable beauty at the still fertile age of twenty six.

"The sarcite produces an aura that resembles what I see at the boundary of Ternaria."

"Those glowy lines?"

"Yes. I've asked all ten of the Moon Faeries nine years or older the same question I asked you. All of them see the aura. None has ever been to the boundary, so I can't say for certain that they would be able to see it, but I suspect they would."

"The monks use sarcite to maintain the boundary with some sort of magic. So you think..."

"Yes. This is the same thing. It would be easier to make sense out of why the Moon Faeries can see it, if I knew why we share the same peculiarities."

"I can't remember if we ever talked about it, but that Vanivoort, at Chive Crossing, told us that the night you were found as a newborn, it was only because there was a full moon."

"I don't believe I've heard that. It's curious, but we're still missing any connection with silver poisoning."

They reached the exercise room. Thirty two students, ranging in age from six to fourteen stood erect in four ranks, eight abreast. As with Gedzik, each wore the school uniform—designed ten years earlier by Riquilda—of a long-sleeved, floor-length lavender tunic with a cowled hood. With their hoods thrown back, the sixteen Moon Faeries among them were conspicuous by their white hair and short stature.

"Oh, Gedzik, before you go on... The reason I came by was to let you know that Vifredo was grumbling again at the council last night about the growing number of Moon Faeries at the school."

"It's been at sixteen for the past eight months."

"I guess another pilgrim made a comment about it."

"Well, it's their own lilac stone that started it all."

"I know."

"I have to begin." Gedzik reached out and squeezed her hand as she departed. When he entered the doorway, the students simultaneously slapped left hands to the scabbards strapped to their waists. At his command of, "First form, begin!" each drew his or her pokewood saber and moved through the positions, their feet striking the polished maple bark floor in synchrony. Against the wall, the cook practiced his lute to their rhythm.

"Partha has been causing problems for the past year," Gedzik said. He stood at the margin of the lilac grove with Pippi, who taught geography at the Academy one day each week.

"But this is different. Chagadi has taken control of Partha's army, and is demanding that Oakhaven and Domes send him a levy of troops and a portion of their tax to support his campaign against the Thistlepix."

"And if they don't?"

"He says he'll take over the villages." Pippi's creation of a map of all Ternaria had served not only to improve travel and trade, but also to encourage the Faeries of some villages to covet the resources of their neighbors. Partha, which abutted the Thistlepix lands seemed, from a quick glance at the map, to have inherited the unfortunate proximity to an unfair degree. "Chagadi thinks they owe it to him for bearing the brunt of the Thistlepix raids."

"So, to protect them from the Thistlepix, who have made no aggressive moves against Faeries for almost two decades, he's threatening to conquer his neighbors?"

"You have a way with words, Gedzik."

"Is he strong enough to do it?"

"The Faeries in Domes and Oakhaven think so."

Shouts arose from the pilgrims that filled the circular promenade within the grove. Overhead, a single wasp and a single apis drone descended. Riding on the drone, a Faerie; on the wasp, an unarmed Thistlepix. Pilgrims scattered in all directions, fleeing into the surrounding lilac. Vifredo, First Tribune of Lilac, and two assistants approached cautiously, their raspberry pikes held ready. Gedzik and Pippi moved closer as well. A Faerie on an apis drone was a rare occurrence in Lilac. The arrival of an unarmed Thistlepix was unheard of.

Both the Faerie and the Thistlepix who stepped down from their mounts appeared quite old. The Faerie, in a beige tunic, seemed to identify the tribune by his white-bordered tunic and approached him.

"Tribune, I am Rath, Elder of Domes. I come on a diplomatic mission to speak with Nebridio." His shoulders hunched, despite holding his balding head erect.

"Is this Thistlepix your captive, Elder?" Vifredo had not yet lowered his pike.

The old Thistlepix wore trousers of dark purple satin and a lighter purple satin blouse with ruffles at the collar. He, of course, had no wings. He walked with a slight limp, his left leg appearing to be slightly shorter than the right. He knelt to hobble the wasp by a front and back leg.

Rath smiled as he placed his hand over the tip of Vifredo's pike and pressed it toward the ground. "This is my lifelong friend, Dobar, King of the Thistlepix. If you would kindly take us to Nebridio."

The gray haired Dobar noticed Gedzik standing nearby and, after staring for a moment, nodded to him. Even among the famous lilacs, Gedzik could detect a scent of lavender.

"I will gladly take you to Nebridio, Elder, but the Thistlepix must remain under guard." Vifredo motioned for his two assistants to watch the Thistlepix.

"You, Tribune," Rath said, not one hand's width from Vifredo's face, "are an ignorant fool..."

"Perhaps," Gedzik interrupted, "King Dobar could visit the Academy—under guard, of course—while the matter is cleared up."

"That sounds like a fine idea," Pippi added. As Nebridio's stepson, Pippi's endorsement left Vifredo with little choice.

"Very well," Vifredo said. "Come with me Elder." Vifredo and Rath headed toward Nebridio's two-level, bark shingled home on the far side of the grove.

Pippi turned to the two guards. "Leave."

"But, sir, we were ordered to..."

"Leave," he said again, more emphatically. Pippi introduced himself and Gedzik to King Dobar, apologizing for the unfriendly reception. The three of them walked toward the Academy.

"Master Gedzik," Dobar said, "you appear too young to be the master of a school, yet too old to be among the blighted babies."

"You seem to know the details of our little secret, King Dobar," Gedzik said.

"Ternaria is a very small place, Gedzik."

"Pippi has actually demonstrated that fact with his maps."

"Yes. Very impressive work. Both of your maps," he said to Pippi, "decorate the walls of my council chamber. Sobering comparison between the two. Ternaria hardly shows up on the map of all the eastern lands."

They entered the Academy, with Vifredo's two assistants clumsily attempting to hide their positioning to observe both entrances. Gedzik led the Thistlepix King to a small conference chamber.

"Bring us some black tea, please," he said to the active majordomo, a duty which rotated at weekly intervals among a group of the oldest students. Once they were comfortably seated, he continued. "I was born the way I am for reasons that remain a mystery. We do, however, have sixteen Moon Faeries—a more euphonious term—enrolled at the Academy. Intellectually, they all seem to be more gifted than those who are unblighted, so to speak."

"If I could interrupt," Pippi said, "I'm terribly curious about the cause for such an unusual visit."

"There are no diplomatic mysteries, Pippi, but I should wait to speak with Nebridio first, as a courtesy."

As the majordomo entered with a pitcher of black tea and three cups, Nebridio, Elder of Lilac, followed her, slightly out of breath. Rath came in after him.

Nebridio looked at those now in the conference chamber and then at the tray in the hand of the confused student. "Go ahead and serve what you have, son, then bring two more cups. King Dobar, I am pleased to finally meet you. I'm Nebridio. My First Tribune has a problem with those who don't look enough like him."

"And with some of those who do," Pippi added.

Dobar stood and offered his hand to Nebridio. "Thank you for seeing me."

"So what is it that brings you here, King Dobar?"

"Chagadi's army has taken Oakhaven, Domes and Nart, a small town just north of Kizikum. Partha now threatens Faerie Ring. He is not yet strong enough to confront us directly, but if Partha conquers most of Ternaria, he will surely send the Parthans against the Pix."

"How is it that he takes these towns so easily?" Nebridio asked.

"A new weapon," Rath replied, "and a new way to use it to advantage. They take the great thorns of the hawthorn, shave their base to make them lighter, then use them as infantry pikes. Because they are three times the length of our pikes, his army can present the points of three ranks of Faeries in front of their battle line. They form into a phalanx that can defend from any side, or all sides at once. Our forces in Domes fled in panic."

"If Chagadi takes Faerie Ring," Dobar added, "he will turn south."

"Is there a way," Nebridio asked, "to defend against the Parthan phalanx?"

"Archers?" Gedzik asked.

"In addition to the thorn pikes," Rath continued, "each Faerie carries a heavy, square shield. When arrows are launched against them, they are able to lock the shields together, like a great tortoise shell. A notch on the side of each shield allows the pike to protrude. The infantry also wears armor made of overlapping rows of small shingles of bark—hickory, I believe. Sometimes crossbows can penetrate it, but ordinary arrows fail."

"His infantry numbers one thousand," Dobar said. "Chagadi also commands five hundred Parthan archers, and a corps of engineers who have built ten catapults on wheels, pulled by mice. These catapults can throw a stone of more than my own weight against whatever defense works you construct."

"How far?" Pippi asked.

"Over a hundred faerielongs," Rath replied.

"If Chagadi already threatens Faerie Ring," Nebridio said, "then we have no more than a week to prepare."

"I know of a Faerie named Tatt, in Elby," Pippi said. "He is said to have a method, using crystal prisms, of directing sunlight to cause fire."

"Send for him, Pippi."

"I have designed a machine, a ballista, that will release three heavy arrows," Gedzik said. "Besides being untested, it would take us too long to build them. But if Joshi could sail the *Luli Shibami* downriver to Shibam, the human jeweler, Hamsa, might be able to build a number of them in a day. The ship could carry eight of them collapsed."

Nebridio scratched his rim of white hair. "If Joshi will do that, then go ahead. I will send Riquilda with a small force to the bridge at Nettle Falls, and a fast runner to Westbog for fish oil and dried peat. Will you help us, King Dobar?"

"I will try. Some of the Pix are content to have the Faeries destroy one another. At the very least, Rath and I can arrange for messages to go to all of the Faerie villages and towns throughout Ternaria." The King sipped his tea.

"Will you leave today," Nebridio asked, "or can you rest for the night?"

Rath and Dobar looked at one another. Both were clearly exhausted. To Gedzik's blighted eyes, they looked even older than Nebridio. "I'm sure," Gedzik interjected, "that you are both eager to go, but that might prove a hardship for your mounts. I believe the apis and the wasp should be allowed to rest and feed among the lilac blossoms."

"Like ourselves," Rath replied, "the apis and the wasp are not as youthful as they once were. If we could impose upon you for—for the sake of our mounts." He winked at Gedzik.

"Of course," Nebridio said. "You are invited to stay in my home."

"If I could divide and conquer," Gedzik said, "I would invite King Dobar to spend the night at the Academy, with the hope of cajoling him to speak to our students before he departs in the morning."

"I am flattered," Dobar replied. "Speak at your academy. I may be a king, but I have never learned to read and write."

"Your words and your mere presence would be a treasured memory for all our young students. Most have never seen a Thistlepix, much less a king. So it is agreed?"

"Gedzik could talk a caracol out of its shell," Pippi chuckled.

Dobar smiled. "I see that. I accept your invitation, assuming your Tribune has not arrested me before then."

"So much of that conflict was because Faerie tribes were mostly nomadic." Dobar strolled through the Academy garden with Gedzik and Pippi. The sun was approaching the horizon, but the sky still provided ample light reflected from puffy, white clouds. "After so many centuries, it has just been within my lifetime that most Faerie tribes have settled in permanent villages and built towns. I believe Lilac was second only to Faerie Ring to do so. As a result, the Pix and the Faeries have ceased to fight, at least until Chagadi decided that Partha should enlarge her territory."

"I suppose it's their good fortune," Pippi commented, "that the hawthorn grows nowhere else in Ternaria." He, like Gedzik, now wore a steel cuirass, and had belted his steel saber to his hip.

"So many of our young died in those needless wars of the past," the king said. "It hurts me deeply to see the senseless killing begin again. We even squeaked through that business with the Saracets without a general war."

"Berenguer would have expanded that war," Pippi pointed out, "but Nebridio and Caluño refused to allow it."

"I have heard that, though not from so unquestionable an authority."

Gedzik drew his saber. "A large bird is approaching." He pointed the gently curved blade to the east. A dark body with enormous wings glided directly toward them.

"That's Kurash!" Pippi said.

Dark wingtips flared, easing the Saracet healer to the ground. Taller than the Thistlepix king, the dark-skin Saracet appeared even taller because of the two curved black horns that grew to either side of his forehead.

Gedzik had met Kurash once before, at the Daiella School in Faerie Ring, but had been told that the teacher never traveled. He returned his saber to its jeweled scabbard.

"I had heard," Dobar said, "that the Saracets were no more."

"Kurash," Gedzik said, "This is Dobar, King of the Thistlepix. Kurash teaches the healing arts at Faerie Ring."

Kurash bowed politely to the King. "Indeed, when I am in my grave, which shouldn't be too long now, the Saracets will be no more. I bring terrible news. The school has been destroyed. Your brother," he directed to Pippi, "is dead. Willi led a small group of defenders in holding back the Parthans so that old Quartrik could escape with the children. He is on his way here with forty. He is hoping to find temporary accommodation for them at the Academy. Faerie Ring will likely fall in the next day or two. Their situation is hopeless."

"Are you certain that Willi is dead?" Pippi asked, anguish in his eyes.

"I am afraid there is no doubt. Three of the oldest students refused to leave, and died bravely at his side."

"I'll go tell Nebridio." Pippi solemnly shook Kurash's hand and Dobar's, then ran from the garden.

"The children," Kurash continued, "will arrive in four days, since their number is too great for the river barge. Chagadi will not be far behind them."

After King Dobar had retired to a guest room for the night, Gedzik posted four of the older children in the corridor outside the door, for his protection. Their scabbards held sabers of hammered steel. Bernaldo, the bladesmith, had made them to order as presentations for these four students, who would be the next to graduate from the Academy. Gedzik decided that the current crisis demanded that they be put into the skilled hands of these four immediately. He was confident that any of them could easily defend against most other Faeries of any size, one on one.

At the moment, he sat in his study, speaking privately with Kurash. "Two years ago, you spoke of the antiquities found beneath Tellia."

"Yes." The Saracet appeared uncomfortable with the subject.

Gedzik placed five small pieces of sarcite in a line on his desk. "Is this the stone you described as forming the handle of some of the human daggers?"

Kurash's brow lifted. "That is the same, I believe."

"Something unusual about my eyes allows me to see the boundary of Ternaria when I approach it. The boundary appears as a filamentous web that glows. No other Faeries can see it, except for the Moon Faeries, who apparently share all my abnormalities. When you look at the sarcite, what do you see?"

"Simply the stones."

"I can see a similar glowing web emanating from the stones. When they are close to each other, as they are now, their strands are shared, reaching from one stone to its neighbors. If I separate them by a hand's width, they no longer share."

"What does all this mean?"

"If, instead, I position five of them as a pentagon..." He rearranged the stones. "...not only do they share, but I can move them to any distance apart, and they still share their strands, and with far more intensity. It requires five stones, no fewer, and in this arrangement. A sixth sarcite will not participate."

"This is interesting, Gedzik, but I still fail to understand its significance."

"The monks of Moss Abbey use sarcite in some way to bring about the magic that maintains the boundaries of Ternaria. It is the magic that I see at the boundary. Sarcite somehow channels magic. The weapons you found were imbued with some kind of magic."

"I suspect that the use of magic is what brought about the demise of Tel and Ternara, the human cities that once were here. Are you sure that you want to explore that path?"

"If it could help to stop Chagadi, yes."

"There were also human weapons mounted with translucent green stone, often on the larger swords. I believe it is jadeite, and suspect that it may have greater power than the sarcite. One curiosity of the ruins of Tel is that, despite there being numerous inscriptions found within them, no books or scrolls are there. It seems that at some point, all of the portable writings were taken away, as though someone wished to remove the knowledge they might have held."

"To prevent the further use of magic?"

"Perhaps. Tomorrow, I will fly to Tellia to request their military assistance. While I am there, I can look for any artifact that might help us, though I'm not sure what that would be."

All thirty-two students of the Lilac Academy rose to their feet in the exercise chamber and applauded as Kurash and King Dobar took their leave. Both had spoken of their hopes for the future and of cooperation in bringing peace once again to Ternaria. Kurash lifted from the garden and flew to the northeast, to avoid any confrontation with

Vifredo, whom he spoke of encountering years before in Tellia. King Dobar, now with Rath at his side, proceeded to the promenade, led by his honor guard of four armed students, and accompanied by Gedzik and Pippi.

"Nebridio was named Dictator by the council last night," Pippi said as they walked, speaking with a somber tone, his eyes reddened. "He refused, saying he would manage the crisis as Elder of Lilac."

"There are few who would be so wise," Dobar said. "Even as King, I would be foolish not to listen to those who disagree with me. Nebridio seems to be more circumspect than his council."

"He named Caluño as Strategus," Pippi continued. "I am Caluño's First Lieutenant; Riquilda was named as his Second. Vifredo was expecting the post of Strategus, and is not pleased with how things turned out."

"I've heard that Riquilda is already at the bridge at the falls," Gedzik said.

"Yes. She will await the oil and dried peat from Westbog, then see which side of the river Chagadi has taken. We can't hold the bridge, so she will retreat with her force." Pippi looked at Dobar as they walked. "It is sad that we should only be brought together by war, King Dobar."

"All wars eventually end. May we end it as friends." Dobar placed the long, slender fingers of his hand on Pippi's shoulder. "I am sorry for your brother's death. I fear that there will be many more before we are through with Partha."

Vifredo approached with six pike bearers as they entered the promenade. "The Thistlepix is to be held as a spy, until this war is over. Stand away from him."

Simultaneously, Pippi and Gedzik drew their sabers and assumed a defensive stance. The four armed students then did likewise.

"That will not happen, Tribune," Pippi stated flatly. "Call off your pikes, or there will be blood spilled."

"I have ordered him arrested, and I shall see that carried out."

Rath stepped forward. "King Dobar is not only our ally in this conflict, he is here under talk truce as a diplomat. What you are attempting violates all decency."

"Stand away, Elder," Vifredo said through gritted teeth.

"Advance!" Gedzik commanded. The student honor guard took three steps forward, brandishing their sabers in figures before them. The pike bearers stepped back, looking to the Tribune for instructions. "Advance!" They took three more steps, driving the pike bearers backwards.

"Stop this!" Nebridio approached, looking haggard and years older than the night before. "Students, sheathe your sabers. What is going on?"

"I have ordered the detention of the Thistlepix as a possible spy."

Nebridio stood speechless.

"Father," Pippi said, "you can't allow this outrage."

The Elder of Lilac looked at the pike bearers. "All six of you, go and help Caluño with the earthworks. There is too much to do and too little time. Tribune, I rescind your order. The King is here as a diplomat and will be respected as such. A simple word in advance would have prevented this...awkwardness." He turned to Pippi. "Would you shame us all by shedding blood on the promenade?" Nebridio cupped a hand against the side of his head. "This is all so unnecessary. Allow me to escort you to your mounts."

"You place too much confidence in this nest of cherry-eye blighters, Elder." Vifredo turned and left.

Once Rath and King Dobar had departed, Pippi said, "You don't look well Father. Are you alright?"

"I've had a long night, too little sleep and too much kaffee. If you need me, I'll be resting at home."

"Pippi!" Joshi ran into the promenade. "Hello, Elder. I've brought the students from Faerie Ring."

"On the river?" Nebridio asked.

"Yes sir. They walked all of yesterday and through the night to reach Nettle Falls. I filled two barges and put the rest on the *Luli Shibami*. With full sail, we made it in two hours. They're unloading now. I wanted to get Gedzik's designs for the ballista to take downriver to Hamsa."

"Did you speak with Riquilda?" Pippi asked.

"Yes. She's below the falls on the west. She has scouts at the top, on both sides of the river. It's going to be a close thing with the stuff coming from Westbog. The inns are overflowing with refugees from Faerie Ring and Oakhaven, so you may have another fifty to a hundred Faeries coming this way before Chagadi arrives. The students I brought down haven't had a good meal for at least a couple of days. I've given Quartrik directions to the Academy."

"Very good." Nebridio patted Joshi on the shoulder and headed for his house.

Gedzik spoke to his honor guard. "Run back and tell the cook we have forty hungry students arriving at any moment. Have the rest of the students make room for them. Those under nine will sleep three to a bed; those nine or older, two. Make them feel welcome. Go."

"Where will we put the refugees from the inns?" Pippi asked.

"It may be no safer here than at the inns," Joshi replied.

In his study, Gedzik unrolled the drawings for his ballista. With his bladder pen, he marked four joints, and wrote from right to left in carefully scrolled Sulalic characters, "remove pin for transport." "Tell Hamsa to search for this note with his thick spectacles. This whole drawing is the size of Hamsa's little fingernail. Also tell him that the measurements are meaningless. We need these to be as large as will fit on the *Luli Shibami*, and as many as will fit." He handed Joshi five rings of gold, then sealed the drawings in a map cylinder. As he handed it to Joshi, he grasped his forearm. "Return as quickly as possible. Otherwise, we may have no use for the ballistae. Be safe, my friend."

When he was alone in his study, Gedzik once again set five sarcites on his desk as vertices of a pentagon and stared at the diaphanous, glowing lines. He moved them as far apart as the surface of his desk would allow. His bladder pen now emanated fine, glowing strands that seemed to connect to those of the sarcites. He wondered what would happen if he were to slowly move the pen beyond the bounds of the pentagon. On its own, without being touched, the bladder pen slid to the edge of the desk, stopping when the web of connections detached from it. At the same time, a deep chill ran through him, as though the stones had somehow fed upon him. He jumped back, falling over his wicker stool.

Gedzik scrambled to his feet and quickly pushed one of the sarcite stones out of position. The intensity of the glowing filaments immediately diminished.

The majordomo entered, carrying a tray. "Your lunch, Master Gedzik."

"Just put it... Here, I'll take it. Thank you."

The tray contained a sliced seed of sweetgrass and a small, shallow dish of toasted sesame oil, as well as a cup of Malagaro black tea. After the student left, he placed the tray in the center of his desk and realigned the five sarcite stones. He could plainly see that the sliced seed, the only item of living matter on the tray, behaved differently. A vortex of diaphanous filaments seemed to roil about it, each filament throbbing outward, as if it wanted to touch the nearest sarcite.

His mind drifted, despite his effort to the contrary. He noted that the sesame oil was seldom hot enough. The sliced seed always tasted better dipped in hot oil. Gedzik could feel his thoughts drawing power from the seed and moving it to the oil, which began to smoke. He tapped a sarcite out of alignment. The wicker tray, at the point where it contacted the dish of oil, had scorched. Then he noticed that the seed slices had shrunk considerably.

Understanding struck him suddenly, like a loose tile from the roof. *Magic is not magical.* Magic is merely the manipulation of nature in a manner that is not clearly seen by most others. Any change must draw power from somewhere. The power of a living thing is more easily stolen from it. Every change is brought about by a change in something else.

Another realization tumbled after. *All things are connected.* The sarcites somehow amplify connections that already exist, allowing his abnormal eyes, and those of the Moon Faeries, to see those connections. It seemed to Gedzik that if he could not see the connections, he could not control the counter-change that brought about the desired change. He could imagine a careless attempt at one result inadvertently bringing about his own destruction.

Gedzik realigned the sarcites into a pentagon, then placed his fingertips on two adjacent stones. Connections to objects throughout his study appeared. He moved the fingers of his left hand to a stone on the other side of the pentagon. The connections shifted their relationships in a way that he could not clearly identify. Bringing the stones closer, to form a smaller pentagon, he contacted three stones, then four, and finally all five stones. With each additional contact, the complexities and subtleties of the connections grew. At five contacts, his senses and his mind were saturated beyond their capacity to take it in. Frightened, he shoved the sarcites into a heap at the back of the desk.

If he had years to understand the intricacies of what he had discovered, he thought, he might be able to use it against Chagadi, without killing himself. If it was to be of help in this crisis, it would have to be something very simple and unexpected by the enemy. Nothing more. He had no idea what that might be.

"Sir..." The majordomo interrupted his thoughts, "...the students from Faerie Ring have arrived. I sent them directly to the dining hall for lunch."

"Excellent. Thank you." He put away the sarcites and walked to the dining hall. There he saw forty Faeries crowded onto benches suitable for thirty-two. They ate ravenously—pickled clover blossoms, soup and dark brown wheat cakes with black tea. Against the wall, a large-framed and very ancient Faerie in a black robe sat exhausted on a stool. Gedzik recognized him as Quartrik, Master of the Daiella School. He carried a stool and sat beside him.

"Gedzik," the old Faerie said, "I've never seen the little scoundrels eat so quietly."

"They've probably never been so hungry. Aren't you having anything?"

"Bad stomach." He patted his gaunt abdomen, and with the other hand lifted the cup of black tea he had been holding. "Kurash says I shouldn't drink so much tea. Is he still here?"

"He's gone to Tellia."

"He has spoken of some nasty relics there from past human wars, like the potion that caused his wings, but killed all the Faeries who drank it. Dangerous business, playing with things we don't understand."

"Are all the children in good health?"

"Yes. Far better than my health. For them, walking all day and through the night was a grand adventure. Oh...our three Moon Faeries were excited to see so many like themselves here. Even among our own students, they sometimes have to endure bullying and ridicule. The other students bring their parents' narrow views with them."

"Here, they are bullied only by the First Tribune, who recently discovered that some of our 'blighters' are sabermasters, and not to be trifled with. Very educational."

Quartrik laughed. "I believe this is as far as the students can go to escape that maniac, Chagadi."

"If we can't stop him here, then we are doomed. There are no villages beyond Lilac that could possibly feed and shelter seventy-two children. There is even worse news. We sent messengers to the south and west for assistance. Two have already returned with word that beyond Wither and Ost there is a pox epidemic. There will be no help from there, and no refuge."

"The walls of Seraz might hold against the Parthans, but that is two weeks away, through scrub and wasteland."

"Have you heard that Willi and the students with him have been killed?"

"I had not, but I was afraid that would be the..." He sobbed. "It's too much to bear. And for what? The greed of Chagadi and Willi's pride."

"We all may share that fate."

Quartrik wiped his eyes and nodded.

Gedzik saw striking green emanations from Kurash's waist pack the moment the Saracet stooped to enter the study. Kurash raised his dark hand.

"I have news that should go immediately to Nebridio."

"Issilla," Gedzik called out. "I have an errand for you."

When the Moon Faerie entered, Kurash seated himself and spoke. "Faerie Ring has fallen. It has been burned to the ground. Chagadi has taken the road along the west side of the Nettle River. The inns at the falls have both been burned, and the bridge destroyed. The Parthans will reach Lilac day after tomorrow. None of them appear to be east of the river. Alketas is bringing one hundred infantry and fifty archers from Tellia, but they are still days away. He will try to bring more when he passes Mount Easley."

"Please repeat that, Issilla," Gedzik said.

She repeated it word for word, duplicating Kurash's intonation.

"Take the message directly to Nebridio. Inform him that it is from Kurash."

"Yes sir." She turned and ran, hiking her ankle-length lavender tunic to her knees.

"And avoid Vifredo," he shouted after her. "Riquilda was to retreat when Chagadi arrived. Did you see any sign of her?"

"There were refugees moving south on both sides of the river. Who they were, I could not tell from high above."

Gedzik pointed to the waist pack. "You brought jadeite."

"Indeed." Kurash lifted a jagged chunk of translucent, milky green stone from his pack. "Could you see it?"

Gedzik was stunned by the intensity of the glowing green mesh of connections that sprouted from the stone and curved back into it. "It looks powerful."

"I broke it from the handle of a human sword of layered steel. This was about as large as I felt I could carry. Be careful with it. No one living knows what it is capable of. Its mere proximity may be dangerous."

"Even the sarcite, I discovered, is dangerous. Thank you for bringing it. Will you stay with us? Quartrik is here with the students."

"I suppose I have nowhere else to go. And you will certainly need the services of another healer, though there are some here who would rather die than be saved by a Saracet."

"Vifredo?"

"Yes. I believe Vifredo would be at the head of that group. Perhaps with seventy two students, we could put them to work making bandages and splints, and crutches, perhaps."

"We have a large quantity of lavender cloth and a small furniture shop."

"Perfect."

"Oh, Quartrik was not looking well."

"He is heartbroken. He laid every stone of the walls and buildings of Daiella School. Even in old age, he continued to mend them himself. I'll ask him to organize the student work details."

When Kurash stooped beneath the lintel and left the study, Gedzik examined the irregular chunk of jadeite, nearly the size of his forearm. By simply touching it, his own body emanated a green aura similar to that of the stone. He drew his steel saber and struck its spine against the center of the jadeite, breaking it in two. For over an hour, he tried various combinations and numbers of jadeite stones. He found the strongest response from a triangle, but it never maximized, even when the three stones were about one faerielong from one another, a distance greater than the span of his arms. Even so, the large triangle seemed to reveal evanescent connections between everything and everything else—a web of nature.

It occurred to him that a fourth stone held above the center of the triangle would itself form the vertex of three additional triangles, in the shape of a triangular pyramid. He placed his stool in the center of the large triangle formed by the three stones on the floor, and stood on it, holding a fourth stone above his head. When it approached the proper height, he could feel a soft vibration in the air.

Everything about him seemed to dissolve into nothing but connections—glowing, diaphanous green connections. He was transfixed by its complexity and its fragility. For the first time, he saw the full boundary of Ternaria—not just those glowing boundaries that reached the ground at immeasurable distances, but the dome of it overhead. The boundary was a large dome! He could follow its strands back to their source, far to the northwest. A huge sphere made of twelve pentagons, a sarcite stone at each of its twenty vertices, was tended by humans. *Moss Abbey*. To his further surprise, the humans who touched the sarcites on the great sphere seemed to be able to see him as well. The shock on their faces frightened Gedzik. He lowered the fourth stone out of alignment, his heart racing.

One further trial remained. He needed to know if the four-stone pyramid configuration was also dependent on distance. If not, and could be made smaller, he might be able to manage some use for it.

Riquilda lay unconscious on a palette in Nebridio's spacious home. The lower level was in the process of being set up as a hospital, though no one had expected a casualty so soon. Gedzik had received word as soon as she was brought in. A blood-soaked, lavender bandage covered her chest below her right breast.

"Where is the healer?" Gedzik asked the orderly, a middle-age Faerie.

"He has already seen her."

"Why has he left? There are no others to attend to."

The orderly pointed to the bottom of his right chest. "Pike to the liver. Nothing can be done to stop the bleeding. She will never awaken, and will be dead soon."

"Surely something is better than nothing."

"I am not a healer, but I have seen many battle wounds, schoolmaster. A liver strike is always a mortal wound. Always. Sometimes it takes hours, sometimes days, but once the victim looses sensibility, he dies quickly."

"Who came with her?"

"Only one other. He is up the steps with the Elder and the Strategus now."

At the top of the steps, Gedzik was stopped by a sentry.

"Let him through," Caluño said. "Go directly to Pippi and tell him what has happened, then report to your unit."

A young adult with blood on his tunic passed Gedzik and descended the steps. Stocky and broad-shouldered, Caluño was still well muscled at forty-five. His face was smudged in dirt, as were his hands.

"Gedzik," Caluño said, "sappers attacked the wagons carrying fish oil and dried peat from Westbog. Riquilda went west of the river to defend them and was cut off by Chagadi's main force. That young private is the only other survivor. Riquilda bears a mortal wound and we've lost nineteen troops. Now Chagadi has our dried peat and fish oil. No doubt he will find a means to return it to us before too long. Do you have any good news?"

"Yes. Tatt has come from Elby. They brought ten prisms, each twice your height. He said he needed to be west of the Parthan battle line to catch the morning sun. I sent him and his wagons to the blueberry hill. Tatt isn't certain they'll be able to focus them to a distant point. They're going to try to practice before the Parthans arrive."

Caluño shook his head. "I guess every little bit contributes. Did he bring folks with him to handle the prisms, or do we have to provide them?"

"Ten prisms, four Faeries. There shouldn't be fighting up on the hill, so I can send six older students to help."

"Good. You might want to post your best saber handlers at the school garden. If sappers manage to come from east of Lilac, that's the first thing they'll come to."

"I've already done that, Strategus. They've been instructed to stay in hiding and, if Parthans come, to cut their heel tendons and run."

Caluño laughed. "Like the bird that snips the grasshopper's jumping legs, then dispatches it at leisure."

"I prefer that children defend rather than kill."

Nebridio had been sitting in silence, staring vacantly at the window. "We took the Great Faerie Army all the way to Seraz to rescue Riquilda," he finally said, fondling the pommel of the bronze sword at his hip. "You found her, Caluño. She was thirteen. Do you remember, Caluño?"

"Yes, Elder, I do."

"You discovered the lilac stone. Riquilda was the only captive spared the humiliation of being seen with blackened skin and shriveled, black wings. We conquered the walled city of Seraz, but we didn't destroy it like Kizikum."

"Kizikum was before my time, Elder."

"There was no mercy at Kizikum. We should always show mercy."

"Excuse me, Elder. I need to speak with Gedzik for a moment." Caluño gave a furtive gesture with his hand, for him to go down the steps. Once at the bottom, he said, "Ask your Saracet healer to examine Nebridio. Our healer says nothing is wrong with him. He has lost his foothold in the present crisis. He's rambled like this all morning. I fear that age has caught up with him. This is all too great a burden."

After Caluño had returned up the steps, Gedzik knelt beside Riquilda. He gently touched her white hair one last time, and whispered softly, "You know I loved you." He kissed her cheek, now as colorless as his own.

The Master of Lilac Academy returned to find an air of wild excitement and fear. Two Parthan soldiers had just been caught sneaking into the garden.

"They're still there," the majordomo informed him.

He walked through the Academy and out the back to the garden. Near the garden gate, two Parthans cowered on the ground, their ankles covered in blood. Neither wore armor. Four student sabermasters stood over them.

Gedzik drew his saber as he approached them. Neither seemed mortally wounded, but true to his own orders, their heel tendons had been severed. "How many more are sneaking into Lilac?" he asked, as he lifted the chin of one of them with the flat of his saber. It was a mere boy, hardly older than some of his students.

"I don't know." The soldier whimpered. "They just sent the two of us down the river to come in from the east."

"So, you are spies?"

The Parthan boy did not answer. He fought back tears as he shrank from the point of Gedzik's saber.

Kurash approached. He whispered into Gedzik's ear. "They can not escape. Neither will ever walk again, unless I sew the tendons."

"Are there any rooms empty?"

"We've filled every corner, sir," the majordomo replied.

"Put them in my study. Don't bother to guard them. Kurash, do what you can for them. And when you're done, Caluño has asked if you could see Nebridio. Resume your watches here and at the front entrance. Don't let word of these two leave the Academy, or they will be hanged."

"Tell the cook", Kurash said to the majordomo, "to boil his two thinnest lute strings in a pot of black tea. I'll need them as soon as they are ready."

At the top of the blueberry hill, west of Lilac, Gedzik watched as Tatt finalized the emplacement of his tall, colorless prisms, each as wide as a Faerie and twice as tall. Each prism stood within a shallow bucket which had been sunken into the ground. The ten prisms formed a gentle arc that opened toward the relatively flat grassland north of Lilac. Just after sunrise, the angle of the sun would allow them to focus the light toward the eastern edge of the expected field of battle. As the sun rose higher, Tatt had explained, the focus line could be directed closer and closer to the hill on which they stood, until about two hours before noon, at which time they could no longer be used until the following morning.

Tatt designated a shrub in the distance as their first test target. "Now!" he shouted. The Faeries standing behind each prism rotated it so that they would all strike the target. Nothing happened.

Visibly annoyed, Tatt stepped behind each prism in succession to check its alignment. "It's pointed at the wrong bush," he said to the first of the prism handlers. "Now this one is pointed at a different wrong bush." He checked the third, then threw his hands up in the air. "They're all pointing at different targets." He looked at the sun. "Well, we'll have to pick a closer target." He turned to Gedzik. "We've never worked them at such a long distance. Each prism has a sight line etched on the front and back to aim them, but I don't know how to point out a target that all the handlers will understand. And at such distance, the sun's angle is right for only a moment."

"I could go out there and mark some targets with different color flags," Gedzik offered.

"I don't think we have time." Tatt pointed to the north.

An undulating tide of thorn tips oozed over the horizon, followed by a billowing haze of dust that drifted eastward. A chill came over him. From his vantage on the blueberry hill, he also saw, beyond the earthworks, a small army, numbering no more than a hundred, fording the river from the east. "I'm going to tell Caluño the Parthans are here."

"But we haven't practiced." Tatt grumbled.

Gedzik sat on a stool in his study, sewing four pockets into one of his hooded tunics—one at the top of the hood, one at each cuff, and one over his navel. The two captured Parthans watched from their floor mats. Kurash had given them opium for the pain, after he had sewn their heel tendons back together.

"That's a strange thing to wear," one of them said.

"But I am a leader. My forces need to be able to recognize me."

"Then why are you sewing rocks into it?" the other asked.

"It's part of the art of command. Chagadi doesn't dress the same as you, does he?"

"He's red," the first said.

"The commanders paint their bark armor yellow, but he paints his red," the other clarified.

"At least you know to get out of the way when they come by," Gedzik quipped.

The two Parthans looked at one another and laughed. "He knows," one said, pointing at Gedzik.

"Wish me good fortune," Gedzik said as he walked toward the doorway, "because if Chagadi takes Lilac, he may hang you for still being alive." He headed for the promenade within the lilac grove.

During the previous afternoon, the Parthans had camped on the plain north of Lilac, five hundred faerielongs from Caluño's earthworks, which stretched from the river, just north of the ford, westward to a point east of the blueberry hill. Five redoubts rose behind the earth and thorn barrier—one at each end and three in between. A trench along the north of the barrier would require attackers to climb the steep slope through a forest of hundreds of thorns embedded into the dirt.

Gedzik had learned that it was Elder Mylis whom he had seen fording the river with one hundred troops from Moonglow, all in sturdy wicker armor. They were nonetheless still badly outnumbered by the Parthans.

Nebridio stood beside Caluño and Vifredo. He issued orders regarding the refugees from the inns at the falls and the provision of water for the troops manning the earthworks.

"When Pippi arrives, we'll begin," Caluño stated. "If Joshi gets here with the ballista, put it on the center redoubt. If there's more than one, go out from the center."

"The Parthans are forming in twenty groups of fifty," Pippi said as he approached. "Their archers are in five groups of one hundred each behind the infantry. They are all positioned as though they will directly attack our center."

"The catapults?" Caluño asked.

"I haven't seen them."

"Mylis, your troops wear the best armor. I want them on the far right, to guard the ford." Caluño took a deep breath. "If any help arrives, it will come by river or across the ford. The redoubt at the river is redoubt one. Pippi, divide our archers in two and place half each at redoubts two and four, so their effective ranges cross at the center. They should be instructed to hold their arrows until the Parthans are well within range and on the move. Put your infantry between redoubts two and three. Vifredo, between four and five, at the far left. I will be on the center redoubt with my forces between three and four. Quartrik is holding the refugee volunteers as a reserve behind the center. Don't count on them. They are untrained and poorly armed. Gedzik, send two older students to me as messengers, and two to each commander. If we fail, take all the children and flee toward Elby. Elder..." He now spoke to Nebridio. "...where can we find you?"

"Oh...I guess I'll be at home if you need me," Nebridio replied.

"Any success with those prisms?"

"They haven't been able to coordinate the...No. None at all," Gedzik admitted.

"Go to your positions. Remember that it is always better to die courageously than to be executed by a victorious enemy."

Caluño turned and strode across the promenade toward the ring of lilacs. A flaming ball nearly a faerielong in diameter roared over the lilacs and exploded in a splash of fire against the south edge of the promenade. A second enormous ball of flaming material struck Caluño full force, crushing him and setting his now motionless body ablaze.

Nebridio turned to Gedzik and opened his mouth as if to speak. Instead, he collapsed to the ground, unconscious. By the time Vifredo and Gedzik had dragged Nebridio beyond the grove, the Elder was dead. The entire lilac grove burned as a great ring of flames that towered three times the height of the lilacs, and reeked of fish.

At a resounding crack, Gedzik turned to see the top half of the great transparent lilac monolith shatter and plummet to the promenade. A colossal crash left a heap of lavender rubble beneath billowing dust.

"There is treachery here," Vifredo shouted. "I declare myself Dictator!" he called out to the remaining commanders. "Man the lines." He turned to Gedzik. "Your Saracet healer has poisoned the Elder. I want you and the rest of your vermin blighters out of Lilac now. If I see you again, I will kill you myself."

As Gedzik knelt beside the dead Nebridio, he struggled to sort out the sudden violence and death from the unexpected words that Vifredo shouted. He rose to his feet. "What are you saying, Tribune?"

Vifredo placed the point of his pike at Gedzik's neck, just above his steel cuirass. "You and your milk-skin squats will leave Lilac now, or be killed."

Anger and outrage swelled within him. In a single, fluid movement, he made a small step backwards, drew his saber and lopped off the end of Vifredo's pike, sweeping the blade in a circle on either side of his shoulders and back into its scabbard. Without a word, Gedzik turned and walked back to the Academy. He felt a strange sense of satisfaction at having restrained himself from immediately killing the self-proclaimed Dictator.

Gedzik first located Kurash to warn him that Vifredo blamed him for Nebridio's death, even though he suspected that not even the Dictator himself believed it. He asked the majordomo to assemble all nineteen Moon Faeries in the garden and for them to bring their wooden sabers.

"Pippi will likely be on or near the second redoubt," Gedzik explained. "Stay clear of the center and left of our defenses. Vifredo will be commanding there."

"With both Caluño and Nebridio dead," the Saracet said, "Vifredo will likely have his way. What are your plans?"

"Elby is the only safe place remaining, for now. We'll go to the blueberry hill and go south from there, if forced. If we flee, there will never be safety for us in Ternaria, regardless of whether Chagadi or Vifredo comes out on top."

An elderly Faerie approached them in the corridor. His right hand worked a cane, which he used to drag the useless left side of his body behind him.

"Ramún!" Gedzik said in surprise. "I'm sorry I haven't spoken with you since Riquilda's death."

"Later," Ramún said in a slow and slightly slurred voice.

"This is Riquilda's father, Ramún." Then to Ramún he introduced the Saracet healer.

Ramún nodded. "I have come to...watch the Academy." He labored over each word. "Vifredo is spreading lies. Bernaldo will come by to help. Go quickly. The Parthan infantry has advanced. Their archers shower the line with arrows."

Gedzik said farewell and ran to the garden, where the nineteen Moon Faeries had gathered. They all seemed too young to be the object of such hatred—the oldest only twelve. When they saw him approach, all of them stared in awe. He remembered then that he bore four jadeites, sewn within his long tunic and hood.

"If you are nine or older, stand to my right."

Eleven moved to his right, including one of the refugees from Faerie Ring. He asked the names of the three refugees, then introduced himself. Gedzik took the two shortest wooden sabers from two Moon Faeries in the older group and handed them to the two younger refugees. "Each of you can see what no other Faerie can see. I carry jadeite stones." He lifted one arm, causing strands of green glow to stretch out toward the stone sewn into the cuff. "You will always be able to see where I am."

He turned to the group of younger Moon Faeries. "All eight of you are a special guard." He led Issilla, the oldest known Moon Faerie, to the younger group. "You must guard Issilla at all times. Never leave her. She is the wisest of all Moon Faeries and must be protected."

Issilla rolled her eyes.

"Go directly to Elby by the south road," he said to Issilla. He removed her practice saber and replaced it with his own jewel-encrusted, steel saber, in its jeweled scabbard suspended by a jeweled belt. Issilla's eyes widened and her chin quivered. "Walk until they can go no further, then rest for only two hours. If you walk through the night, you will reach Elby by morning. Go to the Elder, Mipple, and tell him that we are with his brother, Tatt." He looked again at the eight young students—all six, seven or eight years old. "Present sabers!" he commanded. Eight small hands grasped eight wooden sabers and drew them from their scabbards. "Very good. Now sheath them and stay with Issilla." He nodded to her. "Be careful."

When Issilla led the young ones away, Gedzik said to those ten remaining, "We are going to the blueberry hill to fight the Parthans, not with your wooden sabers, but with your eyes."

"Climb the blueberries," Gedzik said to his ten Moon Faeries, "and bring down one blueberry each. It doesn't matter if they are ripe."

From the crest of the blueberry hill, the raging battle that spread out before him ebbed and flowed silently, like a game of stones, played on a table. The first infantry assault on the center was barely turned back by archers to either side, and a melee near the third redoubt. The Parthan catapults now flung huge stones that, even from this distance, produced an audible thud as they embedded into the ground or into the slowly crumbling earthworks.

More units of Parthan infantry grouped to attack the Lilac right, against the river. Almost in parallel with them, an army of perhaps two hundred moved south on the far side of the river, toward the ford.

"If those are Parthans on the east of the river," Tatt said, "they'll break through."

"With the bridge at the falls destroyed, they would need ten days to reach the ford at Faerie Ring and then come down the east side of the river. They must be allies, maybe from Tellia."

"I hope so."

"Look below the ford. The sails of the *Luli Shibami*. It's Joshi!"

A blueberry rolled beside his feet, reaching nearly to his knees. "What should we do with them?" one of the children asked.

"Right here, bring them right here. Tatt, how far can we aim with the sun's angle now?"

Tatt placed an odd hinged device against the vertical flat of a prism and adjusted its moveable arms. "You see the one, two, three, fourth body of infantry from here. Just beyond that."

"My students are going to aim your prisms." To the Moon Faeries, he said, "Each of you stand behind one of the prisms. Aim it at my mark."

"What mark?" one of them asked.

"You'll know it when you see it. You will need help rotating the prism, so its handler will help you. Just guide them."

Gedzik scanned the focal distance and picked a target. He sat on the ground with a blueberry between his knees and extended his arms so that his cuffs were equally distant from the jadeite sewn into the pocket at his navel, the jadeite in his hood, and from one another. The glow of green connections brightened dramatically. In his mind, he directed the power within the blueberry to pull at the dome of Ternaria's boundary overhead. He struggled to prevent his own body from contributing to that power. A perfect, pointed cone of glowing red filaments descended from the sky into a fine point. "Now!" he shouted.

A Parthan catapult burst into flames half-way across the battlefield. Those Parthans near it ran about in confusion.

"I don't see your mark," Tatt said excitedly.

He lowered his arms. "Only the Moon Faeries can see it." Nearly the entire blueberry had been consumed. The monks of Moss Abbey had seen him tug at the dome of Ternaria's boundary. He worried that they might resist his next attempt to displace a point of it. He rolled another blueberry in place and looked out again. "How far has the angle moved?"

"Maybe three faerielongs," Tatt replied.

He brought the triangular pyramid of jadeites back into alignment. The green glow strengthened. He selected a second catapult, near the first. As his mind tugged at the boundary canopy, it seemed to descend with little effort, almost of its own. *The monks are helping me.* "Now!"

The second catapult erupted in flames. Parthans swarmed like angry insects, searching for the cause.

At the first redoubt, a Parthan phalanx steadily advanced. The army on the east of the river streamed across the ford and joined Mylis' defenders on the Lilac earthworks. Some of them brought a large object from the *Luli Shibami* up to the first redoubt. Showers of arrows arced from the Parthan archers in advance of the Phalanx.

"Give me a line of focus," Gedzik said.

"Half-way into the third body of infantry."

Gedzik saw no large targets. Then a dot of glowing green dropped from the sky. Kurash circled high overhead. At the point where the green glow landed, Gedzik could barely make out a Parthan with bright yellow bark armor. Using the same blueberry, which was hardly consumed, he brought down a pointer from the dome of the boundary, as easily as the previous try. The Parthan commander burst into flame, then exploded into a smoldering heap.

To the left of the first redoubt, the Parthan phalanx crossed the trench and began its ascent of the steep slope bristling with menacing thorns. Suddenly a swath of Parthans fell, as though a great finger had swept from the first redoubt diagonally through the phalanx. The assault collapsed.

"The ballista! Joshi brought the ballista from Shibam. Tatt, give me the current line."

He took measurements of the sun's angle again. "It's right about...um...uh oh. They've spotted us."

The closest phalanx wheeled about and advanced toward the blueberry hill. They were too close for the prisms to be directed at them with the sun's current angle. Gedzik could see two more ballistae being set up on the second and third redoubts. Only if one were placed on the fifth redoubt could it impact the phalanx that now threatened the hill.

"Either Vifredo doesn't see them," Gedzik said to Tatt, "or he doesn't care."

"Should we run?" Tatt asked.

"Not yet." He watched another glowing green dot fall from Kurash and land near a second commander in yellow armor. Gedzik brought down the point of glowing red boundary with ease. "Now!"

The commander's armor caught fire, but because the sun's angle had not been carefully measured, the prisms' effect was only partial. He ran away while tearing the burning bark armor from his torso.

Although three ballistae now worked to slow the relentless onslaught of the Parthan army, Chagadi's forces gained ground, little by little. The phalanx approaching the blueberry hill had nearly reached its base, when Gedzik saw dark dots in the sky to the northwest.

First to arrive were a dozen apis drones, each carrying a Faerie archer. They swooped again and again over the leading edge of the phalanx at the base of the hill, firing volleys of arrows. Though this seemed to be ineffective at wounding the Parthans, it forced them to stop and raise their shields.

Soon, the drones were joined by thirty wasps, two Thistlepix riding each one. The first guided it while the second fired bolts from a crossbow. The phalanx began to fall back from the hill, as the Thistlepix crossbow bolts easily penetrated the Parthan shields and the back of their armor.

"Where is the focus line, Tatt?"

Tatt fumbled with his gadget, then shouted, "The start of the second phalanx."

Now it was close enough for Gedzik to pick out a yellow-clad commander. He rolled in a fresh blueberry, then raised his arms and brought down the red pointer onto the unlucky Parthan's head. "Now!" The victim flared brightly, then dropped.

The infantry was still closing on the Lilac line, their archers close behind. Parthan arrows began to bring down an occasional wasp or apis drone. A group of archers now approached the base of the blueberry hill.

"Stand behind the prisms when they fire," Gedzik shouted.

A volley of arrows struck the ground, some being deflected by the prisms. Then a swooshing thump shook the ground. A catapult had been maneuvered to fire on the hill.

"I believe you can hit that," Tatt said, without sticking his head out to measure.

Gedzik brought down a pointer. "Now!"

The deflected sunlight burned through its taut arm. The frame of the catapult leapt off the ground, followed by a loud clap.

Kurash flew in a tight circle above the ruined catapult. Gedzik assumed that the Saracet had no more jadeite to drop. When he realized what Kurash was circling, he could hardly believe it. Slightly closer to him than the ruined catapult stood three Parthans in yellow armor. In front of them, in a rant, stood one in bright red. He brought down the boundary onto Chagadi's head. "Now!" The monks of Moss Abby showed looks of satisfaction.

The Parthan tyrant's head exploded in a steamy puff. Gedzik moved the same pointer to the nearest of the stunned commanders. "Now!" That one burst into flame and toppled. Gedzik was able to drop one more commander before the last one rushed away from the line of focus.

The nearest company of archers, many of whom saw the destruction of Chagadi, turned and ran from the battlefield. Panic spread like a grassfire across the Parthan host. Waves of long hawthorn pikes dropped to the ground as their bearers turned and fled, some trampling one another. Catapults, packs and even armor were abandoned. None of the defenders pursued them, since no one had anticipated a sortie from the earthworks, and had provided no means of descent forward of the defensive line. Only the apis drones and wasps swarmed at the routed army, pelting them with arrows and bolts.

"Some say it was the last Parthan arrow," Pippi said, "but how it struck him in the back is hard to explain." He stood in the circular promenade enclosed within a smoldering ring of what had once been the famous grove of lilacs. At his hip, he wore his late step-father's bronze sword. "Regardless, I have to admit that I was glad to hear that Vifredo was dead."

"Too many have died," Gedzik said. "I understand that we lost two hundred dead and half the rest are wounded."

"Yes. It was a close thing. Without each bit of help that we received, we could not have held." Pippi looked about him at the destruction and the concentric circles of supine wounded filling the promenade. He shook his head. "This is what victory looks like."

"Many of the wounded that the healers tend to are Parthan." Gedzik looked his adoptive brother in the eyes. "It's what mercy looks like, Pippi. Nebridio would have been proud. Willi would have been proud."

"What do we do now?" Pippi asked. "All of Ternaria is in ruins. All trade has stopped."

"We build it back," Quartrik said, slapping Pippi on the shoulder as he approached, "stone by stone."

Mylis came with him, carrying a large, translucent white jug. "First, with this very well aged gooseberry wine, we drink to victory, which, no matter how bitter, is always sweeter than defeat."

Gedzik walked with Kurash and Quartrik through the luxuriant vegetable garden of the New Daiella School.

"Another hour of that inane bickering," Quartrik said, "and the stone walls will fall down around them." He spread open the neck of his black robe. "Summers never got so hot when I was young."

"Your patience has receded with your hair, Quartrik," Kurash quipped.

"The school is magnificent. You must be proud...and in less than a year." Gedzik stopped in the shade of a pea vine and threw back his hood.

"With a hundred Parthans doing all the work, anyone could do as much in a year."

"Oh, but the stone arches, the timber frames, the tile roofs...It will last for hundreds of years." Gedzik noticed for the first time that the inside of the crenellated perimeter wall, which extended as well around the garden, supported a narrow walkway of timber, that made each crenel dip to waist height on an average Faerie, and the intervening merlons just over the head. A small bartizan hung out over each corner of the wall.

"That's what I thought when I built the first one...as a monastery."

"Did you intend this to be a fortress?" Gedzik asked.

"Quartrik," Kurash replied, "simply wishes to leave...how shall I say it...an impression...on all the honored ambassadors who come to the Hall of Ternaria to debate their concerns."

"That pretty well sums it up," Quartrik stated with a smile. "You might consider it an educational exercise for the Parthans who performed all that unnecessary labor. It's a pity that the citizens of

Faerie Ring merely had to plant their boletus spores to re-grow the town."

"The Parthans did have to rebuild Domes and Oakhaven," Gedzik pointed out, "oh...and Nart and the inns at the falls...and the bridge, not to mention half of Lilac. I think they'll be the first to leap to the defense of what they built with their own hands."

"We really should go back in for the close of the session," Kurash said, placing a hand on Quartrik's stooped shoulder and the other on Gedzik's. "It's the last one of the year."

"It hardly seems like sufficient reparations," Quartrik grumbled.

"They've burnt the hawthorns and rebuilt much of their damage," Kurash replied. "Too heavy a hand would lead to more wars."

They walked back to the general assembly chamber, dubbed the Hall of Ternaria, designed primarily to hold all the students and faculty of the Daiella School, but also designated as the seat of the new Assembly of Ternaria, where twice a year, ambassadors from all of Ternaria would assemble to discuss their needs and common goals. Here, the reparations and restrictions placed on the citizens of Partha had been squabbled over, compromised and ultimately decided to the satisfaction of few.

Gedzik stepped back into the rear of the hall.

Mylis stood at the podium, elected by the ambassadors as Moderator of the Assembly—mostly because of his modest opinions and equally modest power. Seated in the chamber were twelve Thistlepix and dozens of Faeries, all of middle-age or older, representing all the villages and towns of Ternaria, from the northern boundary all the way to Toe Wash. Even the distant cities of Seraz and Kizikum were represented.

At the rap of Mylis' rod of office, the only scrap of hawthorn wood not burned to ashes in all of Ternaria, the assembled ambassadors fell silent. His other mark of office, the fabled bronze sword of Nebridio, hung from his hip. "So, it is decided, the grove of Lilac will be replanted before spring, with two hazelnuts, five wisteria, two dogwoods—both with white blossoms, ten lilacs, um..." His assistant whispered in his ear. "One each of hydrangea, honeysuckle, elderberry, a golden fig—from Toe Wash, sour cherry, a thornless blackberry—from my vineyards at Moonglow..." He smiled proudly. "...and the gift from the jewelers of Shibam, a pair of olives."

The assembled ambassadors of all Ternaria applauded. The rod rapped again on the podium.

"The Parthans are to bring a new lilac stone from the mines of Seraz—a gift of that city, by the way—and erect it in the center of the replanted grove. Finally, a rose from each ambassador will be sent to Partha to be planted around their square. You may send any variety or color—so long as it bears thorns—as a reminder of our suffering and our mercy."

- END -

GLOSSARY OF TERNARIA

Alcalde	The title given to the appointed political leader of Salceda.
Alek	An orphaned student at the New Life Monastery. A poet.
Alfrito	Brother of Nebridio. Lives in Lilac.
Alketas	Son of Darissa. Lives in Tellia.
Almirant	The title given to the naval commander of Kizikum.
Andra	Quarrymistress of Tellia.
apis	A honey bee. Apis drones are trained for aerial transport by the Faeries of Domes.
Archon	Title of the elected leader of Tellia.
Asif	A rural vintner living outside Ost.
Bennik	First literate Faerie. Author.
Berenguer	Elder of Lilac. Dictator during the great war against the Saracets.
Bessa	Younger sister of Britt. Lives in Domes.
Binzo	Trainer of a hummingbird. Discoverer of methods for separating sugars from fruit. Lives in Oakhaven.
Blighter	Impolite term for Moon Faerie.
Blit	Innkeeper of the Earwig Inn at Nettle Falls.
boletus	A thick, round-capped mushroom. Used as dwellings in Domes.
bombus	A bumblebee. Used for aerial transport by some Faeries.
boundary of Ternaria	A magical barrier surrounding Ternaria. It is maintained by the continuous efforts of the

	human monks of Moss Abbey.
Britt	Close friend of Rath and of Bennik. Lived in Domes. Founded the New Life Monastery near Faerie Ring. Older brother of Bessa. Son of Dibola.
Buttercup Inn	Inn situated on the eastern bank of the Nettle River, just below the falls.
Caluño	An orphaned student at the New Life Monastery. Later, Tribune of Lilac.
Cammia	Daughter of Neelian. Skilled vintner. Lives near Moonglow.
caracol	A snail with a spiral shell.
Chagadi	Tyrant of Partha.
Chive Crossing	A small village on the lower Nettle River. Produce chives, pickled clover and sisal.
Chrysanthus	Legendary human wizard.
Claw	A tortoise used by longhaulers to carry cargo between the Warded Mines and Moss Abbey.
Creeper	A millipede ridden by Yori.
Daiella	Beautiful daughter of Dailik. Lives in Faerie Ring.
Daiella School	Later incarnation of the New Life Monastery.
Dailik	Father of Daiella. Lives in Faerie Ring.
Daisy	A tortoise used by longhaulers to carry cargo between the Warded Mines and Moss Abbey.
Darissa	A prostitute living in Tellia. Mother of Alketas.
Della	Mother of Pellana. Wife of Ottus. Lives in Mt. Easley.
Derina, Captain	Captain of the Guard in Elby.

Dianthus	The god to whom Saracets offer prayer.
Dibola	Mother of Britt and Bessa. Lives in Domes.
Dobar	Thistlepix wasp rider.
Domes	Village of boletus houses situated in northwestern Ternaria.
Dunedek	Elder of Westbog.
Dunthum	Crew boss of Alketas archeological dig in Tellia.
Earwig Inn	Inn situated on the western bank of the Nettle River, just below the falls.
Elby	Town in southwestern Ternaria.
Ephor	Title of the high judge of Tellia.
Espiria	Mother of Joshi. Lives at Nettle Falls.
Faerie Lord of Kizikum	Title of the suzerain of western Ternaria.
Faerie Ring	Faerie town of the upper Nettle River. Their boletus homes are maintained in a circle.
Foplin	Father of Tatt and Mipple. Lives in Elby. Inventor of a solar cooking device made of prisms.
fur people	Anthropoid, furred creatures about one third the size of humans. Found east of the lower Nettle.
Gedzik	Wingless, runted albino Faerie. A foundling. Raised at Chive Crossing.
Ginto	Dealer in pokewood lumber. Lives in Faerie Ring.
Gordion	Ephor of Tellia.
Hamsa	Youngest of the three human jewelers of Shibam. Formally, Hamsa ibn Yusuf al Gawahirgi Jubaili.
harvestman	A spider-like acarid, also known as a "Daddy

	Longlegs."
Herrik	Lumber merchant who travels between Faerie Ring and Nettle Falls.
Highbush	The name given by Binzo to his trained hummingbird.
Hometree	The single, great tree that houses all the residents of Oakhaven.
jadeite	A translucent green stone rumored to possess magical powers.
Jardi	Elby youth who was killed by a harvestman.
Joshi	Son of Walto and Espiria. Lives at Nettle Falls.
Kallian	Innkeeper of the Buttercup Inn at Nettle Falls.
Kizikum	A great walled city on the western shore of Lake Willow. Home of the Faerie Lord.
Kurash	A Saracet healer who has migrated to Tellia.
Lake Willow	The greatest body of water in Ternaria. It is situated to the central west.
Leela	Rath's mother. Lives in Domes.
Lilac	An important city on the middle Nettle. Its famous circular grove of lilacs is visited by pilgrims.
lilac stone	Also know as amethyst. Mined by the Saracets from Mt. Gumush and sold to the Thistlepix.
Log, The	A substantial bridge at the outlet of Lake Willow.
longhauler	A Faerie who hauls sarcite from the Warded Mines to Moss Abbey.
Luli Shibami	Sulalic name of the ship, Pearl of Shibam.
Luris	Brother of Cammia and Mylis. Eldest son of Neelian. Lives at the winery near Moonglow.
Mage King	The human tyrant of Tel, in ancient times.

Maha Neruti	Title given to Neruti as Abbot of Moss Abbey.
Mipple	Brother of Tatt. Elder son of Foplin. Lives in Elby.
Mookie	An albino marmot ridden by Herrik to carry cargo between Faerie Ring and Nettle Falls.
Moon Baby	Offspring of Faeries cured of silver poisoning.
Moon Faerie	A Moon Baby older than an infant.
Moonglow	Town of middle Ternaria below the western slope of the mountains.
morchella	A mushroom also called a Morel. Used for dwellings by some Faeries.
mosquito pudding	A blood pudding made from a blood-filled mosquito belly.
Moss Abbey	A human monastery located beyond Ternaria, within the ancient forest of Oldwood.
moss bear	A tiny animalcule that feeds on the leaves of moss.
Mount Easley	A cave village situated at the western crest of the high mountains of eastern Ternaria.
Mt. Gumush	The site of silver mines and the great walled Saracet city of Seraz.
Mylis	Younger brother of Cammia and Luris. Youngest son of Neelian.
Nebridio	Older brother of Alfrito. Diplomat of Lilac.
Nebridio's Bronze Sword	Worn by Nebridio, though never drawn, as a reminder to always show mercy.
Neelian	Father of Luris, Cammia and Mylis. Owner of a blackberry winery near Moonglow.
Neelian, little	Infant of Cammia.
Neelian's Woods	Wooded "wasteland" to the north of Neelian's blackberry bramble.
Nepata	Archon of Tellia.

Neruti	Human monk of Moss Abbey. Later Abbot.
Nettle Falls	The great waterfall of the middle Nettle River.
Nettle River	The main river of Ternaria, running roughly north to south.
New Life Monastery	Operated by Father Britt to interpret the writings of Bennik's Book. Situated just outside Faerie Ring.
Oakhaven	Village of northern Ternaria.
Ost	Remote village in southeastern Ternaria.
Ostrik	Old healer of Tellia.
Ottus	Father of Pellana. Husband of Della. Lives in Mount Easley.
Partha	Town of northern Ternaria.
Pearl of Shibam	Ship of Joshi, built by Talata. Also known as the Luli Shibami.
Pellana	Daughter of Ottus and Della. Raised in Mount Easley.
Perris	Tatt's female friend. Lives in Elby.
Pippi	Younger son of Pellana and Wallis. Raised in Westbog.
Pix	The name by which Thistlepix identify themselves.
Pyxis	Sculptor and artist of Tel.
Quartrik, Brother	Monk of New Life Monastery. Mender of walls.
Ramún	Counselor of Lilac. Father of Riquilda.
Rath	Son of Leela and Reskith. Close friend of Britt. Lives in Domes.
Reskith	Rath's father. Lives in Domes.
Rhodek	Constable of Westbog.
Ringar	Thistlepix King.

Riquilda	Daughter of Ramún. Granddaughter of Berenguer. Lives in Lilac. Rescued captive of the Saracets.
Riverto	Alcalde of Salceda.
Romek	Thistlepix wasp rider. Mentor to Dobar.
Ruprecht	Faerie Lord of Kizikum.
Salceda	Town at the southern end of Lake Willow, specializing in salt, willow furniture and fish oil.
sarcite	A translucent red stone rumored to possess magical powers.
Sardis Run	Rivulet that serves as the northern boundary of Ternaria. To the north is the human land of Oldwood.
sartor	A tailor.
Secundik, Brother	Monk of New Life Monastery.
Seraz	The great walled city of the Saracets, to the far southeast of Ternaria.
Shadhana	Ancient language and script of the Saracet holy book, the Usharashada.
Shibam	A human city at the mouth of the Nettle River, built on the northern bank, beyond the boundary.
shrew	A carnivorous rodent of the dry side of high mountains. Sometimes kills Faeries. Used by the Saracets as a war mount. Dies of starvation if not fed for two days.
silver	A soft metal mined by the Saracets from Mt. Gumush and sold to the Thistlepix. Poisonous to Faeries.
Slug	The name given by the Thistlepix to a particularly obstreperous wasp.
Sorlin	Neighbor and would be suitor to Pellana.

	Lives in the caves of Mt. Easley.
Sorrel Pass	High mountain pass just south of Mount Easley. The east road from Nettle Falls crosses the pass and on to Tellia.
Spall	Saltmaster of Salceda.
Sulalic	Language and script of the humans of the Three Kingdoms of the Banu Sulal. Spoken in Shibam.
Sullis	Elder of Domes.
Sycamore Woods	Formerly known as Neelian's Woods, near Moonglow. Site of the Sycamore winery.
Syrick	Father of Binzo. Lives in Oakton and operates a business selling ladybugs for aphid control. He raises the ladybugs in his rose orchard.
Talata	One of the three human jewelers of Shibam. Formally, Talata ibn Ibrim al Gawahirgi Jakari. Builder of the Luli Shibami.
Tatt	Younger son of Foplin. Brother of Mipple. Lives in Elby.
Tel	Ancient human city thought to be located in the vicinity of Tellia.
Tellia	City in the far east of Ternaria. Translucent white stone is quarried only from this locale.
Tercerik, Brother	Monk of the New Life Monastery.
Ternara	Ancient human city thought to be once located near the center of Ternaria.
Ternaria	An enclave of small beings protected by the magic of the Monks of Moss Abbey. Situated within the "Eastern Lands."
Tewesh	Mispronunciation of the name of the town of Toe Wash.
Toe Wash	Faerie town at the mouth of the Nettle River, on the south bank. Severely affected by tides.

Twitcher	A millipede ridden by Yori.
Usharashada	Ancient holy book of the Saracets. Written in Shadhana.
Vanivoort	Spokesperson of Chive Crossing.
Wab	River village of the lower Nettle, between Wiley and Chive Crossing.
Wahid	Oldest of the three human jewelers of Shibam. Formally, Wahid ibn Ayub al Gawahirgi Jelari. Creator of the Kharita al Sharq (Map of the East).
Wallis	Trader and minnower from Westbog. Mate of Pellana. Father of little Willi and Pippi.
Walto	Operates a crossing barge below Nettle Falls. Father of Joshi.
Warded Mines	Source of sarcite. Located beyond the southwest boundary of Ternaria.
Westbog	Lake town on the eastern shore of Lake Willow. Produces dried peat, dried fish and fish sauce.
Wiley	River town of the lower Nettle.
Willi the Hermit	Hermit Faerie living in a cave south of Mount Easley, south of Sorrel Pass.
Willi, the younger	Elder son of Pellana and Wallis. Brother of Pippi.
Wither	Small town between Wiley and Ost.
Wyranic	Member of the work crew for Alketas' archeological dig in Tellia.
Yori	Weaver of wicker. Handyman. Lives in Moonglow.

www.ingramcontent.com/pod-product-compliance
Lightning Source LLC
LaVergne TN
LVHW050929080826
845145LV00001B/263

* 9 7 8 0 9 7 6 1 5 5 9 5 9 *